The Ink & Chrome Series

Opening Up
Falling Under
Coming Back

The story goes like this: while on pregnancy bed rest, **Lauren Dane** had plenty of down time, so her husband took her comments about 'giving that writing thing a serious go' to heart and brought home a secondhand laptop. She wrote her first book on it. Today, Lauren is a *New York Times* and *USA Today* bestselling author of more than 60 novels and novellas across several genres.

Visit Lauren Dane online:

www.laurendane.com
https://www.facebook.com/laurendane
https://www.twitter.com/laurendane

Praise for Lauren Dane:

'Lauren Dane writes with an emotional depth and authenticity that always leaves me breathless. Simply put, I love her books!' Lara Adrian, *New York Times* bestselling author

'Lauren Dane is a highly talented writer who delivers emotionally charged, deeply sensual tales that are sexy, fun, and intimate' *Night Owl Reviews*

'Lauren Dane books have become a staple in my reading library. Her stories are character driven, emotional and always a lot of fun to immerse yourself in for a few hours' *Romance Junkies*

COMING

Back

LAUREN DANE

piatkus

PIATKUS

First published in the US in 2015 by Forever,
An imprint of Grand Central Publishing, New York
First published in Great Britain in 2015 by Piatkus

1 3 5 7 9 10 8 6 4 2

A CIP catalogue record for this book
is available from the British Library.

ISBN 978-0-349-40986-3

Printed and bound in Great Britain by
Clays Ltd, St Ives plc

Papers used by Piatkus are from well-managed forests
and other responsible sources.

MIX
Paper from
responsible sources
FSC
www.fsc.org   FSC® C104740

Piatkus
An imprint of
Little, Brown Book Group
Carmelite House
50 Victoria Embankment
London EC4Y 0DZ

An Hachette UK Company
www.hachette.co.uk

www.piatkus.co.uk

This one is dedicated to Ray. Because I steal his words and use them to make my alpha male heroes better men.

Acknowledgments

Big giant thank-yous go to pretty much everyone at Forever! With all the upheaval in my schedule, you went out of your way to help me and get these books out—especially my editor, Leah Hulten-schmidt (but also marketing, editing, publicity, art—thank you!).

My agent, Laura Bradford, who has the at times unenviable task of trying to manage me and who usually does so with a pretty convincing smile—I've been thanking you in acknowledgments for nearly a decade now. ☺

As always—my husband, who reminds me that a HEA is not some sort of silly fantasy, but something that's made my life better ever since I ended up in his house for a party nearly thirty years ago.

CHAPTER
One

Somehow, coming to this grand opening party had seemed a lot less terrifying when she'd been standing in her bedroom an hour before. The gleaming Twisted Steel sign beckoned, though Jessi stood still, rooted in place.

Her pulse sped as she realized the sleek, black Mercedes parked near the entrance was the super pricy AMG GT. Adam drove a car just like it.

Which meant, most likely, that Mick *and* Adam both were inside. Hard enough as it was to imagine seeing Mick again after four years, Jessi didn't know if she had it in her to attempt this . . . this reconciliation with both of them at once.

You can do this. You are awesome and you have nice tits and pretty eyes and you know all the words to "Bohemian Rhapsody." You are the perfect woman, she told herself as she marched right up to those big bay doors and into the party beyond.

Inside it was all ink and chrome. Cars and motorcycles parked under lights aimed to cast a gleam and shine on all those curves. The paint and interior design competed with some of the most gorgeous inkwork Jessi had ever seen. The party was full color, men and women rocking a whole lot of ink and piercings milled around. Every imaginable idea of party wear was on display from suits and ties to leather and denim.

It was hard-edged, colorful, a little wild—and though out of Jessi's comfort zone—unabashedly hot.

Jessi tried not to guzzle champagne as she wandered around pretending to sightsee when she was really on the hunt for Mick.

There was no denying the impact of the showroom. Soaring ceilings with fans bearing blades resembling airplane propellers rotated lazily. Large windows at the roof level would flood the room with light during the day, but right then a golden glow warmed the walls from inset fixtures. The floors were gorgeous honey-toned hardwoods with customized tile work.

Jessi tapped the woman next to her as they'd been looking at a '34 Ford. "I need an honest opinion."

The woman grinned. "Okay."

Jessi motioned at herself. "How do I look? I mean, if you had foolishly dumped me several years ago, would you look at me tonight and think about how stupid you were?"

She didn't usually go for the kind of body-conscious dress she wore just then. But she'd wanted to wow Mick, to remind him what he gave up when he ran away. Wanted him to realize he needed her.

"Give me the three-sixty so I can see it all."

Jessi did and the other woman nodded. "He will *totally* be sorry he was so dumb. You look great. I'm PJ." She held out her hand for Jessi to take.

She shook it. "Jessi. Thanks for the opinion."

PJ pointed to Jessi's head. "How do you get your hair so smooth and sleek? I had a long bob like that for a while, but the humidity makes it curl up all the time."

"There's *no* way I could get it to look like this daily. Are you kidding me?" Jessi laughed. "I went to a salon earlier and they did it all. Once I wash it, it'll be curly again."

"I really like that you just admitted that. And that you're not so perfect you can get your hair like that regularly. Okay"—PJ looked around the room and back to Jessi—"who are you looking for? I might know him. I do a lot of paint for Twisted Steel—and full disclosure, I'm with Asa Barrons, one of the owners—so I'm around here all the time," PJ said.

"Oh." Obviously she'd know Mick. "Uh, you do know him. Mick Roberts."

PJ's brows went up and then she leaned in. "I *knew* you'd be gorgeous."

"Me? What? You did? He talked about me?" Holy crap, she needed to find a sentence and go with it instead of word vomiting.

PJ waved a hand and rolled her eyes. "He's a dude, so he hints at lost love. You didn't hurt him did you? I'm pretty protective of my guys, you know."

Jessi snorted. "I'm sure we hurt each other lots of times, but that break was him."

"He's wearing a suit tonight. They all are. So handsome, I made them let me fuss over them extra long." PJ's grin was sort of infectious.

"I'm not sure I've had enough to drink yet for that. Mick in a suit is pretty impressive," Jessi said quietly.

"That's easily remedied. There's a bar station right over there. It's also next to the mini tacos. You should have some of those too. For strength." PJ patted her arm.

This PJ was all right. Jessi liked her pretty much immediately as they headed toward the bar.

Just a few feet away, a wall of incredible-smelling male stepped into her path and she bumped straight into him.

Careful hands took her upper arms to save her from falling. She took a deep breath and looked up into Mick's face for the first time in far too long.

The last time she'd seen him he'd broken her heart.

"Jess..." He smiled and she smiled and the love she'd felt for

Mick Roberts since she'd been fifteen tumbled through her heart, making her a little dizzy.

"I got the invitation. I figured it was a sign," she told him.

He was there. *Right there*. She wanted to bury her face in his chest and never let go.

His smile softened, went sideways. "You and your signs." He hadn't let go and she made no move, just content to take him in.

"Well. Here I am looking at you. So I was right. It was a sign I chose to take note of and my reward is right in front of me. You look very handsome." He'd always had a filter on when he was in public. His eyes were hard, but it was a front. He'd been so pummeled emotionally over his life his only real defense had been to keep people far enough away from his heart that they couldn't hurt him.

But the real Mick, the one so very few people got to see, was the one he showed her just then and it brought tears to the back of Jessi's throat. She shoved them away, choosing joy instead.

"I guess so. It could have been the invitation, though," he teased.

That made her laugh. "I'm really glad to see you. I've missed you so much." This time she'd say all the things she should have been plainer about before. Life was fleeting. She was done letting it get away from her without a fight.

A rush of emotion played over his features right before he pulled her into a hug.

It had been so long since she'd felt like this. Totally happy. A sense of rightness of place and energy. He was the part of her that had never healed over when it was ripped away.

Jessi held on, soaking him in, knowing it would need to end soon because they were in public and standing near the bar. It was his party after all. After one last sniff—holy cow he smelled amazing—she loosened her arms a little, as did he, until they finally broke apart.

That was when she got the full impact of Mick in person. She'd known him since she'd been five. He'd always been bigger, but right then she wasn't sure if he'd always been so very wide and hale and braw or if the time apart had only made him seem so overwhelmingly large.

Despite his size, he wore a pale gray pinstripe suit with a dark blue shirt and a skinny tie. And he worked it. He didn't look like a big lunk wearing a costume. No, he looked like a man who rocked the hell out of his clothes. A little bit of edge, a little bit of business. Yum.

He had ink on his knuckles, *Fists Up*, and red roses peeked from the edge of his shirt cuff at the wrists. Jessi really wanted to know how many other tattoos and piercings he might have and where.

Dangerously handsome.

She knew what was beneath the suit pants. Her nipples beaded at the memory.

Quickly—but not so fast he hadn't noted her attention on his cock—she shifted her gaze up to his face and got stuck. His beard was the same caramel brown as his hair, neatly trimmed a little long, but not anywhere near *guy-who-has-a-manifesto* stage. She liked it. A lot.

Like the hair. That'd had been a new thing when he'd come back from Iraq. Not a smooth shave because he had a perpetual stubble. It was just clipped very close.

She wanted to touch it. Wished she had the right.

Mick had sent Jessi and Adam invitations on a whim and they were both there. Both looking at him the same way they always had, and it was simultaneously the best moment and the worst because he'd left them behind.

He hadn't seen Jessi in nearly four years. Gone was the long dark braid she'd worn daily, replaced by one of those haircuts women made look effortless but probably had to be redone every six weeks. The back of her neck was bare—he'd noticed when they'd hugged—and he'd bet it was downy soft.

The dress was...wow. Something he'd never seen her wear before. At first glance it seemed like a classic cocktail dress. It came to her mid-calf and wasn't cut low in the front. But it had these panels on the sides that offered tantalizing glimpses of one of God's finest things, side boob.

She had ink and a nose ring. It looked good on her. He wondered what she had going on under the dress. Given the fit, he could see there was a large back piece that wrapped around her biceps and shoulder. She didn't wear a bra, and she was even more irresistible than she'd ever been.

She was both the girl he'd known and loved since he was a boy and a supremely alluring woman. He wanted more.

"So." He waved a hand indicating the space. "What do you think?" What she thought was more important to him than he'd realized until the words left his mouth.

"I think this place is absolutely fantastic. I'm impressed and really proud."

"Thank you." Pleasure that she approved hummed through him. "Want a tour?"

He held his elbow out and she took it. Before they walked away, Jessi glanced over her shoulder and waved.

"You know PJ?" he asked.

"I met her a few minutes ago. She was helping me locate you after we had a drink."

Guiding her through the building, pointing out the bells and whistles, he tried to pretend he wasn't keeping an eye out for Adam.

"By the way, I read the thing in the paper about Twisted Steel and how you've been named a third partner. I'm pleased things are going so well for you."

She meant it. Which eased at least a few knots of tension. "Thanks. I've been putting down some roots," Mick said.

Jessi's eyes widened, just a brief thing and then she nodded. "You're back then? For good? In Seattle I mean."

Mick didn't want to pretend away the hope in her tone. "Yeah."

He wanted to kiss her. Wanted to sling an arm around her shoulders and pull her to his side like he had dozens upon dozens of times over the years. There was a hesitancy between them now that there'd never been before, and it was his fault.

Mick had been about to blurt out something stupid when Duke approached with Asa. Both men gave him a look that asked *Who is this?*

"It's long past time you met these guys," Mick said to her quietly. "My other best friends." Then to the dudes he meant, he said: "Perfect timing. I want you two to meet someone. Asa Barrons and Duke Bradshaw, this is my oldest friend, Jessilyn Franklin. Jessi, Asa and Duke are the guys who started Twisted Steel."

"Along with Mick, now," Duke said with an easy smile as he took Jessi's hand to shake.

Asa shook her hand next.

PJ approached and Asa oriented his attention to her. Something stirred deep in Mick's belly every time he saw the way Asa was with his girlfriend. A connection that was heart and soul deep. He craved it.

"I see you found him," PJ said to Jessi.

"He found me. But you were so right about the suits." Jessi grinned PJ's way and the two shared a moment.

Asa gave Mick a raised brow, amusement in his eyes.

"You said she was your oldest friend," Duke began. "What's that story?" He was being so warm and welcoming Mick wanted to hug him.

Jessi turned back to look at Mick before telling the story. "Mick wandered into my fifth birthday party and pretty much has been in my life since."

He heard the emotion at the end. Knew she thought of his absence as well as their long history.

"My family lives on the property next door to the Franklins." He spent so much time there growing up that it was the Franklins' overstuffed household he considered *home*, not the place his parents lived.

"He was so adorable and sweet on my mom we just kept Mick."

His parents hadn't even noticed. Hadn't seen the way he'd drifted away from the heart of their home and into someone else's. They'd been so bent on *correction* they hadn't had time for affection.

"Her parents are self-described 'aging hippie Jesus freaks.' They're pretty amazing, and her dad is the best cook I've ever come across," Mick said.

PJ and Jessi chatted awhile longer. Mick didn't want Jessi to leave so he kept a hand at her elbow and soaked her in.

"Have you seen Adam yet?" he asked her.

She shook her head. "I saw his car outside, though. Have you? Oh, well I guess you have since you asked."

"I did right before I bumped into you. He's mellow tonight. The last time..." Mick didn't finish. The last time he'd seen Adam, Adam had tried to kiss him and Mick pushed him off. Neither of them had been ready.

They'd texted over the last several years. At least once or twice a month. Nothing more than a few lines. Not enough.

"It's okay. We'll talk about this later. In private," Jessi murmured.

There she was, soothing, making things better like she always did around him.

That was what he'd missed the most when he'd been estranged from Jessi and Adam. Belonging.

He had a brotherhood with Duke and Asa, which had saved him more times than he could count. They'd given him a place to land, a safe haven, and he let himself take it for once.

Once he'd stopped fighting needing the safety of the home he could make in Seattle, Mick had allowed himself to belong in the community Duke and Asa had been offering him all along.

But Jessi was something to him no one else was. His first advocate. His fiercest defender. Mick had been hers in all the best ways.

He'd run from this connection before. Twice. He'd thought at one time it had made her happier, but he'd been lying to himself.

"I'm not going anywhere." She said that quietly before taking some food off a passing tray, handing him a little plate of salmon. "This is your night, Michael. I'm here to celebrate with you."

PJ winked at him when he looked toward everyone else once more.

"I should warn you my parents said they were stopping in tonight," Jessi told Mick.

"Your mother called me a few days ago to tell me they were coming. She didn't mention you were visiting." Addie Franklin was sneaky that way.

Jessi laughed. "You're so funny that you think she was going to tell you anything she didn't want you to know. And I'm not visiting. I leased a studio space that also has a small apartment upstairs."

He blinked, surprised and pleased. He hugged her before he'd even realized he wanted to. Mick wanted to tell her he was glad. Wanted to say a whole lot, but she'd said it wasn't the time or place and she was right.

But now there'd be a time and place, which was more than he'd been willing to admit even a month or two before.

CHAPTER

Two

Adam hadn't been expecting to see Jessi. Hadn't been ready for it. So he'd held back at the edges of the crowd, nursing a drink and watching her hungrily.

The way she looked up at Mick as he spoke, the wrinkle of her nose when she smiled, it sent longing spiraling through his gut. How many times had he seen that movement? Done something deliberately to delight her to evoke that smile?

The last time he'd spoken to her it had been as if he'd been in the middle of a fever dream. He'd been at her parents' to celebrate their wedding anniversary. In the years Jessi had been in Portland, Adam had seen the Franklins on a regular basis but managed to keep away when he knew she was up visiting her parents.

Until that party. He knew she'd be there because Addie told him she would be. He thought he could handle it. Until he'd seen her and she'd been so pretty and all he'd ever wanted. He hadn't known how to take it. How to ask for what she'd freely offered.

They'd reconnected, their chemistry had clicked and it was *JessiandAdam* once again. All those empty, bleeding parts inside had been filled and healed.

They'd withdrawn from the noise and crowd and ended up

alone in a dark corner, his hand down her panties, fingering her until he swallowed her cries as she came.

He'd kissed her and she'd trusted him to let him touch her, to give over to him. He smelled of her, tasted her skin, the scent of sex hung between them. It had been so *right*.

Adam had gone upstairs, intending to set up a time to meet with her after the party. They'd work things out because nothing in his life had ever been as important.

Panic had set in. She made him lose control. Or it had felt that way. By the time she'd come back up from the basement, he'd already made his good-byes and was nearly out the door.

A few days later he'd tried to text her to make amends but he'd hurt her so badly he knew her acceptance of his apology was more to be done with him and go off to lick her wounds than really getting past it.

All his life he'd wanted many things. Had achieved a lot of them. The two integral people he'd *needed* stood just across the room.

The question was what he planned to do about it.

Adam ate up every detail, as Jessi's gaze meandered, most likely taking in all the design details. Of course she would. An artist herself, Jessi would be tucking ideas away. Then her attention landed on him, and she started, her mouth curving into a smile.

A smile she had for no one else but him. The sight of it filled him with joy.

She turned to the group she was with and spoke quietly to Mick. He resisted turning to look, but Adam knew he wanted to.

And then Jessi was walking his way.

The dress was hot, the shoes even hotter. She was a casual woman, loving jeans and soft shirts more than hose and heels, and yet, you'd never know it watching the confident, sexy siren who kept walking until she was close enough that he could smell her skin.

"Why are you over here all alone?" she asked.

"I wasn't sure you wanted to see me."

Her expression softened and he regretted his teasing made her sad. "I'd deserve it," he added.

She shook her head. "When are you going to realize you're worthy of forgiveness? I keep wondering when you two are going to figure out who I am. You both always seem confused when I still love you."

He took her hand in his and then pulled her to his body and into a hug. Adam let himself need her. Took that time to draw in the warmth and feel of Jessilyn. "Perhaps I didn't know if I was ready to be forgiven," he whispered as he drew away, pausing to kiss her temple.

"This isn't the place or the time," she murmured, keeping one of his hands. "It's Mick's night."

He tried to pull away, to draw the tattered remains of his defenses around himself. But she held on, shaking her head.

"I'm done letting you run from me." Jessi's voice had hardened.

Adam wanted to pretend he hadn't heard so he could wish away the speed of his pulse. Instead, he let her in because he was exhausted and lonely and she was right there looking at him like no one else ever had.

"And that means what?" he asked.

"It means I'm here in Seattle for good and this is just the beginning of what will continue. In private, with Mick. Away from a crowd. For now, come with me. Mick said he saw you earlier but you faded away. He needs you. So do I. You're my best friend, Adam. Aside from all the other stuff between us."

"Wait." He kept her in place, wanting her all to himself for a few moments more. "You moved home?"

"I did. I've been back about three weeks or so."

Addie never mentioned it. That woman was saucy. Just like her daughter.

Jessi laughed, knowing what he'd been thinking. "She didn't tell Mick either. I asked her not to. I had to..." She shook her head. "Never mind. We'll talk later about that."

"I was an asshole the last time I saw you."

Her smile dimmed and she sighed, nodding. "At least you made me come first."

"I've missed you a whole goddamn lot, Jessi." He cupped her cheek. Let her levity make him feel better.

"Good. You made your bed."

It was then he knew for sure he had no real defenses against her. Not at the point he was in his life. And, given the gleam in her eye, she wasn't going to let him sidle away anymore either.

"At least tell me you missed me too," he murmured, needing it more than he was comfortable with.

Her expression made him smile. He'd seen it a million times as he or Mick had exasperated her over the years. "You know I did. How many times have I said so?"

"You were living with someone in another state. You moved on." Wow, he sounded petulant.

"I'm living alone now. Not even four miles from here. I'm not playing this tit-for-tat game. I'm not interested in fighting with you. Or hurting you."

He could tough through just about anything—and he did on a regular basis—but Jessi never went for emotional manipulation of any kind when they argued. He could deal with faux tears or a pout. Heaven knew he had for the last years he'd been without her.

Jessilyn could be like a terrier when there was something she wanted. She didn't give up, but she was genuine when there was a problem. No manipulation necessary.

What she did since the first time he saw her in their freshman year of high school was take his fucking breath away by seeing him clearer than anyone ever had. There was no hiding from Jessi's gaze.

She finally spoke. "There's been an empty part of my life for four years. Never tease about me not missing you." There was an ache in her tone that was impossible to miss. Adam had put it there. He took her hand, drawing a thumb over her knuckles.

"I'm sorry," Adam said, meaning it for about three hundred things. "Let's go see Mick. His parents are coming. Did he tell you?" They made their way to where Mick stood waiting for them.

"He didn't. I'd like to think they're going to make amends. Maybe they will."

Their sweet Jessi. The kid who picked up every fucking stray she'd ever come across, bugs, birds, dogs, cats, errant boys who weren't wanted in their own homes.

If it had been anyone else, he'd have told them not to be so naïve. But it wasn't. Jessi was a person who couldn't imagine reacting to a child they way the Robertses had.

When Jessi loved you, she loved you hard and to the bone and she would always root for the best possible outcome for you.

But Adam didn't have Jessi's big heart. He wanted to hurt the Robertses the way they hurt Mick. The way they hurt Jessi.

Adam wanted to protect them the way he hadn't managed four years before.

"We'll be there for him either way," Adam said noncommittally, his hand at her elbow, keeping her shielded from the crush of the crowd.

Mick gave up waiting for them, meeting them halfway.

"Look what I found," she told Mick.

Mick quirked a grin at Adam and then to Jessi. "I suppose you're going to want to keep him?"

"He is rather cute." Jessi's tease had both men leaning close to her. And it was as if they'd never been apart. A deep sense of belonging, of satisfaction, hit him and then took root.

"I'm not cute."

Jessi smoothed a palm down Adam's tie and then did something to Mick's pocket square. Adjusting, tidying.

"You're adorable. The more you deny it, the more I know it's true." She winked at Adam. "Mick, PJ is waving at you."

"Oh, announcement time." Mick took her hands. "You're not leaving?"

"Of course not. We'll be here." She slid her arm through Adam's. "Your biggest fans."

It had been years since the three of them had been together this way. United, protective of one another. It spoke volumes that it felt right from the very moment he saw her approach.

They watched as Mick, Duke, and Asa spoke to the assembled crowd. Clapped when they announced Mick coming on as a full partner. Mick looked handsome and happy. Really happy.

Adam was pleased at the sight, but maybe a little jealous too. He'd loved Mick first. Mick was theirs—his and Jessi's. But Adam had let him run and then he'd pushed Jessi away.

Mick had grown a great deal over the last four years. He looked good. Satisfied. The harshly masculine lines of his face worked with the suit. He owned his walk. There was only a shadow of that kid who'd been slowly ground into nothing by his family.

This Mick had seen things. Things Adam couldn't begin to imagine, but when he tried his heart ached.

He had more ink. Each time Adam allowed himself a taste—a few lines of text, a picture here and there—Mick had filled out a little more. The badass, inked-up, pierced guy who fixed cars worked for him.

Jessi's eyes lingered on Mick's face, over the ink at his hands and the braided leather band at his wrist. She smiled and then applauded when their presentation ended, and Mick got swallowed up by his friends and co-workers.

"Let's stay here. He knows where we are when he's ready," Adam said.

"Good idea. Why have you been avoiding me the last four years?"

A burst of joy hit him so hard he had to hug her a moment. Adam made himself set her back or he wouldn't have ever let go.

"I've been wondering when you'd get mad." For whatever reason, it made him feel better when she lost her temper with him. She so rarely did it was like she only trusted a very few people with her anger.

Weird, but it filled him with pride that she'd trust him that way after all the shit he'd pulled.

"I've been telling myself to wait until we were elsewhere before I let myself feel it. But I can't. I'm weak." Jessi sighed.

He scoffed. "Bullshit. *Weak* is the last word I'd use to describe you. I've been in continual awe of you since I was fourteen years old."

Jessi frowned a moment and then rolled her eyes. "Whatever. So? Answer the question."

"I will. But not here. Not now." He wasn't going to do this in public.

"Fine," Jessi said. Which really meant, *Fuck you. I'm not fine and you're going to get your ass kicked very soon.*

He leaned close enough to whisper in her ear, wanting to shake her up. "The first time I saw you I ran home after school to jerk off. I still have that urge."

She turned her head, taking them nose to nose. "Yeah? Me too."

Jessi let that settle in a moment and then moved away from Adam. She needed to clear her head. He smelled so good. Looked sexy in a black suit tailored to every inch of his six-foot frame.

Crisp white shirt that wouldn't dare get dirty. Thin black tie. She wasn't surprised to see his shirt had French cuffs. There was an air of old-school masculinity about him.

Pale blue eyes took her in carefully as she gave up fighting how much he always fascinated her. She knew the jut of his chin, now covered in some seriously sexy scruff. Knew that expression he wore meant he was imagining her with her hand down the front of her panties, rubbing one out.

Knew too, he'd come to some sort of decision about finally standing still long enough for them to actually talk.

"Did you just tell me you masturbated after the first time you saw me?" he murmured with a ridiculous smirk that made her wet.

As always, he seemed to flood her senses when she got close to him. All that testosterone radiating from him. His confident manner a steady hum of sexy in her head.

"Maybe." Then she gave him a look.

His surprised laughter turned heads. She couldn't blame any of the women and men who openly coveted him. He was ridiculous.

As a young man he'd been attractive. All that dark hair and the blue eyes. He had the broody-emo thing going.

The grown man standing in front of her was that times a million. He'd taken the broody thing and made it hot broody. Like he was thinking really dirty stuff all the time. A man who drank excellent Scotch and drove a little too fast, but always ably.

Damn.

"I knew that *I'm fine* meant you were just waiting for the right moment to make me pay. I didn't think it would come quite so fast, though."

"Someone needs to keep you in line, Adam Gulati. I can only imagine—no, I try not to—what you've gotten up to in the time you put me in the time-out chair of your life."

Jessi had intended for that to be a joke but it was so true it hurt.

And he saw it. Softened.

"I'm sorry about the way I left the last time. It wasn't like that. I was the one on time-out."

Just over Adam's shoulder, Jessi caught sight of Mick's father.

"Jess? What's—" Adam turned as he'd been asking. "I see. Should we go over there to run interference or stay here?"

"I don't want a scene." Mick's father was not a person she would ever willingly be alone with again for anything but Mick's well-being.

"When I hear that sound in your voice, Jessilyn, it makes me want to beat that asshole's face in." Adam's sexy growl had gone sharp in his anger.

"It's done and over. If Mick wants them around, we probably need to give them space." She'd watch Mick's face and know. If she had to, she'd barge right on over and intervene, even if it scared her. She'd do it for Mick.

Adam's smile was deceptively mellow, as was his voice. "It's not over when I can see how deep he cut you, hear the fear in your tone. There'll be a bill for that, so don't argue. It's a waste of time."

"You're gone from my life for four years and you think you can boss me around?"

He had to fight against his initial reaction to let her push him back. Instead, he chose to hear the hurt in her tone, the fear of Mick's father. "No. You're mine. To protect. Those people have done enough damage to you and to Mick. I'm back in your life. For good. And I should warn you I'm even bossier. Now, let's head over there. Your parents just walked in, so that'll be extra fun."

She couldn't help her laughter. "I really have missed you."

"I'm fucking charming." He kissed her cheek before tugging her off to intercept her parents.

Just seeing their faces, the way they lit up even more at the sight of Adam at her side, made Jessi happy.

"Hello, punkin!" Addie hugged Adam before kissing his cheeks and then adjusting his shirt collar.

Adam's blush charmed Jessi to her toes. They all fell for Addie Franklin. It was sort of impossible not to. She made you love her.

"Hey, Mrs. Franklin," Adam said.

Her dad gave him a hug next and then kissed the top of Jessi's head. "Where's Mick?"

"He's over there." Jessi pointed. "We thought it would be good to head that way."

Addie caught sight of Mick's parents and her mouth flattened. "I can see why."

Her dad put his arm around her mom's shoulders, keeping their pace leisurely instead of the near run his wife would have them doing.

"It just hurts my heart on his behalf," her mother said quietly to her father.

Jessi's parents were genuinely loving people. They held their faith with deep conviction but a light heart. Her mom always said joy was a balm to everyone's hurts.

And they loved Mick as if he were their own. Which meant anyone who injured him the way his parents had could be counted in that very small number of people her parents truly had no use for in any way.

Mick looked up to see them coming and his face broke into a smile that had her squeezing Adam's hand.

Her parents greeted Mick with hugs and kisses while his mother ignored Jessi and Adam and his father stared.

Adam stared back at Mr. Roberts, narrowing his gaze. Barely leashed rage had his muscles tightening until Jessi made one of her soothing sounds as she rubbed a hand up and down his arm a few times.

She moved her body, angling it to stand between them and steal his attention, breaking the tension. "Hi there. I'd love to get dinner after this. We're going to do that, right?"

"I know you're trying to manage me," Adam said around a jaw that clenched slightly less. It always worked.

She smiled brightly.

By the time he looked away from Jessi and back to Mick, he'd managed to get his shit together.

"Jessilyn, come here. Bring Adam. This is the first time the three of you have been in the same place for a few years. I want a picture," her mother commanded them all, and of course they obeyed.

Automatically, they put Jessi between them, arms around one another, leaning in. Addie laughed and the sound was so lovely everyone's smile got wider.

"You okay?" Adam heard Jessi ask Mick.

He shrugged.

"Do you want us here or away?" Adam asked.

"Here. But give me ten minutes or so while I visit with them. Then maybe we can all talk or...?"

Jessi spoke. "Yes. We'll be right here while you show your parents around. I already extracted a promise of talking and eating after this."

Mick's smile made it a little easier to unclench his fists.

"Good. Okay then. Yeah." Mick blushed just a little, ducking his head as he shifted his attention to the Franklins. "Want a tour?"

Adam was relieved Mick had allowed them to act as a buffer with his parents. Hopefully they'd behave.

CHAPTER
Three

Mick let Addie's questions keep the tour moving. He knew she did it on purpose, to run interference between him and his parents. It made him love Jessi's folks even more.

His father said very little, nodding his head here and there as Mick answered questions or pointed out something interesting. His mother seemed pleased to see him and pointedly ignored Jessi and Adam's presence.

He'd deal with it all.

In time.

There were so many layers of shit, so much debris and pain that Mick couldn't face it all at once. So he'd carved all the stuff on his to-do list and tried to handle it in manageable chunks.

A lot of it wasn't fun, but it was all necessary.

When he'd taken a full circuit of the room they came to a stop near one of the bars. The crowd had ballooned earlier, but since the speech and the grand opening official stuff, things had gotten a little quieter, though still quite busy and full.

Addie gave him a look that asked if they should stay or go. He was an adult. This was his business and there were the people he cared about most in the world all within shouting distance. There were few places that were better than Twisted Steel for Mick to be face-to-face with his parents.

He nodded, indicating it was okay for them to wander off. He knew Addie had a Friday evening thing she did with her friends and that James used that time to sit in the quiet, just enjoying the time alone.

"I know you have to run. But I'm so glad you came tonight," Mick told the Franklins.

"Now that Jessi's finally home, I expect we'll see you more often." Addie gave him a look that dared him to even think about doing anything else. It wasn't necessary, though. He always seemed to find his way back to the Franklins' doorstep.

He smiled, kissing her cheek after she hugged him.

"We're so proud of you, Michael," James said in Mick's ear as they embraced.

Mick grinned at them. "I'll see you both soon."

Without even a glance at Mick's parents—who'd barely roused themselves to respond to the Franklins' hello—James and Addie headed over to where Adam and Jessi stood chatting with Duke and Carmella.

"What do you think?" Mick asked his parents.

"I think a lot of young ladies should be covering up their bodies instead of letting all and sundry see their underpants," his mother muttered.

As Mick happened to like seeing ladies in their underpants, he had no real complaints. And, as his mother was really just complaining to complain, he let it go.

"I meant about Twisted Steel. What do you think of the new showroom and all the work here?"

Mick wished he didn't care what they thought. But he did. They were his parents. He wanted them to respect him.

It wasn't that they didn't love him. They did. Mick was certain of that. But they didn't know how to love him without also making him feel like being bisexual was the worst sort of thing he could ever be.

He served his country in the army. He had a great job and was now a business owner. He'd made good choices when it came to his career at last. Mick wanted them, just for once, to notice that.

"It seems to be successful," his father said. "The paper said profits were up over a quarter from last year." He nodded.

"This new showroom means we'll now have our old showroom space to use for expanded administrative and shop use. Already there's a demand."

His dad had read the article, though. It made Mick happy.

"I'm surprised to see those Franklins and that Gulati boy around. I thought you were finished with them, Mick." His mother frowned.

"They're my family too. You should give them a chance. They care about me."

His father's brows angled down, judgment on his features. "They don't care a thing about your immortal soul. They're too happy to damn you without a thought. He's a lure to your homosexuality and *she's* the source of it all. We never should have allowed you to be around them."

The vehemence in his father's tone, the edge of hatred in it had Mick rising to defend Jessi and Adam before he closed the subject. "That's untrue. It's also something I don't want to talk about with either of you. I love Jessi and Adam, and I have since I was a kid. Mr. and Mrs. Franklin too."

"You have a family the Lord saw fit to bless you with. If you spent more time with us and less with outside influences, you'd have a *wife* and children by now. Instead you're covered in tattoos and surrounded by temptation," his father said.

"This has been a pretty good visit so far, so let's stop now before anything else hurtful gets said. Please," Mick added.

He did need to talk through all this stuff with them, but not in the middle of a party and certainly not when he was in the same place with Jessi and Adam for the first time in years.

His parents nodded, frowning. They made their excuses, including a few about why some of his siblings weren't there. His older brother and sister had come by earlier. They would be there for him, even if they didn't always understand his choices.

The rest of his biological family was a grab bag of messed-up relationships. He was working on letting go of it all. But that was way off in the future. Right then it still weighed on him.

By the time they'd left, so had the Franklins. He tipped his chin and grinned at Asa and Duke after a quick hug of both men's girlfriends, and found Adam and Jessi.

"Ready?"

"Are you sure? There are still people here," Jessi said.

"There are. Most of them work here and are hanging around for free booze and food. The guests are gone. The photographer has headed out. Where are we off to?" He wanted to be with them. Away from everyone else. Felt like he had to or lose his nerve.

"Come to my house," Adam said. "I've got food and a wine cellar."

Mick grinned at him. "We gonna need that much booze?"

Jessi snorted. "Whatever it takes to get you two talking at long fucking last."

They both goggled at her.

"What? It's not that I never say the F word. It's a great word, after all. I'm just more judicious than you two are."

How he'd lived years without her wasn't something Mick wanted to think on just then. She'd been his heart for so long, and then he'd cut her off. That absence had been a raw wound that had never healed.

But there she was and he let himself love it. Love her.

"You're absolutely correct, Jessilyn. You're far more judicious than us in all ways, I'd wager." Mick kissed her forehead.

Adam gave them both his address and they left to follow him to his place.

He was nearly to his bike when Duke and Asa called his name.

Mick could have pretended not to hear them, but as he'd decided to finally talk to Adam and Jessi after all this time, he might as well be open with Asa and Duke too.

Within reason.

He kept walking to his bike, but waved to acknowledge them both.

"So, you want to tell us something? A few things?" Duke asked as they met up at his bike.

"A lot of things," Asa added quietly.

"I know I've been putting you off about this whole thing. And I know I promised to tell you. And I will. It *is* a truly long and complicated story, though. Right now, I'm on my way to Adam's place to talk with him and Jessi, so it has to wait. I've loved Jessi since I was that lonely seven-year-old who she dragged into her birthday party because she saw him watching from the trees."

Duke's expression softened and then hardened. "I want to talk about your parents too."

"One giant life-altering thing at a time. I'm not a wizard," Mick said.

Asa's laughter startled them both.

"As for Adam? Well, that's complicated too, but loving him was one of the things that sent me back to the army. And more. Jesus, a lot more." Mick blew out a long breath.

"Don't keep them waiting. We'll be around when you're ready." Duke tipped his chin before hugging Mick.

"So, *both* of them? This isn't a love triangle situation, right?" Asa asked him.

Mick grinned, glad it was dark so his blush was invisible. "Yes, both. No love triangle."

"Yeah, this sounds like a big bottle of tequila and cigars on the deck sort of story," Duke said with a snort.

A rush of gratitude hit him. Without these two men and their brotherhood, he wouldn't be standing there.

"At *least* one bottle." Mick grabbed his helmet.

His friends stepped back as he got on and keyed the engine to life.

"Call me if you need anything. I know things are still shaky with your brother," Mick told Duke. His younger brother had been going through some rough times and had been in the hospital.

"For now it's okay. Carmella and I are going to dinner with my parents and my sister before they all go back home tomorrow morning. Good luck."

"Thanks," he said to Asa and Duke. He didn't need to add anything else.

Jessi knew where Adam lived, of course. She sent him cards a few times a year, never wanting to fully let go. She might have done a computer street view thing, maybe.

Her stomach tied and untied knots as she sat in her car. And then he came out from the garage and pointed at her car and the space next to his.

"It's fine. I can park here. Then Mick can take the spot in the garage," she said as he approached her side.

"Mick is on a motorcycle. He'll fit anyway. You, inside the garage. It's safe. It's out of the weather."

"You're very bossy."

He arched a brow. "Nothing has changed in that regard, no."

Sighing, she pulled her car into the spot he'd indicated and then got out when he opened her door.

"How hard was that?" Adam asked.

"Not any harder than it would have been to park in the driveway," she muttered.

"Saucy as usual, I see."

"Don't get smirky with me."

Adam paused and then he pulled her into a hug. "I hate how long it's been since I've felt this way," he whispered.

Oh how she wanted to remind him it was his own fault. But she knew it would only wound, and she thought they'd all wounded one another enough for a lifetime.

"Mick's coming," she said instead.

"Okay, you're weird, but you can't possibly know."

"I can hear a beefy motorcycle engine approaching. I'm guessing that's him." She didn't argue with the weird thing. She was totally weird and one hundred percent okay with that.

"Ah."

Soon enough a big bike turned at the end of the street, heading their way. This was a change she totally approved of. He looked badass and gorgeous as he followed Adam's direction and pulled into the garage.

"See? Room for everyone," Adam said, closing the bay doors once Mick had keyed the engine off.

"I should have had you ride with me. Your suit!" Jessi said as Mick joined them to walk into the house. Then again, his suit was fine. He probably rode in all sorts of clothes and stuff.

"Everything is cool." He grinned and then they both paused at the entrance to the main part of the house.

Jessi left them both standing as she wandered into the living room, where the ceiling was open to the second floor. A fireplace dominated one wall with floor-to-ceiling windows to either side.

She cruised past the built-in shelves, loaded with books and small pieces of art, skidding to a halt as she reached something she recognized.

A hand-lacquered box she'd created with some gold and lapis caught her eye and she picked it up.

Adam spoke, "I really can't believe you never told me you did this sort of thing. Imagine my surprise when I was in a gallery and saw this with several others. It was your signature, they had it blown up and in a frame in the display." Adam joined her and soon enough, Mick, without the jacket or his suit coat, showed up on her other side.

"I might have told you if you hadn't avoided me for years." Jessi put the box back, pleased it had a home here on his shelves.

"Fair enough. I bought them all. Two of the collection had already been purchased, so I tracked them down."

"Adam! That's a lot of money for something I'd have given you for free."

He sighed. "Except you deserve to be paid for them because they're amazing."

"Thank you." It was flattering that he'd been with her even in some small way. But at the same time, she returned to the way he'd held himself back.

"I don't know about you two, but I need out of this tie and something to drink and eat," Mick said, interrupting the tension.

"I did promise, didn't I?" Adam looked them both over. "I've got some workout pants and T-shirts if you want to change, Mick. Jess, you look beautiful. But if you're uncomfortable or want to relax, I have some of your clothes so you can see if those fit. Otherwise we can make do with safety pins and my clothes."

"You have my clothes?" She didn't know why, but she was surprised and then deeply touched.

"I had things at my old place. You were there all the time, if you remember. I just brought it when I bought this place two years ago." Adam led them upstairs and into a bedroom.

Adam disappeared into a closet and brought out a stack of things he handed to Mick, and after a brief look through a drawer or two, he indicated she look. "In here. I'm going next door to ditch this suit so I'll meet you all downstairs in a few."

* * *

Mick knew he should go in the other room. Even before anything sexual had happened, they all would have changed in the same space without a thought. The three had been that close.

But that was before.

He was grateful to have something more comfortable to wear, and as a bonus the fabric smelled like Adam. But sweatpants did zero to hide a hard-on, and he'd had one since Adam walked through the doors at Twisted Steel earlier that evening.

After he managed to hang the suit and the shirt, Mick turned his attention to the other side of the bedroom where Jessi'd been standing, staring into the drawers.

How many times in his life had he watched Jessi doing something as ordinary as choosing what to wear? Granted, she usually hadn't been wearing a dress as sexy as the one she'd chosen for the grand opening. But Jessi made everything into a delightful ritual.

She didn't just grab something to put on her body; she pondered Jessi-stuff, like if the day would be cloudy she needed to wear a shirt that had a certain color, or a skirt that reminded her of a flower, whatever. Because it was Jessi, it could be anything at all that inspired the choice.

She dug around a little, pulling a T-shirt free, followed by a pair of funky dad pajama bottoms. Jessi was a clothing thief. Those pants were likely to be a pair she'd lifted from her father years before.

"Can you unzip me, please?" she asked him, looking back over her shoulder.

Not trusting himself to speak, Mick went to her, unzipping the gorgeous dress she had on, unveiling a slice of bare skin as he did.

"Holy shit!" He opened the back of the dress wide and took in the ink she bore. "Wow, Jess, baby, this is gorgeous."

Wings took up her entire back, the bottom tips reaching to her waist, the outer edges at her shoulders, wrapping around her upper arms. At the base of her skull they came to a point, touching artfully.

She shimmied a little so the top of the dress came free and he could see the whole thing.

Mainly in sepia with tones of gray to accent the feathers, the touches of lilac, green, and pink here and there made the wings seem iridescent, as if they caught the light. The detail work was stunning, giving the feathers a three-dimensional quality. It must have taken up hours of her life to have it done.

Because it was Jessilyn, there'd be a reason for this choice. But it suited her, beautiful, magical, strong.

Adam came in, moving to them immediately to look over Mick's shoulder at Jessi's back.

"I could tell you had something big back here," Adam said, his voice vibrating where he leaned against Mick. "Did you give him the story yet?"

Mick turned his head to smile at Adam over the shared memory. "I was about to ask."

Jessi let the dress drop totally, stepping free of the material. She shook it a little before laying it carefully on the top of the dresser.

Adam swallowed audibly as they stood there staring at Jessi in nothing but a tiny pair of panties.

She hadn't turned to face them so they were afforded only the barest glimpse of her breasts while she put on the pajama bottoms.

"You both know how I feel about my angel dreams." She pulled the shirt on—Mick recognized it as one of his—and turned to face them.

"I was riding my bike along a creek trail one day and suddenly there were dragonflies everywhere in this little marsh. Zipping all around in the sunshine. Their wings were so pretty. I nearly crashed!" She grinned as she walked past them and out the door.

They followed her because she'd start talking again, whether they were there or not, and he wanted to hear the rest.

"Kitchen is to your left," Adam called out.

At the bottom of the stairs she waited for them.

"Did you design this yourself?" she asked as Adam flipped on the lights. "Oh!" She did a slide across the hardwoods in her socks that had Mick trying it himself.

Adam weaved his way through them, opening his fridge to peek inside. "I'll tell you the story of this house after you finish telling us about your tattoo."

"Well, that was it, you see. One of my friends in Portland is a tattoo artist. I'd been planning to do the wings for my birthday and then the dragonflies came to me. A sign. I rushed back home and called to make the appointment to get the work done. I feel like they keep me safe. That's the story of my wings. The plumeria on my wrist—ooh, I need some of this!" She dumped a bunch of cheese and deli stuff on the counter before returning to the fridge. "Came after a trip to Oahu and Maui. I made a wedding dress and some other custom pieces for a client. Her father-in-law retired from thirty years of tattooing! Imagine. Anyway, he did the flowers on my wrist."

Adam looked through the items she'd put out on the counter. "I can do something more complicated than sandwiches."

Jessi patted his butt on her way past. "We know. I don't even think we need to assemble anything, just bring the crackers and some bread and go from there."

CHAPTER
Four

Like wayward ducklings, they responded to her directions and before long they were sitting on Adam's couch, readying the first shot of whiskey.

Jessi held her glass up. "Only connect."

The heat of the liquor helped burn through the lump of emotion in Mick's throat. E. M. Forster's words had been their toast since she'd read *Howards End* back in high school.

"That's my shirt," Mick said as they all began to eat and relax a little.

She shrugged. "Looks like it's mine now."

Adam poured them each another shot. "I have nowhere to be tomorrow. I figure being drunk might help us get started with this whole talking it out thing."

"Twisted Steel is closed this weekend so everyone could have a bit of time off after working balls out to finish all the projects we wanted to showcase tonight." Mick offered their toast this time and was rewarded with a smile from Jessi.

"I have a fitting appointment, but it's not until three." Jessi leaned back against the cushions and Adam grabbed her feet, pulling them into his lap.

"Where's your fiancé?" Adam asked her.

"It would serve you both right if I said he was waiting for me at home."

"Stop agitating her," Mick said easily.

"Okay then, where have you been for four years?" Adam challenged.

"What about you?" Mick replied.

"You guys are such babies." Jessi pointed at Adam. "You better have something sweet in this house or I foresee one of you running out to get me a candy bar. No one's too drunk to walk their ass down to that gas station I saw on the way in. I'm just getting that out there."

"How is that even connected?" Adam asked.

"*You guys are babies*. That's pretty much connected to everything. I need something sweet for strength to get me through this so we can fix a mess years in the making." Jessi's tone was patiently amused so Mick eased back too.

"There's ice cream in the freezer," Adam said. "Not everyone is as well-adjusted as you are, Jessilyn."

"Oh fuck off."

Mick cackled. "Twice in one day."

"I'm gifted." Adam sucked in a breath.

"As I was saying," Jessi continued as she sat up enough to pile some ham and cheese on a cracker, "fuck off, Adam. Yes, that's it. I'd rather be well-adjusted and not living with someone who deserved a lot more than a woman who could never love him because her heart belonged elsewhere. What about you?"

Adam got up, grumbling the whole way to the kitchen.

"Ice cream." Jessi said nothing else, winking at Mick.

Indeed, Adam brought in a giant bowl of ice cream with chocolate sauce and some whipped cream on top.

"It's like you knew I was coming," Jessi said, delighted as she took the bowl. Then she frowned. "If you had this stuff because some other someone you've been nailing liked it, I don't want to know."

Adam got to his knees in front of the couch, facing Jessi. "It's not for anyone but me. And now you. I'm grumpy and taking it out on you. I'm sorry."

She held out her spoon, loaded with ice cream and toppings, Mick took it and then she did the same for Adam.

"I'll go first." Jessi tucked her feet beneath her and Adam joined them on the couch once more.

Mick looked to Adam. They'd been the ones to push away, she their anchor. And yet again, she was shouldering something to make things easier for one of them.

He knew Adam felt the same sort of adoration for her at that moment.

"Stop." Jessi put her bowl on the coffee table and shifted to more easily see each of them, her back away from the couch to face them instead. Each man was touching her within moments. Mick, his palm over her knee and Adam twining his fingers with hers, holding her hand.

"It's all right to be weak sometimes." Jessi smiled. "I'd never knowingly harm the bond I have with either of you so I hope you'll trust me to open up, but I'm going first because neither of you seems ready right now. And that's okay."

"I had a lot of conditional affection in my life," Mick said. "We love you, *but*. Or you'd be a better member of our family *if*. You don't do that. You never have."

"I tried not to love you," she admitted. "I tried to put you both in the *people I once loved and will always care about but I've moved on* box. For *years* I tried. But it didn't work. Because I can't unlove you. Neither of you. It's impossible."

Adam lifted her fingers to his mouth to kiss them. "Tenacity. It's a fantastic quality and one of the many reasons I love you."

"He means to say he's glad you can't unlove us." Mick rolled his eyes at Adam. She was in a good mood and they wanted to keep her there, not get her riled up.

Jessi snorted. "That doesn't mean this is going to be easy. I'm not the same Jessi I was before you joined the military and then you left." She indicated Adam with a tip of her chin. "It won't work if we can't open up. I can go first, though."

Jessi looked to both of them, still shocked into delight at random moments when she remembered they were actually together at last. Her lost boys.

So strong and fierce, and yet when it came to this, it was she who could stand as an equal to bear the weight. "Eight months ago I had an audition of sorts. A friend suggested me to the Seattle Opera."

She grinned at the memory of the first phone call. The flattering thrill of something she'd been working so long to achieve.

"They asked for two pieces for their adaptation of *Rigoletto*. I'd been thinking about moving back to Seattle for the last two years or so." Her pride had kept her in Portland long after she'd known there was no running from what she felt for Mick and Adam.

"It was a sign," Mick said. It was a tease, but an inside joke, not in any way making fun. And she was glad because if he'd mocked just then it would have really hurt.

She nodded. "It took a few months so I began to look for jobs up here. I needed to figure out if it was truly possible for me to earn a living in Seattle. And I needed to break things off with Carey. It had been coming for some time. It was totally my fault and I felt awful to do it, but he's actually speaking to me again, so I guess he's forgiven me. Anyway, I moved into my studio, accepted that I was really going to come home. Even if they hadn't loved what I'd made, there's a considerable client base in the Puget Sound, so I began to plan. My place here is in a good retail district with lots of free parking. I moved in at last three weeks ago tomorrow. I sleep in the loft above my workspace. I got the invitation to the grand opening three days before I picked up my keys."

"Another sign." Adam didn't smirk, though.

She nodded. "When I saw your car tonight, I knew I'd made the right choice. Then I sort of panicked that dealing with both of you at once would be too much. And it sort of is, but I guess that's something I like."

"Jess, I'm so proud of you! This stuff with your costuming is amazing." Mick hugged her and she tumbled against him, laughing.

"Thanks," she said, breathless when Adam lay atop her as they both ended up in Mick's lap. "I moved to Portland because you went back to Iraq and then Adam left me a little more every day until we were strangers. I had to go because being here and having Adam look right through me hurt too much."

Adam's intensity changed. No less powerful, his sadness that he'd hurt her flashed over his face as his muscles tightened.

"I fucked up. So much." He shifted his weight so he wasn't resting on her. "I wasn't looking through you. I just lost my shit for a while." Adam brushed the hair from her face.

"Is this the I Fucked Up Olympics? If so, can we do the medal award ceremony and get down to the real issue now?" Mick asked.

"Does that mean you're going next?" Jessi didn't bother to hide her amusement as she craned her neck to look up at Mick.

Mick swallowed hard and decided to be as brave as she'd been. "When I came home from the military the first time and we were together, it changed everything." He'd felt, for the first time in his entire life, that anything was possible. That it hadn't mattered that their relationship didn't look like most.

Just a few times, less than he could count on one hand, the three of them had been together, and it was enough to turn him inside out. Because his whole life it had been, as he'd said to them moments before, conditional love from his family. From his community.

"I thought I had it down. Being with you, the growing thing between me and Adam. And then that scene with my father."

Adam shifted so Jessi could crawl into Mick's lap, wrapping herself around him. Only this time, after a brief moment, Adam also pressed close.

Mick buried his face in Jessi's hair, breathing her in, holding her with one arm, Adam the other.

"I thought I was cool with it. With what I was. Who I was. But after the fight with my dad and the following days, it just made me itchy. Panicked. Like I had to choose, and what if I chose wrong? Had I fucked up the best thing in my life because I let myself have Jessi the way I'd wanted for so long? Adam? Well, I hadn't really let myself consider us being together like that. I didn't feel good enough for either one of you, and I was afraid that if you had to choose, I'd lose you both." And so soon after he'd kicked his pill habit, it had been extra scary.

Jessi spoke, her voice muffled by his shirt. "So you ran."

"I ran because I was afraid to stay. I was afraid of what would happen when reality set in. Ran because I was terrified of what would happen if I chose wrong."

And had been without *this*. For years.

So stupid. Jesus.

"And you're back now? Not just in Seattle, but in my life?" Jessi asked, tipping her head back to see his face.

Mick cupped her cheek and she leaned into him. "I needed to get my shit straight before I made contact." He lifted his gaze to Adam's. "I'm back. In Seattle and in your lives."

Jessi's body snuggling into his after years without her felt so good it nearly hurt.

"I'm sorry I left the way I did. Sorry I wasn't there when you needed me. I was a shitty friend, and I hope you'll let me make it up to you. To both of you."

"Things just unraveled for me when Mick left. Watching Jessi try to process, trying to be there for her and not managing it very well. I felt like an asshole, felt like I'd been tossed away. Felt like I needed to be someone else to see if that's what I should do for the rest of my life," Adam said.

His leaving—the way he'd done it—had been a way to allow himself the space to take what he wanted and gorge on it.

Jessi lifted her face from where she'd been buried in Mick's shirt, locking her gaze on his.

Adam hated that she'd been hurt. Hated that it had been necessary in any case, to step away and be Adam in a completely different context.

"And did you like what you found?"

Adam took her hand. "It was something I had to do. I'm back to you now. For keeps."

Which didn't make it any less harsh, he knew. He had a lot of fucking sins to make up for when it came to Jessilyn Franklin. He just had to hope he was man enough to do what it took.

And that she found it within her heart to understand. One day.

As for Mick, that was still complicated, only in a different way.

"For keeps like we're all close friends again? We hang out and share our lives?" Mick asked, wariness in his voice.

Jessi wore the sweetest confused expression, and Adam refused to think about how terrifying it was that she got to him the way she did just by being herself.

"I didn't want to assume," Adam said.

Jessi rolled her eyes. "You realize that all three of us showed up after years of being apart. We all clicked back together pretty much immediately. And now it's like we're all shy? After all we've shared? That's what this is, then? We're all friends but not like before? We just forget those times? You two want to see other people?"

"Is that what you want?" Adam asked carefully.

"*You* left, Adam. After *you* left, Mick. I didn't want to walk away. You two did. So asking me that question sort of makes me mad."

"You're the one who lived with someone else and was going to get married," Mick mumbled.

"You guys are such assholes sometimes. Despite what you both put me through, I accept that you needed to step away. But you come back to me with this? No, thank you. If you want to just be friends, all right. I can deal. But you need to be up front and you can't be kissing my fingers and Mick needs to stop grinding his cock into my ass. Friends don't do that."

"I just wanted you to know I didn't expect you to hop into bed or anything. I didn't want to assume," Adam repeated.

Jessi looked up to Mick. "And you?"

Mick was smarter than Adam, though, because he hugged her tight. "If it was up to me, I'd want us to all be together. Really together."

"Suck-up." Adam rolled his eyes.

"She's on my lap, though, so I declare that a win."

Adam reached out to snatch her from Mick's lap, bringing her to his own. "Looks like she's in my lap now."

"Something friends don't do," Jessi reminded him.

Adam took her cheeks in his hands and then claimed her mouth before she could say anything else.

It slammed into him so hard—a wave of regret that he'd put this aside—that he gasped, sucking in the sigh she gave him.

A sweet enough kiss. For now. Hunger, barely leashed, filled him. He wanted. Wanted what had been freely offered before he'd truly understood how rare and special it was.

"I'm always your friend," he spoke against her mouth. "But I'd be a liar if I claimed I didn't want *everything* from you. Being away from you only underlined it."

"I was so lonely without you both." She closed her eyes a

moment to avoid his seeing all that pain, but he saw it, felt it cut him to the bone.

"I'm sorry. I was lonely too." Adam had filled every moment with a pursuit of pleasure, but *this* was something totally different. Something he might not have really recognized if he hadn't been without it.

But what he did see was he'd have a job of earning her trust back, even if she was being easy enough right then.

CHAPTER
Five

Mick ran the backs of his fingers down her jawline, to her throat. "That's the worst part. The part I regret the most. I wasn't here for you when you had rough times, and I hate myself for it." He leaned in close to brush his lips over hers as Adam watched greedily.

"I'm pretty sure more self-loathing is the last thing either of you needs," Jessi muttered, pushing back to sit straighter on Adam's lap and look between Adam and Mick.

"You changed in the last four years too." Mick got hot all over seeing it on her. An independence and sass she hadn't possessed before. It fit just right.

"I have. We'll talk about that later. Look, I don't want either of you to hate yourselves. That's a lot of weight to carry. I want to look forward, move on, and we can't if all this negative stuff gets between us." Jessi took each man's cheek in a palm. "I love you and I forgive you—both of you—for everything that's happened."

Mick let out a breath as the words settled in. They needed to do whatever it took to be together and that was that.

Adam looked to Mick and then at Jessi once more. "Thank you. I needed that. And what do you want, then, Jessilyn? We might have run away, but you *loved* someone else."

His favorite crooked-Jessi smile had Mick's mouth returning the expression even as she'd had her attention on Adam. "I've loved two people in my entire life and I'm looking at them. So, what I know is that I didn't want to live my life without trying to heal this wound between us. You and Mick are my best, closest friends, and pride is a small thing to sacrifice if I could just have you back because nothing has been the same since you left me behind." Jessi wiped the back of her hand over her eyes and Adam pulled her close. "Even if we were just friends I'd be all right because we'd be together again."

Mick swallowed back emotion as he hugged her around Adam. He put his head on her shoulder. "Baby, I'm not worth your pride. But I want you more than I've ever wanted anything. All of you."

She turned her head to look at him, remaining wrapped around Adam as he rubbed big circles over her back again and again.

"No one is worth my self-respect. But you and Adam are worth swallowing my pride and making a leap of faith."

Mick kissed her again, calming, relaxing even as his cock was harder than he was sure it had ever been.

"No one has ever made me feel this way," he said against her mouth.

"We're long past the just-friends stage," Adam said, kissing the top of Jessi's head and then, on his way past, Mick's mouth.

Casual. But it staked a claim as well.

A shiver worked over Mick's skin as he licked Adam's lips for one last taste.

"You taste like Jessi. My favorite," Adam said as he moved away once more.

Mick snorted. "My favorite too."

Jessi's eyes had gone half-lidded and glossy. Christ.

Adam stood, putting Jessi on her feet, keeping a hand at her hip. "I should probably warn you both. I'm very possessive," he told them.

Jessi harrumphed and one of Adam's brows rose imperiously slow.

"Did you have something to say?" Adam asked Jessi.

"I said it when I harrumphed."

Adam's smile made Mick's cock throb in time with his heartbeat.

"Love, why don't you use words for me?" Adam's tone had gone down a few octaves, a teasing sort of growl.

The catch in Jessi's breathing was like a tug on his balls. "I don't need to because you know exactly what that sound meant," Jessi taunted.

Mick closed a hand over his dick through the sleep pants he had on, squeezing just so. The interplay between Jessi and Adam was so hot, Mick's cock was already smeared with pre-come.

"Well, here's a thing." Adam tucked her hair behind her left ear. "We've all changed over the last four years. As it happens." He then slid his hand through her hair, sending it into disarray for a moment before grabbing it in his fist and pulling her head back, exposing her neck to his mouth.

"Ohhhh," she said, slow like honey.

"I like to be in charge." He bit and she moaned. "A lot."

"You'll need to earn that."

Jessi's response had Adam standing straight to get a better look at her. "I do?"

"Yes." A smile touched her mouth, not that crazy happy Jessi, this one a seriously sexy one. Cocky even. "Like you said, we've all changed."

Adam's handsome face darkened into a frown.

Jessi's laugh had Mick pulling her into his embrace. "Hi." He kissed her and she wrapped her arms around his neck. "This is the best thing in the world. Right here, right now with you and Adam."

"Yes." Jessi nodded.

"Tell me who you submitted to," Adam said as he pressed himself to Jessi's back.

"No, I don't think that's necessary."

"I really can't understand why you're trying to pick a fight right now, Adam. She's always been our girl." Mick wanted to shake him, demand he stop trying to poke at her.

"Ours." Adam pressed closer, close enough Jessi gave a little grunt as she got squeezed between them.

"Ours," Jessi agreed.

Jessi's head spun with the sexuality in the air. Even before, their first time together and the few days they'd had were more clumsy and wonderful than seriously hot and sweaty. Though that had been part of it.

No, what she'd experienced as a twenty-five-year-old with her two childhood best friends had felt like an extension of what they'd had. They'd stumbled into it, and while it had been amazing, it didn't hold a candle to what it was just then as the air seemed to shimmer with desire and anticipation.

She hadn't actually submitted to anyone. Ever. But she wasn't stupid. Or naïve. If Adam wanted it, he'd earn it. Otherwise why would she do it?

The memory of the sting as he'd grabbed her hair and bent her back rushed through her.

Her boys were there. With her. Their hands and mouths on her. The ache she'd pretended away for years had been slowly easing as just being around them had made her feel better.

She'd eaten, had ice cream, and now was about to have a hot-damn three way with the two people she loved most in the whole world. And they looked even better than they had when she saw them both last.

Between the inked-up, rough-and-tumble Mick and Adam, the debonair dom, she was totally screwed. But like, in a good way. This sort of thing they made together was a kind of magic, and there was nothing she could do but love it as much as she loved them.

"Did you both learn lots of things to do to me?" she asked, unable not to laugh at her good fortune.

Adam's growling laughter was met by Mick's groan.

She tipped her head back to stare up at Adam.

"I'll endeavor to keep you satisfied," he told her, kissing her forehead.

"It's a big job," she assured him.

"I probably need to get started then. Come on up to my bedroom, where we can spread out. Mick, bring the liquor." Adam stepped back and held a hand for her to take, which she did.

Mick took her free hand and they let Adam lead them to his lair. She tried to pretend she did this every day, which was naturally a pretty big lie. But it was Adam and Mick. They wouldn't hurt her.

Not in a way she didn't like anyway. It was pretty clear to her that Adam ran to the uber–alpha male territory, so she was fairly sure he could hurt her in ways she *would* like a lot.

She'd deal with the uglier feelings about him touching anyone else later. Right then every part of her just wanted to be with them, bare and exposed.

His bedroom took up half the second floor. A big bed dominated the room, but there was a sitting area near the fireplace with shelves, an overstuffed love seat, and a lamp perfect for a rainy day of reading inside by the fire.

The rugs on the hardwood floor were Persian. She'd been with him when he bought the one she stood on. The room was a sanctuary. A really luxurious one, no doubt. But this was about Adam's inner life. Sumptuous fabrics, leather, gorgeous textiles created a space she knew without even asking he spent a lot of time in.

Probably not always alone. But again, she shoved that aside because it didn't matter. Not right then and most likely not anymore.

"I want to smear all your make-up." Adam said this as he drew the pad of his thumb over her bottom lip.

"Do I have any left?"

Adam's severity seemed to wisp away, replaced by a sweeter expression. "You do. Enough that you're going to have smudged mascara when I'm done." One corner of his mouth hitched up and she sort of forgot what she'd been thinking about. Make-up? Whatever. When was he going to take his clothes off?

Mick burst out laughing—most likely at the confusion on her face as Adam got her all sex addled—as he tugged his shirt over his head and her mental dialog skidded to a halt.

Shoulders that had grown impossibly wide ridged with muscle. The muscle of a man who worked with his body on a regular basis.

And a lot of that taut, muscular skin was covered in tattoos. She held one hand out to stay him while she clutched at her heart with the other. "You're enough to startle a girl."

"Or a boy," Adam said.

She was *so* lucky.

It was Mick's turn to wear that cocky grin as she and Adam looked their fill at him. His belly sported a snarling, badass orange-and-black tiger's face with numbers below it.

He slid his palm down his belly, over those numbers, and she huffed a sound, like a desperate wheeze. *More please* and *oh-my-god-stop* all at once.

"Look at you," Mick said with the tip of his chin.

"I'd rather look at you," Jessi said, meaning it with every fiber of her being. "The tiger is new."

"Your nose ring is new."

"It is. The numbers, it's my birthday." She crept closer, looking at the roses and thorns rippling down his forearms, ending at his wrists.

"I had it added year before last."

He'd kept himself apart from her for years, but he hadn't let go of her in his own way.

"The way you look at me..." Mick drew a deep breath he slowly exhaled as if trying to center himself. "I'm different now. But you look at me with that light in your eyes. Now I'm just nervous about regular stuff, like how long I'm going to be in you before I come."

Heat flushed across her skin at his words.

"I've got faith in you," she murmured. "You're not all that different. More ink and piercings, but it's sexy. Your heart is the same."

Mick looked over her shoulder to Adam, who nodded.

"What? What does that mean?" She pointed a finger back and forth between them.

"Nothing," Adam said, but he laughed and blew his cover.

"Oh really?"

"Really," Adam grabbed her around her waist and pulled her back against him. His cock seemed to burn against her skin. "We're going to look at one another like that because he and I love you."

Well. She liked that.

"Now you." Mick gestured her way.

"Shirt off, Jess," Adam whispered in her ear like a fallen angel luring her to temptation.

"Just because it's off doesn't mean it has left my custody," she told Mick as she whipped her shirt up and over her head. If she was expected to give back all the clothing she pilfered, she'd be naked a third of the time. She stole them, they were hers. That was the rule.

Mick's grin made her tingly and swoony. Honestly, how could she ever have thought happiness was possible without these two people in her life?

"I'd never think to steal my shirts back once you have them." Mick stepped close enough to slide his upper body against hers.

"Oh!"

Laughing, Mick reached around her to get Adam's shirt free as well. "You too."

Jessi turned in their arms so she could get a look at Adam, and holy cow was she glad she had. Tawny skin played over his upper body. No ink but on his inner forearm at his elbow.

Jessilyn. In her handwriting. He'd shown it to her the last time she'd seen him.

"I never told you why I put your name there," Adam said as she slid her fingertips over his skin.

She waited for the telling and when she did, he smiled, grinding his cock into her.

"You're my addiction. The thing I need more than anything."

Always so tough. So taciturn and grumpy. And yet, so very tender it broke her heart sometimes. Hell, *he'd* broken her heart more than once too. It came with loving him, she'd finally accepted.

"Is that why you denied yourself?" She gave in and combed her fingers through his hair. "And denied me too, I might add."

"I had to work through a lot of shit, and I couldn't do it with anyone else. I had to do it alone." His voice was rough, full of guilt and anguish.

"I hear the guilt in your voice. Let it go." Selfishly, she wanted him to be unfettered when he came to her at long last. So she'd know he was there for good.

"So you don't hate me?" he asked.

Startled, her eyes widened and she tugged on his hair to get his attention. "I could never hate you, Adam, and if I did, I wouldn't be here. I'm here because I've always been here, just waiting for you to remember that."

He pressed into her body as Mick gave no quarter at her back. Being squeezed that way kept her immobile.

And it was delicious.

He said nothing else before he bent to kiss her. At first slow, teasing, sexy kisses that heated her belly and made her knees feel like noodles. He licked at her lips, teasing her mouth open until she sighed happily.

Mick played his fingertips up her sides, brushing over the curve of her breasts. "When I saw these tonight I knew you'd worn that dress for me."

"I admit that when I tried it on and it had all that tasteful side boob I knew you'd appreciate it," Jessi said as Adam moved away from her mouth.

"Who *doesn't* appreciate it?" Adam asked as he stepped back enough to grab the waistband of her pajama bottoms and shove them down her legs, along with her panties. "As far as side boob goes, yours is aces."

Jessi laughed and then got nervous because they both still had pants on and there she was naked as a jaybird.

"Mick, why don't you lead our angel to the bed?" Like a switch had been thrown, Adam took charge. He drew authority around himself like a cloak.

Mick backed her up slowly, caressing her shoulder before pressing kisses across her skin.

It was really happening. After years of going through the motions, here it was, the moment she'd been waiting for since she'd woken up to find out Mick had reenlisted.

Desire made her limbs heavy, left her movements languid as Mick shifted to lay her back on Adam's big bed.

"I'm naked and neither of you are," she said, proud she'd remembered all her words. She got snagged up in the details. The muscles and ink. Both men's gazes roamed her face and her body and there was *no* mistaking just how happy they were to be right there.

The inner walls of her pussy contracted on nothing, sharpening the ache.

"Patience," Adam said.

She raised a brow his way. "Are you new here?"

Mick, laughing, bent to kiss her.

A *crack* sounded and Mick groaned into her mouth as he moved forward. Did Adam just spank Mick? Jeez, they had to hold some of this super hot stuff back or she'd burn to cinder.

She opened her eyes to watch Mick straighten, a flush on his neck. Adam liked it too, getting caught up for a few moments before turning back to Jessi.

"I'm not new here, no. I know you're impatient and greedy when it comes to orgasms."

Jessi grinned at Adam, knowing there was a *but* coming along soon.

"But I'm in charge. You'll get what you're begging for. When I'm ready to give it to you."

One of those *sort-of* orgasms, the kind you had in dreams, stole through her as she squeezed her thighs together. He was going to kill her from desire. Or something. She really couldn't wait.

CHAPTER
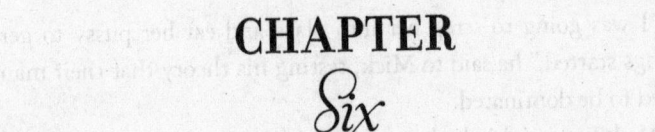
Six

Adam sucked in a breath, wresting his control back. The way her pupils had flared, the dark, hard nipples on tits she thrust his way when he spoke. The parting of her lips on a gasp. *Everything* she did incited him.

He was good at this, damn it. The control always snapped into place, his ability to wield it had never been in question.

But Jessi did something to him. He wanted her to love his dominance as much as he loved dominating her. She looked up at him with trust naked on her features. Willing wasn't what she was. It was so much more.

No one looked at him the way she did. It made him feel ten feet tall. It didn't matter that he wasn't worthy. Jessilyn ignited something in him from the start.

Adam had tried to live without her. Without this. And while he'd learned a hell of a lot about himself during those years, he'd never felt as whole as he did right at that very moment.

"Okay," Jessi managed to breathe out.

Step one in his earning her submission, he supposed, stifling a smile. She'd been right of course, real submission wasn't taken, it was given. And he wanted it. All of it.

Mick moved at his left and Adam turned to take him in, this man who'd surprised him over and over.

His pupils were as wide as Jessi's. As he waited.

Adam pressed the heel of his hand against his belly as he considered the bounty before him.

"I was going to strap her into place and eat her pussy to get things started," he said to Mick, testing his theory that their man liked to be dominated.

Mick's mouth hitched at the right corner.

"But we have you. So for now, I don't need straps," Adam told him.

"He should be naked for that," Jessi added and it made Adam snort.

"I think you're right. Get those pants off, Mick."

Jessi rolled to help and Adam grabbed her ankle. "Ah, no, angel, I didn't tell you to move."

She raised her left eyebrow at him in a very fine echo of what he'd done to her just minutes before. But she stopped trying to get to Mick and eased back to where she'd been.

He straightened again and turned just as Mick's cock sprang free from his shorts.

"My. That's bigger than I remember," Jessi said.

Adam couldn't help but laugh.

"It wasn't *that* long ago," Mick said, grinning at the compliment.

"I only got to play with it a few times before you ran off." Her tone was prim but her gaze flicked from his face to his body, taking her time as she reclined on the bed.

Broad, muscular thighs dusted with hair led to similarly rock-hard calves. The cock was, as Jessi said, big. Adam hummed his pleasure at what he saw.

"You can play with it all you want, Jessilyn." Mick gripped his cock at the base, squeezing slightly.

Jessi laughed, the sound filling Adam with a peace he hadn't felt in some time.

"When *I* say you can. Keep your hands where I tell you, Jess. For now, Mick, get behind Jessi and hold her wrists for me."

"I can put my head in your lap. You know, for ease and all," Jessi told Mick as he moved.

Adam still had a hand wrapped around her ankle so he held her in place, sliding one of the straps at the foot of his bed around first her left and then her right. It would keep her body exactly where he wanted it and still allow her to struggle without hurting herself.

All her sass seemed to drain away as he worked and by the time he straightened and took her in, her eyes had gone heavy lidded, her mouth open slightly.

Mick crouched at her head, his fingers around her wrists, holding them to either side of his body. A guardian, a co-conspirator. Beautiful and fierce.

Adam bent to kiss each one of Jessi's ankles and then up to first one knee and the other. Her skin was soft and warm and smelled just exactly as he'd remembered. It seemed like he'd been dreaming this smell forever. And there she was. He needed to relearn her, though. He hadn't done as much as he'd wanted before things had broken.

Now he had the time. Time to play. To adore and cherish and devour every delicious bit of her. To show her he was ready now, to be hers in every way.

And he'd damn well take it and do his job to keep her right there in his bed.

When he reached her pussy, Adam paused to breathe her in as he spread her labia to expose that soft, wet flesh to his gaze. That's when he noted the small silver ring and bead piercing her clitoral hood. A full-body shiver of desire took over and stole his words for long moments.

"So beautiful," he whispered. "When did you do this?" He tugged gently on the hoop and she gasped.

Mick leaned forward and cursed at the sight.

"Your pussy is pierced. Baby, when?" Adam asked, proud his voice hadn't cracked like a fourteen-year-old's.

His sweet and sexy *Jessilyn* had a silver hoop gleaming against the dark, slick flesh of her pussy. He'd honestly never seen a sight that turned him on more.

"Seven months ago," she managed to say, though her words were slow and slightly slurred.

"Later you'll tell us why." He knew there was a reason. This was Jessi after all. "For now I'm going to eat you until you scream. And then Mick can play with you." Adam's gaze flicked to Mick's.

Mick had always owned a part of Jessi that was far older and deeper than Adam did. Adam wanted to make her come first, begin to heal what they'd torn apart. Maybe heal parts of himself too.

Somehow.

For the moment, though . . .

He took one lick, and then another, and one more until it was all he saw and felt. Her pussy, her taste, the sound of her indrawn breath. Everything he'd ever wanted and now could finally trust himself to possess.

Everything he'd never, ever let go of again.

Mick watched Adam's mouth on Jessi's cunt, his breath short, cock impossibly hard.

Jessi was pierced and inked and *right there*.

Damn.

He allowed himself to believe, to hope and trust. It was the only way he saw himself being happy because he'd been pretty damned empty without her. Jessi had been part of him for so long and then he'd tried to hide on the other side of the planet because he'd been a damned fool.

The ache of her absence in his life had gotten heavier—deeper—each passing day until he'd seen her again.

A sexier, more grown-up version of his best friend. A woman confident in her sexuality. A woman who knew her appeal. Still his kooky, silly Jessi, but more.

He'd let himself need her and she'd stormed right back into her—rightful—place in his heart.

The woman arching, licking up the side of Mick's cock whenever he let himself get near that mouth eased Mick's concern that he was too dirty for her. That what he and Adam made with her was more than she could accept.

She opened her eyes, locking her attention on him and whispered, "*Please.*"

It tore at him. Needing to please her. Needing to answer her call. But Adam had a plan. That much was totally clear, so Mick managed to wait.

Just barely.

The domination stuff was new, though Adam had always possessed a great deal of charisma and people tended to look to him to make decisions.

But straps rigged underneath his mattress? That air of leadership and take-charge attitude? Unexpected, and he had no complaints. Given the way Jessi writhed against Adam's mouth, she had none either.

Her hair, cool and silky, brushed against his thighs and balls. Delicious agony.

Mick watched her nipples harden and darken as the scent of her rose on the air. He gripped her wrists tighter and she opened her eyes, tipping her head back enough to look up at his face again.

Her cheek brushed the side of his cock, bliss and pain at the same time.

"I'm next," he murmured to her and she licked her lips, nodding.

Mick continued to alternate between her face and the way Adam's hair would fall forward to hide what he was doing for a few moments. Each reveal was a sensual punch to the gut.

Every time she surged against his hold and the straps at her ankles, he got harder.

She made a sound, a near snarl as Adam held her ass up, serving himself her pussy as the rest of her arched, coming so hard Mick knew exactly what she was going through. The rush of her energy, nearly electric, seemed to explode from her, sucking Mick in, making him want her more than he'd ever wanted anyone or anything the whole of his life.

Adam, appearing as shaken as Mick was feeling, looked up the line of Jessi's body, caressing her face and then up to Mick's.

She was the bridge between them. Mick knew it better than Adam would admit to himself most likely. But he'd known Jessilyn longer. Had been hers from the moment she'd pulled him from the stand of trees and into her life.

Adam petted his hands up her ribs and across her belly. "Now, I feel so much better that we've taken the edge off."

Jessi's laugh made Mick smile. "My edges are just fine if either of you needs yours to be handled. I should also probably say I have no plans on a cock in each hole."

This time, Mick burst out laughing. The stuff she said, Christ it made him so glad he'd finally accepted how much he needed her.

"Even if I told you to?" Adam asked.

"I'm totally fine to have you boss me around and be in charge. I'll even obey you most of the time. But I still have likes and preferences and hard nos. A cock in my ass and one in my pussy is a hard no."

Adam nodded, kissing her belly. "Fair enough."

"If you two want your cocks that close, just do it. And let me participate or watch."

Mick bent to kiss her quickly. "We'll keep that in mind. But for right now? I told you I was next."

Jessi's pupils swallowed the color in her eyes for a moment as she nodded, solemnly. "I'm all yours."

She was.

How fucking lucky was he?

Mick looked to Adam, seeking . . . permission? A blush heated his skin.

"I had no plans in this direction," Adam murmured and Mick stared, waiting.

"Because you're the debonair dom now, and you figured you and Mick would top me?" Jessi asked.

Adam's gaze flicked to Jessi, a smile playing at the corner of his mouth. "So what exactly did you get up to with your fiancé?"

"Notice how he ducked the question?" Jessi was taunting Adam deliberately. In a way Mick was fairly sure no one else dared to do.

"Who's ducking questions now?" Adam's voice was a seduction.

Mick moved from his place behind her head, letting the two of them continue their little back-and-forth. He wanted her and he wanted her right then and he planned to take her. "I've waited so long to see you this way." Trailing his fingertips over her hip bone, he groaned at her sigh of pleasure.

"Still such a hedonist when it comes to touch." Mick bent to kiss her there, licking a trail where his fingertips had been.

Jessi got to her elbows to watch him. "I'm a hedonist when it comes to you two."

"Get your fingers nice and juicy from your pussy," Adam said, the command wrapped in a hoarse caress.

He hadn't relinquished control. Not totally.

Mick began to turn, feeling territorial, but she caught him up when she spread herself open for them both, circling her clit and that fucking dirty-gorgeous ring with her fingertips.

Adam pressed himself to Mick's back. He licked up Mick's neck before biting his ear hard enough to bring a grunt from Mick's lips and a jut of his hips.

"Not trying to stand in your way," Adam murmured.

"Better not be." He'd tolerate lots of things, but he'd not let anything get between him and Jessi ever again.

Adam drew blunt nails down the wall of Mick's chest and it was Jessi who gasped in delight.

"It won't be easy to share. But we can work it through. I expect Jessi will be generous with herself so we get enough." Adam snaked a hand down Mick's belly to his cock. He jerked Mick slow and loose as his stubble tickled the skin at Mick's shoulder. "But I don't share control."

Jessi licked her lips before she bit her bottom one. "You boys are so sexy." Her voice had gone dreamy. "What if I want to be on top sometimes?"

Her tone was partly teasing.

"Harder, yeah, fuck." Mick leaned his head back into Adam as they both watched Jessi finger herself.

"Me? Or him?" Jessi tipped her chin toward Adam.

"He meant me." Adam gripped Mick's cock a little tighter. "You don't want to be on top, angel. You *need* to be worshipped. Adored. Cherished. I need to do the adoring."

He let go, stepping away from Mick as he stripped his shirt off and climbed on the bed with Jessi. "Get your nipples wet for me."

Mick watched, transfixed as Jessi obeyed. Her breathing had changed and her skin bore a pretty flush.

"Mick needs to do the adoring too. Sweet Jessi, you have two bossy men to handle now."

Mick got between her legs, sliding his palms all over her. *His once more.*

They'd both top Jessi, but when it came to the relationship between Mick and Adam? Did Mick want to bottom?

"You think you can handle us both?" Mick asked Adam.

Adam's expression changed to that of utter certainty. Cocksure, arrogant, and hot as fuck.

"Yes, babe. Bet on it." Adam bent to lick over Jessi's nipples. Mick caught the flash of his teeth as he tugged hard enough to make Jessi arch into his bite.

"What will you do to him?" Jessi asked, her attention on Mick, though she'd asked Adam.

Adam looked him over, a look on his face that told Mick maybe yeah, he might like to bottom. To whoever Adam had allowed himself to finally be.

"I've known you both a long time, but I'll need to learn you all over again. Have to keep you both satisfied. I expect you'll keep me very busy." Adam tugged her nipples hard enough to send a gasp of pain from her lips.

Mick's skin flashed hot as Adam bent to lick her nipples again. This time the only sounds she made were full of pleasure.

But she hadn't taken her eyes from Mick. He knew she paid attention. Always had. Jessi had a way of making him feel known. No one else in the world came close.

He got to his knees, nudging the head of his cock to slide through the furls of her cunt. He'd meant to do it quickly, a tease, but the heated honey that slicked his way dug in deep.

"Please tell me you have condoms," Mick muttered, looking to Adam.

Adam tossed him a foil packet. This was for her. He'd protect her until he knew it was safe to be naked inside her.

Fisting himself a few times, he slicked his cock with her lube before suiting up.

Through this, she'd continued to watch and wait. Adam had traded places with Mick, settling in at Jessi's back, leaning her against him so she could continue to wait for Mick's next move.

Mick flicked the ring and she gulped.

"You like that?"

He tugged it, along with her clit and got even harder as her breath came out on a sigh of longing.

She nodded, her hips churning as she ground herself against his fingers.

"What will *you* do to me?" Jessi asked Mick, a smirk on her delicious mouth.

"I'm going to fuck you hard enough to watch your tits bounce. And then, well, who knows?" Mick looked from that beautiful pussy up to Adam for a brief moment.

"Feel free to unstrap her if you please." Adam's voice seemed to vibrate through Mick's balls. "The trunk at the foot of the bed has all manner of delights inside."

Jessi continued to watch Mick as he knelt between her thighs. His hands spread at her hips to hold her in place.

She frowned and he tried not to laugh. "What's that face for?"

"You moved your hands. But I like the way you look holding me. I like the way your ink looks. So I'm probably going to be all right momentarily."

Mick leaned over her body to kiss her long and slow before he broke away to find Adam's face just in front of him.

Before Mick could worry about how to respond without scaring anyone away, Adam's hand caught the back of Mick's neck to haul him the final inch to meet in a kiss that took over Mick's brain.

Adam's lips were nearly as relentless as the edge of his teeth and the flick of his tongue. Mick gave over to it, let himself fall under Adam's spell, let Adam set the pace.

Between them, Jessi wrapped her fist around the base of Mick's cock, slowly jacking him. The other hand traced over his balls before sliding back over his asshole and up to his sac once more.

He groaned and Adam swallowed the sound. Mick pressed closer.

Jessi squirmed and both men broke apart slowly moving away a little so as not to smother her.

"Sorry about that," Mick said, craning his neck to get a better look at her nestled there between them.

"I would like very much to have two things," she told them both.

Adam looked to Mick, grinning, before answering Jessi. "What man here could refuse you anything, angel?"

"You still have pants on. I've tried to remain patient here, Adam, but really now." Her long-suffering sigh brought a laugh from Mick's belly.

"She has a point, Adam." Mick gripped the base of his cock as he shifted back a little. Brushing himself over her clit and the ring lazily, he gave her a smile as her gaze blurred a little more with each stroke of her clit with the head.

"If you both insist." Adam leaned out to kiss Mick again and then Jessi before he moved to the floor to shuck the pants. He wore no underwear so his cock sprang free immediately.

"Oh. Yes, that was worth insisting over." Jessi stared at Adam, her nails scoring over Mick's balls.

Adam was as beautiful naked as he was clothed. Long and lean, he'd run track in high school and college. Powerful legs said he still worked out. The flat belly too. Though his metabolism was one that made him one of the genetically gifted who seemed to be able to eat anything and never be concerned.

His cock bent in a way she'd remembered very well. Mick's grunt echoed her gasp of delight when Adam fisted himself a few times, preening for them.

"Satisfied?" Adam asked them.

"I was. Now I want more." Jessi blinked at them both. She wanted everything. It was all she'd be willing to settle for.

"Does this relate to your second demand?" Adam moved to the bed so she grabbed his cock with her other hand. He was thick and so very hard.

He raised a brow her way and she laughed, so full of joy it made her drunk. "I think this is the most perfect example of embarrassment of riches ever."

Only with them could this be so hot and dirty and sexy, and yet sweet and comforting all at the same time.

"My second request was that someone put a cock in me and very soon." She smiled prettily between them. "I know it might seem greedy of me since I've already come once."

Mick scooted back, playing his cock through her pussy, driving her into near incoherence. Her breath seemed to slow to that same rhythm as she and Adam watched Mick.

"His stomach is rather delightful," she whispered.

She felt Adam laugh at her back. "I completely agree."

"I would look at the three of us doing sex stuff in a mirror all day long." They were each so incredibly handsome but in totally different ways. Mick with his broad shoulders and muscles. Acres of tattoo ink spooled over his skin. Both nipples were pierced by a silver bar.

Leaning back against Adam, Jessi reached to Mick, touched him. He was there. Real.

She pushed the regret away that he hadn't been for too long.

When she twisted the bars gently he made that sound again—part groan, part grunt of command to give more. It made her dizzy just being with them.

Mick's hardened expression wisped into amused affection. "Mick, I love your tiger. Which isn't a euphemism for your penis. Though I really like that too."

Mick thrust into her body in one hard movement and she arched, pleasure tinged with pain zinging through her. She wanted to wrap her legs around him, drive herself to meet each thrust, but she couldn't.

Her legs still immobile, he pulled her to his body, fucking her onto him. There was slack enough in the ankle straps to bend her knees a little, which got him deeper. Deep enough that he grunted each time he got in fully.

"So tight, Jess." He nearly panted as he slowed his pace, but kept deep with his strokes.

"It's been a while."

She should have been coy probably. Allowed for some mystery that she was a hot property or something. But they made her so addled she forgot everything.

Adam slowly drew the tips of his fingers up her inner arms and brushed them back down again. Over and over as she watched Mick take her. Own her like he should have done years before.

Claim her because she'd never belonged to anyone else but these two.

Mick's cock was so thick, so big it filled her to the point where it nearly hurt. But not quite. That delicious knife-edge he kept her on as he fucked into her body meant all she could do was let herself feel.

How could she have gone through the last years without this? How could she have ever believed it was possible to be happy without it?

"I can't believe I didn't do this for four years," he muttered.

Jessi tightened around him as hard as she could, underlining that. He grunted, one corner of his mouth lifting in acknowledgment of her point.

Adam began to add his nails to the strokes up and down her arm. Lightly scoring the sensitive skin but nothing more. It made her sleepy, heavy lidded even as pleasure began to edge toward climax.

Mick drew close too. His expression had gone from affectionate to furious focus on his goal.

"You first," Mick managed to say.

"Want some help?" Adam asked and Jessi wasn't sure which one of them he was asking.

Mick answered, though. "Can you reach her?"

"Baby, never underestimate the lengths I'll go to touch our sweet Jessi." Adam scooted forward a little, wrapping his arms around her so he could slide one hand to her clit and the other found her left nipple, tugging and circling in time with Mick's thrusts.

She wasn't sure when she ended and either of them began as her world became pinpoint focused on the three of them, right then, right there, and when she came, trying to arch, being held in place by one man at her front and the other at her back, the pleasure was unrelenting as it swamped her.

Mick snarled a curse, speeding his thrusts until his fingertips dug into her thighs hard enough to bruise and came, burying himself with a groan as they struggled to breathe.

Adam, one arm holding Jessi to him, reached out to grasp the back of Mick's neck to haul him into a kiss once Mick had come back from disposing of the condom. It had been meant to reassure, but within seconds, it lit every cell in Adam's body.

Mick gave over so fucking beautifully it spurred Adam on, wanting more. Mick was bigger, shoulders broader, outweighed him by at least twenty-five pounds and yet when Adam shifted to get Mick to his back on the bed—and away from crushing Jessi, who was still strapped at the ankles—he rolled immediately, looking up at Adam with a smirk.

Adam dragged his nails down Mick's sides, over all that tight, colorful skin. "Jessi, unstrap your ankles and come here." He spoke without looking away from Mick.

A few moments later and Jessi hopped from the bed and nuzzled into his side. He turned to kiss the top of her head. "In the top drawer of the nightstand there are condoms and lube."

He turned to watch her move, noting Mick doing the same. She had no discernable problems with her nudity, a fact that made him very pleased indeed because he most certainly liked her naked. Especially in his bedroom. In his space.

She brought the tube and a packet back to him. "I wish I could paint. Because this sight would make a masterpiece," she murmured as she looked back and forth between Adam and Mick.

Adam caressed a line up her back as they both watched Mick. He blushed a little at their attention. "Someone better be touching me soon."

"Impatient." Adam raked his nails over the bars through Mick's nipples. "You just came."

"True." Jessi waited, her gaze sliding all over Adam's hands on Mick. "You're the only one who hasn't come yet."

"Don't worry, love. You and Mick will make it all worth the wait." He might be sated. After a few weeks. "Jess, get the condom on my cock and then let's get Mick's ass ready for me."

She made a soft *ooh* and Mick grinned, jutting his hips forward, already beginning to get hard again.

"That what you want, baby? Hmm? My cock in your ass? Fucking you incoherent?" Despite the rough words, he meant it. Wanted to hear Mick ask for it.

"Yes," Mick snarled. "That's what I want. Fuck me."

"Gladly."

Jessi got the condom rolled on and then lubed him over the latex.

"Want this face-to-face," Mick said.

Jessi climbed to the bed, settling in, ass perched on her heels as she kissed Mick and whispered in his ear. Mick's eyes closed and his lips lifted into a smile so sweet Adam immediately wanted her to make *him* smile that way.

"I told him watching you two was the best fantasy come to life," Jessi said quietly as she got her fingers slick, pouring the lube over them and Mick's asshole at the same time.

"Yesssss," Mick groaned out as she slowly worked one finger in. "It's been a while since I've had more than fingers or a toy in there. *Fuck yes*," he told Jessi as she added a second finger.

Adam didn't say out loud that he'd only fucked other men to prepare himself for Mick. It was the same for Jessi. His cock hurt, he was so hard, needed to come so desperately.

His hands still smelled of Jessi. He tasted her on his lips. Watched her with one fist wrapped around Mick's cock while the other hand slowly opened his asshole. The sheer taboo of it juxtaposed with how right it felt because it was Adam/Jessi/Mick made the hotness nearly mind-blowing.

"Love." Adam stepped between Mick's legs. He moved the fingers Jessi had been using on Mick and replaced them with his own. Needing to gauge how ready Mick was.

And then he was pushing his cock in ever so slowly as he tried not to come immediately at how hot and snug Mick was.

He'd take Jessi too. Needed to mark her as much as he needed to mark Mick. It was enough for the time being that he still smelled of her, enough that the three of them were together again.

"More," Mick urged.

"I don't want to hurt you." Adam tried to hold Mick back from pushing himself completely onto his dick. "Not like this," he added.

"The burn is part of why it feels so fucking good." Mick wrapped his legs around Adam's ass and hauled him all the way in. Adam nearly shouted a curse and Mick arched on a groan.

Jessi watched, flushed, eyes wide, her hands clasped on her lap.

"You like what you see, angel?" Adam asked her.

She nodded.

Adam bumped against Mick's gland and they both grunted.

"Yes, yes, yes," Mick intoned, nearly a prayer as Adam gave up trying to hold back. He wanted this. Mick was hard again, red and flushed, his belly slick from where he'd been leaking.

"Jerk yourself for me," Adam said.

Jessi gave him a little lube and settled again, just watching, smiling like a girl who got everything she wanted for her birthday.

Inside, Mick tightened on each thrust Adam made when he hit Mick's sweet spot. Over and over as Adam got closer and closer to climax. Mick's movements, which had been sure and steady, got erratic as his body tightened so hard around Adam he had no choice but to come.

Adam kept coming as Mick shot all over his belly and chest, thrusting until he finally managed to stumble back to pull out and head to the bathroom quickly.

When he returned, Jessi had cleaned Mick's belly and chest off and they'd settled onto his bed talking quietly. For a moment he reacted to their connection, which had always seemed a little surreal. But they turned to him and smiled. Jessi held her hand out. "You're back. Come over here."

And he did.

CHAPTER
Seven

W here are you going, angel?" Adam's sleepy voice reached her as she got to the door leading to the garage.

He was beautiful as he came to her in nothing more than very low-slung sleep pants. Rumpled. Even his hair was cocky.

"I have to go to work. Lord above, Adam, you are so beautiful." She smiled, caught up in him.

He pulled her close, burying his face in her hair at her neck. "When will you be done?"

"Not until the evening." She had a fitting and then finish work on a wedding dress she was set to deliver to a bride in two weeks. She also hoped he didn't realize she'd stolen one of his button-down shirts.

"Will you text me when you're finished? Or come back?" He touched his forehead to hers.

"If you want me to, yes."

The sex had been great and she'd woken up feeling better than she had in years. But it was still wobbly and she didn't want to be the one who screwed up first.

"I do want you to. I know we're all busy, but we need to make time. Text me when you're ready." He kissed her. "And for the record, I don't want you leaving without saying good-bye."

"You both looked so peaceful I didn't want to wake you. You were both very busy making me come all night long."

He gave her a look. "I don't want to wake up not knowing where you are. I've done that more than enough for the rest of my life."

She cupped his cheeks and tiptoed up to kiss him once more. "Fair enough. I did leave a note. It's on the table. My address and info are on it along with an extra key I had. You two have to share until I get another made." Not that they'd want to be in her tiny little space when Adam's giant bed was available. But she wanted them to always feel welcome.

"Not that I'm complaining, but what is it I have to share with Adam?" Mick joined them, coming to hug her from the side, kissing her temple.

"I only had one extra key to my place. I left it on the table with my note. I'll get another one made soon."

Mick frowned. "You're going somewhere?"

She laughed. "I have to meet a client in about an hour and I need to change and get ready. I already told Adam I'd let him know when I finished up in case you wanted to do something tonight."

"Of course we do."

Adam rolled his eyes. "See?"

"Okay fine. Sheesh. I have to go or my client will see me do the walk of shame."

They both walked her to her car and Adam opened the door for her. She promised, once more, to let them know when she finished up and then drove away with a big smile on her face.

Once she got home—or her temporary home until she found a bigger place—she showered, tried not to obsess over all the pretty marks they'd left on her skin, and got her head back into work.

The next hours were filled with a fitting, a lot of hand sewing of sequins, and detail work, so when she looked up to find it was nearly ten p.m. and she was alone, cross-legged on her bed with a backache and eyestrain, she wasn't surprised.

How many times had Carey found her this way and chided her to eat or take breaks? Jessi put her work away and stood, stretching her muscles, realizing now how hungry she was.

Her phone had texts on it from Adam, asking after her schedule. She smiled as she noted how pissy he got the more he asked. *Someone* hated it when things were out of his control.

He'd always been a take-charge person. Always dominant. But the way he was now was . . . more. Like he'd grown into himself. It was sexy as hell and it fit him. But it meant Jessi would have to figure out how to manage all that bossiness or he'd take over.

She texted him back that she was done and if he was still awake she'd love to grab late dinner with him and Mick.

He texted back, "Mick and I are standing outside your front door."

Sighing, she headed down to find, yes, two gorgeous men standing outside. She unlocked and smiled. "You have a key I told you to use."

They came in, Mick grinning as he kissed her quickly. "We just got here and figured we'd knock the first time."

Adam waited not so patiently for his hug and kiss. He looked her over carefully. "Do you usually work this late? This neighborhood is dicey."

She rolled her eyes. "This neighborhood is *not* dicey. Like at all."

"Who are those guys down there?" He indicated the couple a few buildings down unloading what looked to be groceries from their car.

"Don't know. Want to go introduce ourselves?"

Adam narrowed his eyes at her for a moment, but she blinked and smiled innocently. He might be the debonair dom and all, but she'd been handling his grumpiness since she'd been in her early teens.

Mick rolled his eyes. "Give me a tour?"

She locked the door and turned to them. "It's not that big a space really. This out here is where I plan to have a few retail pieces. I figure at prom time I might have some dresses, some of my cocktail and wedding stuff too."

Jessi led them through to the back where her workshop was.

Adam paused at the costume currently on the form to his left. "You made this?"

She nodded. "What do you think? It's for an opera." It had taken hours and hours to get all the seed pearls placed just right. But it would glimmer in the stage lights perfectly.

Adam was awed by her work. He knew she was talented, but this was so much more than he'd expected. This was art.

"I think it's fantastic. I'm stunned that anyone could actually make something half this good."

She let out a breath. "Thank goodness. I was worried when you got quiet for so long."

Mick snorted. "He was wowed by it. Like I was. So you make this stuff regularly? Enough to have this as a job?"

"That's my goal. It looks like a realistic one right now. The more I do this, the more people will refer me if they like my stuff. I..." She shrugged.

Adam pulled her close. "You what?"

"I tried to do other things. I had a *real* job while I did sewing on the side. It wasn't enough. And I'm trying to be done with not enough."

He kissed her. "Love." He never had all the right words when it came to her. It was all what he felt so he put it into the kiss.

He'd hurt her. More than he'd thought. It humbled him in a way that only Jessi could manage.

"You're amazing. You deserve everything."

Mick watched them, several expressions crossing his features.

They were more careful, though certainly that comfort level had simply clicked into place the night before.

She hugged Adam and then turned. "Anyway. I have ideas about expanding. But for now this pays the rent on the space and I've been sleeping in the loft while I look for an apartment. My parents offered me my old room, but honestly I'm here so late sometimes it's easier just to sleep here until I find the right place."

Adam frowned at Mick, who looked similarly annoyed.

"I live ten minutes from here. There's no reason for you to sleep in some closet when I've got four thousand square feet to share." Adam realized after he'd said it just how much he wanted it.

"I said I was looking, and it's not a closet. It's actually cute. Come on and look." She tugged away, leading them up a rear stairway to a studio-sized apartment with a speck of a kitchen and a bed she'd clearly just been working in if the project still on the coverlet was any indication. There was a small café table and two chairs, lots of bookshelves, and a television so ancient he couldn't believe it still worked.

"What the hell? It's freezing up here." Mick was truly pissed off when he turned to Jessi.

"I had the window open for a while. I like the way it smells when it rains. You know that." Her chin jutted out slightly as she finished, and Adam's dick liked it.

Adam growled. "Look, either find this miracle apartment or stay with one of us. You don't need to live in a tiny space with no damned heat. It's getting cold. That fridge is making a sound I can hear from here. This neighborhood isn't safe." It actually wasn't bad, but damn it, she had no need to live this way. "Is it money? I know you're touchy about this, but let me at least loan it to you."

"Touchy?" Mick asked.

Jessi threw her hands up. "Oh my god. I am so hungry! I told you I was hungry, and we're in here and you two are trying to tell me what to do when, take a look around you, I can do my own living just fine. This place is plenty warm. This neighborhood is just fine, and so is the fridge."

"What exactly are you looking for in an apartment? A double rainbow? A prophetic dream? Jesus, angel, why punish yourself when you have all these offers? At the very least let me get my real estate agent on a search for a place for you to rent." Adam wasn't going to let this go. He wanted her safe.

She crossed her arms over her chest and glared. "I know you did *not* just make fun of me. Feed me or go away."

Mick sighed and got between them, sliding his arm around Jessi's shoulders. "He's just worried. He didn't mean to make fun. Let's all go get something to eat and then we can talk. Pack a bag, Jessi, you can sleep over with one of us. Please?"

Her lashes swept down and then she squared her shoulders and nodded.

Mick kissed her quickly. "Adam and I will go downstairs to wait. Unless you need help carrying anything?"

"No, I'm fine." She turned without looking at Adam again and began to gather some clothing.

Mick shoved him out of the room and they headed downstairs to wait.

"We can't let her fuck around and play. She either finds a place better than this or moves in with me. I have the room. You both should move in," Adam said quietly.

Mick snorted. "We just got back together yesterday. Let's slow our roll here. You can't just boss her around like that. Especially with the mocking. I'm not cool with you hurting her feelings."

Adam blew out a breath. "I shouldn't have mocked." He knew how much Jess believed in her signs and dreams, and he'd just been worried and gotten pissed.

"Amateur."

"Rub it in." Adam was extra grumpy because he'd been a

dumbass and Mick looked smooth in comparison. And because Mick had been right. "I was without you both for too long. I'm being careless." Adam shoved a hand through his hair.

Mick caught him around the shoulders to still his pacing and hauled him close enough to kiss him quick and hard.

"We'll work this through. It's Jessilyn. She'll be laughing and snuggling in fifteen minutes if you just *ease back and be nice*," Mick said quietly as they turned at the sound of Jessi coming through to where they waited.

"My car is out back. Where are you two?"

Adam held a hand out and she gave him the overnight bag to carry with a shrug.

"It's already ten thirty. I know a little place that's open until two." Mick tipped his chin. "Follow me to my house and we can head over from there. Since I rode in with Adam, I'll drive with Jessi so she doesn't get lost."

"I'm much better at that stuff now. I have a GPS in my car that tells me step by step where to go." Her pout was irresistible, even though she was annoyed with Adam. He took a risk and kissed her quickly.

"Works for me," Adam said as they headed out.

CHAPTER
Eight

I know he hurt your feelings. He didn't mean it the way it came out," Mick said as they headed to his place.

"I know." She continued to drive.

"You're still upset."

"I'm agitated. Not upset. I think that's called *hangry*. You know how I feel about being really hungry."

He hid a smile. "I do. We'll get you fed soon. I promise."

His house wasn't very far away from her shop, about fifteen minutes or so. Enough time for him to chill out and reassure himself she was all right.

Adam pulled up behind them.

"He thinks I don't know he parked me in so he got to drive," she muttered as they got out.

Mick took her hand. "He knows you know."

She harrumphed, but there was a ghost of smile on her mouth.

"She's hangry now, she tells me," Mick called out to Adam as he came to join them. "I propose we just walk to the diner now to feed her."

Adam took her other hand and they walked together the few blocks to Toulouse Petit.

Several people inside waved to Mick as they arrived, including someone he'd taken home a few weeks before. Mick put an arm around Jessi's waist to underline that he wasn't there for anyone else.

"I'm having a cocktail to go with my food," she said as she looked through the menu once they got seated.

"As many as you like, love. Mick and I can carry you home if that's necessary." Adam winked and she smiled at him, easing the tension.

"What did you two do today?" Jessi asked them both once they'd ordered.

"Fucked. Slept some more." Mick looked Adam over and then shifted his attention to Jessi again. "Waited for you."

"I'm jealous. The closest I got to sex was measuring inseams." She buttered some bread and bit into it with a sound that had Mick breathing deep to keep his cock under control. Watching Jessi do anything she loved was this way.

"Let's talk about your living situation," Adam said and Mick kept his sigh as quiet as he could.

"Let's keep it nice and easy because of course we know Jessi is smart and capable," Mick said, smiling at the server as their drinks arrived.

"Of course she is." Adam raised his glass. "Only connect."

They clinked their glasses and sipped.

The cheese plate arrived and they dug in, not speaking about anything deeper than how good this or that combination was.

She perched on her chair like a little bird, the pleasure at everything she tasted written all over her. How it was that one person could be as joyously beautiful as Jessilyn, Mick had never been able to fully understand. So he'd fought it because it was scary to imagine it might not be real.

Her hair was a wavy, nearly unruly mass of dark silk. But it wasn't disheveled. It was unbelievably sexy. When he saw her he thought about Sundays in bed. All day. She moved with a sense of whimsy and wonder in a way he'd never seen in anyone else.

"Don't think I'm unaware of the shirt you thieved from my closet this morning," Adam said.

Jessi laughed. "It's a great shirt. I'm going to wear it with a belt and jeans, I think. Otherwise I might just tailor it. Take it in at the sides."

"If you lived with me, you could borrow my shirts every day."

Mick would give that a solid eight as far as attempts to get Jessi back on topic went. But Mick had long ago realized Jessi put a lot more thought into what she did and said than most people.

She was stronger willed and more deliberate than pretty much anyone he knew, and he knew some hardheaded motherfuckers. Jessi was just adorable when she did it, which led to most people being charmed by her, though a lot of people underestimated her.

"I can borrow your shirts every day no matter where I live. Oooh, gnocchi!" Jessi smiled up at the server, who blushed as he set her plate down. "Thank you."

He stood, simply staring at her for a few seconds more before Adam cleared his throat and the guy snapped out of it and finished what he'd been doing.

"I've missed watching you charm everyone, Jessi." Mick bit into his po' boy, glad they'd gotten past their tension.

"You know what my mom says about manners and being gracious."

Indeed, Addie Franklin had very definite opinions about how to treat other people. Her heart was big and her ability to love seemingly infinite. He had a woman who'd given birth to him, but Addie had been his mother in more ways than he could count.

"So, about finding a place," Adam said again.

"Why are you suddenly so interested?" Jessi turned her attention to Adam.

"I'm always interested in your safety."

"We've already established there's no real safety issue with my place. And you didn't care about my safety three weeks ago. Or six months ago," Jessi said.

"Ouch. I did. But I had no right to say anything one way or another about it. You were with someone else six months ago."

"No I wasn't. Anyway, what's past is past and I don't want you to feel awful. I just want you to explain why it is you get a say in where I live."

"I know what your neighborhood in Portland looked like. I know he has a good job and you seemed to be happy. If I couldn't be with you every night to be sure the doors were locked, at least I could know you were with someone who would do it in my stead. Obviously not as well." Adam sniffed and Jessi tried not to smile as she rolled her eyes.

"We only just got back together yesterday. It's foolhardy to jump into something." Jessi frowned as she said it and Mick knew why. She was a terrible liar.

"Bullshit. We've been together from the start. You *know* me. I can't hide from you. You look miserable when you say that because you don't believe it." Adam's voice was calm enough, but no less emphatic for it. He turned to Mick. "For that matter, *you* live in a garage apartment, for fuck's sake. Both of you need to just give in and move in with me."

"He's lived there since he came back to Seattle. He must like it. Unless he was just waiting for us." Jessi looked up at Mick. "Which is it?"

"I needed to get some shit straight. I'm still working on it. But maybe part of me was waiting for this. Hoping. My life is different now than it was before I went into the army. I'm different." Adam's house was sleek and modern, and while Mick liked it there, he wasn't so sure they'd want him and all the rough-and-tumble that came along with him these days.

"Like you breed goats in the kitchen? More tattoos won't affect living with me." Adam shrugged. "The garage floor has been treated, so if you want to work out there, there's room. Make it yours. If it's not right, you're living with an architect, I think we could work out a design that would."

"I think goats are adorable." Jessi finished her food and sat back with a sigh.

"Of course you do, Jessilyn," Adam said.

Mick spoke. "I don't breed goats anywhere. But I like to race cars. I like to box and brawl. I work late more often than not, which means I'm a night person, and you have an office job."

"I think I'd really like to watch you race cars," Jessi said, her face flushed.

Mick brushed the backs of his fingers down her throat and she sighed happily. "I think I'd like to race knowing you were watching me."

"I work from home several mornings a week, and even when I have to be at an early meeting, it's not like I can't go to bed before you get home. Look, I don't want to control your lives. Just what we do in bed." Adam paused as Mick and Jessi leaned in closer. "I like, very much, the idea of the three of us sharing a home. Having you two with me last night made me realize how big the place was. I want to be part of your life, Mick, and I understand it comes with new friends and experiences. And before either of you can retort that this is sudden or whatever, that's crap. You both know it. You and Mick have been headed here for over two decades. My time away from you both helped me figure out a lot of stuff. Chiefly that I hadn't been ready for what happened between us the first time. More important than that, I am now."

"I like the idea. In theory. But I work late too. Pretty much every night. I can't be tussling with either of you over my comings and goings. Sometimes I'll need to sleep over at the studio. When that happens I'm not having any sort of debate about it. I'm a grown-ass woman and I'm building a business."

"I'm sorry I mocked you earlier." Adam took her hand briefly, turning it to kiss her wrist before letting go again.

Mick watched their interplay, contenting himself with stroking his fingertip up and down the back of her neck, where it was oh-so-soft.

Jessi kept quiet for a while as she considered everything that'd been said. Waiting for Adam to say more.

"You're also right that you're a grown woman and you shouldn't have to debate what you need to do to keep your business thriving. I want to control you when you're naked and sweaty and aching for me to make you come. I don't want to control your job."

Mick shifted, trying to get comfortable as his dick hardened at Adam's words.

"I've spent enough time without you, Jessi. I want you with me. I want to be with you and Mick in our house, even if that comes with racing and the sound of a sewing machine at one in the morning. I'd been thinking about adding guest quarters out back, but we could use that to make you a workshop. I'm *not* saying you have to give up your lease and where you are now, so don't start to argue."

"I'll argue when I want to argue," she said, mouth stubborn, daring to be kissed.

Adam must have agreed because he drew even closer, nearly touching his nose to Jessi's. "I know."

Jessi laughed, quickly kissing Adam.

"If you move in with me you can have animals," Adam tempted.

She perked up, as Mick knew she would. "Carey got the dog. I hated to leave her behind, but she loves that yard and the house and the dog park. He needed her more."

"No goats, though." Adam might be a pushover for her, but he sounded pretty serious about the no-goats rule.

Her nose scrunched up just a little and Mick tried not to laugh.

One day they needed to buy some acreage and build so she could have her goats if she wanted them.

"Your floors are pretty gorgeous for a man who just offered to let me have a pet." Jessi raised a brow at Adam.

"Does that mean you're going to do it?" Adam asked.

"Can I have two dogs? Small ones."

Adam knew resistance to her wishes was futile when he made the comment about her having animals at his place.

Hell, he'd have agreed to goats if she'd actually wanted them. Not that he'd say that out loud and give her ideas. He had to run from his car to her parents' front door sometimes if those damned geese were lurking around.

"No geese," Mick said, reading Adam's thoughts.

"Believe me, I'm with you. Mom's the only one they don't terrorize." Jessi shuddered.

Adam had to force himself not to demand an answer right then. He knew it seemed sudden, but he wanted them both to see how they were meant to be together all along.

He settled on "We can't all fit in your bed, love."

"Or in mine, even if I wanted to fuck you both in a garage apartment at my brother's house. Which I don't," Mick said.

"Let's start with spending nights together and go from there. You live alone. Your house is perfect. I'm not perfect, as you know. I don't make my bed. I wear shoes in the house. I leave my stuff out on the counters. I'm a terrible mess." Jessi looked quite pleased with herself, and Adam had to admit, she had some points.

"I'm not saying it won't take work. But I'd like you to give me a chance to do so." Adam wanted the opportunity to prove to Jessilyn that she'd done the right thing.

Jessi blinked back tears. "Okay. But I'm going to remind you of this when I get nail polish on something."

Adam scrubbed a hand over his face but remained grinning. "Can't wait." And he wasn't lying. He didn't give a fuck about his floors or unmade beds. He wanted to soak in everything about her. Wanted her bright, beautiful energy all around him. She made him feel like he was home.

"Yeah? Can you wait until we tell my parents?"

Both men stared at her. "What? Why now?" Adam asked as he grabbed the check to pay it and tried to figure out how he thought they'd react.

"Because I tell them stuff. And they're absolutely going to want to know what's going on since last night. The only reason my mom wasn't on my doorstep today is that she and my dad are up in Bellingham visiting a friend with a new baby." Jessi allowed Adam to take her hand as they left.

They'd had a bump and had worked through it. They'd both given in to him, Adam knew. Which made it even sweeter.

"Well, let's think about that tomorrow because I'm not going to have your mom in my head for what I plan to do to you next," Adam said as they got outside.

"Mick! Hold up!"

They turned at the hail of his name and soon after, Mick realized who it was and resolved to speed this along. He put an arm around Jessi's waist and Adam framed her other side, their hands still entwined.

Retty looked Mick up and down with blatant sexual interest, but Mick greeted the others first. His night with Retty was regrettable in a few ways, chiefly because they were all in an extended community of friends, which meant Mick had to see the guy at least once every few months if not more and had no plans for a repeat of a drunken grapple and an unspectacular blow job.

"Good to see you guys, but we're off. Just had a fantastic dinner." Mick wanted to keep this moving.

"Why don't you stay for a drink or two with us? If your friends are going and all," Retty said and then gave Mick's cock a good long look.

Long enough that Jessi blinked at him, clearly annoyed. Retty didn't really pay her any attention, though. But Mick knew better. She could be sweet and all, but once you pissed Jessi off for real, she could burn shit down.

"Ah, no thanks. I have plans and they can't be broken." He leaned down to kiss the top of Jessi's head, making a declaration as he propelled them down the sidewalk, away from the others. "See you at the track!"

They kept walking until they got to Mick's place. "Let me get some stuff and we'll head to your house, Adam," Mick said.

"You didn't introduce us," Jessi said as they all went inside.

"Not about you. About them. They're assholes," Mick told her.

"One of them played doctor with you." She walked around the tiny apartment as Mick began to toss things into a suitcase.

"*Played* being the operative word. Past tense. It wasn't that good anyway."

"I don't expect you to pretend you didn't enjoy sex with anyone who wasn't me," Jessi said as she picked up a framed photograph. "Look at how young we were!"

"I'm not saying that I didn't have any good sex. I'm saying he doesn't know what to do with his teeth."

Everyone winced at that.

"It *is* pretty big. Kind of hard to keep teeth out of the way with such a mouthful. I can see why he couldn't remember his manners." Jessi shrugged.

Adam burst out laughing. Jesus, the stuff she said.

"Nobody gives compliments like you." Mick swooped close to hug her and, laughing, he continued to pack. "Anyway, he's just someone I passed some time with." And yet another encounter that had left him empty.

Jessi shrugged. "It's not like I thought you were both chaste after we broke up."

Mick zipped the suitcase and walked to her, dropping it so he could pull her into his arms. "You're upset."

"I'm not. Not in the way you think." She cupped his cheek and then petted his beard a moment.

"So how are you upset then? I love you. I've loved you longer than I've loved anyone else. Fucking is just...fucking." Mick searched her features as he cupped her throat, his thumbs brushing against her jaw, over the space below her ear. "You know what we have is different, right?"

"I do, yes. I'm just sad at the loneliness in your eyes when you talk about your life before."

He took a deep breath, casting his gaze to Adam briefly. "I've known you forever, and it's sort of crazy that you can still surprise me with how big your heart is."

"Look, I *am* bummed we had years apart. I want us to be honest about that. I never expected you to be pining for me. I'd be lying if I said I really wanted you to find someone else to love. But my heart hurts to know you were sad."

He hugged her one more time. "I'm not sad now." In fact, he wanted to fuck her right that very moment.

"I can sort of tell how happy part of you is," she said against his chest.

"It likes you."

Adam laughed as he got closer to them.

"It likes you too," Mick told Adam.

"Good to know."

There was a brief knock at the door, and as they sprang away from one another like schoolkids, Mick's oldest brother came in.

"Hey, saw your...oh, I'm sorry!" John winced.

"It's okay." Mick slid his arm around Jessi's shoulders to keep her from backing away.

"Jessilyn, it's really good to see you," John said with a crooked smile. "Adam, you too."

The oldest Roberts son wasn't as closed-minded as the rest of their siblings when it came to Mick's sexuality. He didn't care, as long as Mick was happy. It hadn't always been easy between them, but over the last year when Mick had been back in Seattle, he and his brother had been able to work through a lot of shit.

It made a big difference, even if it was just one of his siblings.

Jessi nodded with a wave. She wasn't her usual bubbly, friendly self and Mick didn't blame her. It'd be a while—if ever—before Jessilyn and his family would be comfortable around each other. Hell, *he* wasn't entirely comfortable around his family, and he was born to them.

"I was going to remind you about Kate's birthday dinner later in the week. I'll text you about it," John said.

"Great. I'll be there." Mick had long since given up hoping his family could be as open and welcoming as Jessi's was. But they were his family nonetheless. Kate was his sister-in-law, and so of course he wouldn't skip out on a birthday dinner for her.

"I'll take your stuff down to the car. Jess and I will see you at the house, okay?" Adam knew he'd probably want to talk with John alone.

Jessi eyed John carefully and then turned to Mick. "You're okay?"

He loved that she'd done it in full view of John. Mick wanted his brother to see what being with Jessi meant to him.

"Yeah." He kissed her forehead. "I'll take my bike over if you can handle my suitcase, Adam."

They left after a good-bye to John.

"Mom called. Said they'd been at your grand opening. She was worried about your soul." John leaned a hip against the edge of the couch.

"My soul is a lot happier when I'm with them." Mick shrugged. "My whole life, when something big happened to me, good or bad, it was Jessi I turned to. Jessi has never rejected me for being who and what I am."

"You don't have to defend her to me. I know she cares about you. Thinking back on it, I'm fairly sure I've always seen it. But you know how Mom and Dad feel about the Franklins. If you're hanging around with them—or more—this whole business from four years ago is going to come back. You ready for that?"

"Can't say I'd ever be ready for it. But if and when it comes up, I'll deal with it. I don't know exactly all of it right now. Or even how to begin to describe it. It's complicated, but pretty much the most right thing I've done in years. This time I'm not running."

John nodded. "I don't pretend to understand your personal life. But you're a big boy, and I figure your soul is your business, and I don't much like seeing Mom and Dad being so mean-spirited. I probably should have stepped in between you and them more often."

Surprised, Mick found himself shrugging.

"You're not the only one who grew up over the last four years, Mick." John clapped him on the shoulder. "When it comes up, as long as they're good to you, I'm on your side. Okay?"

Mick swallowed back emotion. "Yeah. Cool. Thanks." He waved a hand around the room. "And for this."

"I'm your big brother. That's what big brothers do."

They walked out together after Mick locked up. At his bike, he paused. "I'm going to be spending most of my nights away. Eventually we'll be living together. We're taking the moving-in part slow. I'll see you Thursday night for dinner."

John grinned as he shook his head. "I don't think you've done a boring thing your entire life."

They bumped fists before Mick backed down the driveway and headed to Adam's.

CHAPTER
Nine

Jessi had been wrapped up in a blanket on the back deck, stitching something, when she heard a knock on the door at the side of the house. It was late. Or, really early to be more precise.

Her boys had fallen asleep just after two, but she'd always found it good to think while she worked, so she headed out to the deck with her materials and lit some candles for light.

She put aside her things and headed through the house to the side door. When she looked out, a woman stood there, surprised to see Jessi.

"Is Adam home?" she asked through the door.

"It's four in the morning. He's sleeping." Jessi didn't know who the woman was, but it wasn't too hard to figure out she'd come for a little late night booty call. Too bad for her, Adam's booty was taken.

"Who are you?" the woman asked.

"I live here and you should probably go home now. Don't bother coming back. Adam's penis is spoken for." She let the blind over the window in the door fall as she walked away.

Everyone thought she was *sooo* nice. And she was. Usually. But that woman should have pretended she had the wrong house because clearly if she was there at four in the morning, she'd been with Adam and that was just plain rude of her.

Adam and Mick were excellent catches. Jessi had no plans to let them go, and she knew being with them would entail watching some boundaries because she knew both men would have lots of men and women in their pasts looking for more.

It took a while. Plenty of tears and heartache, but she'd made a claim and they'd done the same. For too long she'd left it up to others, but this time she was taking matters into her own hands.

So they could knock on the door at four in the morning, and the next time she wouldn't even bother answering.

Adam awoke at six like he normally did on a Monday. But today was different because *they* were here with him.

Mick looked fantastic naked, the sheets to his waist exposing his back and all that ink. Even sleeping he looked like a king. Jessi, though, wasn't in bed, which meant she was either up or had curled up somewhere for a nap.

She'd gone out to the living room when he and Mick had gone to bed, so he pulled on a pair of pants to go look for her.

It didn't take long. In the living room he found her curled up on the couch, and the sight sent a wave of tenderness through him.

She wore one of his shirts and a tiny pair of panties, and her hands were clasped under her cheek. The blanket she'd been using had fallen to the floor, so he picked it up and covered her.

"You had a guest earlier," she said as she opened her eyes.

Concerned, he picked her up, blanket and all, and sat, settling her on his lap. She snuggled into him, her face in his neck and he let it mean everything.

"What happened? Why didn't you wake me?" Adam kissed the top of her head, already used to her being back in his life.

"It was four in the morning. She only showed up for your cock. I told her it was taken and to go home."

He cringed. It wasn't usual for his partners to show up at four in the morning, but he knew who this was.

"I'm sorry. That shouldn't be happening. Blond?"

"Yes. Six feet tall probably. Great taste in shoes." Her voice was sleepy and not that annoyed, so he went with it.

"She doesn't like being told no."

Jessi laughed at that. "Since I *know* you sure don't, I imagine this wasn't a match made in heaven. Too bad, so sad for her. Are you going to work now?"

"I have a client meeting in a few hours and I need to go in and make sure everything is ready. Although I'm seriously considering taking the day off and rescheduling the meeting because I like being here like this with you and would be totally happy right in this spot for the rest of the morning."

"Long as we had time for a doughnut break." She ran a hand down his chest in her way and he moved into her caress. "But I have work to do too. I just went to sleep an hour or so ago, but I have a lot on my plate today."

"You need your rest, Jessi." He frowned.

"I had planned to sleep until nine or so and then go in to my studio. I'll have time to nap later on."

"What time will you be home tonight?" he asked, brushing the hair back from her forehead so he could press his lips there.

She shrugged. "Dunno. My mom is coming out to help me later. She's so fast with things it really helps." Jessi's voice had gone dreamy. He stood and carried her up to bed and put her in next to Mick, who turned toward her without even waking.

"Text me to let me know your schedule. Maybe we can grab dinner or something," he told her quietly.

Damn, he really wished he didn't have to go to work because the two of them in bed looked a hell of a lot better than a day at work.

"Okay. I'm always up for dinner." The smile on her face said she expected him to join them, but he needed to get moving. So he contented himself with a slow kiss before tucking her in and heading off to shower and leave.

*   *   *

When he parked his car before going into the office, Adam had a moment of thanks that he'd achieved all he had. After years of feeling like everything he did was because of his family's money—that he hadn't earned any of it except what he'd been given—it was something to be grateful for.

Gulati Design was his. He built it with his hard work and dedication. It had helped that his father's name brought in some clients. But that was the least his old man could have done. It was Adam's talent that brought them back, made them refer friends, and had catapulted him into the place he was then.

To have his business going so well and to have Jessi and Mick back in his life made him feel like humming a tune as he began to get ready for the meeting. He didn't of course. He saved silliness for Jessi, who appreciated it like no one else.

It wasn't until the afternoon that he finally had to face the situation at his door at four in the morning. Christina Paul had been a woman he'd played with a few times. For her it had been far more serious, and he hadn't realized it until toward the end. He wasn't looking for anyone permanent in his life. He'd been clear about that, but Christina was a beautiful woman with a beautiful body and a fantastic mouth. She didn't like being told no and had shown up a few times to tempt him.

It wasn't okay for her to keep coming by, and it sure as hell wasn't cool with him that Jessi had to deal with that, especially when he'd just gotten her to agree to move into his house.

"Christina, I hear you were at my home earlier this morning," he said by way of greeting when she answered her phone.

"I bet you did. She seemed rather put out that I was there." She put a purr in her tone and it bristled.

"I'm rather put out about it myself. We talked about this several times. Things are over between us, and you can't come to my home." She wasn't in stalker territory. Not yet. But she was edging closer every time she showed up after he'd told her to stop.

"Who was she? At the door, I mean?"

"Everything. So, I don't want to be an asshole, I just need you to be respectful and appropriate. I wish you the best in life, but I won't be part of it. Are we clear?"

"Things are good between us, Adam. You're fooling yourself to think anyone can do for you what I can."

He'd seen her and they'd fucked around no more than a few weeks. He'd broken things off five months before, and he hadn't missed her.

"Not really interested in what you think about my life at this point. So let's dispose of the niceties and be real. Stay away from my house, my business, and my woman. You're intelligent and beautiful, you won't have any problem moving on once you make that choice."

Christina snorted. "You know where I am when you get bored." She hung up and he sighed.

If she stayed mad, hopefully she'd keep out of his life for good. If she came back again, he'd have to take more steps.

Jessi woke from a super hot sex dream on the verge of an orgasm. But it wasn't a dream, it was Mick, touching her slowly, caressing, as if he were trying to remember every single curve and dip.

"I should apologize for waking you," he said quietly when she opened her eyes. "But I can't do it convincingly. I want you too much."

"I'm yours, Mick. Take what you want." What was sleep compared to this?

"It's worse when you're so fucking beautiful and responsive."

"Worse?" she managed to gasp out as he found her nipples and began a slow pinch and tug that she felt right to her clit.

"I feel stupid. More stupid because you're everything and I knew it. I had it and I ran."

"I'm here now. You're here now. Touching me like I've wanted. It's okay." Reaching up to cup his cheeks, she held him and looked right to his heart. "I don't want your guilt, Mick. I want your heart. And your dick very soon too."

He laughed, kissing her. He was sleep-warm and so substantial she never worried about floating away. He anchored her.

And then his hands were on her sides, over her ribs, down her hips to her thighs, which he pushed open—with no resistance, obviously. He scooted down to kiss her belly and over her hips before he stood and pulled her from the bed and into the huge bathroom.

"I need to shower for work. You do too. We should conserve water."

"I'm fine, but you'll be needing to satisfy my insatiable hunger or we don't have a deal."

His grin changed and made her shiver. "I promise." But he made the X over her heart instead of his. "On your heart instead of mine because you gave it to me and I want you to know how seriously I take that."

Damn it. When he was like this, she had no defense. He broke down everything she'd thought she'd fixed and put away.

He kissed her hard as he turned on the water and ushered her into the giant shower stall.

"Benches will come in handy," he murmured. "But first let's get you all clean so I can dirty you up."

Like she'd argue.

He drew her under the dual shower heads and as she got warmed up and wet everywhere else, he began to slowly wash her. Strong fingers massaged shampoo and then conditioner into her hair before he slicked her body down with soap. That part seemed far more detailed than was truly necessary to get clean, but she had no complaints because his hands on her were the only thing she wanted.

Once she was rinsed off, she did the same for him, paying extra attention too as she fisted his slippery cock first in one hand and then the other.

She had no real idea how big Mick was until she'd been with someone else. His cock was fat in her hands. Hard. She wanted it everywhere all at once.

Soon enough he moved her hand and pushed her to sit on the bench before he went to his knees between her thighs, his hands gripping her ass to haul her pussy to his mouth.

"Yes," she managed to say as he licked over her clit before sucking it gently, abrading it with his teeth. She grabbed his head for purchase, but she didn't necessarily pull him closer.

Didn't have to. He couldn't seem to get enough. He ate her like there was nothing more delicious he'd ever tasted. Like he needed her on the same level as oxygen.

Steam curled around them as he devastated her with his mouth. Licking every part he could reach, fucking her with his tongue, licking against her perineum and then over her asshole before coming back to her clit.

Her back was arched as she held on, orgasm so close, so huge it built up like a fucking storm and when it hit, she actually yelled out his name.

"I want that every time," he said in a near snarl as he got to his feet.

Jessi licked her lips as she took his cock in from eye level, but he clamped a hand on her shoulder. "Don't. You'll make me come before I'm ready and I want to fuck you."

He arranged her, on her knees facing the low tiled wall and the glass through which she could see everything in the mirror that took up the opposite wall.

"Brace your hands on the ledge," he said. Ordered.

She did, waiting, excited for whatever he had planned.

The condom wrapper ripped and Jessi shivered.

Then he was back, pressed against her as she held on. It was a good thing she wasn't standing, though, because when he thrust into her in one hard movement she might have fallen over with pleasure.

"Love you like this," he murmured before licking over the edge of her ear. "Soft, willing, open to me. You're so fucking hot inside. I want that all over my dick."

She exhaled on a sound because she was out of words. She loved it when he talked dirty. Loved it because she knew it was just for her, not a script. Loved it because it was theirs.

He thrust, deep and slow, taking his time. The air was warm and the water rushed over one side of her. The ledge she held on to was smooth and cool, a contrast to the scratch of the wiry hair on his thighs against the backs of hers.

She lost all sense of time, all there was was his cock inside her, his hands at her hips, fingertips digging into the muscle there would leave a mark, and she loved that.

He kept up a stream of sweet words mixed with the dirty ones. He loved her body. Wanted to touch her all the time. These compliments settled in, and she believed them.

He made her feel beautiful. Sexy. Desired. Loved.

"You need to come again, baby," he rumbled as he sped his pace.

"I do?"

He bit her shoulder, just to the side of her throat, and pleasure she hadn't imagined stole through her. Breathless, she pressed back, wanting it again.

"Gonna leave a mark," he said, but it was a question. Did she really want more?

"Make me yours. Mark me," she answered, and he did on the other side.

Damn. What *was* that? It was so good.

"Hand on your clit. I want you to make yourself come all around me."

She did, not needing to be told again.

"Do you have any idea how hot it is? Feeling your pussy all around my cock, knowing your fingertip is on your clit? You tighten and get even hotter and it kills me. But I want that. With you. Jesus," he snarled as she realized she was far closer than she'd thought.

Climax tore through her this time as she tried to move away and yet get closer to him. Her wrist hurt because she worked her fingers on her clit so hard and fast. She let go after the first big bloom of climax but he took her through another, smaller one as he began to fuck her in earnest. Hard. Hard and fast and deep. She grunted with each thrust and it was fantastic.

Pain hovered nearby, but all he gave her was sharp pleasure as he came at last, sinking his teeth into the muscle of her back.

"Damn. I think living here is going to make me be in a far better mood going to work every day." He kissed the top of her head and helped her to stand.

Outside the shower stall he wrapped her in a towel and dried her carefully before he did himself.

Muscles loose, heart full of love, she got dressed for work with him. Really glad she'd made the choice to stay with Adam and give this living together thing a try.

"Want a ride?" Mick asked as they headed downstairs. "One of us can pick you up later. I'll probably be at work until seven or so. But it's Monday so sometimes it's much later. But I can make a run to swing you home at any time. And I'd like that," he added before she could argue.

"I don't want to have to interrupt anyone's work."

He took her hands. "I want to. I want to take care of you. You don't have to, obviously. But I want to or I wouldn't have offered."

"Okay then. Sure."

"Car this morning instead of bike. It's rainy and you don't need that."

"I'm not made of sugar," she told him. One of her mother's favorite sayings was that a little rain never hurt anyone and her kids weren't made of sugar, so they wouldn't melt.

Mick grinned. "Maybe not. But you sure are sweet."

She rolled her eyes. "Sometimes."

He cupped her pussy. "Right here? Always."

She had to close her eyes a moment and he stole a kiss before they left.

CHAPTER
Ten

Mick strolled into Twisted Steel with a smile on his face. Things were so damned good he was afraid to trust it. But he had no choice because once he'd allowed himself to admit how much be needed Jessi and Adam, there was no way he could deny it any longer.

That morning, waking up to her snuggled beside him only underlined how fucking good a thing he had. He would not fuck that up.

He stopped by Carmella's office to check in. They had their Monday morning staff meeting every week to discuss timelines and shop projects, and Carmella was so fantastic at keeping them all in line it made Mick's job as shop manager a thousand times easier.

Today she looked so pretty, as she often did. Her red hair was twisted up in a bun at the back of her head and the blue and white she wore only brought out her eyes. It was easy to see why Duke had fallen in love with her so hard.

"You're the second best thing about this morning, Carm." Mick winked at her as he picked up the paperwork waiting for him.

"Only the second?" She winked. "Does that mean the first is lovely Jessilyn?"

Mick nodded. "Yeah. Jessi's been the best thing about every day since I met her."

"You should tell me the whole story. I love happily-ever-afters." And she should, since she and Duke had one of their own.

"I will when we have the time."

"I'm excited to get to know her." They both stood, gathering their things to head to the break room for the meeting.

Mick realized he was excited for his Twisted Steel family to meet and welcome Jessi and Adam. They would, he knew, because they were all his friends and because Jessi and Adam were loveable.

Duke and Asa were already there, coffee mugs within their reach, several boxes of doughnuts on the counter had been doled out on plates at the table.

"Saved you the lemon ones," Asa rumbled as they sat. Mick tipped his chin in thanks.

"People know I like them and steal them. Assholes."

"That's why we saved you some, whiner," Duke joked as he sidled next to Carmella, who tried to send him a look to remind him they were at work. A look Duke pointedly ignored.

She rolled her eyes, but there was a smile on her lips, so it wasn't so serious.

"Business first, and then we want details about your weekend," Asa told Mick as he started the meeting.

After half an hour talking cars, invoices, and schedules, Carmella headed to her desk while Mick remained in the break room with Asa and Duke.

"You and Carmella have a good weekend away?" Mick asked Duke.

Duke nodded. "We needed it. She sure as hell did. We took my parents to the airport and headed west. Stayed on the beach. Took a few long rides on the bike because the weather was so nice."

"Your brother?" Mick asked. Duke's brother had recently attempted suicide and he'd been out of state dealing with it until just several days before.

"My sister says he's a little better. He's got a ways to go before he's really okay. But for now, it looks like he's at least trying to get there. Carmella and I, though she doesn't know this yet, are going to road trip down there in the spring to visit. That way Ginger can come so Carmella won't worry. I want my family to know her. Not the dog." Duke snorted. "Carmella."

"I think we figured that out," Asa said before turning to Mick. "Now you. This woman we met at the grand opening, this is the one you've been hinting at?"

"Yes. We got back together this weekend. But ... it's complicated."

Duke broke in. "Complicated how? She married? Addicted? What?"

Mick laughed without humor. "Of all of us, Jessi is the one who is fine. I'm complicated. Adam is complicated. Jessi is perfect. Weird. Delightful. But three? I dunno. It's what drove me away, part of it anyway. But I can't fight it anymore. Don't want to. And once I'd touched her again there was no turning back." Which was the truth.

"So, you and her and the dude?" Asa asked. There was no judgment in the tone.

"The complicated part I referred to includes that."

"You're not going to fuck this up and run off, right?" Duke tipped back in his chair.

"I already did that and nearly lost her." In the two days they'd had together, he'd cast off so much shit and had been so happy he knew there was simply nothing to be done but admit he loved them both.

"Your family?"

Mick winced. "Yeah, not going to be so accepting. My parents hate Jessi and her family as well as Adam. My brother knows, but I haven't said anything to anyone else yet."

Eventually he'd have to.

"Why should you?" Duke asked him.

"Duke," Asa warned, "chill."

Usually it was the other way around: Duke was genial, while Asa pushed.

"Fuck chill. His family are assholes. He has us. And he has Jessi and Adam now, so whatever. They didn't want him loving anyone. You think they're going to be loving when they find out? He's not just bi, but with two people at the same time?" Duke, fully agitated, let his chair right itself and leveled his gaze on Mick. "Do not let them tear you apart."

"We won't let them," Asa added.

Mick looked back and forth between them, these two brothers he'd been lucky enough to have in his life.

"They came to the grand opening," Mick said. "Which is more than I thought they'd do. My dad had read up on the shop. I'd like to think they'd come around. Or be civil at the very least."

Empty words.

Mick knew they wouldn't come around. It wasn't the bi thing when it came to Jessi. It was that Jessi dared to love him in her own way. And in doing so, made his parents face their own shortcomings. So they clung to their religion and used that, but it was really because Jessi did what she wanted and no one could stop her. Adam would tear shit apart to make her happy, as would Mick.

Duke lowered his voice because the sound of people streaming into work would hit the off button on this conversation after not too much longer. "You have a family. Some of them are the ones born to you and the rest you've collected. You don't need these people to make you feel like shit all the time."

They headed out to the shop floor. Asa paused at the front end of a '59 Chevy he'd been slowly coaxing back to glory, pounded-out dent by pounded-out dent. "Bring them to the track Wednesday night so we can get to know them."

"They're family too?" Mick teased.

But Asa's expression was serious—to be fair, it was his go-to expression—as he shook his head. "No fuckin' joke. You are my brother. Like Duke is. Of course they're family. That's how we get through shit."

That meant more to Mick than he could ever put into words. So he nodded. "Thanks. I'll ask them."

There was still a knot in his stomach. One he'd had most of his life. The knot that told him he was different. Not good enough because he refused to be the same as everyone else.

But it was smaller than it had been a year ago. Smaller than it was just five days before.

He allowed himself to believe that someday it might be gone.

Wye Oak had been playing very loud as Jessi and her mother worked together in her studio to finish the seed pearls over the bodice and skirt of the wedding dress she hoped to finish by week's end.

"I do love this music, Jessilyn," Addie said. "But perhaps it's loud because you don't want to talk about whatever might have gone on between you, Adam, and Mick Friday evening." Addie continued to work. "Of course, if you don't want to talk, it's all right. You don't need to hide from me under loud music."

Jessi turned the volume down to a far more reasonable level. "I'm not avoiding so much as I just don't know how to even begin to talk about it."

"Are you worried that Daddy and I won't love you anymore if we find out you're in love with two men who love you back with the same depth?"

"It would be nice if sometimes you didn't know exactly what I was thinking," Jessi muttered. "I'm not really worried you won't love me. But it's not a usual relationship. Mick's family is going to freak out. Adam's, if they notice, won't be happy either."

"None of them are us. Jessilyn, we love you. We respect you. We're proud of you and the woman you've grown into. Daddy and I trust your decisions. And we love Mick and Adam. I just worry they'll hurt you again."

Jessi shrugged. "It's unavoidable that we'll hurt one another. We did before they ran off scared too. It's how things work. Mick is like..." the other half of her heart. The person who she'd turned to more than anyone other than the person sitting across from her.

They continued to work as Jessi thought, but her mom didn't push. Another thing she loved about Addie.

"When I'm with Adam and Mick, it feels right. But I know there are things that'll come up and challenge us. I worry about Mick's heart when it comes to his parents. It's not only that they'll disapprove, his father will make that known in ways that could devastate Mick."

"Why don't you tell me what happened between you and Michael's father? It's clear there's something you've been avoiding talking about. More than whatever happened to drive Mick away."

Which had been bad enough. As for the other confrontation? Jessi hadn't told anyone the details other than there'd been an exchange of some harsh words. The details, the big ones anyway, she'd never told anyone. And now she'd been boxed in because love had made her relax and get lazy. Addie was loving and sweet, but she was sharp. Didn't miss anything, and Jessi had a feeling this time she wasn't going to be able to talk her way around it.

"I told you. He was unpleasant. He said unpleasant things." She didn't want to stir any more shit. Didn't want any more angry words. Didn't want to remember how helpless one person could make her feel.

"What unpleasant things?"

"Mom, drop it."

Addie put her work aside. "Sweetheart, now I most certainly can't. Does Mick know whatever happened?"

"It's over and done with. There was no point in telling Mick."
Mick had gone anyway.

"Did you tell Adam?"

Jessi sighed. "No. He knows something bad happened, but not specifics. And I don't want him to. They'd be so angry, and there's absolutely nothing they can do to make it go away. It's in the past, and it needs to remain there."

"That's not how life works. You understand that better than most anyone I know. It's one of the most wonderful things about you. What did that man do? Tell me now, or I will go over there myself and demand he do it instead."

Addie would do it without hesitation. Which is why she'd never told them about what happened to start with.

But that was past now because there was zero way to get around it. So she told her mom, trying to edit as well as she could, knowing her mother would sense it if she hedged too much.

At the end, Addie Franklin was angrier than Jessi had seen her in years. She stood and began to pace.

"Why didn't you tell me sooner?"

"I just didn't want this. This right here! You upset and feeling bad. *For nothing because you can't change it.* I didn't tell Mick or Adam for the same reason. I stay away from the Robertses with the exception of the only one worth a damn. It won't happen again."

"You're darned right it won't."

Uh-oh. "What does that mean?"

"It means that man hurt my baby and it's my job to *make sure* it never happens again."

Great. Addie Franklin in savior mode. She'd burn everything down and salt the earth once she got this far.

"Mom, you can't. Please. Please leave it alone. It'll make things worse, and Mick will feel like it's his fault. You know he will. And his father would be glad of that. Adam has enough guilt too. I'm sorry I burdened you with this, but I'm begging you to let it go."

"Only if you tell them. Mick and Adam need to know. If you tell them, I'll let it go unless they get anywhere near you. That's as good as you're going to get from me, so I suggest you take me up on my offer with a smile, a hug, and a thank-you. I need the hug anyway. I'm so sorry."

Jessi went into her mom's arms and let herself be a little girl for just a moment. "Thank you. I love you, and you don't have anything to be sorry about."

There was no awkwardness, only that sense of comfort that being around her parents always brought. They continued to work for several more hours, taking breaks here and there, until her mother headed home.

Jessi didn't *want* to tell them. She hadn't actually promised her mother she would. But that felt dishonest, and eventually Addie would circle around to be sure Jessi had done it.

She almost felt sorry for Mick's parents the next time they came face-to-face with the Franklins. Almost. It would come out eventually, and to try to protect Mick as much as she could, she had to tell him.

But not right that day or anything.

It was already after six thirty and to be totally honest with herself, she wanted to be with Mick and Adam, so she texted them to see what they were up to. In five minutes, Adam stood at her door with a smile.

"Hi." She took him in as he moved toward her. In a suit. He looked fantastic. Like sex on legs. Wearing really great shoes.

"Damn. Today has been a Monday and a half, and here I am with you and it just fades away. How you do me, angel." He smiled as he came close and pulled her into his arms. "You look like everything I need."

A thousand compliments couldn't mean as much as one from this man. "Sorry it's been a hard day. But I'm glad you're here, though I have no idea why since I just texted you to see what was going on in your world."

"A nearly impossible to please client. Permitting issues. The usual. I came because I was on my way home when you texted. I wanted to see you. Touch you. I've been thinking about you all day long. Earlier today Mick texted me to say he'd driven you in this morning, so I thought I'd give you a ride home tonight."

"Here I am," she managed to say when really all she wanted to do was drag him to a flat surface and have her way with him.

"Have you heard from Mick tonight?" he asked brushing her hair out of the way to drop kisses on her neck and ear.

"He says he'll be leaving work at seven and is coming straight home."

"Let's meet him there. Plus if we get home first I can have you all to myself. I've wanted you riding my cock since I had to leave you with Mick this morning."

She hummed her agreement with that idea.

"Let me lock up and grab my stuff. I'm bringing more to your place." She'd intended to make this a statement but it sounded slightly uncertain at the edges.

"Why do you make that sound like a question when you know I want you there?" Adam's expression softened.

Maybe she knew, yes. But. "There's what you know here." She tapped her forehead. "And what you know here." She indicated her heart. Jessi wanted to fling herself into this because it was truly everything she wanted. But she restrained herself because being cast aside again would break her heart into so many pieces there'd be nothing left.

"Okay. I understand. I'm frustrated by it, but I understand. I want you with me. Always." Adam cupped her cheek and she leaned into his touch.

"I want that too." Which was the truth.

He smiled. "All right then. We're in accord. Let's get your stuff and go home."

Adam hated that question in her gaze. Hated that she had every right to have doubt because of how he'd acted.

Once they got home he opened her door and took her hand before they went inside. He'd simply show her more of how much he wanted her. She needed to know. Deserved to know.

"Was thinking of grilling tonight. What do you think?" he asked, settling on the bed to watch her move through his space, filling it with her scent, her things.

"You cooking for me? I think, yes please." She turned from the drawers she'd just filled with her clothes. "I can do the sides. What are we grilling?"

"I've got some steak."

"Yum. I'll take a cruise through the supplies to see what sorts of things I can put together to go with."

It was totally, wonderfully normal. A dinner with his woman.

And his man. That part was a little extra. Not abnormal by any fucking stretch, but certainly not usual. And yet, right.

Her phone beeped and she reached over to look at the screen. "It's Mick. He said he had to take care of something last minute and was hoping to be here in an hour or so."

Adam didn't mind. Not really. One-on-one time with Jessi would be a good thing. "Tell him we'll keep his dinner warm."

She texted him back and put the phone on the dresser.

"Want music?" he asked.

"Yeah, that'd be nice."

He got up to turn on the promised music, and once TV on the Radio's "Careful You" began to play, he went to Jessi.

Taking the clothes from her hands and putting them aside, he pulled her to his body and began to sway.

Adam had missed this. This sense of belonging he hadn't felt anywhere in his world except with her and Mick.

Jessilyn Franklin was his *home*.

"God damn I love you, Jessi." He pressed a kiss to her temple.

"Show me," she said as she tipped her head back to look up into his face.

He would. Every moment of every day.

He pulled her shirt free, shoving the cups of her bra down to pinch her nipples until her gaze went glassy and her breath caught.

The urge to shove her to her knees and fuck that beautiful mouth tore through him with so much force he nearly grunted.

Her focus sharpened, which made him even harder. She paid attention.

Adam buried his face in her neck, breathing her in as she smoothed her palms down his back for a moment.

Then her nails found him. Digging in, urging him.

Inciting him.

Deliberately.

He bit her hard enough to leave a mark and she cried out. But it wasn't a distressed sound by any means. No, Jessi loved what he'd done.

He licked and nipped his way over her collarbone, pausing at the hollow of her throat before ending up at her opposite shoulder.

"Get these jeans off," he told her as he made himself step back.

She pouted so prettily he leaned in to pinch that juicy bottom lip between two fingers for a moment.

Triumph shone in her gaze.

"Careful how far you push me, angel. I've got years to make up for. Every man you've been with needs to be stripped from your memory as nothing but inferior."

The laugh she gave was breathy, a little shaky, and he liked that a great deal. Wanted to affect her the way she got to him.

Once her jeans were off she looked up through her lashes at him. "What if I want to strip all other men and women from *your* memory the same way?"

He hauled her close with a hand at the back of her neck. "None of them ever could have been a shadow of what you are to me. You're indelible, Jessilyn."

Startled by how much he'd just said, exposed to her, he was silent as she watched him. "Good," she said at last. "I only share with Mick."

Again, she'd known exactly what he needed. A little tease to ease the emotional vulnerability.

But that didn't mean she couldn't still shake him to his core.

"And for the record, even when I was living with someone else, there wasn't anyone for me but you and Mick. Now, panties too?"

He shook his head, amused and delighted. He should have known it would be a matter of days before it was as if there'd never been time apart.

There was a bright, beautiful love within her. She brought it into every place she went. Into the lives of each person she was around. It made him want to bask in her.

So he did. One brow cocked her way, he tipped his chin to answer her question about underwear. "I want you totally bare."

She hooked her fingers at the sides of her tiny underpants and whipped them from her body.

"Beautiful." And she was. Strong and soft all at once. Smart and serious. Ridiculous and whimsical. Protective. Fierce. A total marshmallow. All contradictions that mixed up to make her perfect.

She blushed with a smile edged with a shyness that wasn't in any way calculated.

"You too."

He'd taken his tie off long ago, but the jingle of his belt buckle caught her attention as he undid his pants and pulled his cock free.

One-armed, he hauled her up to the vanity counter in the area outside the bathroom. "Perfect height," he muttered as he traced his fingers through her pussy, already hot and slick.

Jessi grabbed his cock, scooting closer to the edge to touch, to drag the head against her clit and down, circling back up. He had to clench his jaw to keep his control.

"This condom business needs to end as soon as possible," he muttered.

"I want you in my mouth," she said.

"I'll be there soon enough. Right now I want inside your pussy. But you can pout if you like."

She did, but this time there was amusement there too. "Fuck me then!"

He flicked his gaze to her face as he rolled the condom onto his dick. "I think we need to remember who gives the orders around here."

Her moan and then the way she caught her bottom lip between her teeth made it a lot more difficult to hold on to his control.

"There we go." He drew a palm over her head to her neck where he shifted to collar her throat as he thrust into her body slowly but surely. "Trust me to give you what you need," Adam told her.

She managed to nod twice but she went a little blurry when he traced a fingertip over her clit as he set a pace that kept them both dancing on the edge.

Her nails dug into his side, urging him on. He wanted that. Wanted *her* to mark him too.

"Harder," he nearly snarled as he pulled her even closer.

Jessi was so flushed, so prettily pink and fuckdrunk that she took a bit to register what he'd said. Confusion led him down to that sweet, sexy O she'd been making with her lips. Drove him to possess it for a hard kiss.

Pressing himself into her nails on his right side he repeated, "Harder."

She dug in until it stung, then with an annoyed sound, she pulled his shirt free, a few buttons popping off.

"I can fix that," she said before she dug her nails back in, this time against his bare skin.

Jesus. The power she held. She couldn't possibly know how much. And yet, he understood she'd never use it against him. Even after he'd left, she had never done anything but love him.

Her inner walls squeezed and fluttered as he brought her closer to climax with that fingertip on her clit.

That humbled him. The way she loved him and Mick had kept him from drifting too far down the rabbit hole of pleasured abandon he'd launched himself into after they'd all broken up.

Control had been a hard-won thing. But he'd had to lose it before he truly found it.

Control over this beautiful creature was the most glittering, enticing thing he'd every imagined. Everything he'd done and felt up until that moment had been a dress rehearsal.

"Very soon I'm going to take you from behind right here. I'm going to have you bound, and I'll be in charge of everything, even your balance," he growled into her mouth as he kissed her.

"Yes," she sighed and he stole the sound, taking it into himself like air. "*So close.*" The words a plea.

He pressed that fingertip over her a little harder, enough that she clamped around his dick as orgasm rode her. The legs wrapped around his thighs shifted, her calves hooked up over his ass, urging him closer, deeper, harder.

He muttered a curse as he came so hard his teeth hurt.

Downstairs the door opened and Mick called out a greeting.

That made Jessi laugh as she kissed Adam's forehead.

CHAPTER
Eleven

A few nights later, Mick got ready to go to his sister-in-law's birthday dinner, and Jessi tried not to show how nervous she was for him. Mick didn't need the weight of her worry on top of whatever he was struggling with.

"I'm sorry. I should have insisted they invite you both," Mick said to her.

"It's a birthday dinner for someone I don't even know. Of course you shouldn't have. Unless you need allies there. Do you?"

Adam sighed and she turned his way. He gave her the *be quiet* look.

"What? Am I supposed to pretend that's not an issue? I thought we all promised to stop that."

Mick snickered. "It's okay, Jess." He smiled down at her before he stole a long, drugging kiss that left her dreamy. "John and I have come a long way over the years. He's in my corner. I'm not going to hide you and Adam. But it probably won't come up. It's not the time."

It wasn't. Which was why she thought it best for her and Adam not to be at the dinner. Things were tense enough when it came to Mick's family, the last thing Jessi wanted was to ruin his sister-in-law's birthday dinner.

She gave a last, critical look at Mick's shirt. She needed to make him some nice, tailored shirts. Maybe for his birthday.

He tried not to smile but he couldn't help it. His grin brought one of hers in answer. "Next time you lose buttons or have a tear, bring it to me and I'll fix it." She smoothed a hand down the front, needing to reassure them both.

"If it's wrong to get hard while watching you mend shit, I'm the wrongest dude who ever wronged." Mick winked and then kissed her forehead. "I'll be home in a few hours."

"I might be at my parents' house," Jessi said before tiptoeing up to grab another kiss.

"I'd much rather be there," Mick said as he frowned slightly.

"They'd much rather you be there too. Have a good time. Let your family love you in their own way. But. If they hurt you, they'll have me to contend with." Jessi meant that with all her heart.

"You know where we are if you need us," Adam said as he came to stand with Jessi, his arm around her shoulder.

"If you're done and we're still at my mom and dad's, it's not like you can't show up late." In fact, her mother would love it.

"The dinner is at John and Kate's place, but I may be in dire need of your mom's snickerdoodles after tonight."

"I'll bring you home some just in case you don't make it by." Jessi hugged Mick, trying to pour all her love and calm into the embrace.

He hugged Adam and then headed out while she watched from the front window.

Adam spoke, startling her. "I hate them."

She nodded.

"You're not going to admonish me to try to love them?"

"If I did it'd be about you, not them. But I'm not. Because they deserve to be disliked." She'd tried for years upon years to understand them. To find a way to get them to see what they were doing to Mick.

It hadn't worked.

And then, after years of cold, severe condescension, it had exploded and she'd been...

Jessi shook her head to stop that train of thought.

"I sort of feel bad for them now." Adam pulled her close, wrapping her in his arms, so she snuggled against him, taking comfort. "I'd hate my life if you didn't like me."

"Everyone thinks I'm nice. But I'm not."

He laughed. "Shut up. You're totally nice. It doesn't mean you don't have a temper or that you aren't protective. You have a spectacular temper and are ferocious in defense of those you love."

Okay, well, that was a pretty good save.

"I'd love to be grr, scary like you." She tried to scowl, but it apparently didn't work very well because he snickered. Then she thought about the woman at the door and he nodded, approvingly.

"There you go. Clearly you're thinking of something very unpleasant."

Hmpf. If he only knew.

"This is making me horny. We need to go now or we'll never leave."

"Adam, everything makes you horny. It's like your superpower."

His grin went dirty at the edges. She sighed happily at the way he looked at her.

"I can't get enough of you. But that doesn't seem to scare you."

She heard the vulnerability there, the wonder. "The only thing about you that scares me is you walking away. That you want me all the time? That's not scary at all."

"The things I want to do to you..." He nearly snarled.

"Are all pretty damned fun so far as I've experienced."

"I want to rut. I want to mark you. Bruise your skin. Bite you. I want to see rope marks in your flesh. I want my come all over your tits. Your face. I want to debauch you. You should be afraid."

But she wasn't.

Her heart pounded in her ears as her body heated, her pussy slick and ready for any and all of those things.

"I'm not afraid of what you want to do to me. I'm not going to break. I want everything. Dirty, filthy parts as well as the way you put gas in my car without my even asking you to."

Jessi didn't want him holding back.

Which may have been a wee bit hypocritical because she hadn't told him or Mick about the stuff with Mick's dad, and she'd promised her mother.

He knew there was something wrong and caught her chin to give her a look. "What?"

"It's not any of the sex stuff. Just something I remembered."

"One of your most charming attributes is that you're a shitty liar." He took her hand and pulled her to the living room couch. Keeping her close.

"I'm not lying!"

"Neither of us is a lawyer, love. Stop hopping around the subject and just tell me. You can say anything to me. You know that."

"It's not about you." And probably she should tell them both at the same time. But that sounded overwhelming. They'd both have feelings about it. If she told them separately they'd be upset. If she told them together they'd be upset too.

"All right. Who is it about? You know I'm not letting up now so you might as well just tell me."

"It has to be when we're all three together." That would stave the inevitable off for a while longer. "Don't look at me like that. Mick will be upset if I tell you first, and it'll be hard enough to share, I don't want to do it twice."

"You see, *now* I'm angry. Not at you, though I have to say I'm annoyed you haven't told us this whatever it is yet."

That scared her. And then anger hit that she'd been scared.

She shoved off his lap and began to pace. "You don't get to do that."

Adam looked her over carefully, one palm up. "I know what I'm mad about. But not what you're mad about. Want to share?"

She wrung her hands a few times. She'd never really hesitated in telling them how she felt before. But things were different now. It'd left her a little shell-shocked, she supposed.

"What are *you* mad about then?" She turned the question back onto him.

"If it concerns both Mick and me, it's probably something more than a few days old. And whatever it is, it's got you all worked up and jumpy. It takes a lot to get you so shaken up. I don't like seeing you freaked-out and jittery. I'm angry someone has done something to you that's created this. I'm angry at myself for not protecting you from whatever it was. Hell, maybe it's me. But you said it wasn't. So I don't get to do what, angel?" He stood, approaching her slowly. "It tears me up to see you upset. Let me fix it."

It was the last two sentences that helped her get past her anxiety enough to speak once more.

"I'm afraid sometimes that when you get mad, you'll get mad enough to leave. Again. It's stupid. I know. But it just felt . . . for a brief moment . . . like a threat."

Adam sucked in a breath at how small her voice had gotten. At the pain in the words.

Pain he'd put there.

"I'm not leaving. And I'd *never* use that to make you do what I wanted you to do."

"I know. But I just had a moment."

He sighed. "I'm sorry I've given you more than enough reason to doubt me. But I want you to tell me when I do things that make you feel bad. I can't—we can't—fix things going forward unless we're being honest."

"I don't see the point in hurting anyone's feelings. What's done is done."

Of course that'd be her concern. Their feelings, not hers.

"If only reality worked the way you wanted it to, eh, Jess?"

She frowned at him. "Stop poking fun."

"I'm not poking fun. Not right at this very moment anyway. It's not all in the past. Everything we've done to one another has brought us here. We can't pretend it away."

"All right. Point taken. I'll tell you and Mick about the thing when it's right."

Adam scoffed. "You're going to avoid telling us until you can no longer hide from it."

She smirked. "Well, you know I have something to tell you. It's not like you're going to let me avoid it."

Oh, how he loved it when she got saucy like this. When she provoked him on purpose, teasing him right straight between her thighs, where he'd rather be than anywhere else on earth.

He wanted her. Every moment of the day. Just looking at her, hearing her voice or scenting her on the sheets made him ache to possess. Claim.

But they were due at the Franklins', and as much as he wanted to fuck Jessi silly, he never wanted to be the one to put disappointment on Addie's face. The Franklin women were his best girls.

"You get me all worked up, and I can't take you right now. Torture, that's what it is. Come on. Your mother is going to start calling in less than ten minutes."

The Franklins' house was an anchor for Adam. A place he'd spent pretty much every free moment he could once he'd met Jessi in high school and she'd drawn him into her life and her family.

It sat on a rise as they approached up the newly paved driveway. A big front porch. Lots of trees. The tree house where he stole his first kiss from Jessi still existed. Still made him smile every time he saw it.

Lights blazed through the windows, and once they'd parked and headed toward the back door, he caught sight of activity inside.

"Full house tonight, looks like," Jessi said.

He took her hand and she paused, turning his way with a smile. So joyous to be with her family. The Franklins were the real deal. Their kindness and easy affection weren't manufactured.

If they told you they loved you, they meant it. It meant their door was open to you at any time. There'd always be a plate at their table for you. The kind of people who offered to take you to the airport and help move.

They gave him a family, and even when he and Jessi had broken up, he'd come to this place at least monthly.

"Is everything all right?" Jessi asked.

He wanted to be worthy of the place they'd made for him in their family. Hated the thought that if they came in together, he'd remind them of the years when Jessi had lived three hours south. Because she'd run from him and the hurt.

"In the time we were apart, they never made me feel unwelcome."

"Of course not. They love you."

Adam loved the surprise on her face at the very idea of her parents making him feel unwelcome.

"What was between us—how it broke—it didn't have anything to do with your connection to them. If you'd have harmed me or betrayed me in some way they'd have poisoned your potato salad, though." Jessi winked.

The sound of music and laughter rose as they got to the door and then went inside.

Immediately the fantastic chaos that was the Franklin household reached out to embrace Adam and Jessi with hugs, exclamations of welcome, and the promise of food.

James Franklin pushed the ugliest pair of glasses Adam had ever seen back up his nose, a smile on his face as he headed to Jessi.

"There's my baby." He dwarfed her in a hug before he twirled her out and then back. "Charlie's in the garage with your mom."

Jessi clapped her hands at hearing her big sister's name. She hugged her father one last time, squeezed Adam's hand, and scampered out the door leading to the garage.

James gave Adam a hug. "Come help me bring chairs up from the basement."

They never treated him like a guest. Adam was family, which meant they put him to work like they would any of their kids.

"You broke your glasses again, didn't you?" Adam asked, hiding a grin.

"Lost 'em. Addie made me order two pairs this time. These are just fine, but she gets mighty annoyed when I wear them."

Adam laughed. "You do that on purpose!"

James winked as he handed over the chairs to take up to the dining room. "Gotta keep her interested. Woman like my Addie, well, she'd get bored if you didn't poke at her now and again."

"Must be where Jessi gets it," Adam muttered.

James laughed. "That's *exactly* where she gets it. Now, move your butt, boy."

Once they got back upstairs Jessi had her nephew on one hip while she handed him bits of apple and some cheese.

"Oh good. Hi, sweetheart." Addie kissed Adam's cheek before she indicated where she wanted the chairs.

"Hey, Adam." Charlie came in with a platter of food.

He took it from her, accepting her one-armed hug. Jessi's big sister had the same chilled-out demeanor as her father. A wisdom and humor that made most everyone want to be around her.

"Hello, hello, Franklins!"

"Hamish! I had no idea you were here."

Jessi's delight should have made Adam happy. Instead the dumb, cocky Scottish asshole strolled into the dining room with his arms full of flowers, bags, and totes of wine, food, and presents and sucked it all away.

Jessi launched herself into the other man's arms and he caught her up, managing not to drop a single thing he carried, laughing as he hugged her, leaving kisses over her nose and cheeks.

"Fancy that. I had no idea *you* were here." Smiling, Hamish put her back to her feet, his hand at her waist to steady her.

"Adam and I came to dinner." The way her smile changed when she looked to Adam soothed his annoyance.

That part of her belonged to no one else but him. It enabled him to be smiling easily when he focused on Hamish.

"It's like old home week." Hamish tipped his chin in Adam's direction. "How's it goin', mate?"

"Good. You?"

Adam had no need to reach out to show his claim on Jessi. She looked at him. *Looked* at him, and there was no one but him. But the deep, burning need to punch that asshole's fucking face never totally went away.

Addie and James welcomed Hamish, taking the flowers and packages, Addie excitedly thanking him for the treats.

A cat wove its way through Adam's legs and he snorted. "I haven't seen you before, cat. You're a newbie, aren't you?" He went to his haunches to pet the top of its head.

After orders to wash hands and get to the table, Adam stood side by side at the big kitchen sink with Jessi, who bumped him with a hip. "Hi."

"Hello." He tried to keep his voice normal, but all he could think about was licking her pussy.

"You're going to get me in trouble if you keep looking at me that way," she said quietly, handing him the towel after she'd dried up.

"God, I hope so."

They headed into the dining room, sitting where Addie told them. Much like her youngest daughter, Addie had *reasons* for everything she did, which meant you never knew where you'd be sitting or what you'd be eating at the Franklins' table.

So you went with it, because who wanted to make any Franklin woman sad? Jessi ended up across the table with a toddler on one side and her father on the other.

"Thwarted by a two-year-old," Adam said.

"Plenty of me to go around," Jessi said, laughing as she kissed Rynn's fist.

"Made to have a baby at her hip, that one," Hamish said in an undertone that was so carefully casual it was pointed.

Adam wasn't taking the bait. "Maybe. But not right now."

"Sure. I suppose in the meantime she can raise you and Mick."

Adam barely withheld a growl, and Jessi looked him over carefully. Concern for her and respect for the Franklins meant Adam got his shit together and barely held back a sneer in Hamish's direction.

James said a quick blessing for the meal and soon enough, the platters began to shift from person to person.

Jessi continued to glance his way as she cut food up and put it on Rynn's high-chair tray.

"Jessilyn, my queen, your father tells me you've gotten yourself a job making costumes for the Seattle Opera. Congratulations. I couldn't be happier for you. Tell me what you're working on right now," Hamish coaxed.

Jessi blushed and it charmed the annoyance right out of Adam once more.

Something had gone on between Hamish and Adam, that much was clear. Adam's brow had furrowed—he'd have a wrinkle there by the time he was forty, and it would look sexy—and his back had stiffened.

Hamish had that smug little smile he got when he successfully needled someone.

Jessi's father had found Hamish living in an alley near their local grocery store. He'd been thrown away by his family and had nowhere to go but the streets. James and Addie Franklin had slowly tamed Hamish. First with clean clothes and food. Then they'd invited him for lunch on a Saturday and let him use their washer and dryer and the bathroom to clean up.

It had taken about eight months before he'd moved into the garage, taking over what had been a shop-type space James hadn't ever really used. But it had been a safe place for the boy, who lived there for another two years on and off until he headed out to make it big with his band.

And he had. Oh, not for years and years. But the scrawny, jumpy, and seriously moody teenager who'd watched everyone as if they'd be bound to disappoint him had grown into a man confident in his craft though still guarded except with a very few people.

He and Adam weren't friends, though in Jessi's opinion they should be. So much alike, those two.

"I'm finishing up a gown for *Don Giovanni*. Spent what feels like a thousand hours on the bodice of a wedding dress. She loves sparkles. I told her about this dream I'd had about her wrapped in starlight. And do you know her fiancé is an astronomer? Right?" She grinned at her mother, who exclaimed happily.

Hamish dug into his food, which made Jessi relax a little. On and off over the time she'd known him, he'd struggled with various addictions. The last time she'd seen him, he'd been too thin, a ball of nervous, fuzzy energy.

That night he looked good. Healthy.

"So I've embroidered and dealt with crystals until my eyeballs want to fall out. But it's the stars in the sky the night they met. I mean, obviously not perfect, but close. And the magic is there."

"It's good to see you so happy, Jessilyn." Hamish meant it. No smirk as he needled anyone.

She looked over to Adam and smiled. He'd been watching her as he ate. Listening, giving her his attention.

"Thank you. I have to admit, my life is pretty wonderful. I'm home, surrounded by all the people I love. Doing a job that makes me happy."

"You deserve it, angel." Adam lifted his glass of iced tea her way. She was so very blessed.

"What are you doing in Seattle? Visiting? Doing a show?" she asked Hamish during the next lull in conversation.

"I'm playing here in a few weeks. I'm thinking of buying a house. Portland, Seattle, maybe Vancouver. I need to be away from New York and London."

"He called a few hours ago. Asked if he could stay in the guest room." Addie gave Hamish a censuring look. "Imagine. *Asked*, like he was a guest instead of family."

There was no mistaking the affection in her mom's voice. Even better, Hamish accepted that affection so freely offered.

She didn't need to ask Hamish what he'd meant when he'd said he needed to be away from London and New York. Jessi knew they weren't always the safest places for him to keep his life together.

He'd come home. Not a luxury hotel or a long-term rental, but to the Franklins' modest, chaotic ranch-style house to sleep in Jessi's old bedroom. He was running scared—from what she didn't know, but she'd make it a point to find out the next time they were alone.

It was enough to know he'd sought out that protection as she watched both Hamish and Adam begin to relax and stop eyeing one another like they were thinking about throat punching.

She hoped Mick was all right. Wondered if she should text him. Decided not to until after dinner. Just a quick check-in after she helped Charlie get Rynn cleaned up and changed into pajamas.

Mick didn't reply, so she wasn't sure if his phone was off, or if he was in the middle of something or maybe on the way home. She sent a picture of herself smiling at him, hoping he could see how much she loved him, and tucked the phone in her pocket before heading back out to the living room.

An hour later they said their good-byes and headed back to Adam's place.

CHAPTER
Twelve

Mick tried not to make a lot of noise when he got home, but he obviously failed because Jessi came downstairs with a frown, Adam on her heels, telling her to hold up.

Mick laughed because it was exactly what he'd needed. Them, concerned about him. Adam being Adam. Jessi wasn't going to wait upstairs because Jessi did whatever she wanted to even if Adam told her to do otherwise.

Mick *needed* the way they both looked at him now.

"Hey," he said as he dropped his jacket on the back of a chair.

Adam's gaze went to it, and then back to Mick's face.

"Did you drive like this?" Jessi demanded, one hand on her hip.

"Like what?"

Her eyes widened and then narrowed into slits that a smarter man would have recognized. "Are you *kidding* me right now?"

Adam watched the scene, one brow raised in Mick's direction. Watching Mick drive himself off the goddamn road as he pushed Jessi like a fool most likely.

"I drove home a few hours ago. You weren't here so I *walked* down to get a drink. And I *walked* back."

"You went to have *a* drink? Two hours ago I texted you to see where you were and you ignored me and instead went to have a lot more than one drink with strangers instead?"

"Why are you on my fucking case?" Mick demanded, pissed that she knew him so fucking well. Then she flinched a little and he cursed himself for getting so damned drunk.

Adam stepped between Mick and Jessi, his gaze intense and unhappy. "I know you didn't just speak to her like that. You obviously understand how disrespectful that tone would be to someone you just promised to cherish just a few days ago."

The pain of that truth sent nausea through his belly. Jessi continued to watch Mick from around Adam's right arm.

"I'm sorry." Mick rubbed his palms over his head.

"Why do you punish yourself so hard? Hmm?" Jessi asked softly as she pushed herself forward.

Adam gave up trying to shield her with a sigh, encircling her with one arm, hugging her close to his side.

Jessi leaned out and hooked her finger through one of Mick's belt loops and tugged him closer.

"I'm on your case because I love you." Jessi shook her head. "You can't scare me away with your pissy attitude."

"What happened at dinner?" Adam asked this time as he brought Mick the last inches separating him from them with a hand at the back of Mick's neck and then hummed, satisfied at the contact.

He brought Mick from a singular to a plural again with that last bit of space between them all gone. He'd accepted Jessi knowing him so well, but Adam got to him, understood him better than he'd realized.

"I don't want to talk about it." If the words got free they'd tear from the place he'd walled them into. He didn't want that kind of pain.

Adam shook his head. "You don't need to drink yourself into oblivion. You can find oblivion in better ways."

Mick's nipple hardened as Jessi drew her nails over it and the bar piercing it. He moaned, pressing into her touch. "Harder."

Jessi cupped his cock through his pants but he'd had more to drink than his sluggish dick preferred. The rest of him throbbed, wanting more.

"You don't have to punish yourself to get the pain you crave, Mick."

Adam's words sent a ripple of lust so hot and sharp it seared through Mick's body.

The palm he'd had cupping the back of Mick's neck shifted to collar his throat, squeezing enough to make a point.

"Whiskey dick displeases me," Adam said into Mick's ear.

A sound—yearning—broke from Mick's lips.

"You're damaging what's mine when you drink like this."

Adam brushed his mouth over Mick's, licking and then biting his bottom lip so hard Mick grunted, his hips jutting forward, wanting more.

"Get these clothes off and into the washing machine. Then jump into the shower." Adam let go, stepping back, taking Jessi with him. They turned to head upstairs, leaving Mick standing in the living room, staring after them.

"Keeping me waiting isn't something that gets my dick hard, Mick," Adam called out at the top of the stairs.

Mick could pretend to be macho. He could refuse to bottom in this kind of way. But he couldn't lie to himself at the way Adam made him feel just then. The dark, sweet temptation of giving over.

This was far more than a cock in his ass. This was submission on a different level. He wasn't sure what it meant or what it said about him.

Jessi's moan drifted down to Mick, spurring him to take that first step. And then the second as he began to strip on his way to the laundry room. Less than five minutes later he walked into their bedroom only to stumble to a halt at the sight.

Jessi on her knees in the middle of the bed, totally naked. Adam leaned against the nearby doorjamb wearing pajama bottoms and nothing else.

"Jessi turned the water on for you so it's hot," Adam told Mick.

"You two should join me in there." Mick stepped to the bed, reaching out to touch Jessi. "You look so pretty here on your knees." And she did.

Adam spoke. "No touching. Jessi and I have plans. We've been waiting for you to get started, but I'm done waiting now. The quicker you obey me, the quicker you'll get to play with us."

Adam's words were a whip, snagging Mick's attention. Compelling him to obey.

He might have a case of whiskey dick, as Adam so delicately put it, but if anyone could revive his cock, it was Jessi, who made such a picture on her knees in their bed.

Mick hurried past to the bathroom, leaving the door open to watch them as he got into the shower.

Even the steam on the enclosure couldn't hide the way Adam took Jessi in. He spoke to her and she nodded, sliding her palms all over her upper body, her head tipping back as she did.

Quickly, Mick rinsed off, never taking his attention from Jessi on her knees, her hands cupping her breasts, caressing her shoulders and upper arms, back arched, head tipped.

The water and brisk dry-off woke Mick up, drove the drunken lethargy away, letting desire fill that space instead.

When he got back out to the bedroom, Adam pointed at the chair to his left.

"Jessilyn, love, keep touching yourself."

Mick settled on the chair, naked, cock half-hard—no quitter, his penis—marveling at what a gorgeous creature their woman was.

Jessi pinched her nipples, her eyelids drifting closed as she did. She hummed her arousal and it sang up Mick's spine.

"This is what you can't have when you abuse yourself, Mick."

Adam got close enough to Jessi to gather her hair in his fist and yank it, forcing her to arch deeper. Thrusting her tits higher. Mick's breath gusted from his lips when Adam bent to scrape the edge of his teeth over that pale skin. His fingers tightened on his knees when Adam licked over her nipple.

"I can make you feel good. Both of you," Mick replied as he gripped his cock. Good. But not enough.

"You can. And you do." Adam continued to watch Mick over Jessi's body. "If you weren't so set on cutting yourself to shreds at the bar, you could be here with us. I could be giving you pain. Not from disdain or anger, but because you want it, because you need it, and because from me it's beautiful."

Jessi's right hand stole between her thighs.

Entranced, Mick was unable to tear his gaze away when Adam growled and delivered a sharp, loud slap to her ass.

Mick gasped at the same time Jessi did.

But she didn't take her hand away.

Taunting.

Playing that game she and Adam played so very well.

Adam's smile went feral at the edges, and Mick's skin went hot and cold at the same time.

"Tell me what you want, love." Adam grabbed her wrist with one hand and with the other he delivered two sharp slaps to her pussy. There was no disguising how wet Jessi was. Or how hot she found the sting when she groaned, a flush building from her throat.

"Touch me. Fuck me. Let me touch you." Her words ran together slightly but there was no mistaking what she needed.

And no doubt Adam would give it to her.

Mick wanted to *help*. Wanted to be part of what was happening. Needed to have them touch him too.

He stood but Adam shifted to stare at him. "Sit."

Mick attempted to be outraged by that casual order.

Instead his dick throbbed to life a little more as he sat.

As he'd been told to.

"I *am* touching you, love," Adam murmured to Jessi.

"Let me touch you both," Mick said.

Adam got behind Jessi on the bed. He hauled her to his body as he caressed every part of her he could reach. All while he never looked away from Mick.

Mick swallowed hard, mouth dry as he took them in. Jessi, so beautiful in Adam's arms, nipples hard, skin pink and desire flushed, her gaze gone blurry. Adam firmly in control. There was a light in his gaze and Mick knew it probably meant something really good for him.

The need for that, for whatever Adam planned to dole out, terrified Mick.

Not as much as it intrigued him.

Not as much as he *wanted*.

He'd started out just wanting to drink the night off his mind. Planned to come home, roll around with them a bit, and pass out. He'd had more than he should have, yes, but he didn't drive anywhere. He hadn't puked in the front room or cheated.

Mick hadn't expected Adam to be angry. Maybe annoyed. Long-suffering even. But not angry.

"I'm going to make Jessi come all over my hand. And then I'm going to fuck her from behind. All while you watch. I'm in charge here, Mick. And you don't get to fuck yourself up. Only *I* get to do that."

Mick's cock seeped pre-come. "Looks like I'm revived enough to participate after all," he said hopefully.

Adam's answering look told Mick that wasn't going to happen. At least not on his schedule.

"Look, I said I was sorry," Mick told them.

Adam stopped what he was doing. "You did not. Further, you don't even know what to apologize for right now. You just want to get your dick wet."

"I had a fucked-up time at the old family home tonight. Is it so wrong that I needed to have a few drinks?" Mick asked.

Jessi pouted and Mick regretted that he'd been so loud.

Adam's fingertip still moved on Jessi's clit. His gaze lasered onto Mick's, but Mick couldn't tear his attention from how Adam's hand looked, olive tones against her paler skin. So big and capable.

Jessi sighed, grabbing Mick's focus, and he caught sight of the way she tipped her head back onto Adam's shoulder as she rolled her hips.

"Give it to me, love."

Adam's murmur seemed to tear something loose from deep inside Mick.

"She's got a hoop in the piercing today. The bead, oh naughty, does the bead rub your clit?" Adam asked Jessi, who nodded.

"Not as good as you do," she said lazily.

Adam's smile—*damn*—always had made Mick a little dizzy. But the ones Adam gave in intimate moments were his favorites.

He pushed her a littler further, the muscles of his forearm cording a little as he fingered Jessi's clit harder, faster. Her breath hitched and Mick watched, enchanted as she came. So beautiful. So dirty and sexy. Jessi gave herself over to Adam totally.

Adam petted her as she drifted back down, but he kept his gaze on Mick. Seeing right through him.

He got up from the bed long enough to strip off his sleep pants and grab a condom, rolling it on easily.

Jessi looked over at Mick sitting there in his chair, too far away to touch.

"You're so beautiful," she told him.

"He is." Adam didn't get back on the bed, though, he helped Jessi off, leading her in Mick's direction. One severe look, though, told Mick he wasn't going to be touching any time soon.

"Keep frowning at me like that. I'm usually opposed to punishment. I don't want to be your daddy. But you sure do tempt me." Adam's mouth hitched up in one corner. "I'm inclined to give you what you think you want. But not right now."

Jessi stood between them, naked, her skin warm enough that Mick could feel it against his knees and thighs.

"With this temptation right here in front of me I'd agree to any punishment you ask," Mick said, his focus leaving Jessi's mouth and shifting back to Adam.

"Brace your hands on the back of the chair to either side of Mick's shoulders," Adam told her.

She obeyed, which brought her tits level with his mouth.

"This is torture. I'm sure it's a violation of the Geneva Convention," Mick snarled as Adam bent her a little more and then thrust into her pussy hard and fast. Not so fast that Mick missed the sound of flesh hitting flesh when he seated himself inside Jessi fully.

A puff of air from Jessi's exhaled *oooh* was electric against his temple.

"*This* is what you get when you bring your shit to us, where it belongs." Adam licked over her shoulder.

"I didn't take my shit anywhere. I had a few drinks. Just what do you think I did down there anyway?"

Adam's fingers shifted from where he'd been collaring Jessi's throat to grasp a handful of her hair and yank, exposing all that sweet, warm skin just below her ear where she liked to be licked.

Mick ran his tongue over his bottom lip, his fingers digging into the arms of the chair so hard one side creaked.

"I think you drink this much to punish yourself all while lying and claiming you need oblivion. Hurting yourself by getting so drunk you can't get hard isn't oblivion. It's a cheap, lazy substitute. And it keeps you apart from us, from the people you promised to love."

Denial sprang to his lips but he couldn't lie. Not with Jessi's whimpers puffing against the sweat at his temple. Not with Adam daring him to tell the fucking truth.

Adam kept Jessi bouncing so tantalizingly close Mick may have whimpered a few times too. Each thrust underlining the choice he'd made.

"I didn't want to bring it to you. I wanted this," Mick waved a hand to indicate the three of them, "free of my family's bullshit."

"If you need oblivion I'll give it to you. You need a little pain to feel better? Why is that so much harder for you to accept than my dick inside you? You sleeping with not just one person every night, but two?"

Adam bit Jessi where her neck met her shoulder and she groaned. Mick knew that groan. Knew what her pussy felt like around his cock when she made it.

"Jessi likes it a little hard. Do you find her less beautiful for that?" Adam's voice was deceptively smooth and calm. Mick knew it was a trap and yet he couldn't resist.

"She's magnificent because of it."

Adam nodded, reaching past Jessi to slide his fingers over Mick's scalp, scoring lightly with the edge of his nails.

"Because she's full of light and joy and sweetness and at the same time she's dirty. Beautifully dirty, and we get to see that. She trusts us with that. With that dark, twisty part that responds to fingerprint bruises on her ass because I wanted to be inside her so deep. The part that gets so very hot and wet when my teeth dig into her skin."

His words, like a spell, had Mick nodding. He'd sobered enough to know he'd feel like absolute shit tomorrow at work. Hell, the only thing keeping him from feeling like absolute shit right then was the sight right in front of him.

"You know how much I love it when you make yourself come around me," Adam said as he bent his body around Jessi's, bringing his face nearer to Mick's. Jessi shifted, leaning against Mick a little as she moved her right hand to her pussy.

Everything he'd ever wanted was right there. Was his already. He hated bringing any of his family's shit into that.

"If you want to burn the guilt away with some pain, Michael Roberts, you'll damn well get that from me." Adam continued to underline his point in a way that left Mick utterly disarmed.

Jessi's sweet begging finally broke Adam's defenses. He whispered that he was right there, soothed her as she moaned her way through her orgasm. Adam wasn't far behind, his attention on Jessi.

Adoration was stamped all over him before a strangled moan broke from his lips.

Mick held his breath as he watched Jessi come and then Adam. The next breath he took was full of the scent of sex.

Adam led Jessi back to the bed and helped her make a nest in the pillows so she could curl up and watch whatever he was going to do with Mick. He loved it when Jessi was like this. Pliant and warm from climax, like a cat in a patch of sunshine.

It continued to fill him with wonder that she shared his life. That he actually was loved by this woman.

"Are you warm enough?" Adam asked her.

She smiled up at him. "If only everyone knew you were such a pussycat beneath all that grump."

That she said all this with stubble burn on her shoulders and back, bite marks given to her while their boyfriend watched, only made him love her more. God help him.

"Only for you." He kissed her forehead.

And when he turned to face Mick all the whimsy she'd filled him with subsided.

"Stand at the foot of the bed. Facing Jessi." Adam walked past the chair and into his closet. Since he'd come, since Jessi has soothed his agitation, he was much more clearheaded.

Adam pulled several things from a series of drawers and headed back out to the bedroom.

"Jessi, love, will you please bring Mick a glass of water?" Adam asked and she scampered off quickly. "I'm assuming you weren't drinking water and I want you hydrated."

"Yeah? What exactly do you have planned?" Mick tried to tease his way around the subject but Adam only stared back at him until he sobered a little.

"Now then." Adam laid the English tawse on the bed, followed by the leather slapper with the holes, and, lastly, the flicker whip. Each made a different sound. Each had a different sort of sting. Each felt different in his hand.

Adam knew which he liked to use best, but that wouldn't necessarily be what was needed.

Jessi came back in with a carafe of water and several glasses on a tray. Adam thanked her, and she climbed back into bed, freezing as she caught sight of his toys.

He knew she wanted to ask, but she didn't. She got that this was about him and Mick and left it to them, settling back into her nest of pillows.

"Well." Mick drank his water but it didn't disguise the interest in his gaze as he looked over the implements on the bed. "This seems like someone's had an expert level or two unlocked."

"Practice makes perfect." Adam shrugged. "Each tool has a purpose. In this case, all suit mine so I'll let you choose."

Mick looked up at Jessi. "Which one do you think?"

Jessi spent several moments thinking before she answered. "You can't stop looking at the one in the middle."

The leather slapper with the holes.

"But."

Adam and Mick both waited for Jessi to finish.

"I think you *need* the one to its left." Jessi nodded as if she'd made a firm decision. "Yes. Both of you need that one."

Mick turned his head to look at Adam. "Okay then." His voice wasn't entirely steady, but it wasn't the liquor.

Mick wasn't drunk anymore. He was exhausted and harried enough by his troubles that he was finally letting go. And Adam needed to keep his attention perfectly focused. This was a balancing act and he was feeling his way along with Mick the same as they were with him.

Every choice mattered.

Adam picked up the tawse, testing it in his grip. He made a few strikes through the air just to hear the sound. So *Mick* could hear it. Jessi's pupils were so big Adam could see them from where he stood.

He drew the edge over the back of Mick's head, down his neck and spine. "We've both had an achievement unlocked. This is an English tawse. Have you ever felt one in action?"

Mick shook his head.

"Have you ever given in to your desire for pain?" Adam asked quietly.

"Some."

Adam heard the anticipation, the desire, and a little fear. He tucked it away. "The safe word is *red*. Now, let's learn one another. Brace your hands on the footboard and lean forward."

Mick was beautiful. Naked, firm all over, ink and piercings, some scars. He closed his eyes and Jessi shifted just slightly, to get a better view.

The first strike was an easy one. More for the noise than anything else. The split leather made a distinctive snap when it made contact with skin. Adam needed to test Mick's limits. Figure out what he liked and didn't. What his pain tolerance was.

He took it slow because this was a seduction. Adam needed to coax Mick, help him get to a place where he could accept what he liked. Where he could get what he needed in a healthier way. In a way that built him up instead of tore him apart.

Pain had a way of doing that, of burning through the bullshit.

A sheen of sweat made the tattoos on Mick's back seem to glow as his ass cheeks got pinker with each successive snap.

Adam didn't fail to notice how fucking hard that dick that couldn't be roused just an hour before was getting.

He dragged the edge of his nails down Mick's left side, loving the shudder he got in response.

"Sometimes pain helps us see the truth." Adam bent the tip of the slapper and let it go.

Mick grunted, pushing back into the strike.

"I don't want to punish you. I want to please you," Adam whispered into Mick's ear. "You need it to hurt for your own reasons? That's what I'm here for. You let a bottle do it or your fucked-up family, and that means you're turning your back on what the three of us have."

Jessi moved to her knees just a few inches away. Her hands clasped in her lap. She didn't interfere, but her presence helped Adam keep his control and let Mick lose some of his.

The hair on top of Mick's head was long enough to grasp, though Adam couldn't wait until it got longer so he could wrap it around his fist as he fucked that sweet mouth.

He growled and Mick sighed with so much longing Adam found himself hard again.

"Would you like to kiss him, angel?" Adam asked Jessi.

She licked her lips and blinked a few times, as if she'd been dreaming. "Yes. Very much."

"Go on then. I think our Mick needs a kiss right about now."

Adam needed to see it as much as Mick needed to feel it.

Jessi bent forward and cupped Mick's face. She kissed over each eyelid and then across his browline, down his temple, and across to his mouth. All the while she whispered endearments as Adam continued.

Mick's muscles began to tremble so Adam slowed down, leaning over to blow across the heated skin of Mick's ass.

Mick whimpered and Jessi kissed it all away.

"Your eyes are so dreamy," Jessi murmured as she sat back. Then she looked to Adam and smiled. "Yours too."

He'd had partners who liked a little pain before. But this between him and Mick was more intense.

Intense was a stupid word for it.

But it was what he had at the moment so he went with it.

Adam led Mick to the bed, helping him ease onto his belly. "I need to come so bad," Mick said into the mattress.

Jessi's cool, steady energy seemed to keep them all on an even keel as she lay facing them both just a few inches away.

"Can you?" Adam asked as he settled on Mick's other side.

"I'm so fucking hard, I'm going to puke or come. I'd rather come."

Jessi wrinkled her nose and Adam suppressed a snicker.

"Go on then," Adam said as he kissed the back of Mick's neck. "Jerk yourself off." This wasn't about being lazy and not wanting to make Mick come, but letting Mick have some control back.

He'd been shaken by his reaction to the spanking. Hell, Adam was too. But this was a careful dance, tiny steps and giving more trust with each experience. They'd all learn together.

Jessi's distaste had disappeared. Her eyes had gone wide and her nipples darkened as Mick turned his face to her and slid one of his arms beneath his body.

"Don't want to get jizz on the bedding," he mumbled as he began to thrust into the fist Adam knew Mick had wrapped around his cock.

"You could get it on me," Jessi teased.

Mick groaned but moments later made it to his knees. His cock was shiny with pre-come as he fucked his fist. "So sweet and dirty."

Jessi rolled to her back and Adam moved to her other side, not wanting to miss a moment.

"Is that what you want? To dirty me? Mark me?"

Jessi's words seemed to suck the air from Adam's lungs and Mick's grunt and the way he sped his movements said he felt similarly.

"You both marked me a long time ago. Inside." She ran her hands over her torso, holding her tits up for Mick. "So go on, use me. Make me yours on the outside too."

With a strangled curse, Mick came all over Jessi's breasts and neck before he collapsed on the bed, careful of his ass so he stayed on his side, panting.

"I'm afraid this isn't just a take a shower moment. I need to wash my hair and you probably need to change the sheets," Jessi said as she scampered off to the bathroom, leaving Mick and Adam laughing.

CHAPTER
Thirteen

Jessi went in the side door at Twisted Steel like Mick told her to and nearly knocked Duke Bradshaw over.

He caught her, laughing. "I'm sorry about that, sweetheart! I was staring at Carmella and forgot the rest of the world."

It filled her with happiness to hear those words and the love behind them.

"You're looking for Mick?" Duke asked.

"Yes. He left this on the counter at home, so I offered to bring it by on my way to work." Jessi held up an accordion file folder.

"The master of the universe schedule." Duke grinned. "He keeps us all in line with that. No wonder he looked like ten miles of bad road today."

That and drinking so much the night before.

Duke called Mick's name, and he popped his head around a corner with an annoyed look on his face.

Until he saw Jessi and smiled, loping over as she took him in, breathless. Even hungover he looked good.

"Thanks for bringing this by." He took the folder and hugged her.

"Sorry it wasn't sooner. I worked at home for a bit this morning, so I didn't see it until I was on my way out."

Mick snorted. "Hush. Do you have a few minutes for some coffee? I was just headed in to grab some."

"Sounds good," Duke said, and Mick shot him a glare.

"You're not invited. I see you all the damned time."

Duke scoffed. "You see her all the damned time when you don't see me. Then again, I can see why you'd rather see her. She's softer and smells better."

Jessi laughed, really liking Mick's friend.

"There are doughnuts," Carmella called out and Duke drifted her way, grinning.

Mick put an arm around her shoulders and walked her around the edge of a huge shop floor where people worked at various points on several different projects.

Arctic Monkeys' "Knee Socks" played loudly over the din, like spice on the meal, and it made Jessi pause at the top of a three-step landing to look out over them all.

"The energy here is very good. You're all working together. I like it that you work in this place."

Mick kissed her quickly and someone whistled in the background. "Thank you for saying that."

He led her to the break room, where Carmella and Duke had taken a seat already.

"I don't want to share," he mumbled.

"The doughnuts, the girl, or the friends?" Jessi asked.

His grin was what she'd hoped for. A reminder that she was his and always had been.

"He's afraid I'll be so charming you'll realize he's a mug," Duke said as Mick gave in and they sat with a coffee and their doughnuts.

"As if." Mick rolled his eyes.

Carmella ignored them both and smiled Jessi's way. "Hi there. How are you?"

"Hi, Carmella. I love that color on you." Most redheads didn't wear orange, but Carmella did and it worked. Bold and sexy all at once.

"I found it at a garage sale. I paid three bucks for it."

"What are you up to after you leave here?" Mick asked when she turned her attention back to him.

"I'm going fabric shopping. Don't be jealous." She winked and he sighed happily before sipping his coffee.

"Did you invite her and Adam tonight?" Asa said as he cruised in and headed straight for the coffee.

"Oooh, to what?"

Duke grinned. "I like this one, Michael. She's got a good attitude."

"You and Jessi are the two most Zen people I've ever met." Mick turned back to Jessi. "We're all going out tonight for sushi. Before that we're having a few recreational brawls. You and Adam are invited to one or all parts. Whatever you prefer."

"*Recreational* brawl? I feel like we might have different understandings of the word *recreational*." Only Mick would think fighting was a fun game.

But this was his life, and she was part of it now. Which meant all of it, especially parts she may not understand. Plus it would be hot.

"A fight league. We have rules," he amended quickly at the look on her face.

"I can vouch for the general hardness of his head. And the size of his fists is pretty much in his favor too," Duke defended Mick.

Jessi shrugged. "He's a grown man in charge of his life. I'm sure Adam and I will be there. For both parts, as long as we aren't cramping your style or whatever."

Mick looked like he'd eaten something sour. "Since when does having a gorgeous woman and a handsome man count as cramping style? Because as far as I can tell, that's the fucking coolest thing ever, not embarrassing."

"You're so good at that," Jessi said as she fought a blush.

Carmella laughed. "It's like seeing a whole different part of Mick when he talks about you. I like it. Though I totally agree with you, Jessi, that recreation should mean swimming or baseball. Not face punching. But they all seem to really love it."

"At least it's not eating paste, I guess."

"I never ate paste!" Mick protested over everyone's laughter.

"You drank bong water once." She mimicked the dry heaves.

"It was a dare." Like that was an actual reason.

"This might be why you enjoy getting punched in the face, Mick."

Duke and Asa laughed harder.

"I rarely get punched, though." One of his eyebrows rose, and she was filled with silly, wonderful love. "I do the punching."

"All right then. Text directions to me or Adam." She finished her coffee. "I need to get moving."

"I'll walk you out," Mick said as he joined her. She told everyone she'd be seeing them later before Mick led her out a back door.

"Thanks again," he said as they got to her car.

"Of course." She wouldn't ask him if he was feeling up to brawling that night. He had to be in charge of his own health. Even though he had to be hungover and feeling pretty rough.

"Adam tells me there's something we both have to be present to hear. I'm trying to get out by six and go home straight from here. Then you can tell us before we go out."

Oh that would be a delightful pre-dinner conversation! She couldn't wait.

Ugh.

Instead she nodded. "Okay. I'm hoping to be finished by then. Hamish is coming by late in the day to be fitted for some new stuff to wear onstage."

Mick's face darkened. "He's visiting?"

"Staying with my parents for a few weeks. Says he's going to be house hunting while he's here. He loved the pants I made for him two years ago and wants more."

"Don't give that cock a discount."

Jessi frowned. "He's not a cock. He's *family*, which means he gets a discount. Now, stop this ridiculous pouting. You and Adam both, so ridiculous. As if I even had *time* to get up to anything with Hamish! Who is like my brother, so ew."

Chastened, Mick stopped his scowl and kissed her instead. "I'm glad Adam and I keep you so busy."

"You should be. Go back to work. Drink lots of water and I'll see you later."

He hugged her. "I love you, Jessi."

"I love you too."

Adam came home to find Jessi bent over Mick's shoulder as he sat at the kitchen island.

Artie Shaw played in the background. The fireplace sent golden light through the room, and the whole house smelled really good.

His elegant, simple showcase of a house had always filled him with pride. But Jessi had filled it in a way nothing ever could have. Bits and pieces of her began to make appearances. She'd left little stones here and there in windowsills in groups of three. An oxblood throw with gold chevrons lay over the back of one of the chairs near the French doors leading outside. A framed picture of the three of them from the night of the grand opening sat on a shelf in their bedroom.

It meant she was moving in. That she felt safe enough to put roots down and make it her space too.

Most of all, though, Jessi made this a home. Just being there made him happy. Like walking in was a damned hug. Her touches had warmed the space like her presence had done to his life.

She laughed, pressing a kiss to Mick's neck, and stepped away. Or tried to. Mick moved quickly and grabbed her, pulling her back for a more thorough kiss.

They were beautiful, his angel and his man.

Jessi sighed and turned her head, but when she noted Adam there her face lit with a smile and she launched herself at him.

This is what it meant to come home every night when you had the life you needed.

Laughing, he caught her and kissed the taste of Mick off her lips. "That's what I call a welcome."

"I thought it was pretty good myself."

He put her down, giving her ass a final squeeze as he met Mick halfway across the room and kissed him hello too.

Adam moved to step back, but Mick held him in place long enough to place one more kiss on Adam's forehead first.

"I was just telling Jessi that coming home to her was better than any drug. And then I got a double dose," Mick said.

Adam was relieved to have that easiness between them unchanged, that chemistry and connection that bound them together still strong. The night before had been incredibly intense in a number of ways. For all of them. Mick had been exposed and vulnerable, and Adam wanted to be sure the trust between them hadn't been broken.

But Mick looked him dead on when they spoke. His kiss had been easy, sexy, and the kiss on the forehead had been something Adam'd needed without even knowing it.

"When do we need to go?" It had been a big deal that Mick had invited them that night. Their going would also be a public declaration of a relationship to Mick's community. Adam knew he'd have to do the same at some point, though he wished his family were more like Jessi's.

"We've got about an hour and a half. It's up north tonight, near Edmonds. We move around from time to time. One of the guys at the shop just bought several acres, so we can get rowdy without getting the cops called."

Jessi sighed with so much longing both men looked in her direction. She blushed. "What? I know! Okay?" She threw her hands up and started pacing.

He had *no* idea what she was talking about, but he did love to watch her move.

Mick snorted. "Angel, help us out here."

"It's sexy, okay?" She ended on a near wail and Adam couldn't help laughing. "It shouldn't be. I should be worried for Mick. Though, okay, I am. But it shouldn't make me all 'mmmmm, hot stuff, let's go to bone-town' when he talks about punching people. I'm a terrible person."

Mick had to put a hand over his mouth, trying to wipe away his smile as he smoothed over his beard. "You're a lot of things, Jessi. Terrible isn't even on the list. I *like* that you get hot over my love of fighting. It's a regular part of my life so, I mean, all the better for me if you think it's sexy. Bonus."

"I can assure you, Jessilyn, that your wanting to go to *bone-town* is never going to be counted as a negative by either of us," Adam said.

She flipped them both off but smiled. "Okay then. What should I wear? I've never been to an open-air brawl before."

"I think we need to sit and have you tell us whatever thing you said you needed to tell us both." Adam pointed at the couch.

"Well, how about we wait? Until after? It's Friday night. We'll get home and then I can tell you after we've enjoyed ourselves. It's better that way."

"Jessi, cut the shit." Mick threw himself onto the couch and she frowned but shuffled over to sit on the big chair nearest the fireplace.

"I want to emphasize that what I'm going to tell you happened in *the past*. I wouldn't even be telling you now but my mother found out and she made me promise to tell you both or she would. I don't think you need to know, to be honest. But I'd rather you hear it from me."

Adam braced himself. Whatever she was about to say was going to be hard for her to share, so he tried to keep his face relaxed and the anger from his muscles.

"Jessilyn, you can tell us anything. How many times have you listened to us? Put us back together when we were breaking apart? If your mom gave you that ultimatum it's got to be bad. So up front I want to emphasize," Mick echoed her words, "that we love you and we'll deal with whatever it is."

She took a deep breath. "Two months after we'd all broken up, your father showed up at my front door."

Adam had already been exiting from her daily life by that point, but he hadn't heard this story. He knew enough to understand he wasn't going to like the rest.

"We had an argument. He said mean things. It's over." She recited this with her eyes on her toes.

Mick shifted to get to his knees in front of her. He took her hand.

Adam moved to her other side. "I know this is hard. But if you can, will you give us more detail?"

"And the *full* story." Mick kissed her palm and the inside of her wrist. "Don't hold back to protect me. Or because you're afraid of me."

She blinked quickly and Adam noted the unshed tears. He had to ignore his instinct to demand she tell them immediately, so he could set about making Mick's father pay for whatever the fuck he'd done to her.

"He shoved into the apartment right when I opened up. I would have asked in him anyway. So we could talk about you. I wanted him to know how wonderful you are, how much you meant to me. I thought we could connect through our love of you." She licked her lips. "He'd been drinking."

Shock rippled over Mick's face and then so much pain Adam

didn't know what he wanted to do more, comfort them or hurt that asshole for doing this to start with.

"He said ugly things. Broke some of my furniture. Threatened me."

"Tell me the details. All of them." Mick's voice was thick with emotion.

"Mick, it's...I don't want to put that look on your face." The anguish in Jessi's voice drove at Adam. At the need to defend and protect her.

But he hadn't been there either. Not at the time and not enough that she trusted him to seek him out. Adam blew out a breath as he rubbed circles on her shoulder with his thumb.

"He said I was the reason. That I'd tempted you to sin from the first. That even at five I was a whore."

Adam barely leashed a growl.

"He said you'd confessed to your wickedness. That you left because I wouldn't stop tempting you. Said if I got near you or tried my witchcraft, he'd burn my parents' house to the ground. *Please don't tell my mom about that part.* I didn't want to scare her." Jessi paused a second and then continued. "There was a tussle as I tried to get him out. My shirt ripped and he started screaming in my face. He grabbed me and shoved me against the wall. Accused me of trying to seduce him. My neighbor heard yelling for help and came out. Your father ran away when he heard her tell him she was going to call the cops."

Tears had broken free and she wiped the back of her hand against them.

Adam had seen her fear at the sight of Mick's father, but he'd chalked it up to how he'd been when he'd walked in on the three of them and they'd had the initial blowup.

"*Did* you call the cops?" Mick asked.

"No! He was drunk and out of control, but he was your dad and I didn't want to tell the cops what he'd said. I was embarrassed."

"You kept this to yourself. All these years." Mick had tears of his own. Adam pushed up to pace.

"I didn't want to hurt you. Like I just did." She tried to wring her hands, but Mick hadn't let go.

"You shielded that piece of shit to protect us." Adam didn't ask it, he knew it.

"Was I going to run to you? When you kept pushing me away? It would have felt like I was manipulating you to get you back. And by the time Mick and I were communicating again it didn't matter. It didn't need to be shared. It happened. It's over. I'm sorry I had to hurt you with it."

Mick exploded to his feet. He didn't pace, but stood, humming with violence and fury. "No. You don't get to be sorry for *what he did*. All his talk about how precious femininity is and how it should be cherished and protected, and he assaulted you."

"He didn't. Well, not really," Jessi interrupted.

"Enlighten me then. How did he rip your shirt by accident?"

When Jessi looked away for a moment, the knowing settled into Adam's belly. Shredded through him, washing away all his control in wave after wave of rage.

"He called me a name or two and I tried to move back, to get out of his reach. To get to the door."

Mick's father was an easy six and a half feet with the build of a guy who played linebacker from age nine all the way through college.

"He grabbed me, to underline his point, make me listen, whatever. He was really angry and I was afraid, so I moved toward the door and he got startled and grabbed out at me. The shirt ripped then."

Mick blew out a shaky breath, but not in relief. The tension in the air continued to build.

"He didn't rip the shirt on purpose." Her story stuttered to a halt and Adam knew she was holding back.

And so did Mick. "And then? Once it did?"

"I think he was shocked by that. He snapped. Then he started screaming at me that I was trying to seduce him. He shoved me back against the wall in the hall, but I'd been able to get the door open and that's when the neighbor came out."

"Before or after he threatened to burn down your parents' house?" All that emotion in Mick's tone had been honed into brilliant, calm rage. "He assaulted you. He shoved you. He's twice your size. I can't let this pass, Jess."

She covered her face with her hands. "Oh god. No. Please. If you bring this out now it'll only stir up problems. I never expect them to like me. They don't have to. I just don't want them not liking *you*."

"Jessi, he put his hands on you. He terrorized you." Mick headed for the door but Jessi followed.

"Please! I never ask you for anything like this. I don't want to get between you and your family. But I'm begging you right now not to rush off."

Unable to stay out of it, Adam stepped between them, placing his hands on Mick's shoulders. "I'm angry too. But she's right. If you go now it'll end badly. I'm not saying we won't hold him accountable; that's a must. But if you leave now she's going to feel responsible and never tell us anything again. And, baby, I just don't want you rolling up and getting entangled with all that hate."

Mick's features softened. "I want to beat him for hurting her. For having the gall to see her at the grand opening and not throw himself at her mercy to beg her forgiveness."

"He never bothered me again after that. I'm sure he was ashamed. I know he's had some trouble with his sobriety over the years. I just let it go because in the end, it was awful, but it was over. Everyone makes mistakes." Jessi was torn up and it made Adam antsy. She shouldn't be feeling any guilt over this. But being who she was, of course she did.

"Now would be a good time for you to share the rest of what happened last night," Adam said to Mick, coming back to the couch. "After you two come over here because we all need to be touching one another right now."

Hopefully they could calm down.

They settled Jessi between them.

"I spent most of the night working not to let my father goad me. John kept getting in between us, making him back off. Mom hid in the kitchen for most of the night. He asked about you a few times. I didn't announce that we were all back together over a toast or anything. It was someone else's birthday dinner. My dad said the prayer before we ate, and family values figured prominently."

"By this point he must think she's never going to tell you or that you know and don't care." Adam figured Mick's father for a coward, so he'd go with the former.

Mick groaned. "I'm so sorry, Jessi."

She shook her head. "Didn't you just tell me not to be sorry for him? You don't get to be either."

"I set it in motion and left you to deal with it alone."

"Just like I did. Only you were on the other side of the world and I was just a few miles away," Adam said. "It's my turn to apologize."

Jessi started to cry in earnest. Mick looked as panicked as Adam felt.

It was untenable that she be this torn up. Adam wanted to punch something, preferably the person at fault here, Mick's father.

"This is why I never said anything. You're both upset over something that can't be changed. Look at us."

Adam did. He thought about the whole evening and then he sighed, nodding.

"Yeah, look at us. Right here, being there for each other like we should have been. This is good, Jessi. This is us being us. And we can't make it un-happen, but we can deal with it honestly now. *We don't have to break.* We bend and fortify. Because no one is going to break us now. Do you understand me?" Adam tipped her chin up. "Together we can get through anything."

"I never expect you to be in the same room with him again." Mick shook his head. "I will handle this so don't ask me not to, Jessilyn. But not tonight. Tonight we have a date. If you're feeling up to it, that is."

"Should you fight when you're upset?" Jessi asked.

"I can think of worse ways to burn off steam."

Jessi shrugged. "Okay then. If you're sure."

"Are *you* sure? You just told us something really terrible and you're upset. I can beat on people any time I want or need to." Mick kissed her quickly. "So if you'd rather stay in and hang out just the three of us, that's cool too."

"I want to get to know your friends."

Mick stood. "Let's do this."

CHAPTER
Fourteen

Maybe it was all the testosterone in the air, or having Jessi with him after she'd related that story about what Mick's dad had done to her, or the way Mick looked—all dangerous and angry—but Adam's blood seemed to hum with the need to possess them both.

The three of them walked up from where they'd parked to a field behind the house with a boxing ring set up in the center. The group resembled the one at the grand opening of the new showroom for Twisted Steel. Only with less formal clothing.

People stood around in knots here and there, drinking from red cups or from bottles, their breath misting in the growing cold.

Mick towered over most people—including Adam—and he used his size to barrel through anyone who might bump into or otherwise bother Jessi. Adam had seen this in action hundreds of times over the years. Had always respected Mick's dedication to Jessi in that gesture.

But this time Adam was included in the way Mick ran interference. That the same man who bulldozed through the crowd with an easy grin that didn't always make it to his eyes was one who begged to be fucked by Adam only made the situation hotter.

Adam hadn't been entirely sure how this would work in the end. A relationship between the three of them when Jessi had been the heart of it had been natural enough. But the Adam and Mick stuff? It had been part of why he'd lingered longer than he should have before finally owning how much he needed them *both*.

What he'd come back to over and over since the night just one week before was that yes, Jessi was the heart of it, but not at the *expense* of his connection to Mick.

There was *AdamAndJessi*, but there was also *AdamAndMick*. There'd been a growing sense of Adam/Jessi/Mick since they'd all met, that stable foundation of love and protection he felt for both and for their friendship of three. But the deepening of that friendship and connection to love and committed romantic relationship had been a delightful—if surprising—result. Better than he could have imagined.

They came to a stop where Carmella and PJ stood with Duke and some other guys.

The women welcomed Jessi, which visibly relaxed Mick. Adam really didn't have much doubt that Jessi would find her place in Mick's circle of friends. Adam, though? He'd have to see.

It wasn't that he was uncomfortable. But this was an entirely new social situation for Adam. He was there for Mick more than he was there because he wanted to watch his lover beat someone up.

Though it sort of did sound sexy now that they stood feet away from the ring. Violence and sweat hung in the air, and damned if it didn't make his dick hard.

"Right on, you're here. You want to go next?" Duke asked Mick. "Asa's getting ready to go in. If you take the next slot, we can clean up and be out of here in an hour."

"You're really hungry, aren't you?" Mick asked him.

"I haven't eaten since lunch." Duke shrugged.

Mick and Duke had an ease, a back-and-forth that was borne of deep, intimate ties. Not sexual, Adam was certain of that. But Duke saw Mick as a brother. So despite Adam's concern that maybe he didn't fit into Mick's new world, he'd do whatever it took to make it work. He was relieved Mick had Duke and Asa, especially in a place like the middle of a goddamn war halfway across the planet.

"What do you think, angel?" Mick asked Jessi. "Should I go next?"

She looked him over. "You have a lot of energy you need to work out." Jessi took his hands in hers, bending his fingers to make a fist. She kissed each one. "We'll be here when you're finished."

Mick exhaled and Adam knew there was a terrible storm inside Mick's heart. It was terrifying at times because Jessi said things, things you needed to hear but weren't always ready for. It wasn't to manipulate or scare. It was just how she was.

Duke took this scene in, Carmella at his side. Her smile brought one to Adam's face. She *got* Jessi.

Mick bowed his head a little, resting his chin against Jessi's hair for a moment.

"Next it is, then. Jessi's hungry too, and she's cranky if you wait too long to feed her." Mick kissed her quickly and she rolled her eyes.

A group of dudes drifted into the edges of the circle they'd made with Duke and Carmella.

Mick tipped his chin at them but didn't say more. It was enough that Adam knew there'd been something between him and at least one of the guys. Though probably not the one looking at Jessi's tits like he'd never seen breasts before.

Jessi noticed and turned her body away from the guy. Adam stepped between them, glaring at the dude. Yeah, they were great tits and all, but a person didn't need to be disgusting about taking in their majesty. It was never acceptable to make a woman uncomfortable.

Especially when it was Adam's woman.

Asa tossed his shirt to PJ and then stomped back over, pulled her to his body roughly, kissed her hard enough that at least half the people there got a little tingly, and then headed away, wearing a smirk.

Adam recognized a dominant man when he saw one. And Asa had probably been one from birth.

"I need to warm up a little," Mick said quietly to Jessi and Adam. "You'll be fine here out of the fray."

Jessi smiled up at him. "Is it weird that I get super turned on when you use words like *fray* on your way to get into a ring and punch someone for fun?"

Adam laughed. "If it is, angel, I'm weird along with you."

Mick's smile promised lots of dirty fun as he took a step back.

"Kick some ass, Mick," Jessi said. "I'll probably say bad words if you get hurt. So, you know, don't get hurt or my mom will get mad."

It was the most Jessi-type sentence ever. It meant fifteen different things, and all of them were exactly what Mick and Adam had needed for all sorts of reasons.

Mick, still grinning, kept walking backward, facing them for several long moments more before finally turning and heading around the other side of the ring where Asa had gone.

"Beer?" Duke, wearing a sexy grin, held two out Adam and Jessi's way. Jessi took hers, clinking it with them both before she sipped, her gaze roving over the crowd, lighting here and there as she took the place in.

"Looks like she's cataloging every last detail," Duke said to Adam.

"She's a costume designer, so most likely she is. Taking mental notes about this or that thing she'll end up using at some point in the future. She's like a magpie. Always collecting ideas."

Duke nodded. "I like that. Sunday at my house Carmella and I are having a barbecue. I told Mick earlier this week that I wanted to invite you myself. Except I forgot."

"Which is why Mick is so awesome, because he and I work

together to remind Duke of things like the time he invited thirty people over and forgot to tell me." Carmella leaned around Duke, her arm linked through his. Her expression was one of affection, not annoyance, though.

A big red-haired dude got into the ring and announced the first bout. Asa and some other guy the size of a boulder ducked between the ropes and met in the middle with the announcer.

"He better not play around with this fool," Duke groused as he tugged Carmella to his side.

"I've got snacks in my purse, you know, if you can't possibly wait."

"You do?" Duke asked her.

She dug around and pulled out a bag, handing it his way. "Cashews."

He beamed, kissing her hard before making quick work of getting the bag open and half the cashews eaten in one bite.

"Don't get excited. I only have an apple," Jessi murmured into Adam's ear.

"I bet it's the tastiest fucking apple ever."

She laughed, kissed him, and turned to watch as the fight began.

PJ moved forward, but Duke reached out, grabbed her belt loop, and pulled her back.

"She gets all worked up. Asa gets distracted. She gets mad that we didn't stop her from bounding up to the damned ring like she's Tigger and Asa ends up with a black eye because he looked her way. So she makes us promise to keep her back," Duke explained.

"Not his face!" PJ yelled. "Jeez. His face is so handsome! I like it unbroken."

"Does that work?" Jessi asked. "If so I guess we both need to yell at the next guy not to punch Mick's face."

"The point is not to get punched in the face," Duke said easily.

Asa didn't take too much longer before he was declared the

winner. PJ scampered over to Asa, who held the ropes for Mick to take his place.

Jessi leaned back into Adam's body as he wrapped his arms around her, grinding his cock into her ass.

Their man looked ridiculously hot. Shirtless, his ink over all those damned muscles managed to be menacing and beautiful at the same time. He, like Adam, had a lot of anger and guilt to work through.

"He's so sexy right now. I don't know what to do with myself," Jessi said quietly.

Adam bent to speak into her ear. "That's all right. I always have ideas about what to do with you. And I definitely have many about what you should do with yourself. In fact, I have something in mind for later."

Mick gave in to the need for whatever he got from doing crazy and or dangerous shit and moved with grace even as he took a punch and barely even moved.

Adam's protective streak went into high gear when it came to Mick and Jessi. He wanted them to be safe. But Jessi was . . . Jessi. And Mick, well, Mick's edges came with the whole package. He was driven by demons Adam figured he and Jessi would spend the rest of their lives helping him slay.

"Did you see how many people checked him out? Not that I don't get it. I mean, look at him." Jessi waved a hand in Mick's direction and winced when Mick got nailed in the face. "Kick his ass, Mick!" she yelled.

Part of Adam bristled. Mick was *theirs*. And yet it was undeniably sexy that others wanted but couldn't ever have him again.

Asa and PJ came over to them once more to catch the rest of Mick's fight. Mick and his opponent were very evenly matched in size and relative power. Both had landed several solid hits but showed no real signs of slowing down.

Jessi put her hands over her eyes after a shot to the gut sent

Mick back a step. But he recovered quickly, and soon enough she was peeking around her fingers.

"He's a tank," Asa said quietly before he squeezed Jessi's shoulder. "No one can take a punch like Mick."

"It's all that anger," Jessi said and the truth of it made the men go still. "You can get told you were broken your whole life, but it's going to leave a mark. If you want to survive, you give up and acquiesce, even accepting a life that's a total lie, or you build yourself armor."

She licked her lips and stopped speaking. Adam knew she'd never want to reveal things about Mick that he didn't want shared. Hell, even Adam hadn't known all the details, and as he learned earlier that evening, the Roberts family seemed a bottomless well of bullshit behavior.

What they'd done to Mick had been bad enough. But the way Mick's father had treated Jessi could not be tolerated. Adam would find a way to handle this situation so Mick and Jessi would be safe from people who hurt and called it love.

He hugged Jessi tighter, and she ran her hands over his forearms a few times to soothe him.

"He'll win." Jessi's words had no doubt in them. She was totally sure and Adam couldn't argue. Especially as they continued to watch.

He got close to her ear, choosing love over the anger roiling in his gut. "And we'll soothe all his aches afterward."

She shivered as she nodded, her gaze never leaving Mick, her eyelids growing heavier as she chewed her bottom lip. Thinking of sex.

Their sweet angel was so, so dirty.

The hair on the top of his head that Mick'd been letting grow out had been pulled up into one of those things Jessi called a man bun. Whatever it was, it rang Adam's bell as much as the ink, sweat, and look of utter violent concentration of Mick's face.

"Mick's looking mighty fine tonight," said one of the guys with the dude who'd been stupid enough to stare at Jessi's boobs to Asa, who barely looked his way but did move his body to block him out.

This guy again? Obviously either Mick had fucked him or the guy had really wanted it. In any case, the past was past.

"He hasn't been around much," the guy continued.

Asa continued to ignore him.

Mick and his opponent were totally beating the shit out of each other, though Mick seemed to have squarely gotten the upper hand.

There were rules of some sort, Adam knew. But this was... feral. The violence between those two men squaring off seemed to radiate from them.

Mick took two pretty solid punches to the kidneys and then his gut. Jessi yelled something Adam couldn't quite make out because the noise of the crowd rose.

"Who's the gash?" the guy asked Asa. *Meaning Jessi.* "She some passing fuck toy? Mick likes cock. Does she know that?"

Adam spun, shoving Jessi toward Duke as he headed right the fuck into that loser's face.

"What did you just call her?" Adam's anger at anyone disrespecting Jessi, especially in such a misogynistic way, surged through him.

Asa didn't get between them. Instead, he settled at Adam's left, both forming a line between where Jessi stood with Duke and this asshole.

"What's it to you?" The guy made a decent enough sneer, but Adam wasn't overly impressed.

Adam didn't even think before his fist was already making contact with the guy's face.

"That's what it is to me." Adam's hand was going to hurt like hell the following day.

The guy lunged at Adam, but while he was rougher, Adam was pissed off and defending what was his, so he stepped to the side and tripped the dude, punching him as he went down.

"She's a fucking queen, that's who she is. And Mick is taken," Adam snarled.

He knew Duke and Asa would keep Jessi from interfering, but he heard her in the background, and despite the situation, he wanted to laugh at how pissed off she sounded.

So he let himself. Let go of the laughter in his belly, of the nervous energy of his rage about what Mick's father had done, of the possessive, protective things they both made him feel.

The little fucker who was about to come at Adam yet again stilled at the sound of Adam's less than calm laughter.

But still didn't mean silent. Much to his misfortune. The guy looked over at Jessi and then back to Adam. "Taken? By a *chick*? I think not. You think you're the first one to try to scare others off with a bullshit claim?"

By that point the crowd had shifted their attention from the official fight to the one happening between Adam and this douchebag.

He was already seeing red after Jessi's story earlier, and this asshole upsetting her more was the last push into full-blown rage. He fisted his hands and it felt *really* good.

"I'd really like to punch your face again. So keep coming at me," Adam taunted, meaning every word. The darkness he kept at bay roared into his ears.

The guy was bigger, but Adam was angrier. He had a reason to fight that was more than a hard cock.

The guy was also dumb. He failed to see those things and came at Adam, giving him the perfect opportunity to clock the stupid fucker right in the face, sending him to his knees.

"You sure do know how to fit in, babe."

Adam turned to Mick, who stood, grinning, covered in sweat

and blood. Jessi hopped up and down, but Asa and Duke had her penned in.

They'd have to pay for that, Adam knew. She was safe, though, so that was enough.

"He called our girl a very unpleasant name."

"That so?" Mick stepped closer, but Adam slid an arm around his waist.

"Handled. Did you win?" Adam asked Mick as they turned their backs on the piece of shit being helped away by his friends.

"I did. What happened?" Mick looked over at Jessi, tipping his chin at Asa, who let her out.

She stomped over and poked Adam in the side. "I'm not okay with being penned in like a puppy."

"He referred to her as a gash."

Mick went very still and then spun to take in the asshole, who was limping away with his friends.

"No!" Jessi took his arm. "It's over. Jeez. Adam already punched him in the face. Twice."

"Let's skip the next round and get going. Dinner sounds like a good idea, don't you think?" Carmella asked with a smile. "Adam probably needs to ice his fist."

Jessi's emotions were stamped over her features, and Asa paused after a look from PJ.

"I'm sorry you're mad at me," Asa said to Jessi. "Mick would kill us both if you got hurt in any way."

"You can't be sorry for how I feel. You can only be sorry for what you do."

Asa's mouth quirked up at the corner. "Jesus, you're going to fit in just fine, aren't you?" He slung an arm around Jessi's shoulders and hugged her quickly. "I'm sorry I made you upset. I'm not sorry I kept you out of the fight."

Jessi nodded. "Fair enough."

"We okay? I don't have to watch my junk?" Duke asked her. "What? You all laugh, but you think Carmella or PJ wouldn't be just as dangerous?"

The chuckles died down.

"As long as you'd have had Adam's back, we're cool."

"You and Adam are with Mick. That makes you ours too. Of course we had his back." Duke's expression was sincere and Jessi nodded.

Jessi tapped his fist with her own, making Adam like Duke even more.

"Right on. Let's go get dinner now while everyone is ahead."

CHAPTER
Fifteen

Mick sat out in his car for a long time before he finally went around to the back door of Jessi's studio. It wasn't quite eight and she'd been up late the night before. She'd spent the night there to meet a deadline.

Back at the house, he and Adam had slept fitfully—though they'd had dinner with Jessi and hung out at her studio until after midnight.

He got it. She needed to work. Sometimes he had to work long hours too. But he missed her.

And he needed her.

Unsure if she'd be awake, he paused until the scent of freshly brewed coffee hit him.

"Jessi?" Mick called out as he headed up the stairs to her studio loft.

She met him as he got to the top, music drifted out at her back.

"Hi! Come hug me." Jessi reached toward him and he met her in one more step.

She smelled like sleep and sex and everything that made him feel better. "Good morning, angel." He kissed her before they headed toward her tiny kitchen area.

"Want a cup of coffee? It just finished brewing about two minutes ago."

He nodded and she made them both a cup before joining him on the bed.

"I was going to eat pie and tell you I had a kale smoothie. I'm still going to have pie, but I'll share it with you." She held up a bakery box and two forks.

"You have secret pie?" Sipping his coffee, he was so glad to be there.

"You know. So it's not a secret. Duh. Because I'm being healthy I'm forgoing ice cream."

"When you put it like that it's much clearer." He dug into the pie along with her.

"So. You're here to visit me and I'm not complaining because I love being with you. But it's not as if we aren't going to see one another tonight. What's wrong?"

It had been a week since she'd told him and Adam about the incident with Mick's dad. A week with a lot of thinking.

"I need to talk to someone about this situation with my dad. And I have friends to do that with. People I can trust, like Asa and Duke. Adam too, of course." He chewed his bottom lip a moment, and she put her mug aside to get a little closer.

"But none of them know the whole truth of it. Of what it was like for you."

He shook his head. "Only you know. Only you know it all."

"But you feel like you can't tell me because, well, because it happened to me. I can't pretend to be unbiased. Not ever when it comes to you, and certainly not when it comes to what happened between me and your father. But I've been your best friend a very long time. I love you, and I promise to do my best to listen to you and tell you the truth."

"But you didn't. Not for years."

She breathed in slowly. "No, and if it had been up to me you'd never have found out."

He had been upset with her for not telling him. Years and years had passed and she'd kept her silence. He'd gone to see his parents, never knowing his father had treated Jessi that badly.

"I keep coming back to how I invited you to the grand opening and you came. You came and you were there for me. Excited for me. You knew they'd be at the event."

Jessi shrugged. "I'd hoped."

"That they'd be there? Really? Why?"

"Because you needed them to be," she said with infinite patience as she ate her pie.

"That's . . ."

"Complicated." Jessi laughed and patted his knee. "I'm entirely capable of disliking your family and also hoping they do right by you because you love them and want them to love you back."

"This is where I needed to talk to you most. Because." He stopped speaking, knowing once he said the words out loud there'd be no more ignoring them.

Jessi got up to top off her coffee, doing the same for him. She fiddled in the fridge and brought over a plate with some fruit and cheese on it.

"Pie is awesome and all, but some protein might help your blood sugar." She nudged the plate toward him as she settled back in across from him.

"After you finished telling us last week, the words just sort of rattled around. Echoing. Vibrating and getting louder and louder. I was ashamed because he mistreated you. He used his size and your gender to hurt you and scare you. Because of me."

"Not because of you. No one made him do it, Mick. Your father made his choices."

He held Jessi's gaze for long moments. "Exactly. So guess what? You don't get to feel guilty for it either."

She flipped him off. "Are you new here or something? Do what I say, not what I do."

Mick stole a quick kiss and then took her advice and ate some of the cheese and apple.

"I can't remember a time when I ever felt comfortable around my father." He'd always been on guard with his behavior. Even before he'd come out at fifteen, Mick had been different. He loved to read. Loved to draw.

But his father mocked anything he saw as womanly. Mick had to draw in his room, always taking his sketchpad to school in his backpack so it wouldn't be found in his absence and destroyed.

He asked the wrong questions at Sunday school. He was curious about things, always asking how and why. Until the age of seven or so, when he'd finally shut up and did his asking at the library.

Which also made his family suspicious.

Mick hadn't really known how good it felt to be hugged and touched all the time until he'd started to spend time with the Franklins. He got his hugs there. He asked his questions, debated philosophy with Addie until the late hours as a teen.

"And I see now that you didn't tell me because you know me so well. Know how much I wanted them to finally fucking love and accept me for who and what I am. And I'm not mad. I'm head over heels in love with you, and that's just the epitome of why."

She smiled, but it was sad at the edges.

"So a few days ago rage burned into a sort of clarity. The man who did that to you isn't someone whose respect I need anymore. I've realized at long last that things are never going to be what I hoped for. They'll never be satisfied. There's no future with them where I'm comfortable or at home."

She sighed, grabbing his ankle, her touch reassuring.

"I feel . . . nothing. No, that's not exactly it either. Whatever there was between us that kept me bound to them, that's broken. I can't—no, I won't—hide being in a relationship. I could have been circumspect and respectful of their beliefs, but they will always want total capitulation from me. Nothing short of a total denial and discernable absence of anyone they disapproved of would be enough. Eventually, even if I went along, left everyone I cared about to play their game, they'd still find a way to be unhappy."

"That's your place. In the family, I mean. Your role is to be the one who doesn't measure up. And because you refuse to pretend to be straight, they get to be even more disgruntled."

"I should have come to you before now," he said. Jessi always managed to help him think clearer after he talked to her about his troubles.

"You couldn't because you didn't know about that thing with me and your dad. And you weren't ready. Not to see this all so bluntly. I'm sorry. For whatever that's worth, I hate that they don't see you for how amazing you are."

She did, though. Which made him love her even more.

"But before I cut them off, I need to confront them about what he did to you."

Shock flittered over her face, and then resignation. But he knew she'd try to sway him anyway.

"Okay, but why? Will it change anything? He's not going to react the way you want him to. He's going to try to hurt you on the way down." She clamped her lips together, and Mick shook his head.

"Oh *no way* can you do that. What were you going to say? You promised honesty. Remember?"

"I don't want any more hurt for you. Not today. Give yourself a break."

"You shred me to pieces without even trying." Mick blew out a shaky breath. "It's fucking terrifying to be loved by you sometimes, Jessilyn. You're just so damned good at it."

Her smile was nearly shy. "Terrifying?"

"I ran from this." He indicated the two of them. "You see me.

Flaws and all. My ugly parts. My weak parts. And you love me despite that. I'm afraid of fucking it all up. This thing with my father…I should have protected you. If I had stood up for you then, he'd have never come to your doorstep. I failed you by running off the first time. Now that I have this again. Now that I've allowed myself to imagine forever with you I'm freaked I'm going to screw it up. It would crush me to do that. To see you look at me with disappointment in your eyes."

She wiped her tears on the corner of her shirt, which exposed her breasts a moment, scattering his thoughts like birds exploding into flight.

"You've gone through a lot of shit. Dealt with casual cruelty over your life. Everything you've experienced is part of who you are. It's made you the man I love. The heart of a warrior. Dinged in places, maybe a little rusty here and there, but it's strong. I love all the parts of you. Even the annoying parts like opening the milk cartons the wrong way."

Mick laughed, feeling so much better than before he'd walked in earlier. "So. Honesty. You promised. I promised. Tell me what you censored yourself from saying about my father earlier."

She relented finally. "He's a spiteful man. Petty. Mean. He's always slicing you just to keep you wounded. He did what he did and he's not sorry. If he was, he could have apologized at any time over the last four years. Why give him any more chances to wound you? If you're done, be done. Let it go and save yourself the hurt."

Why indeed?

"I've been thinking about this a lot. Pretty much constantly. I know he's not going to apologize. I understand it's going to be unpleasant to have to confront him. I need the closure. For me, not him. I need him to know I see his hypocrisy and I'm done. And I want him to know what he did to you was unacceptable. Not because he'll see it as wrong, but because *I do*. And because you're mine. And because you've protected me over and over. You and

Adam are my family. Important enough to me to defend. I need to draw a very clear line for him."

"Do you feel like you can move forward if you do this? If you protect me and Adam and confront your father, is that what you need to happen to get closure?"

"Yes. What do you think? Not as Jessi my girlfriend, but Jessi my best friend."

"It's hard for me to tell. I'm so wrapped up in this with you. I'm worried about you. I have negative feelings about your family. I'm so biased. I can't pretend otherwise. I think Jessi the bestie and Jessi the girlfriend are all linked now." Her smile was cockeyed. "I think you need to be free of this. And it feels to me like you believe this will help you begin that process. I don't think this one thing is the end of it. Grief doesn't work that way. People don't work that way. You'll have other trials to face. But we'll handle it when it comes. Will you at the very least meet him in public? Or have John with you? Or Asa, since he's probably more liable to punch your father's face in than your brother would be."

"I can handle him." But it probably would be good to have someone around, just for everyone's benefit. "I'll ask John," Mick amended.

"I'm glad you and your brother have been able to have a closer relationship," Jessi told him.

"He's a pretty smart guy. A better dad than the one we had growing up, that's for sure. You don't think I'm a monster for cutting myself off from my parents?"

"I don't think you're a monster for wanting your life to be filled with people who are positive forces within it. You get to want love and respect. You deserve to be able to set limits. You deserve to be loved." She shrugged like it was the simplest thing in the world.

And maybe it was.

"I hate that this happened to you."

"I hate that you can't see that the fifteen minutes I experienced with your father is nothing compared to the decades of what he's done to you." Jessi cupped his cheek for a moment.

"It's not that. It's that you don't . . . you weren't exposed to it so long you grew calluses on your heart. You're tender. Not fragile. Jesus, never fragile."

She smiled, triumphant.

"You grew up in a house where your mother sang you songs to wake you up until you graduated high school. You Franklins and your goofy dance parties and cookouts filled with people you've collected and made yours over the years. I'm used to what my father does and says. You shouldn't have to endure even a second of it. You're better than that."

"If you're tossing your dad out of your life, can you please toss out your self-loathing along with it? No kid should grow up in a home the way you did. You should have had goofy dance parties with your family. Instead your father made you kneel on hardwood for hours and hours at a time as he castigated you and tore you down. You are his child. You are a fine, courageous man who served his country. He should be proud of you!"

She was so passionate in her defense of him and Mick was feeling so much better after their discussion that he let himself think about the sight of her tits when she'd wiped away her tears earlier.

"I'm done talking about it for now. Let's change the subject so we can have sex." Mick put his coffee and the plate aside as he brought her to the bed, his body against hers. "God, that's so good. It's sexy when you defend me. And safe."

"Leave no one behind."

He kissed her.

"Will you ever tell me about the army?"

"Not when I plan to fuck you." He pulled her shirt up over her head after doing the same with his own. "Only good stories now. I missed you."

"You saw me less than twelve hours ago when I chased you and Adam out of here." But she smiled, giving over to him right away.

"Eleven hours and forty-eight minutes too long. How is it you're so much in such a small package?"

"I'm told I'm a dynamo."

That was her nickname among her siblings, and it was as accurate as calling her angel.

"You are. Until I said all that out loud I hadn't really faced why I left. I'm still so scared of messing up. You deserve for me to be fearless."

He'd meant to stay on sex, but it was important to tell her all the things he didn't before.

"I don't think any smart person is fearless all the time," she said. "Or even most of the time. You did mess up. But I'm here. The moral of the story isn't don't ever be afraid. Or even don't screw up. It's that screwing up isn't the end of the world. I'm here. I said that again because it's important. Most screwups can be gotten past. We all need to trust one another to do the work."

He kissed it away. Took her promise, believed it because she'd never given him reason to doubt.

She helped him from his jeans and shorts before grabbing his cock and squeezing. "You brought breakfast."

"I'm going to be late for work, I think," he said, nipping her bottom lip, settling between her thighs on his knees.

Jessi, high on the joy of loving this man, just took some time to look at him. She knew he loved to fuck her this way, so her back would arch and her hips canted up so he got in deep.

"You're quite literally the perfect bad-boy fuck fantasy."

His intensity didn't dim at all when he smiled, pleased by the compliment.

"Is that right? Want to share yours with me?" He grabbed his cock at the root and tapped the head against her clit until she went all blurry with just how sexy he was.

"You're the best kind of bad boy."

"The kind who's going to make you beg for it before I give it to you?"

Jessi now knew where the text term *guh* she used with her friends came from. She made that very sound when he talked dirty and ordered her around.

"The bad boy who's actually a nice guy with rough edges. You have a custom motorcycle *and* a great job. You give up your seat on the bus to the elderly. You helped me run my animal hospital."

He'd been frowning, always so reluctant to believe wonderful things about himself. But when she mentioned her mom's potting shed, where Jessi had set up a space to tend to her animals who might need help, he smiled.

"Your dad is a vet, angel. I just followed your orders and fed birds with medicine droppers. He did all the heavy lifting."

Mick ran his hands all over her torso. Bringing sensation in the wake of his touch.

She didn't hate very many people. Hate took up a lot of energy and emotion. But she hated the way Mick's father had shaped his son into a man who, despite being a success, had such difficulty hearing a real compliment.

"You're the only bad-boy fantasy I've ever had. Why else would I think of anything else? You look at me like you're going to burn yourself into my skin." She gasped as he pinched her nipples.

"I've got grease under my nails."

"Occupational hazard, I wager." Jessi would beg for him to fuck her. She wanted it. He wanted it. But he wanted to tease her first. Since she wanted that too, she dug her nails into his thighs, urging him on.

"You're so fine. Delicate and I'm not."

She wriggled to rub herself over his cock, inciting. "What?"

"I was just saying you're too good for me." He aimed at a charming grin, but she frowned, annoyed that he'd believe such bullshit.

And she told him so. "If you're not right for me, that means you also think I'm dumb."

"This is turning into one of those very special episodes with Jessi and her logic that takes me a long time to figure out, isn't it?"

"Not if you want to put your dick in me."

He grinned, teasing the head of his cock just barely inside her, rocking gently. "Feisty."

"Yes. Which means *you are perfect* for me and I'm perfect for you. So I'm not dumb for loving you and choosing you. I'm brilliant."

"Okay, so I figured it out pretty quickly, but it was a Jessi-type conversation, you have to admit."

"Every conversation with me is a Jessi-type conversation."

He rolled a condom on. "True. But not every one is a delightful meander through a myriad of topics until at last, the point becomes clear. After a while."

Laughing, she pinched his side. Or tried, but because he was all muscle it was hard.

His hand splayed against her thigh, holding her where he wanted. So big and strong. She'd seen him punch people with that hand. The vivid color of his ink stood out against her skin. The leather cuff he wore on his wrist, a gift she'd given him for his eighteenth birthday.

"You think you're not good enough for me because you work with your hands? Or because you find some measure of comfort and relief in using those hands to punch people for fun or in defense of those you care about? Because you say dirty things?" She knew she'd hit home when he closed his eyes a moment. "What you miss is that I say dirty things too. Things like, *please put your cock in me. I need you to fuck me.*"

His attention snapped into place as he paused, still only barely inside her.

"Please," she added prettily because it got him hard.

He sucked in a deep breath and then thrust deep.

"You and Adam think I'm an angel, but I'm just as filthy as you two are. I can be that with you. I can beg you and know you'll ease my pain."

He snarled a curse as he tapped her mouth with his fingers. She sucked them inside, her taste on his skin. "Get them wet so I can finger your clit."

She did.

He brushed his now slick fingertips against her, tugging just perfectly on the hoop she had in.

"You have no idea how many times you've saved me over the years in some way or other. You're so fucking perfect and beautiful. That you love sex and trust us enough to tell us what you need is perfect and beautiful. That's why you're our angel. Who else but you shelters guys like me and Adam from the storms of our lives? Angels are warriors, you know."

He did something fancy with his fingers that made her lose coherence for long enough that she could have let it go.

But she didn't. "It's the other way around. You two who save me all the time. Now, hush up with all this fancy talk and fuck me. Please."

"Hands above your head and keep them there," Mick said as he added a flick of the pad of his middle finger to her clit right before he squeezed it and then pulled back, tugging on her piercing. "All that sweetness makes the spice even hotter. We'll be out and about and I'll look over and remember your pussy is pierced. And then I have a hard-on at work and have to think about something gross."

"Like when you think you're biting into a chocolate chip cookie but it's raisin?"

He snorted. "Or shredded carrots in Jell-O."

"This is the weirdest conversation I've ever been turned on by," Jessi said on a gasp as he sped his thrusts in time with whatever sorcery he had going on with his fingers on her clit.

"Wait until you see what's next," he murmured right before he did some sort of squeezy-rubby thing with his fingers and hit some sweet spot inside her pussy with his cock and it was too much.

She needed to back off, but it was so good she couldn't work up the will to fight it. Jessi went sideways and upside down all at once and she let it, the orgasm rolling through her body so hard and so good she arched, squeezing his cock with her inner muscles, holding him deep with her calves wrapped around his waist, pushing him as hard as he'd pushed her until his head tipped back as his hips jutted impossibly further, getting so deep it nearly hurt.

Jessi watched muscles on his abdomen and chest flex and bunch, his neck and shoulders tense until finally he groaned her name as he came.

When he got back from getting rid of the condom he rummaged around in her freezer until he found the ice cream, bringing it back to bed with two spoons.

"Damn, you're so handy," she told him as she set the lid aside.

"I figured you earned a splurge. Have to keep your strength up for work."

"One of the many reasons I love you."

CHAPTER
Sixteen

Jessi opened the front door to find Adam's youngest sister, Denise, standing on the doorstep. She barely spared Jessi a glance as she walked into the house, leaving the front door wide open.

"Can you fetch Mr. Gulati? I'm his sister," Denise asked, looking over the room with a critical eye. It was still Adam's cool guy house, but Jessi's presence was clear, as was Mick's.

Denise apparently didn't know him well enough to understand how the house had changed, only that it seemed a little different.

"Adam!" Jessi called out. She could have easily gone to get him, but Denise had always been snooty. She'd ordered Jessi around without ever having looked her in the eye. Or saying please.

Apparently she hadn't changed one bit from the spoiled young woman she'd been.

Startled, Denise turned with a gasp and then froze when she finally realized who she'd been ordering around.

Jessi waved. "Hi, Denise."

"What, my love?" Adam said from the kitchen. He'd been retrieving something from a hall closet before they went to pick up Mick to head out for the ballet. He was amused by her bellow of his name, that much was clear in his tone and on his face.

"Your sister is here." Jessi indicated Denise, who hadn't bothered to reply to Jessi's hello. Instead choosing to curl her lip slightly like Jessi had been picking her nose or something.

Adam noted Denise's body language and lack of even basic manners in Jessi's direction. He frowned at the sight before looking to Jessi again.

"I'll get Mick on the way and meet you at the restaurant," Jessi said and then kissed his cheek. "You're okay?" she asked quietly, for his ears only.

He nodded. "Drive safely. See you in about an hour." He walked her out and then came back into the house, where his sister waited, the look of shock still on her face.

"I'm sorry for my manners. Hi." He hugged his baby sister. "Come on through. Want something to drink? We've got cider, beer, soda, water, wine." Perhaps if he kept civil she would too.

"Why was that woman here? I thought you'd finally cast off Jessilyn Franklin."

"I never cast her off. We broke up for a while, went our separate ways. But we never totally lost touch. We're together now. She lives here."

He considered telling her about Mick too, but figured he'd go for one step at a time.

"Lives here? Adam, you can't seriously let that creature move in. Before long all your beautiful furniture will be covered in Day-Glo flower stickers and gurus will be setting up camp in your backyard."

"Don't be a snob. Our money isn't old enough for that."

"Those people are charlatans. Crystals and energy readings and chakras or whatever. She's full of it. I thought you were dating real adults now."

Adam repressed a sneer. Barely.

So much like her mother and their father. Cold and calculating.

Everyone in her life went through that benefit-cost analysis. What could they do for her? Someone like Jessi didn't care about that sort of capital, so she existed to be belittled and mocked.

"Enough. She's with me. I've told you that. I don't care to hear any more of your bullshit about her. Why are you here?"

"Touchy. I'm just looking out for my big brother."

"I will always be touchy on the subject of Jessilyn," he warned.

"Fine, fine. You haven't let Mom know if you'll be at dinner this weekend."

He resisted the urge to remind Denise that her mom was not *his* mom. Katherine herself had reminded everyone of that fact enough in the years since Adam's father had been married to her, so he left it alone. That and he was a grown man, not a boy in high school.

"I don't know. I told Katherine a month ago that my schedule's pretty tight."

"It's your *father's* seventieth birthday. You can take your girlfriend out but not give your time to the man who gave you life. *Most* people would be there. He wants you there," Denise chided.

"I'm not most people. He'd be the first to tell you that. If he noticed my absence at all."

"You're his only son. Of course he'll notice. What will people think if you're not there? His friends from work will be at the party. Family from all over the country too. You can't even spare a few hours?"

That's what it was really. How it looked. Not how it *was*. Then again Paul Gulati had always preferred looks to substance, so it wasn't so much of a surprise.

Adam blew out a breath. "Don't count on me for sure. I have a business to run. I'll let you know toward the end of the week."

"We need a definite. That way we have enough. You know how this works. It's not like I'm ordering a hoagie from the deli."

Hell, if she did, he'd probably go.

"Bring your—whatever she is. Bring Jessilyn. Or not. If she needs clothes I can give her the name of a few places in town she could locate appropriate cocktail attire."

"She's a costume designer, so I'm quite sure she'll find something to throw on." He'd have said he was bringing Mick too, but Mick would *loathe* an event like this party, and he wasn't much of a fan of Paul Gulati anyway. "I hate to push you out the door, but I do need to meet Jessi and Mick for dinner. He lives here too," Adam told her as they went toward the front door.

He had no idea why he'd just said that. It would most assuredly cause a fracas. Which is possibly why he said it. Like a boy in high school.

Adam was better than this silliness. But he was relieved to have told her. Whether she believed him and how she'd react he didn't know.

"Have you started operating as a B&B suddenly, Adam? Do these people need money? You're suddenly their ATM machine?"

"ATM. *Machine* is already in the word, it's the *M*," he said absently. "And no they're not in need of money. Though if they were, I'd give it to them instantly. Do you really want to know why they're both here?"

Her eyes darted around the area as they stepped out onto the porch. "You're making me nervous, now. What on earth are you talking about?"

"I'm in love with Jessi. I have been since I was fourteen years old. She's given me another chance, and I aim to never make her regret that. And I'm in love with Mick. I sort of wondered if he'd be the guy who came along with Jessi, the one I had to share her with. But really, I absolutely love him. Funny how that works. I'm happy. Yes, it's not what most people do. But it's what I'm doing and it makes me satisfied. So. Anyway. He won't be at the birthday thing. But Jessi will be."

"What's gotten into you? Are you on something?" Denise looked him over carefully.

"No. I'm sorry." He hugged her. "I'm not on anything but love. I told you to poke at you. But now that I've said the words, I'm glad I did. I hope you'll give Jessi and Mick a chance because they're both worth knowing. And because I love them."

Denise's expression was sour. "You can't be serious. Adam, this is absurd. You can't live like this. It's bad enough you'd live with a woman like her, but with a man? At the same time? There's no way. It's unacceptable. You'll embarrass everyone."

"Turns out I don't give a rat's ass if you're embarrassed by something that doesn't involve you." He'd wanted her to be happy. Even though it had been a long shot, it still hurt. "I'll see you at the dinner party."

She shook her head. "You can't bring her. If you come, you can't . . . not either one of them."

"You're uninviting me to a party? To our father's birthday celebration you were just telling me I had to come to or I'd shame the family?"

"Yes I am." She hitched her expensive handbag up onto her shoulder. "You can't expect anyone to accept this . . . this whatever you're doing. Get your act together, Adam."

His sister stomped down to her car and sped away.

"Well. I guess I'm free of a whole lot of social obligations I never wanted anyway."

Jessi made quite an entrance, Mick had to admit. Normally she was pretty. But that night she was fucking gorgeous.

Twisted Steel got pretty busy on Saturdays as people came in to finish up things. And that day was no different, only more. More as she walked—click, click, click—in sky-high heels. A switch in her step that sent her ass swaying from side to side.

The dress, a simple, dark gray number, seemed to caress every curve as it left plenty of her legs exposed.

She waved and he moved through the workshop floor, ignoring all the dumbasses he worked with who stared at her, besotted.

By the time he reached her, Duane had given her a hug and had made her laugh. But Mick noted the strain around her eyes. She was worried about something. As the three of them had begun to settle in to life together, Mick noticed each one had rough patches as they worked through things.

Any romantic relationship was complex, and theirs was most certainly that and more.

"You look beautiful." He gave her a hug.

"Me? You worked in a garage all day and you're in a suit, looking suave." She linked her arm through Mick's. "Adam's going to meet us at the restaurant."

Which most likely was connected to whatever had her looking worried.

"I'll drive." He held out his hand for the keys. With a roll of her eyes, she dropped them into his palm.

"See you later, Duane! Have an awesome date."

Duane blushed and smiled. "Thank you, sweetheart. You enjoy the ballet."

Several other guys who'd been working around the shop called out their farewells to her as they left.

"I have to beat them off with a stick every time you come around." Mick held the door open for her and she got in.

When they pulled out of the lot, heading toward Queen Anne, Mick spoke again. "You knew I'd want to drive, so you brought my car on purpose. Didn't you?"

Jessi snorted. "I pay attention. Nothing more than that."

"You make it sound like it's no big deal to pay attention when the sad fact is, most people don't. It takes a lot of energy to listen."

"You just finished with this car a few months ago and you love to drive it. It's not motorcycle time anymore, and Adam will obviously bring *his* car."

"Thank you for paying attention. What's going on at home that made Adam have to meet us there instead of coming with you?"

"Right as we were about to leave, Denise showed up at the door. She wanted to talk to Adam, and so I told him to meet us at the restaurant. I didn't want him to feel rushed into whatever they had to talk about."

"His sister Denise?"

"Yes, that one."

"She must have been thrilled to see you." Mick laughed. The baby of the Gulati family had never been anything but unpleasant. Entitled. Spoiled.

"Honestly, I don't know why she doesn't like me. I've never done anything to her. Anyway, she didn't even notice me until Adam came into the room. I was just this person she told to *fetch* Adam. Actually, she said Mr. Gulati. I guess I look like a butler? Or whatever."

"Did you get a sense about whatever her issue was?" Adam's mother's family were good people. Warm and supportive. But the Gulatis were another story.

"She couldn't even be bothered to say hello to me. Though, I should be fair and tell you she might have just been surprised to see me after all these years."

"Maybe, if she was a normal human instead of a cyborg."

Jessi laughed as they parked and he gave the car one last look. The '65 Chevy Impala had taken him pretty much the entire year he'd been back in Seattle to restore. A lot of money. Thank god he'd been able to do a lot of the work himself on the side and had help when he'd needed it.

The tangerine paint had a metallic fleck and the chrome rims made it more than a restoration. It was *Mick's* car. He couldn't drive it every day, but he'd only had it done for just about a month and the joy of it hadn't even begun to get old.

"So shiny." She sighed the words and he got off on the fact that she loved it as much as he did.

"You also wanted to drive my badass car, and coming to pick me up gave you a reason."

She laughed. "Just because I listen to you doesn't mean it didn't also suit my purposes. Your car has good energy. It pleases me to be in it and it's totally badass. People just get out of the way for that car. And orange goes with the gray of my dress, don't you think?"

In the alcove of the restaurant, Adam stood waiting, looking handsome in a deep blue suit.

Jessi smiled at him as he approached. "I didn't expect you for a while more."

Adam bent to kiss her quickly and then, much to Mick's surprise, Mick as well.

"As it turns out, she didn't need very much time."

Mick waited until they'd been seated and drinks had been ordered before he pursued it. "What did she want?"

"They're throwing my father a birthday dinner thing. She and her mother have been hounding me to say yes."

Jessi sighed and then clamped her lips together. It was adorable and infuriating all at once.

But Adam didn't miss it. One of his eyebrows, the right one, slid up very slowly. "So, I did say yes, and then I got uninvited."

"What?" Jessi exclaimed before Mick got to say anything.

Adam explained that he'd said Jessi would be there but Mick wouldn't and that he loved them both. His sister—predictably—hadn't handled it well.

"That's awful! I'm sorry. Go without me. I'm not offended. I know they don't like me."

Jessi would most likely be relieved because Paul Gulati was a braggart of the worst order. If you broke a leg, he was in traction once after climbing Everest. If you just bought a new house, Paul had a multi-million-dollar mansion built for himself.

Mick found it exhausting as well as pitiable.

"I'm not going." Adam waved it away, and when Jessi made a little growl he drew his fingertip up her neck to her chin to hold her gaze. "Angel, I'm absolutely not going, so don't argue. I had a twenty-five-year-old who's never held a job she wasn't *given* tell me to get my life together. Because I have the audacity to love two people instead of just one. I don't know if she was more horrified that one of the people was gay or that one of them was Jessi."

Adam and Mick laughed, but Jessi didn't really find it funny.

"Most people think I'm fun."

Adam took her hand and kissed her knuckles. "I definitely think you're fun."

"They don't like you, because they can't own you. You're not after all the things they think are important." Mick winked at the bread guy, and Jessi gave him a look. Mick grinned to tease her, but she remained frowning. "You can't possibly think that's serious."

Adam ran a palm over Mick's head and Mick leaned into that touch like a cat. "He's so pretty. They all can look as long as they don't touch."

"I would like to point out that if I flirted as casually as you both do, you'd lose your shit. Back to your families not liking me. It's dumb. Carey's mother *loved* me. She still does. Especially now that Carey's dating again and seems a lot happier. All my boyfriends' families have loved me except for the two of yours."

"My mom loves you," Adam said. "So does Lissa. The people who count in my life." After the mention of his mother and sister,

Adam cocked his head as he examined Jessi's features. "I'm sorry. You're more upset than I thought you were. What can I do to make you better?"

"I'm just hungry." She looked down to her menu and Adam's gaze flicked up. Mick shrugged. She'd been tense on the way over, but he'd assumed she'd be better once she saw Adam.

Their server showed up soon after and took their orders.

"Once the appetizers arrive, we can talk about what's bothering you," Adam told Jessi.

"Nope." Jessi took her hand back and placed her napkin in her lap. "Both of you need to quit looking at me like that. I'm cranky and hungry. Let me eat and stop glowering at me."

Mick handed her a piece of buttered bread.

"Thank you." She ate it in three bites and downed the rest of her drink.

Of course Adam never obeyed anyone, so when the first round of food came out, and everyone had eaten a little, he circled back to her mood.

"Feeling better?" Adam used his silky sex voice. Mick's cock loved that voice. He wasn't sure about the rest of Jessi, but he'd been inside her when Adam had used it on her and he knew her pussy liked it too.

"I don't know whose day wouldn't be improved by a bacon tart and some scallops." She ordered another round.

"I haven't seen drunk Jessi in a very long time." Mick sat back to settle in. "Good thing I've got a first aid kit in the trunk."

She sent him a prim look and then stole one of his crab cakes, replacing it with a scallop the size of his fist.

"Sharing is loving."

Mick couldn't help but laugh.

"Maybe not drunk Jessi when we have to sit still for a few hours," Adam said. "Drunk Jessi needs room to run and be free."

"Mock all you want."

Adam laughed. "I thought we were already doing that."

She muttered something and the words Mick was able to make out sounded suspiciously like *stab* and *fork*.

He swiveled his body to shield any soft bits should she make good on her ruminations of fork stabbing.

"Oh for god's sake," she snarled.

When Mick turned to see what had prompted her outburst he saw a tall blonde who appeared to be making eyes at Adam.

"What's going on with that?" Mick asked.

"She's his ex. Showed up at the side door at four in the morning a while back. I informed her Adam was taken. As long as she keeps her butt over there, everything will be fine."

Was it weird he got hard at her jealousy?

"I called her the day after she did that and told her to not come around anymore. That you lived there and I was with you. She has an office nearby, so this is a place she probably eats in often." Adam kept his tone even, and not once did he look over in the blonde's direction.

Jessi harrumphed and Mick struggled not to laugh.

"Were you this cranky earlier and I missed it? Or has my sister's visit ruined your day? Or, do I need to correct your mood?" Adam's smile went very dirty and Mick hoped she chose the last one so they could all go home right then.

"You two have your cranky moments. I'm having one right now that I don't need permission for," Jessi said.

"You're absolutely right." Mick squeezed her hand and gave Adam a look that he hoped said, *back off.*

It was rare for her to be like this. Agitated, spoiling for a fight. Since it wasn't that rare for Mick and Adam, he wanted her to get through it. She had a reason, even if it turned out to be some twisty Jessi-reason. She wasn't prone to snits and when she was mad at them it was sort of hot, and it showed she trusted them.

But Adam, well, Jessi was his and it was hard to see her unhappy.

They had dinner, and once they'd left Jessi alone awhile, she relaxed a little. By the time they needed to leave to get to McCaw Hall for the ballet, she was tipsy but not drunk and annoyed, not mad.

And she still looked fucking gorgeous in that snug gray dress with those towering heels.

CHAPTER
Seventeen

Jessi couldn't shake her mood. Even before Denise had shown up at the door, Jessi had experienced bouts of being overwhelmed. But in the five days since, she'd needed to hide out to try to get herself in order.

She believed she had a life she was supposed to be living. She believed being with Mick and Adam was a choice she'd been meant to make since the first time Mick had ever kissed her and Adam had punched him and kissed her too.

But all sorts of stuff rattled around in her head. So much had happened in the last month she found herself overwhelmed by it. It made her cranky.

She took care of people. It's what she did. Jessi wasn't used to not being totally sure about everything she did. She liked it when she was the one doling out wisdom.

Late nights and a push to finish two dresses for upcoming winter formals at a local high school gave her the excuse to sleep at the shop. Mick and Adam both prowled around her, dropping by to make sure she ate. Adam brought her coffee at least twice a day, and Mick napped on her bed while she worked downstairs for a few hours after he'd been at the track with his friends.

They knew something was wrong but she'd told them both to back off, that she was trying to process a bunch of things.

But they'd only let her avoid them so long and as Adam was a bossypants, she was now heading home after delivering both dresses. She'd take off a few days, sleep in, catch up with her boys, watch a lot of television.

The house was empty when she arrived, so she got a load of laundry started, went up to the bedroom, and crawled into bed, burying her face in their pillows and snuggling into the space that was meant to be hers.

She woke up sometime later when she was pulled into someone's arms. Adam. She knew his smell, the way the hair on his forearms felt as he brushed his skin against hers.

When she opened her eyes it was to find his handsome face looking back at her. "What time is it?"

He kissed her, easing her back to the mattress and settling his body against hers.

"It's a little after six. When did you get home?"

"Two. I finished up, closed the shop, and headed here after tying up loose ends. I just planned to close my eyes awhile. *Oops*. I have the next two days off. You feel good." Jessi snuggled into his body, relaxing a little bit more with each breath.

"I have one appointment I can't miss, but I'm all yours otherwise. I saw your car in the garage and it made me so fucking happy. I know I said I'd be cool with you spending the night at the shop when you got busy, but I hate it when you're not here. And I especially hate it when you use your work to keep your distance."

She stilled for a moment.

Downstairs, the door to the garage opened and Mick called out. "You answer. He missed you too."

"We're upstairs!" she called out. "You act like I was gone a month. I saw you both every single day of the four I was less than five miles from here."

Mick's footsteps sped up the stairs and down the hall until he burst into the room and jumped into bed.

"There's a gorgeous stray in our bed, Adam." Mick winked.

"I suppose you're going to want to keep her?" Adam asked, reminding Mick of the same words *he'd* given Jessi about Adam just a month before at the grand opening.

"I'll feed her and keep her clean." Mick kicked off his shoes and then shucked down to his skin and got under the blankets with her.

"Will you always get her exactly the kind of candy corn she likes and not that—and I quote—waxy crap that is a disgrace to the name candy corn?" Adam smirked.

"You guys make fun, but it tastes like eating a candle your grandma has had since 1977 and brings out every Christmas." Jessi felt that candy corn was serious business, and there was no crime in having standards.

"That sounds like a very specific thing. Like maybe you ate a candle once." Adam was so suspicious.

"Who has a candle that looks like a piece of candy?" She shook her head, disgusted.

"The burned wick wasn't enough for you, angel?" If Adam thought she didn't notice the way he tried not to smirk, he was a dumbass.

"You're kidding, right? It was a decorative candle. It's probably in my mom's Christmas crap in the garage right now. With a bite mark that she just put red fingernail polish over. Still unlit."

Mick laughed. "I think I've seen that candle." He hugged her and she rested her head against his shoulder.

"She never throws anything out. She might need it in ten years and then what? It's not like you can buy candles at any old store or anything." Jessi rolled her eyes, laughing as she thought about her mother.

"She's taken the next two days off. I'm taking them off too except for the few hours I need to be at a meeting," Adam told Mick.

"I can shift my schedule around to do the same. I might have to go in for a while tomorrow, but otherwise I can be here with my two favorite people. Having sex. A lot of it." Mick ground his hard-on into Jessi's side just in case she wasn't clear.

"First, though, we have talking to do."

Jessi and Mick both groaned at that.

"What? Should we ignore the fact that she ran away for several days?"

"No. But you can show some finesse. Jesus. You dress like you'd have some. You drive a car like you'd have some. But you just barrel through at Jessilyn every time and she automatically says no because it's your weird relationship cadence."

Jessi and Adam both looked to Mick.

"That's pretty astute." Jessi shrugged.

"You're too nice to her. You let her get away with too much," Adam countered.

"Except neither of you is my dad! Ew. Letting me get away with what? *Letting?*"

"See?" Mick tipped his chin in Adam's direction. "You use words you know will set her off. I think you like it when she gets mad."

Adam made a face. "She doesn't get mad enough. She holds it in and lets it eat away at her heart. Puts everyone and everything else first. If she's mad, she can let go of whatever the fuck it is she's been pretending away."

"Hi. You remember me? I'm Jessilyn and I live here. I can also hear when you're discussing me as if I'm not even in the room. So, guess what? Lucky you, I'm mad."

"What the fuck, Adam?" Mick sat up.

* * *

"Finally," Adam said as that feisty, pissy side of her came out. He shrugged as he turned to Mick. "It needs to be dealt with. She'll avoid it otherwise."

"So you poked me into being mad after snuggling me awake?"

"The snuggling is just as valid as the dealing with whatever is bothering you."

Adam knew her tendency to smooth things over would make it hard to open up about the things that had upset her. The only way to get her to do it was if she cried or got really mad. He'd far prefer her mad to crying.

"I know you, Jess. You want everyone to be happy all the time. The only person you don't insist on that with is yourself. Here's a thing, though. I want everyone to be happy all the time too. You're mine. Mine to take care of, and I can see you're struggling with something. The only way this can work is if we share the load."

She frowned. "You should have admitted to making me mad on purpose after I told you everything."

He risked his safety and stole a quick kiss. "You knew it anyway. So, tell us."

She sucked in a breath. "We need pizza. With artichoke hearts and sun-dried tomato."

Mick curled his lip. "I'll get more than one pie, obviously." He got out of bed and went off to call in their order before coming back with three beers.

He also tossed Jessi a Snickers bar. Adam had taken to keeping them in the freezer because that's how she liked them.

She kissed Adam quickly. "Thank you for thinking of me." And clinked her beer to Mick's. "You too."

"Pizzas will be here in an hour. She seems less cranky. Did you make her come or something?" Mick winked.

"Not yet." That would happen after the telling. "Now, your

pizza has been ordered, you've been given chocolate and alcohol," Adam said. "So time to get this over with and tell us what's wrong."

"Or. I have an alternate suggestion. Let's roll around and kiss a lot until the pizza arrives and then we can eat and I'll tell you." She got to her knees and whipped her shirt off. "I'll let you get to second base."

"Shirt off is more than second base, isn't it?" Mick, grinning, put his beer aside and used his body to take hers to the mattress.

Adam took her beer, put it and her frozen candy bar off to the side, and dove in.

An hour later, Adam handled the delivery and even brought up new frozen candy bars to replace the one they'd put aside before making out.

Once they'd eaten a few slices, he gave her a look. "You need to get talking now."

She growled, but mainly because she knew he liked it. "Nothing's wrong. Not really. It's not like I'm mad at anything. I'm not even mad, I'm just...Ugh!" Jessi jammed half the frozen candy bar into her face, and he worried a moment she might choke. "Damn," she mumbled around a mouthful, "forgot they were this hard when frozen."

Mick burst out laughing. "You know what? I had nothing this wonderful in my life when you weren't around."

"So why did you live here for a year without coming to see me a single time?" Jessi asked once she'd managed to chew her candy bar.

Mick's laughter faded.

Jessi cocked her head. "See, you guys say you want me to be honest and then I make you sad. It's really hard for me to make you sad."

"I needed to hear it." Mick hugged her. "It's been there, unasked, between us since we got back together."

Adam needed to hear the answer too.

"I'll tell you. I promise. But it's your turn right now." Mick told Jessi.

"As I said, it's not that I'm mad. It's just . . . things are jumbled. I don't like that jumbled feeling in my stomach. I try to follow my heart. It's important to me."

She washed down the rest of her candy with a few swigs of beer. "I know you two think I'm a kook."

Adam interrupted. "No, you don't know that. You *think* that. Incorrectly."

"Or we make you feel that way," Mick answered.

"Fair point." Adam took a deep breath. "For the record, I think you're amazing."

She smiled. "It's weird for you two, huh?"

"What is, angel?" Mick asked her.

"Jessi the girlfriend is different from Jessi the best friend."

Adam guffawed.

Jessi's eyes widened, but before she could get worked up, he shook his head, holding his hands up. "It's not a bad thing. It's just a true thing. We're both learning that."

"In most ways, it's the same as it's always been. I'm comfortable with you both." She paused, clearly frustrated. "That's not really the right word, *comfortable*. But it's the only one I have right now. I just feel like I can be who I am with you."

"There's a but coming. I can tell," Mick said.

"This is complicated." She waved a hand around. "We've all used that word and said that very thing. So, I understand that we've got a lot more hurdles than we would if there were just two of us and there wasn't this backstory between me and your parents. I *hate* that your families don't like me. It's awful that your sister uninvited you to your father's birthday. You're both having to give up a lot to be with me. It's chaotic and full of so much drama in the worst way."

"It's totally complicated." Adam shrugged. "Did it never occur to you that we'd have trouble with our families? Especially with what happened with Mick's dad four years ago?"

It had been Mick's father who'd burst in on them. Having sex. He'd hauled Mick out of bed, screaming, red faced. Jessi had tried to calm them down, but Mick's dad had shoved her out of the way.

At the time, though Adam had been angry, he'd chalked it up to the chaos of the moment and the tussle between father and son. Now, given the way he'd treated Jessi after that, Adam wasn't so sure it hadn't been on purpose.

"I don't want you having to choose. It was one thing when there was general dislike, but this, this cutting off and being shunned? Because of me? It's breaking my heart. I'm stealing something from you that I don't have a right to." Jessi's voice had gone thick with emotion.

Mick sighed, softening because neither of them wanted to see her hurting. "Angel, I made half-assed choices for years. All the while trying to find some middle ground. Long enough to know it's not possible. So, I made my choice and I haven't regretted it. Have you?"

Jessi got to her knees to kiss Mick and then Adam before sitting once more. "*My* family loves you both. They already assumed that since we were all together again as friends it was something more. I don't have to give them up. They'd never expect me to, maybe. Hopefully. No one has uninvited me from anything. Family is important."

Adam agreed. "Family is incredibly important. And you come from one that's fantastic. Close. Loving. Your family greets you every time you walk in. They're genuinely pleased to see you and spend time with you. The loss of *that* would be a terrible thing indeed. You must know as you've been out in the world that your family isn't what a lot of people have. It's not what I have with my father and most of my sisters. So what am I missing out on? Huh?

You said you stole something? You can't steal what's freely given. Moreover, far from theft, you've brought me everything, even Mick." He smiled Mick's way and closed their circle once more. "*You* are my family. Mick is my family. Losing you two would fell me. Not going to a party I never wanted to attend to start with? With people who don't know me and have no desire to? Fuck that. Sometimes you have to make hard choices in life. But this one wasn't even mildly difficult."

Part of him was relieved that he had a reason to just let all that go and sever ties totally.

Mick broke in. "As for *my* family." He was silent awhile. "Your mom and dad have been there for me a million times more than mine ever have been. I don't have to give anything up. Being with you is a plus, not a minus. I put a lot out of my head, things my father did and said to me over the years. To survive."

Adam cupped the back of Mick's neck. Steadying.

"But since you and I had that talk at your studio week before last, I've been letting the memories free."

Jessi scooted closer to Mick, taking his hand. "And how are you dealing with it all?"

Given what Adam knew and what he'd suspected given the things Mick had said and done over the years, the memories of something like that coming back in a short time could cause havoc.

Mick sighed, letting the tension go. "I'm working on it."

"Which is why you've been at Twisted Steel twelve hours a day and when you're not there you're working out or punching something?" Adam had been watching Mick's energy amp up over the weeks since Jessi had confessed to them about what his father had done.

"What did I tell you about that?" Adam tightened his grip at the back of Mick's neck. And as he'd expected, Mick's gaze went glossy. "You come to *me* when you need this burned from you."

Mick turned his heat to look at Jessi. "You want to know why I was back for a year without contact?"

"Only if you want to tell me right now."

"Oh, sweet, sweet Jessi." Mick smiled. "You were so ferocious about knowing when you first asked. But now you'd let it go?"

"To save you heartache? Yes. Of course. But eventually, if you don't give it words and release it, it's going to eat you alive."

Mick sucked in a deep breath. "Right before I came home the first time I had some trouble with pills. Okay, a lot of trouble." Mick ran a palm over his head, the scratch of the close-cropped hair at the back sent a shiver through Adam.

"I ended up in the hospital. Then I had to accept what had happened and why and get my shit together."

Adam noted Jessi's shock. So Mick hadn't told either one of them.

"I came back and we all got together and then my dad came in and I ran. I ran because I was afraid to fall again. I was afraid I couldn't keep it together. I wasn't strong enough. And I know you, Jessi. I can tell you're thinking right now that you were right not to have told me about my dad."

She sighed. "I contend that if I had, given that you'd run back into a war zone and Adam was back to living on his own, it would have felt manipulative. And once we started the contact we did have, I loved it so much, wanted more of it, missed you so much I wasn't going to ruin it. I'm not sorry I didn't tell you while you were in the army, and knowing all this stuff about the pills only underlines that."

"All those glimpses, the cards, and letters you sent, they kept me going."

"Which is why I never put anything negative in them. I worried nonstop about your safety. I said a lot of prayers for you. I sure as hell wasn't going to load you down with anything else when you needed all your wits to survive." She had that defiant set to her mouth that Adam knew well enough to understand she'd have done the same thing over again.

"That last tour wasn't so dangerous. Not as bad as it'd been before. Most of it I wasn't even in Iraq. After about a month or so I knew I'd have fucked up seriously if I'd stayed in Seattle. I also knew I'd left wrong and that I had to fix it. But I needed to fix myself first.

"I had to know I could do it on my own. Be healthy. I had to find a strong enough sense of who I was. I'm not saying this right. I'm not eloquent. But I didn't feel strong enough to be anything other than a soldier. I knew I could do that and not fuck it up. I knew the routine. I knew how to get along. So I did. I built myself back up. Each time I'd stumble a little, I'd get a card from you, Jessi. I learned about myself. That I was good at running projects and with supervising others. I'm excellent with my hands."

Jessi hummed her agreement and Adam smiled her way.

"When I came back I was steadier. But I had a stumble at first with PJ and Asa. It fucked me up, made me seriously question my judgment. In the end it was what was supposed to happen because I realized I was only partially okay when I got back here. I couldn't come back to you or ask you to come back to me until I got my shit straight."

"Pain," Adam said.

Mick nodded. "I tried with fucking. I wasn't an angel when I was away from you both. But I'd given my heart away to Jessi, and it wasn't ever more than fucking. Pain, though? I *need* it to hurt. When it hurts, when it's fast and hard and dangerous, I'm alive. They're things I can feel that are okay to feel. I'm not harming anyone. I'm not victimizing anyone, least of all myself."

"But it's not enough," Adam said.

"Sometimes it feels desperate. I don't want it to be desperate. I wanted us to be back together without that. It's why I stayed away."

"You make bad choices when you're desperate," Adam agreed. "So, from now on you get what you need here. From me. You can keep on punching people and racing. That's part of you. But the kind of pain you need, I can deliver. I *like* delivering it. It doesn't always have to be sexual. But it's always what you need."

Mick stared at him for long moments, as if afraid to believe.

"So we get what we need here, right? Jessilyn? You too. People like Mick's dad and my sister, they want you to feel bad. They want you to be unhappy. Are you going to let them decide when I'm telling you otherwise?"

"You think you can handle us both, mister?" Jessi's mouth quirked up at one corner.

"I think it's exactly what I'm meant to do. So the choices have been made. Not because you insisted, but because other people put that choice out there. We're all here. Like we're supposed to be."

CHAPTER
Eighteen

I'm really glad you came out with us this weekend," PJ said to Jessi. Asa and Adam were building a fire with Mick and Duke looking on.

Carmella handed Jessi a soda and joined them in the ring of seating clustered around the fire pit.

Duane's vacation cabin—*ha*, if cabins had six bedrooms—was only ninety minutes outside Seattle but it felt a million miles away. It was surrounded by forest on all sides but the rear of the house, which faced the lake about three miles down the hill.

It was cold up in the mountains in late October, so they'd put on some layers and headed out to enjoy some time by the fire.

"How are things?" Carmella asked.

"We just hit our one month back together. So much has happened. It's very fraught. I'm not a fraught person. But I love them. Both of them. I'll deal with fraught if it means I come home to them every day."

"That's hella romantic. Also, exhausting. Adam and Asa are starting a friendship. At least I think it is, since neither of them says much other than to give imperious looks and gestures to order everyone else around. I don't know how you deal with Adam and Mick both. Don't get me wrong, I bet it's pretty awesome when it comes time to be naked."

They all three laughed at that, and the men turned their way to see what was going on.

"Damn," PJ whispered. "Look at all that. So much fine-ass man over there it's sort of stupefying."

"God, I hope they aren't comparing tips."

PJ waggled her brows at Jessi. "I bet Adam's got some tricks up his sleeve Asa hasn't tried yet. I'm all for Asa trying new things on me. Unless of course Adam likes something like being puked on."

"What? You don't think that's hot? You never know until you try it," Jessi said, managing to sound totally serious.

PJ appeared caught between wanting to apologize and wanting to be horrified. "Nuh-uh. He's kinky, that much is written all over him. But not that kinky. He smells too good and has great teeth."

"So do you look for a puke smell and bad teeth in a potential guy?" Carmella asked.

They all laughed again. Jessi missed girlfriends. She had several in Portland, but it had been hard coming back to Seattle because it was Mick and Adam who'd been her best friends there. They were who she'd turned to for so long.

But Carmella and PJ were fun. Open. Friendly. Being around them reminded Jessi she had a life to build too. *With* Mick and Adam, but also friends for her own emotional health.

God knew that two men kept her busy enough. Being able to talk about men with friends was a good thing.

"So you don't think it's weird that I'm in a threesome? I mean, that's not normal."

Carmella snorted. "Normal isn't the aim, is it? And I'd say *normal* is a relative term anyway. I can tell you in the last month Mick has been happy. Happier than I've ever seen him. I obviously know him better than I know you, so maybe you're always like this. But you seem pretty happy every time I see you. Are you?"

Was she?

Jessi nodded as she looked over the scene. Men and fire. Good lord.

"I am. I love them both—have loved them both—a long time. I feel like I'm meant to be where I am right now."

The sky above was dark and they were far enough away from the city to see the stars in their glory.

A sign.

"If you don't mind my asking—and please tell me to butt out if I overreach—how does your family feel about all this?" PJ asked.

Carmella nearly choked. "She will totally back off if you tell her to. Then again, she's super nosy so she'll be back to it in a while once she thinks you've forgotten."

"I'm an enthusiastic friend." PJ gave a bright smile. "It's just that Mick mentioned they were religious. When I met them at the grand opening they seemed lovely, and clearly they had deep affection for Mick. But I didn't know if they were..."

"They're good-hearted people whose faith is central to pretty much everything they do and who they are. They met in the Peace Corps. My mom and her friends spend a few hours every week knitting and sewing things to give out to shelters and homeless along with food and hygiene kits. So, they love me and my boys, and they want me to be happy." She shrugged.

"Your parents sound amazing," PJ said.

"It didn't occur to me how amazing until I was living a few hours away. I realized how much time I spent with them on a regular basis until I couldn't." She'd learned a lot about herself in those years in Portland. "I do a lot less taking them for granted these days."

"Sometimes you have to be without something before you understand its importance," Carmella said. "I'm envious. My parental situation is...not like yours, so it makes me happy to see what I always thought was the ideal."

Jessi laughed. "I don't know if I'd say ideal, but it's pretty close. I just wish their families were more open."

"Asa gets so tense any time he mentions Mick's family his jaw actually clicks," PJ said.

It was hard not to gossip or reveal too much about Mick's and Adam's families, but she was relieved that Asa had the same opinion of the Robertses as she did.

"The nice thing about being in love and building a relationship is that you can do things better when it's your turn, you know?" PJ said as she never took her gaze from Asa. "You can make your own family and hopefully screw up less. I know Asa makes me feel a million things at once, and not one of them is unsafe or unloved."

Jessi reached over to hug PJ quickly. "Thank you." She hugged Carmella next. "You both made me feel better."

Mick called her name and held up a bag of marshmallows.

"S'mores!" Jessi hopped up. "Let's get some."

"Duane has official marshmallow roasting forks." Duke handed them out and Mick impaled Jessi's for her while Adam got her chair and moved it closer.

"No offense, but we're stealing Jessi back," Mick told PJ and Carmella as he sat on one side of Jessi, while Adam took the other side.

"Did you just lure me with chocolate?"

"Dash it all. Jessi's figured out our ruse." Adam's voice was dry but he winked, making her snort-laugh.

"I haven't had s'mores over a fire in two years. I went camping with my oldest sister, Charlie. Our last trip before she started popping out kids."

Carmella leaned into Duke for a moment, clinking her beer to his. "If this is what camping was like, I'd find myself available the next time Duke asked me to go. But he likes tents and cooking over a campfire. It's fucking *cold* out here. Camping means my only solution to cold is a tent. Ugh. Here? I can go inside and be warm in three minutes. Indoor plumbing too. No peeing in the woods."

"There are four bathrooms. All have heated floors," Duane called out.

"See? Duane knows how to do things. Am I right?" Carmella looked to them both.

"I prefer campers or cabins. But I like being out in the woods like this. It's so peaceful and it smells good." PJ took a deep breath.

"I like to camp. Like in tents and cooking over a camp stove. Campfires are nice, but a camp stove is easier. I also like air mattresses." Jessi was glad it was dark so her blush wouldn't be that evident.

"Here's a fun fact about Jessilyn. She's a camping freak. I've never had more fun camping than when it's with her." Mick smushed the marshmallow and chocolate together into a melty, gooey sandwich with graham crackers and handed it her way.

"Dude. You just made her a sandwich." PJ tipped her head back and laughed. "I love that."

Jessi grinned over at Mick. "Once, when I was nine, my sister's freshly toasted marshmallow dripped onto the back of my hand. I still have a scar from where I tried to brush it off because it was so hot, but it got several layers of my skin too. So Mick always does my s'moring for me."

Mick kissed the top of her head. "Her designated smusher."

"I should get a plaque for your door at work. *Jessilyn Franklin's designated smusher, so back off.*" Jessi nodded. "Yeah, I like that."

"It's no secret I'm your designated everything, angel."

"Good. I'd hate to have to embarrass someone by wiping the floor up with them after getting grabby with you."

"Maybe so. But I'd pay to see it." Duane laughed. "Mainly because you're a tiny badass. It's always the nice ones or the quiet ones. Also, because I think people need to see that not only is Mick taken, but by someone worthy. And you are."

Jessi stepped over to hug Duane. "You have an awesome heart."

Adam and Asa shared a look, and Jessi groaned internally,

wondering if they'd be sharing alpha male tips and if she should be excited or scared by that.

PJ always looked happy, so Jessi supposed it was fear but in a good way.

"This place is fantastic, Duane. How long have you had it?" Jessi asked.

"I bought the land ten years ago. It was a gift for my girlfriend. A wedding present."

Since there was no wife or girlfriend in his life now—she'd asked early on, and Mick had told her not to be a matchmaker— Jessi braced herself for the rest of whatever he was going to say.

"Took another few years to get the structure up as we built on weekends and during the warmer months. The house has been mine longer than she ever was by this point."

"And it's here for you when you come by, which is also more than she ever did," Duke said. He was so rarely negative or even mean-spirited. Even when he fought he did it with humor. But he clearly didn't much care for Duane's ex.

Duane guffawed. "Yes, well. The sex was fucking magnificent."

"Which is always why relationships with women like her last way longer than they should." Duke raised his beer.

Carmella gave him side-eye, but he kissed her quickly, hugging her to his side. "Not that I know anything about that because my lady is wonderful in every way."

"PJ, I had a dream with you in it," Jessi said.

Mick slid an arm around her shoulders.

"Was it a sex dream?" Asa asked, and Adam raised a brow her way.

"It wasn't a sex dream! Jeez. One-track minds. In the dream you had purple gloves on. After I woke up I've been thinking about those gloves a lot."

"Were they awesome? Purple is my favorite color. Now I think I need purple leather gloves for winter." PJ held her hands out like she was already seeing it.

"Sometimes my dreams tell me things my conscious mind doesn't hear. It's fine, I'm not going to get woo-woo on you or anything. I just wanted to tell you in case it meant anything. Also because they were awesome purple gloves. Like the color of the outside of a ripe fig."

"Hmm, nothing springs to mind. I wasn't worried about woo-woo. You don't strike me as flighty. Just whimsical. And also the sort of person whose dreams would tell her things her conscious mind didn't hear very well."

Mick let go of Jessi and pulled PJ into a hug, whispering something into her ear before stepping back.

PJ smiled his way and then over to Jessi.

"God, all this love shit is making me tired." Duane heaved himself over to one of the chairs and flopped into it with a sigh that sounded more satisfied than tired.

Duane was one big softie, and it made him happy to be in his house with his friends.

Mick picked her up, sat, and brought her down into his lap. Adam pulled his chair closer to theirs, stretching his long legs out as he grabbed Jessi's, pulling them to rest on the arm of his seat, leaving his hand around her ankle.

Safe. Happy. Protected.

Adam slowly circled her ankle bone with the pad of his thumb, sending wave after wave of sensation over her skin.

Desired.

They petted her in their own way, she supposed. Mick arranged her so she leaned against his chest and side, his arm holding her upright without any real effort.

Damn, that was hot.

He was so fucking strong. And big. And ferocious.

Most of her life she'd been protected and adored by Mick. In so many ways that had never changed, only gone dormant until they'd seen one another again the month before.

But it was different. This was some sort of cell-deep connection. As if he were a big cat and he'd claimed her because to him she was the smartest and best and most beautiful in all the world.

Some primal thing seeped through her. A pride that she was his and Adam's. A pride that Adam couldn't keep his hands off her. Confidence in her appeal to men such as hers.

It was the sexiest, most romantic and exhilarating thing she'd ever experienced.

"Did Jessi tell you about the *Weekend* piece that had one of her costumes in the photographs accompanying it?" Mick asked.

"I'm sorry. He tells *everyone* about that." Jessi covered her face with her hands.

"Sorry? You should be sorry you never said anything before now," Carmella said. "Tell us about it."

Jessi described the general tone of the article that had been in the local arts magazine. Adam pulled his phone out and pulled up a copy of the photograph, and they all passed it around.

"You made that? From a pattern or . . . ? I mean, wow." Carmella smiled so broadly it filled Jessi with happiness just to see it.

"You sew?" Jessi asked her.

"Not at this level, no. But I've made a lot of my own clothes and linens since I was a kid. I'd love to see your work in person."

Jessi turned to face Carmella and lean toward her. "Really?" Oh, that was delightful.

"Yes, really."

"I don't have any costumes in the shop right now that are finished, but I'm working on two for Halloween. One's nearly done and the other is about halfway there. I've actually brought some of the hand sewing with me."

"You promised." Adam's voice was teasing but underneath was truth. He was going to make her pay for bringing work when they both agreed to leave theirs behind for the two nights they were up at Duane's place.

"I know. I haven't even taken it out. I just brought it in case I had any extra time. Halloween is next week. Wait. That was a crappy apology. I'm sorry. I did promise and I broke that promise."

"Damn, how can you ever be mad at that?" Duane asked.

"It's nearly impossible. Even when she brings work and thinks I didn't see her work tucked into her bag before we leave the house." Adam winked at her and Mick laughed.

"Okay. I was going to ask to see it, but I can wait until next week." Carmella's expression was one of someone who loved something. Which only endeared her to Jessi more.

"I'll be there pretty much all day every day until next Saturday. I had an assistant, but she moved to New Mexico to help take care of her granddaughter, so it's crunch time. Luckily, my mom is pitching in to help, as is my sister. They're both the ones who taught me to sew."

"If you have a need here and there for an extra hand, let me know," Carmella told her. "I'm happy to help. I mean it. I love to sew. I mean, you can see some of my work before I started anything of yours, obviously."

Asa held up some cigars. "Anyone up for a smoke?"

Adam grabbed the bottle of Balvenie from the nearby table and his glass. "I'd love one."

"There's a hot tub here," PJ said to Carmella and Jessi as the men passed around cigars. "I vote we pass on cigars and have a soak and talk about boys."

Jessi didn't really mind cigars, but a soak in the hot tub with the forest all around, surrounded by her friends, new and old, sounded like something she would far rather do.

They all headed inside to change.

CHAPTER
Nineteen

Adam came out to the small waiting room at his offices. Asa was there with two cups of coffee.

"Sorry to give such short notice. I appreciate you fitting me in," Asa said, shaking Adam's hand.

Asa had called him about half an hour before asking if Adam had time for a cup of coffee and a chat.

Adam was interested to know what brought his new friend over in the middle of a workday. "No problem at all. Come on back to my office."

His three-person firm took up half the second floor of a building in Eastlake, and Adam's office overlooked Lake Union in the distance.

"Some view." Asa sat, his body language easy enough that Adam let go of any worry there was something negative between them.

"I watch the float planes land and take off. Makes up for how old the building is and the lack of an elevator."

Adam put some sugar from the packs Asa had brought with him into the coffee before settling back. "Not that I mind a coffee break, but I get the feeling this is more than just a just-passing-by-let's-have-coffee situation. What's up?"

"I did need to come down here for something. I had to renew my tabs. But I did come by with something specific to tell you. We had a visit at the shop earlier. Mick's father showed up."

Adam sat forward. "Why?"

"Mick wasn't there when he came by. He was up in Lynwood grabbing a part. John Senior came at Duke pretty hard. Which was a pretty big mistake. Duke's all *right on* and laid-back until he's pushed too far. Then he's a fucking machine."

Adam bet. He'd seen Duke fight, and all his laid-back demeanor melted away. Underneath it he was a beast.

"What's his beef? I mean which one specifically. The man has many opinions, and none he's shy about sharing. He's professionally disgruntled."

Asa grinned and snickered. "Perfect definition. He's all up in arms over Mick's soul. Duke told him to mind his own salvation and get the fuck out of the shop. By that point I'd come over and Carmella had the phone in her hand, set to call the cops. I asked her to wait and waded in. Normally I wouldn't say anything. I figure you know what a festering shitlord Mick's father is. He's not worth Mick's emotion."

Adam laughed. "I have to use that one in the future. Shitlord indeed. What made this time different than others where you'd have let it go?"

"In my opinion—Duke's too—he's really focused on Jessi. I'm just concerned and wanted you to know. I'd tell Mick, but to be honest, I've been so happy he finally cut his parents from his life I didn't want any setbacks. They abused him enough, and I don't want them to do it anymore. But I sure as hell don't want Jessi in danger. So I'm here because Mick is my family and you're his, which makes you mine too. And Jessi. Plus, PJ overheard, and she's so pissed off she said if I didn't do something she would."

Adam nodded. "She's scary."

Asa tipped his chin. "Oh yes, she is."

Until then, Adam had sort of been more of the *just cut them off and never speak to them again* camp when it came to the Roberts family. After his initial anger had passed, he thought more about Mick and how it would hurt him more to confront his father about something everyone knew he wouldn't ever apologize for.

But now he was worried about Jessi. "I appreciate the heads-up. I'm going to ask you to tell Mick, or let me tell Mick. You may not know this, but Jessi had a run-in with Mick's father four years ago and we only just learned of it, so everything is a little raw right now with not being told stuff."

"I didn't know. Fair enough," Asa said.

"How about if I show up at the shop in a few hours and we can all go to lunch? Do you have the time? I know it gets busy around there." As much as Adam chafed to just fix things on his own, Mick would feel like he was being patronized. Or spoken around. Or worse, he'd feel out of control, and it would lead to bad choices.

"I'm never too busy for lunch." Asa stood. "He's more centered than I've ever seen him. Less frenzied. Whatever you're doing for him is working."

Something passed between them. They'd spoken enough that it was pretty obvious both men liked to be on top in the bedroom. It was nice to know that maybe in the future he might have someone to share tips with. Or whatever. It wasn't like you sprang free from the womb totally good at topping someone. It'd been a learning process, lots of stumbles in between.

They made plans to meet up at one thirty at a teriyaki place near Twisted Steel, and Adam tried to get back into his work project but failed.

He didn't want to just show up at Jessi's studio. In fact, he didn't want to bring her into this whole situation until he'd talked with Mick. She'd be pissed they kept her out of it, but until he and Mick talked, Jessi was keeping her pretty little ass out of trouble.

As much as they could manage anyway. Jessi took orders fantastically when it came to sex. Otherwise, she did what she wanted, when she wanted. And if she felt like Mick's father was out to hurt Mick, god only knew what she'd do.

But they couldn't keep it from her entirely. Just momentarily. As much as he wanted to shield her, they'd made a promise to share and be honest with one another and that's what he'd do. Otherwise, she'd hold back at some other point and then be able to say it was because of this.

He took a drive over to the arboretum just to be outside awhile. He needed the fresh air and the time to think. Normally he'd have hunted down Addie or James. They both gave great advice. But Jessi was their daughter. And their allegiance would be to her.

Jessi and Mick were out for the same reason. This adult relationship business was hard work.

Four years ago he'd run from that. The responsibility of it seemed too much of a joke after Mick had left. He'd thought himself strong, but he'd been so fucking weak. He buried himself in pussy. Tried all sorts of things he'd never done. Most of them were overrated.

Being a man worthy of love wasn't something he understood innately. He certainly didn't count learning how to block a punch when his old man had too much to snort and decided to slap Adam's mother around.

He pulled his phone out and texted Mick that he was coming by for lunch at one thirty and all the details. Mick texted back immediately that he'd be there. Then Adam called Jessi.

If she was consumed by work, she'd have her phone off. But she picked up on the second ring.

"I was just thinking about you," she answered.

"Was it extra dirty?"

"As a matter of fact, yes. Want to come over and make my fantasy a reality?"

"Oh, that's a very fine offer." Fuck, if it weren't for his lunch and then an afternoon visit out to a building site he'd already be at her door. "Sadly, I have to decline. Or rather, postpone until this evening. I just had some time and I wanted to hear your voice."

"Well if I can't have you fucking me from behind I suppose a lovely piece of flattery will do in a pinch. Is everything okay?"

"What makes you ask?"

"You're not as smooth as usual. You're normally caramel and expensive Scotch, but right now you're more like juice and cookies."

"Like a kid?" He laughed.

"Not in that way. Like, I don't know, what they give you after you donate blood. You know what I mean? Also you're engaging with me in one of my so-called Jessi conversations and haven't made a single syllable of sexual innuendo. Not. Normal."

"I opened the conversation with sexual innuendo!"

"Not since we entered into this topic. Now, you're avoiding answering me. Which only means I'm right. I know it and you know I know you know. So there."

Only Jessi could make a bunch of words like that actually make sense. "I'm fine. Just busy and distracted and sad I can't come over and fuck you from behind as you so colorfully described."

She harrumphed, not believing him. But he was going to tell her that night anyway, so he didn't try to push it any further.

"I'll probably be home around nine or so," she said. "I think I can finish tonight, which means my workload is manageable tomorrow and I won't have to be up at four or spend the night here."

"I'll expect you at nine then. Text me when you leave work so we know when to look for you," Adam said.

She sighed this time. "I went to and fro every day for years, you know. I'm not *that* flighty."

She was absolutely fucking flighty. But she wasn't a bad driver because of it. She loved to pull over to look at a lot of stuff, though, so he and Mick often did the driving instead. Especially if they had a schedule to keep.

"I love you. I'll see you tonight and expect that text when you leave work."

"I love you too. And I will."

Mick headed over to the teriyaki place with Asa and Duke. Adam waited there already and Mick didn't think twice before giving him a hug and a kiss before grabbing the chair next to him.

"Hey. You look handsome."

Adam cupped the back of Mick's neck briefly. Enough to establish that connection but not so much that anyone else would have noticed. Mick's cock sure did.

Adam knew it too. "Thanks. I had a client meeting first thing and I'm going out to a job site after this, so I'm the boss today."

Mick leaned close, pretending to examine the menu over Adam's arm. "You're the boss every day," he murmured.

Adam's mouth hitched up, but he kept reading the menu.

Being a small place, the food was up, piping hot and fresh, in about ten minutes. That it was also really good and served in huge portions made it a favorite lunch spot for Twisted Steel employees.

"Your dad came by the shop earlier today," Asa said as the food arrived a few minutes later.

Mick, who'd been busily demolishing his gyoza, stuttered to a halt in a nearly cartoonish fashion. "The fuck he did."

"That was pretty much my reaction upon seeing him demanding that Carmella find you. As if we'd been hiding you," Duke said.

"Why is this only being told to me now? Is that why you're here?" He turned to Adam.

"I'm here because I wanted to have lunch with you and our friends. But also, yes, because of your father's visit."

Dread settled into his gut as he pushed his plate away. "Tell me all of it."

As Duke and Asa did, it just made him tired. And concerned. "So essentially he's saying that Jessilyn made me gay? That's the fucking logical place he's coming from? That a five-year-old Jessi pulled me into her life to send my soul to hell?"

Mick blew out a breath. So much for finding a way to put all this stuff behind him as Jessi had been begging him to.

"Okay, so what do you all think?" Mick asked Adam. "I'm so close to this. I just want to flip tables and burn shit down."

"Normally, I'd shine it on and wouldn't have even mentioned it except that he seemed so focused on Jess. As Asa pointed out to me, your father is a festering shitlord. So it's not like we should be surprised he's being one when he can't push you into breaking things off with us. He's a bunch of words and hate." Adam shrugged. "I'm usually of a mind to keep that shit as far away from my life as I can. And it's not like you're going to ever change his mind."

"Guys like him, they're all bluster. Ignore it and he'll find another thing to do," Duke advised. "He feeds off the attention and the drama. Don't give it to him. Keep an eye out for Jessi, obviously. But instead of rushing into some sort of confrontation over this—like he wants—think about it. Be smart, Mick. This guy is an emotional vampire. You want to keep feeding him by letting him control your emotions some more?"

Duke was really smart about people and he gave excellent advice. But Mick chafed at not popping his father one in the nose for talking shit about Jessi.

"I can see you fisting your hands over there," Asa said. "Much as I'm normally in the punch-him-in-the-face camp, I think Duke has a point, as does Adam. Fuck this clown. He's been a piece of shit to you your whole life. Even before you came out. He's never going to be satisfied with you. The only thing he wants is to torture you more. For kicks."

"If he gets anywhere near Jessi we change tacks," Adam said. "But he's striking out because you're not coming when he beckons you these days. If you go to him and call him out over the bullshit he pulled four years ago he's only going to blame her more. And know his little ploy to manipulate you has worked."

Duke stole one of Mick's dumplings. "I told him if he came back to Twisted Steel I'd beat his ass and then call the cops."

Mick knew how scary Duke could be when he got pushed too far.

"Okay. But . . . are we going to tell Jessi?"

Adam winced. "I spoke to her earlier. She's in a really good mood. Finishing up something earlier than she thought, so we have dinner plans for nine. I hate to alarm her. And it's not like he said anything he hasn't already said in some form or other."

Asa snorted. "I can tell you from experience that if you sandbag something, she'll find out at some point and all will love her and despair."

"I find it so weird that you quote *Lord of the Rings* as often as you do." Mick sighed. "Let me think about it. You too, Adam. There's no use telling her if it's not face-to-face anyway. And if we do, it should be more like Mick's dad was a jerk and dropped by Twisted Steel, but luckily Mick wasn't there, so nothing bad happened."

"That's pretty good." Adam nodded.

Mick started eating again, feeling better now that they'd gotten to that point. "We'll monitor this and if he steps over that line we set, we act. Otherwise, hopefully he'll find someone else to condemn to hell."

CHAPTER
Twenty

Adam left Mick and Jessi cuddling on the couch, letting them know he'd call them up when he was ready for them.

Mick was stressed-out and worried. His energy was all over the place, so before he did anything stupid, Adam planned to help him out and exorcise some of the demons his father had visited upon him.

Involving Jessi would help her too. Though they'd used the more casual "oh by the way, Mick's dad showed up at work today" way to tell her, she was agitated. Concerned for their little family.

Mick's gaze held shadows.

Adam aimed to push the darkness back because Mick deserved to live in the light with them.

He drank a glass of red wine as he prepared the guest room where he'd finished installing the suspension bar at the foot of the bed. It'd go perfectly with the cuffs he'd picked up from JT's Stockroom with Mick in mind.

After he'd made them wait long enough, he called them both up.

Laughing, they tumbled into the room shortly after that, but Jessi's eyes widened when she took in the toys spread out on the bed and Adam standing there in the low-slung sleep pants he liked to wear when he played with them.

A surge of possessiveness rushed through Adam as he took them in. Mick's blush, not a shy one, and Jessi's excitement. They were his as surely as he was theirs.

"Jessilyn, you need to be naked and kneeling on the mattress. Close to the foot so you can help me with Mick."

Jessi got naked quickly, sending Adam a look over her shoulder as she walked over to the bed.

"Michael." Adam said his name like a command and Mick took two steps until he was right in front of Adam. Waiting. "Naked."

Mick preened for both of them as he got rid of his clothes and came back to where he'd been standing in front of Adam.

"Normally I'd use some arm binders on you," Adam told Mick. "And I will. But not tonight. Arms up." Adam adjusted the bar so Mick wouldn't get hurt if he struggled.

Mick's pupils got so big Adam was helpless to do anything but lean in and kiss him, tasting all that delicious anticipation.

He then held out his wrists so Adam could put the cuffs on. "You're so beautiful when you're bound," Adam murmured as he adjusted, making sure the fit was snug.

Mick's cock was rock hard already, which pleased Adam greatly. And it got even harder when Adam had finished connecting the cuffs to the carabiner and then to the bar itself, slowly raising it until Mick's arms were above his head, but his shoulders and general positioning were safe.

"Wow," Jessi breathed out as she looked Mick up and down.

Already Mick's eyes had gone glassy, which told Adam how much he needed this.

Adam had been pushing Mick's limits for the last month, testing out his pain tolerance. Seeing what he liked and didn't. Hell, figuring out what *he* liked too. Adam never really thought about delivering pain the way he did with Mick.

At first he wasn't sure if he could give Mick as much as he

needed. And truth be told, Mick would be racing and brawling until he was ninety most likely. But it would be Adam who burned off the worst of it.

"I'm not done," he whispered to Mick as he held out the silver in his palm. "These clamps fit around your piercings best. And you turn it to tighten like this."

Mick gasped when Adam danced his fingertips up to his left nipple and then fit the square clamp over the bar and then the nipple just right and began to tighten.

Adam followed with the right nipple, getting the clamp in place before picking up the flicker whip. He snapped it through the air and Jessi moaned at the sound.

Their sweet angel didn't much like pain, but she loved watching Adam deliver it to Mick. In her lap, she twisted her fingers together, wanting to touch but not having permission yet.

"Do you see how she looks at you, Mick?"

Mick focused on Jessi.

"Like you're the most beautiful and sexy thing she's ever seen," Adam said as he moved around behind Mick, trailing the tail over his shoulders.

"You both are," Jessi said.

Mick grunted.

Adam chose the flicker whip because the sound was one of his favorites, but also because he could increase the pain and sensation as they went along to a very vicious sting. One he'd been feeling more and more that Mick needed.

It would take him further than they'd gone so far, but still within parameters Adam was confident in.

He pet down Mick's back, pressing a kiss to the space between his shoulder blades.

And then he struck. Three quick flicks of his wrist, each successively harder until pretty red welts rose.

"You need to tell me if your shoulders hurt. The bar should be set just right, but I can't fix what I don't know about. Get me? I'll hurt you, baby, but I don't want the wrong kind of pain."

Mick whimpered a little, but nodded.

"Jessilyn, would you like to help me?"

Adam alternated between strikes in the air and those against Mick's ass and the backs of his thighs.

"Y-yes," she managed to say. The power of it surged through Adam. That he could affect them both this way was a gift.

"When I tell you, you can kiss, bite, lick him wherever you like as long as you like or until I tell you to stop," Adam told her.

Mick groaned, the sound ragged with need.

Jessi nodded, the smile on her face a temptation like no other.

"Go on then."

Jessi leaned forward and licked up Mick's side from hip bone to nipple. He let out a shuddering breath, and she squeezed her thighs together. She blew over his nipple and when he made a sound she licked softly.

The tension in Mick's muscles seemed to bleed away a little more each time Adam's flicker whip—a pretty name for something that made such a wicked sound—made contact.

She found his lips and he fed on her mouth hungrily, his tongue dancing inside briefly, teeth catching her bottom lip as she pulled away.

He was beautiful there. A little dazed, he bent forward as he watched Jessi. His arms were above his head, wrists all bound up in badass black leather cuffs.

His skin gleamed with sweat and his cock was the hardest she'd ever seen it. Dark red, smeared with pre-come, balls tight against his body.

"You make my mouth water," she said as she dragged the pad of her thumb over the head of his cock.

Adam made a sound that time and she basked in it for a

moment as she brought her thumb up to lick the taste of Mick away.

"Enough for now, angel," Adam told her in a rusty voice.

Mick's moan this time was one of alarm and disappointment.

Jessi sat back on her heels once more, licking her lips as she watched. Waiting to be allowed to touch Mick again. As she did, Adam slowly demolished all the impotent anger and pain Mick had built up over his family situation.

Adam had used the term *burn the pain away* a few times, but when she saw it in his hands—took him in as he slowly and with total focus concentrated on what Mick needed from moment to moment as well as by the end—she understood.

All the fighting and the high adrenaline stuff like racing and even dangerous stuff like multiple tours in Iraq were Mick's way of punishing himself. But in Adam's hands, the pain was a caress. It was a loving way to wash away all that loathing, all the toxic, vile stuff his family made him feel.

She loved them both so much right at that very moment she thought she'd burst like those stars she'd seen when they'd been up at the cabin the weekend before.

Mick gave over to the bright, nearly overwhelming sensation each strike of the flicker whip gave him. He fought it at first and then gorged himself on it until it threatened to be too much.

And each time, Adam adjusted so Mick could find equilibrium. The sweet ache of it, the sharp, precise edge that took him three steps from pleasure and into pain, where he felt as if he were flying.

That perfect physical/chemical balance that was better than any substance he'd ever used. All the poison turned to ash in the wake of each searing sting against his skin.

And then Jessi's mouth on him. Her hands. The things she said with such dirty sincerity were a palate cleanser. As Adam knew they would be.

She teased him with her kisses and licks, gave him an anchor so he could float and not worry about drifting away.

Then Adam would tell her to stop and she'd settle back to watch once more.

Over and over again, interspersed pleasure and comfort along with the pain. Mixing in a way that felt a lot like magic.

This was why he submitted to Adam. No other thing he'd done burned away all the poison the way Adam did. Mick began to feel renewed, revived, even as his body continued to fill with pleasure.

"Again, angel." Adam reached around and pulled the clamps free and a wave of sensation swirled through Mick, rendering him light-headed for a few moments.

Mick gasped as she got to her hands and knees and crawled his way, her tongue darting out to lick around the crown of his cock, taking him in a little deeper each time.

His head hung forward as he watched his cock disappear into her mouth over and over again. So pretty he never wanted it to end.

So good it had to pretty damned soon.

Adam moved to the side, tossing the flicker whip to the night table.

He lay down next to Jessi and took over, saying to Mick, "You were so good, let me reward you for that."

Adam swallowed Mick's dick, getting it nice and wet with spit. One hand cupped his balls just right as he got a good, hard rhythm set.

He knew Mick didn't have any use for subtle at that point. Knew Mick *needed* to climax.

Adam sucked hard, much harder than Jessi usually did. A shouted grunt came from Mick's lips as orgasm claimed him, digging in with claws so sharp Mick struggled against his cuffs as his back arched and he stuffed as much of his cock down Adam's throat as he could.

Moments later Adam freed Mick from the cuffs, massaging his shoulders and biceps as he helped settle Mick facedown on the bed.

Mick wanted to say a lot of things, but none of them seemed to come to mind. So he smiled and slurred that he loved them both.

Adam kissed Mick and whispered in his ear, "You might want to move your head so you can watch me fuck Jessi."

"Now you're talking," Mick managed as he turned to catch sight of Jessi. "So pretty. Hi, angel."

"You sound high."

"He's high on all sorts of body chemicals. And from your beauty of course." Adam pulled her to her feet on the other side of the bed—now that he'd gotten rid of his pants and was there in all his naked glory—and bent her forward. "You told me earlier that you had a fantasy about me fucking you from behind. Well here you go."

Adam shoved her forward and then grabbed a handful of her hair while he slammed into her with one stroke.

Jessi wheezed the F word, which made Mick laugh.

Adam fucked her in hard, slow thrusts. Her tits would bounce and then he'd wait, pull back, and thrust again.

Jessi squirmed and Mick knew she'd be hot and tight inside, pulling at him, clamping her muscles around Adam's cock to lure him back in.

There was no denying her allure. No denying whatever urgency that took hold once you were deep inside.

Mick saw the moment Adam fell, the moment of no return. He hitched Jessi's leg up, changing his angle and giving him access to her clit and that pretty hoop they both loved so much.

Her moan went very deep and guttural, and Mick's cock thought very hard about reviving.

"Do you know what a temptation you are? Hmm? Your mouth on his cock. He needed it so bad. I needed it so bad," Adam snarled.

"And now you both have it," she said as she pushed back against him.

Mick couldn't tear his attention away unless the house was on fire. The two of them so raw together. Adam ran covetous hands over her skin as the backs of Mick's thighs had settled into a dull burn. The kind that seemed to throb like a heartbeat.

The kind he loved.

"You first," Adam insisted, and whatever he did, Jessi responded by a surprised yelp of pleasure and then a gasp as it got her pretty close pretty fast.

"No fair," she said, panting, "I was already close watching you work on Mick."

"Fair? What's fairer than all of us coming so hard we see stars?" Adam asked.

Jessi cried out, reaching to tangle her fingers with Mick's as Adam drove her over the edge and followed right after her.

Adam pulled out and helped her back up to the bed. "Be right back. I'm getting arnica and some ice. You're going to bruise, most likely, but that should help some and also with the pain."

Jessi helped Mick turn his head toward the right end of the bed and got settled. "You can be in the middle tonight. It's a good place for highest levels of snuggle."

He needed that. And there they were, giving it to him. The impulse to punch something was gone. He was lazy and happy and totally relaxed.

"Life is pretty fuckin' sweet," Mick said as Adam came back with the arnica and ice.

CHAPTER
Twenty-one

I can't believe you downplayed how good you are," Jessi told Carmella as she looked at some work she'd just given her.

Carmella smiled, pleased. "Oh I just mean I'm not hand sewing and hand beading and making ballet and opera costumes. I'm pretty handy with most sewing jobs. You're like a Jedi master. How'd you end up doing this anyway?"

Jessi laughed. "I tried a lot of jobs after I got out of high school. I went to college but decided it wasn't for me after two years. Worked at my dad's veterinary practice. He was pretty bummed I didn't want to take after him. Charlie, that's my older sister, and Leif, he's the youngest son, both work with him, though. My mom runs the office."

"How many siblings do you have?" Carmella asked as they headed over to the coffee pot in Jessi's studio.

"Three. Samuel is the oldest. He's a cameraman. He works for the BBC in crazy war-torn places that make my mother pray a lot. He's fearless and super smart. Then Charlie, who is the oldest daughter and also a vet, then Leif—surprise—a vet too. I'm the youngest. So they're all super achievers. And I was average. Anyway, because I did my dad's marketing and was pretty decent at it, I got a job in sales and marketing for a hospital. Which enabled me to luck into a job doing the same in Portland, only for a regional producer of plays, musical theater, and ballet."

"This was after you'd broken up with Mick and Adam?" Carmella didn't have pity in her tone, only curiosity.

"Yes. I'd been looking for a new job for a while. I wouldn't have considered Portland at all before the breakup because they both lived here. So anyway. Through that whole time I was sewing and started doing more work on the side to do custom pieces. Weddings, prom, that sort of thing. After a while, people in the industry began to come to me and see my work and I lucked into getting work up here, which is where I wanted to be and had been working at doing. Now I'm here. My profit is pretty much nothing, but I'm not in the red and I think if things continue to go well, I can have an actual career doing this. Which is pretty damned cool."

"That is pretty damned cool. And you're in love."

Jessi nodded. "Truth be told I've loved them both for a long time. I wanted to move on, believe me. But in the end, we came back together when we were ready. I truly think that."

"I bet this threesome thing isn't for amateurs. I mean, in a having to deal with public opinion way. Not sex." Carmella groaned and put her hands over her face a moment.

"I know what you mean. And yes, that's what I mean. I don't know that I'd have been able to deal with all this stuff, the issues with family, four years ago. I was a different person then."

"I definitely think there are times—setbacks—where it's dark while you're going through it, but eventually you figure out why you had to survive that dark time. I hate that you had to be so sad. But I'm so happy for you now," Carmella said.

"I like you, Carmella. You have such wonderful energy." Jessi hugged her. "I'm so glad I know you."

"That's a nice thing to say. Thank you. I'm glad I know you too."

Jessi moved past Carmella over to the worktable, where pieces of a bodice lay. The early November day was clear and sunny, so she had the blinds up to let the sun in while she worked.

"I bet that guy got locked out of his house or something," Jessi said, tipping her chin toward the dark gray sedan that'd been parked at the end of the block. "He's been out there an hour already."

"Or he's waiting for someone. My mother used to be late all the time. So I've been him a time or two. Waaaaaaiting for someone to show up somewhere."

"Probably." Jessi snorted. "Will you be at PJ and Asa's tonight?"

"Yes. Duke just texted me a few minutes ago to say he was already there. Asa's got four or five racing channels, how that's possible I don't know. But they love to sit over there for hours, staring at the television and eating stuff. PJ and I are so happy to have you around."

"They're like a family. Twisted Steel I mean. I like that." Jessi really loved that Mick has such a fantastic support system.

"When I first started working there, it was after coming from a shop my uncle owned and ran. And Twisted Steel feels like that did. Like a family business. They punch each other a lot. My god. But they love each other and protect each other and it's magical to be part of." Carmella looked out the front windows again as she headed to the sewing machines.

"You're a part of it now too. They do that when one of the crew really falls for someone. Those big tough boys in that shop who bring me magnets from the trip they took their mom on to Branson when they think no one is looking aren't fooling anyone. They're teddy bears with massive fists and an alarming addiction to things that often leave them bruised. You're ours, which means they'll break stuff at your house too. Don't worry, PJ and I have learned that these guys are handy so they either fix it or have the connection to some contractor who can."

There was so much affection in Carmella's tone. It helped Jessi listen to her heart better.

"Can I confess something to you?"

Carmella smiled. "Of course."

"I don't think I've ever wanted anyone to like me as much as I wanted you all to."

"It's not hard to like you. Especially if you know Mick well enough to see the change since he's been back with you and Adam. Duke and Asa both know how much you meant to Mick, so even if the others were on the fence they'd have opened our group up to you. But each time you're around and we get to know you, and see you with Mick, it's blatantly plain you're meant for him. You've both earned the respect and acceptance of the Twisted Steel family."

Jessi knew a lot of people, but she only counted a very small few as her pack. Her family both biological and chosen. Twisted Steel was Mick's pack, which made them hers and Adam's too.

"He loves you all. It's a relief to find acceptance in his life," Jessi said.

Carmella sighed. "So how are you dealing with that? Duke said Mick's father yelled at you."

Jessi took a deep breath. "I never liked Mick's parents. Even when I was a kid. I try hard not to be a negative person, but they make me fail every time. I tried to see them in ways that would explain how they treated Mick. I tried since I was five and I'm twenty-seven now. I still haven't been able to. So it's hard for me to see this without bias."

Carmella waved a hand before she ran the seam through the machine to finish it before cutting it free and trimming it up. "Everyone has a bias about things that involve them. How can they not?"

Truth.

Jessi continued. "Not liking is one thing. I don't like nuts in cookies, so I just don't eat them that way. But I have trouble finding a way to tolerate how much pain they put this person I love so much through. It's unconscionable for anyone to treat a child the way they have and call it love. But I also don't want to be the reason Mick is estranged from his parents."

"What if they're shitty parents? What if being estranged from them is the best way to keep him safe and healthy?"

There was a knowing in Carmella's tone.

"Part of me believes that. A big enough part that I believe it more than I don't believe it. The thing is, his dad isn't just going away. His experience is that he's bullied and abused his son and called it parenting. Every time I come into the picture things get dicey between them. Mick and his brother are close, and he told the rest of the family to back off for a while because Mick didn't want to have any more fights with them. Which is apparently what set John Senior off."

"My mom has struggled with mental illness and addiction over most of her life. She's destructive and toxic and obsessed with my father, who is a career criminal in and out of prison and also has a history of addiction," Carmella said as she began to pin a hem. "I've been her caretaker since a pretty early age, and a few months ago I had to finally break away from her to protect myself. In my limited experience with John Roberts and knowing through Duke that he treated Mick terribly, Mick is better off on the other side of a self-imposed moat to keep them out. They will rip him apart. Through you if they have to. So I have no sympathy for them. You can't just shit all over someone and expect them to take it forever. Mick deserves to be happy and healthy. You bring him that. Don't ever feel guilty for being what he needs."

"I would like to keep you around all the time. In case I need a really good pep talk," Jessi told her. "I needed to hear that. I knew those things, but I needed to understand it's not just my perception. And I'm sorry about your mom, but glad you're doing what you need to to stay healthy."

"Duke has been there for me through the whole thing like a

charming, laid-back pit bull. Don't let that slow drawl fool you, he's as alpha as they come when you push him. But by the time I figured it out I loved him. It was too late." Carmella shrugged with a lovestruck grin. "And I'm available any time you need a pep talk. You have my number, you know where I live and work. I'm good for it, as long as you'll do the same."

Jessi held out her pinkie and they swore on it.

Adam sat with Asa as they watched over the group below. They smoked their cigars and had some bourbon, something that had become common when they visited one another's homes. Which happened a lot, as it turned out.

At Duke's they hung out on his back deck, as they did at Adam's. But here the landing they sat on was bookended by casement windows Asa had thrown open so the smoke had an escape.

Before Mick had come back into his life, he hadn't spent time multiple times a week with the same group of friends. Before getting back together with Jessi, Adam had only allowed himself a certain amount of time with the Franklins, and now they were around him with the same frequency as the Twisted Steel folks were.

He'd gone from quiet nights listening to music and fucking near strangers to this, a house full of people all talking and laughing and his new friend, who also happened to be dominant.

And taciturn like Adam. So their conversations weren't as animated as the ones Jessi or PJ got into, but it sure was nice to have someone around who got him on a level most people wouldn't.

"If anything gets broken, PJ's going to kick my ass." Asa didn't seem worried about it, though.

"Mick did warn me before the first time you all came to our house that the art would be fine, but sometimes windows and furniture got broken."

Asa laughed. "Only rarely. Things okay with the Robertses?"

"Been quiet for the last few days. I'm sure Mick told you he talked to his oldest brother, who turned out to be pretty support-ive." Adam had been pleased that something positive could come from that mess.

"Yeah, he did. I was glad to see John Junior step in over this bullshit. We'll see if he stays away or not. I will call the cops if he won't leave this time. Mick doesn't need that asshole in his life."

"Amen to that," Adam murmured. Downstairs Mick stood, leaning a hip against the couch Jessi sat on. He sifted his fingers through her hair over and over as she leaned into him.

That thing—the most essential thing, their connection—grew stronger each day. And as it did, each one of them began to accept their relationship would make it through bumps and bruises because it was real and forever. Mick wasn't always so amped up, especially now that Adam took him in hand to keep all that vio-lence from overflowing.

Jessi was well . . . Jessi. She bloomed, vibrant and beautiful. She soaked up the love they gave her and gave them back twice as much. She was fierce and passionate about the things she loved. Their family, or their pack as she called it sometimes, was at the center of her heart and she guarded it.

Which simultaneously pleased and distressed Adam. He loved it that she cared for them and their little family. But he worried it would get her hurt or upset.

It wasn't like he could really stop her from doing something once she set her mind to it, so all he could do was his best to shield her from the worst of it should things blow up with Mick's family.

Woe to them if they did, though. Adam'd had enough of John Roberts Senior, with his holier-than-thou bullshit. The man was a bully. A petty, hard-hearted lout. If that asshole showed up on their doorstep expecting to bully or abuse anyone Adam loved, he'd soon find out the error of his ways.

Duke caught sight of them and headed up, joining them with his own cigar and a beer. "Noisy down there."

"It's all nice music. Nicer from up here." Asa shrugged. But Adam didn't miss the way Asa's gaze returned to where PJ sat with Jessi and Mick, with Carmella on their other side.

"I have no idea how you handle two of them," Duke said to Adam. "Mick's like a fucking Dalmatian puppy. So much energy."

"He and Jessi do seem to have a calming effect on him," Asa said. "He's always pretty together at work anyway. But you two gave him something to steady his heart."

"That and all the sex," Duke added.

There was something chemical and magical about the way they all fit together. Adam had stopped questioning the reality of it. He'd probably always wonder at how it could be so special.

They hung out until nearly midnight and finally headed home.

"I like your friends," Jessi said as she came back into the bedroom after brushing her teeth. She had on fluffy socks and a long nightshirt-type thing.

"They like you right back. Guess you'd say they're your friends now too," Mick said sleepily. He slept in nothing. Neither Jessi nor Adam had any objection to that. He was hard and sexy and Jessi loved that he gave off so much heat.

Plus, Adam got to look at the bruises.

That had been something he'd struggled with. Finding it hot when one bruised someone's ass and thighs wasn't an emotion he'd ever imagined having, much less how to process it.

But it had been Mick who'd loved it. Mick who Adam caught looking at them in the mirrors in the master bath. Because Mick had wanted it, had found it desirable, Adam was able to accept it.

She turned off the lamp on the table and looked out the window. "Wind is coming up now. Oh, weird."

"What is, angel?" Mick asked as he got into the spot in the middle he and Jessi traded back and forth according to a timetable only the two of them seemed to understand. Adam didn't question it.

She slid beneath the blankets and snuggled up to Mick's side. "Just a car outside. Second ten-year-old dark-colored four-door I've seen today with some dude sitting inside it. Must be the day for getting stood up."

Jessi yawned and nearly fell from the bed when Mick sat straight up. "What? Where did you see the other one?"

Jessi gave him a look as she got settled again. "Outside my shop. In front of that fourplex on the corner."

With a stealth that gave Adam a shiver of fear, Mick seemed to melt from the bed to approach the window. "Was this car to the right or left?"

Jessi didn't argue. "To the left. In front of that house with the blue shutters and the barking basset. Oooh, that's a lot of alliteration."

Mick carefully looked out without even disturbing the curtains. Looking at the man in the shadows of their bedroom, Adam saw Mick the soldier.

"He's pulling away from the curb." Mick cursed. "Couldn't see a license plate number."

"What's going on? Did something happen with this car thing today?" Adam asked.

"No. Carmella and I figured he either got locked out or had been stood up. You know how that goes. We only noticed because we were working out front to catch the sunshine and we saw the car from the windows."

"Was it the same car?" Mick asked.

"I ... I don't know."

"Earlier today was the car doing anything? Or the guy? Did you see him well?"

Jessi thought and then shook her head. "No, he didn't do anything wrong or weird that I could tell. He was just out there. For all I know he was listening to an audio book or stop-smoking CDs."

"The guy outside tonight, did he look the same? Was he doing anything?"

"I didn't see any features, but I thought maybe he had on glasses." She shrugged. "He wasn't doing anything. Just sitting out there. He could have just pulled over to take a phone call. Normally I see those things, but you two were in bed and I was all schmoopy. Was it something important? Did I mess up somehow?"

Mick ushered them all back to bed. "You didn't do anything wrong. But you're observant. If you thought it was worth mentioning, it was worth a look. But there's no one out there now that the car left, so I'm just going to check all the locks before we go to sleep."

Jessi's eyes widened and Mick took her cheeks in his palms. "Hey, it's all right. There's nothing wrong. It's in my nature to want to protect you. Now I just want to be sure we're all locked in and then I'm coming right back."

He and Adam checked all the doors and windows. Everything was locked up tight. The motion lights were working and hadn't gone off, so there was no reason to be alarmed.

"I'm sure it was just a coincidence. She's right," Mick said, as they got back upstairs.

Jessi had taken the middle and they all got back under the covers.

"All is well. We're here safe and sound. Sleep. I'm betting Adam wakes us up for sex before he goes to work," Mick said as he buried his face in Jessi's neck.

"Counting on it," she mumbled.

CHAPTER
Twenty-Two

Adam was just leaving Sazerac after a business lunch downtown when he bumped into his father as he headed toward his car.

"I was beginning to think you were a figment of my imagination." Paul Gulati gave his son a handshake and couldn't resist that macho squeeze at the end. Adam ignored it.

"Nope, I'm still here. What brings you downtown?"

Paul had long been a handsome man. Even at seventy he commanded attention with his looks. The fiery anger that had marked Adam's childhood had faded into a deeper, more ingrained sense of entitlement.

He was still an asshole, but less a physically violent one. No, the richer he got, the meaner and more vengeful he got.

"I was at my accountant's office and then I had to stop by Tiffany and pick something up for your mother. You're upsetting her," Paul said.

Adam was quite glad no one else was nearby so he could speak freely. "I had no idea you were speaking to my mother at all."

Paul cocked his head and the mean stirred just a little. "I meant Katherine, and you damned well know it."

"Why would your wife be upset with me?"

"You yelled at your sister and kicked her out of your house. You're her big brother. You owe her more than that."

Adam laughed. "I did *what* now?"

"Denise came to your home to invite you in person to my birthday celebration and your girlfriend was rude, and then you threw Denise out for saying so. I raised you better than not defending your sister. Especially to trash like that Franklin girl."

"You need to listen to me when I warn you to never speak of Jessilyn that way again. As for this fantasy about kicking someone out? Denise came over to invite me and when she learned who I was living with, she uninvited me. We were already on the porch, leaving my home, when she did this and left. I was raised to tell the truth and stand up when I made a mistake. I imagine you'll be addressing this with Denise and her mother."

"Not so fast, Adam. She seems to believe you're in some sort of tawdry mess of a relationship. What do you have to say about that?"

"I say I'm a grown-up and what sort of relationship I'm in is my business. I'm not taking lessons from Denise on how to run my private life."

"So you are in some mess."

"There's *nothing* tawdry about what I'm doing."

"Have you stopped to consider how your actions reflect on the rest of us, Adam?" Paul pretending to be logical and paternal pushed his buttons, even as he knew he was being manipulated.

But Adam wasn't Paul. He reined it in.

"No, can't say as I have. Because who I love and in what combination isn't anyone's business but my own. If other people judge you or Denise for what I do, I can't help it. People are often nosy assholes, Dad."

His father's paternal frown shaped into a lip curl. "You're not twenty-two anymore, Adam. You can't live like you're in college when you're in your thirties. You can't seriously expect anyone who matters to accept this, this whatever you want to call it."

Adam counted to ten, remembered this was important and the people he loved gave him more family than this man in front of him ever had. Paul may have shaped him in a lot of ways Adam hated, but he made the choice not to *be* Paul and had spent the rest of his life since finding control, honing it, and keeping his shit together.

"If you're genuinely interested, I'll explain," Adam said.

His father's impatience broke through the fake paternal concern. "I'm on my way somewhere. Call the house and make a time to come to dinner. We can figure this out then."

"Figure out what?"

His father sighed. "How the hell you'll get yourself out of this mess. Haven't you been paying attention?" He snapped his finger in Adam's face.

Adam barely wrestled back his impulse to break the fingers his old man used to snap. He fucking hated the snapping.

But he didn't hide the lip curl. "I'm in love—and in a relationship—with Jessilyn Franklin *and* Mick Roberts. We all live together. I have no plans to get out of anything. This has nothing to do with you. So if you want me to come to dinner, it wouldn't be to get your advice on how to run my romantic life."

"Jesus Christ, Adam!" Paul exploded and Adam was done.

"I'll see you around. Happy belated birthday." He turned and crossed the street, leaving a sputtering, angry Paul on the other corner in his wake.

But he didn't head back to the office, instead he found himself driving over to James Franklin's vet practice over in Maple Valley. The drive enabled him to have himself together by the time he arrived.

Which was later than he'd thought it would be before he remembered it was nearly three on a Wednesday, so traffic had already started to build and a heavy rain was coming down, which only made everything worse.

The big guy was in the front drive of the vet clinic as Adam pulled up. As Adam got out of the car, James called his name and came over to give him a hug.

"You're an unexpected sight! Come on inside. I was just helping load a horse into a trailer before you got here."

Inside, the scent of freshly brewed coffee competed with medical and animal smells. For whatever reason, though, it always made him feel better.

"You just missed Charlie. She headed over to North Bend to tend an ailing sheep." James pointed to the coffee pot. "Want a cup?"

Adam shivered. "Yes, please. Cold and wet out there."

"I'll be surprised if we don't at least get some wet snow at the higher elevations tonight." James stared at Adam over the rim of his cup a moment. "What brings you here? Leif isn't around. He had an eye appointment, so he left about twenty minutes ago. Addie took him because they have to mess with his pupils. So, just me and you."

"I just ran into my father downtown. It was as unpleasant as it usually is." They sat in James's office, and Adam took a cookie from a plate on the desk.

"I'm sorry he can't be what you need in a father. I'm sure he's probably not too happy about my daughter and Mick being in your life. He might come around in time."

That was the thing about the Franklins, they were passionate about what they believed in, but they really did make an effort to be positive, even when things were negative overall.

"I'm not sure I care." Adam blew out a breath. "I hate to be that guy, the one who has daddy issues."

James waved a hand. "That's bunk anyway, son. You don't have daddy issues. You want your father to respect you and be a positive influence in your life. Just because you're an adult doesn't mean he's not still your dad. It's unfortunate he doesn't seem to understand that your desire for his affection and acceptance is a good thing. It's what parents usually want."

"So, you're okay with me and Mick and Jessi? Really?"

"I have four grown children. They're all wonderful in their own way. Unique. A joy to me and their mother even when they turned all my hair gray. If Jessi was in a relationship where she was being hurt in some way or not being true to who she was, I'd be unhappy. But I've known you and Mick for years, and I know my daughter. She made her choice. She doesn't make a lot of mistakes when she goes with her heart. Addie and I raised a daughter with a good heart. She helps others and goes out of her way to make life better for pretty much everyone she comes across. That's what her mom and I care about most. Is she the best person she can be? That she's in love with two men or one woman or one man, none of that matters to us as long as there's love, respect, and honesty. You both make her happy and you'll protect her. That's why I'm okay with it, yes."

"I had to leave the first time. There wasn't a lot of control when I was growing up. I had all that anger like him. I needed to figure out how to get myself in check and keep myself on an even keel."

It was necessary that James understand.

"Do you have any plans to walk off and hurt her again? Or to be like your father and use your strength to hurt her?"

"I only want to use my strength to protect and love her. I'm here for good. I don't know how we'll configure things eventually as far as legalities. That's a level of difficulty and complication that I'd want to talk with an attorney about with Mick and Jessi as full participants in the process. But yes, we're all in this for the long haul. I know this isn't conventional, but I already made my promise to Jessi and Mick and them to me. I want to love them both the way they deserve to be loved."

James nodded and grabbed another cookie so Adam did as well.

"That's all I ask for. For you and them. Tell me about your father. What happened? I imagine you argued about Jessi and Mick?"

"Pretty much. It wasn't so much of an argument as him blustering, losing control, and me having the awful realization that this back-and-forth he and I have is ugly and petty and I need to cut it out of my life. To be fair, it's not like Mick's situation. My dad's never done anything to Jessi. He might have tried to get physical with me years ago, but he won't now." Not after the last time he'd pulled his father off his mother to stop him from kicking and punching her.

"What do you mean? John Senior or that wife of his did something to Jessi? When was this? What was this?"

Oh shit.

"I assumed you knew. Jessi is going to kill me." Adam scrubbed his hands over his face. This was what happened when you let emotion get to you and overrule your logic. You got lazy and did something that was going to make his girlfriend, and most likely her mother, really mad at him.

"Not if I get to you first."

Thing was, a violent man like Paul spouted off shit like that all the time. Bravado. But when a peaceful, thoughtful man said something like that, you had better pay attention.

Adam told James, omitting the burning the house down part because that would be up to Jessi to reveal. He was already going to have enough explaining to do. He also told him about the visit to Twisted Steel the week before.

"Why am I only learning about this now? I saw John Senior at the grocery store a few days ago. I wish I'd known this then," James said.

"She didn't tell anyone for a number of years. Her reasons aren't convenient for me or for Mick, but after thinking about them for a while, I've come to the conclusion she did the right thing. It would upset her deeply if you went off and did something in reaction to this. She'd be a lot more hesitant to share things, and you know Jessi, she *wants* to hear what other people think about things."

"Addie knew and didn't tell me."

"In case you hadn't noticed, Jessi is a lot like her mother," Adam said, pleased he got to say something wise.

James growled but sat back once more. "Setting that aside for a moment. We were talking about your father before we got off track."

"I don't plan to make a big deal of it. But I just need to keep some distance between me and my father and his family. I have my mother—who I need to speak with in person when she gets back to Seattle. It's not a phone-type conversation." Adam's mother spent the winter months at her condo in Ventura, a few miles from his sister Lissa and her family.

"Is this what you want? Truly?" James asked.

"For a long time I've had this relationship with him that's all reaction. It's all triage and defensiveness. It's not healthy for me or for him. They're never going to accept what I have with Mick and Jessi, and I'm just exhausted by it. Like I said, I don't want to make a huge thing about it. I just want to drift apart gently and quietly. Do you think that's cowardly?" What Paul thought was irrelevant. But what James thought about Adam mattered immensely.

"I was thinking it was compassionate." James shrugged. "You're not trying to hurt anyone or be vindictive. It's absolutely acceptable, in my belief, to only open your life to people who will treat it with respect. Just because someone is responsible for your biology, doesn't mean you owe them the opportunity to wound you over and over. Despite whatever John Senior wants to say, I do not believe the Lord created any of us to be miserable and hurt by those closest to us. If at a later date you want to come back to this again to see if things have changed, you still can."

Adam let it go then. That last bit of energy he spent trying to adhere to someone else's ideas of respectable and successful.

And it felt fantastic.

"I'm going to talk to Addie about this, but I won't go off half-cocked. I can't make promises any further than that. But I'll do my best to be compassionate too. Even when the thought of that man yelling in my daughter's face fills me with rage."

"You're not alone," Adam assured him. "Thank you for listening. And for your advice."

James took a bracing breath. "You're part of our family. I'm grateful that you came to me to share your troubles, and I'm glad I could help."

CHAPTER
Twenty-Three

Jessi bowled a strike and did a little jump that had her jiggling in all the right places. "Life is so fuckin' good," Mick said as she approached wearing nothing more than a long-sleeved thermal shirt, underpants, and long socks.

"This gaming system was the best idea ever," Adam told Mick, patting Jessi's ass on the way past.

"You have to wear pants at most bowling alleys." Jessi snuggled up to Mick as they watched Adam take his turn.

"That you do, angel." Mick kissed her quickly as he got up to take his turn. "I missed the 'video games are way more fun when your girlfriend plays them in her panties' memo."

"What *isn't* more fun when your girlfriend does it in her panties?" Adam asked.

Jessi snort-laughed, which made Mick laugh too. Before this, before they'd all found their way back to one another, he'd have been out drinking and carousing. Trying to feed his need for sensation and never really succeeding.

Now he still played hard, but this was the center of his life. This is where he got what he needed.

"My mom called today," Jessi said and Adam winced. Mick

took his turn, wiped the floor with them both, and then folded his arms and looked to Adam.

"Oh, don't look so panicked. She told me you slipped and mentioned the thing with Mick's dad years ago to my dad, who she hadn't told yet. She's not mad at you. I, however, am totally annoyed that *she* told me instead of you." Jessi managed a censorious look.

"I know, I know. I meant to tell you when you got home. But you brought baked goods and then I bent you over the couch and forgot everything. But your dad was a great listener and gave me good advice as usual." Adam licked his lips and told them about the thing with his father.

Jessi frowned. "This is terrible."

Mick walked past, picked her ass up, and settled on the couch, keeping her in his lap. "You quit right now, Jessi. I can see you're already making yourself sick with guilt."

"Mick is totally right. We knew this would have a bumpy road. And this isn't about you." Adam sat across from them on the low table. "This is about me and my father. You had nothing to do with the critical breaks in the foundation of our relationship. I don't have much to do with him as it is. He's going to sulk for a while, and maybe at Christmas or around my birthday or Father's Day, he'll remember he hasn't seen me for a while. I'll handle it then. It's not negative. I've needed this last push for some time. I'm telling you the honest truth, Jess. Cutting this last bit of tie with him isn't from an angry place. I'm saving myself. And really, him too."

Jessi thought awhile as she remained a pleasant, warm weight on Mick's lap. Her hair smelled like green apple candy. His favorite Jolly Rancher flavor.

"I'm trying to find a way to be all right with this. But I really hate it."

Mick nuzzled her neck a moment before speaking. "It wasn't as if Adam or I were even close with our families. Not before you, not during, not after, and not now," Mick said. "I know you hate it. But we already covered the fact that the three of us have our own family. *I'm good*. That you can take credit for."

She frowned, clearly arguing with herself in that head of hers.

"Haven't you seen any signs? Or had dreams?" Adam asked. "Hmm?"

Jessi gave them both a very careful look.

Adam said, "I'm sorry I've made you feel suspicious."

His words were so heartfelt he and Jessi both leaned out to be closer.

"I'm sorry too, angel." Mick squeezed her and she leaned her head back against him for a moment.

"Thank you. Mainly I know you both are just teasing, and it's funny." Jessi hesitated.

Adam spoke the rest. "But sometimes we hurt you. And though we didn't mean to, we did. So we'll work on it. That's what couples do."

Mick agreed. "Back to the complicated thing. It's like the toilet seat. Or the way Jessi kicks her sheets free and Adam opens windows even when it's cold enough to snow."

"Not that Mick is bothered by that." Jessi's deadpan delivery made them all let go and move forward.

"Look at us adulting hard-core." Adam grinned. "I vote we go to the living room so I can start a fire. I like fresh air, but I don't like you cold." He stood, bending to kiss Mick and then Jessi. "Jessi was about to tell us something."

"Living room is closer to the cheese popcorn Hamish had sent today." Jessi hopped up and scampered from the room.

"That fucking guy," Adam groused.

Mick snorted. "Suck it up. She loves him, as do Addie and James. For what it's worth, I believe he loves them too. He wouldn't do anything to hurt them."

Adam headed over to turn on the fireplace, and Jessi came back in with a huge bowl of popcorn. "You want a soda or a beer? I got root beer earlier. It's that kind you like."

Mick was on her in two steps, sweeping her into his arms. "I'm so lucky." He kissed her until they both were breathless.

"Wow. Note to self, always remember to buy root beer for Mick," Jessi said faintly.

"You think about what makes me happy. It pleases me." It filled Mick with warmth and a sense of belonging.

"Oh. That. Well of course. I keep telling you people I love you." She headed into the kitchen to get drinks for everyone and a package of red licorice ropes for Adam. "I went a little snack food heavy. Hormones. Least you two have each other when my monthlies come. That's what my grandma Franklin used to called periods. Hilarious that woman. Sort of nutty and mean sometimes too. She had this walking stick, and if anyone gave her lip, it had better have been outside her reach 'cause she'd wield that thing like a ninja."

Jessi stopped talking long enough to tuck herself on the couch in between Adam and Mick. They handed her the popcorn and her soda once she got the blanket just how she liked it.

"So, when I asked you about signs, I meant it," Adam said, tossing his feet up to the coffee table.

"Last month when we were up at Duane's place the stars were so beautiful and bright. You can't see them as well in the city, of course. So I was sitting there with my friends and my loves and the stars wheeled above our heads, bright and hot."

She ate popcorn awhile. Mick had learned years before to just let her tell the story in her own time and her own way. She hated to be rushed.

"We're like that."

"Stars burn out, though, angel," Adam said with a frown.

Jessi shook her head. "After eons. We don't have eons. We can burn bright and hot as long as we live."

Mick saw the moment Adam got it. It changed his face.

"Okay. I like it. Yeah." Adam nodded.

"Oooh!" Jessi jumped up and rushed to the side door, flinging it open. "Snow!"

She danced out to the deck despite not having pants on. Laughing, Mick and Adam followed her out.

Big, fat fluffy flakes fell heavily to the ground, a hush of quiet followed. They stayed out for another minute or two before Jessi complained her socks were getting wet and went back in.

"Seattle snow. The best kind." Came on a Friday, was gone by Monday. "Still cold, though." Jessi burrowed back under her blanket.

Adam jogged from the room, returning shortly after that with a pair of socks. "Change out of the wet ones."

She smiled at him. "Thank you." Jessi managed to switch them over and Adam even took the others into the laundry room.

"Now." Adam came back to settle on the couch as they all watched the snow through the windows. "Warm, dry, fed. If you can call popcorn and soda fed."

"Which you do unless you're a grumpy old man," Jessi said as she tore into the licorice.

"The last time you called me that you also threw a drink in my face," Adam said to her.

"You're lucky I didn't run you over with my car." She shrugged.

"I missed this story. Enlighten me," Mick told them.

"About six months after we broke up we ran into each other at a bar." Adam's expression told Mick it wasn't necessarily a happy memory.

"He stomps over to me, tells me I've had plenty to drink. I told him he was a grumpy old man. I wanted to say more, but the woman he was with came over to rub herself all over him."

"So she threw her drink in my face." Adam shrugged, but there was a ghost of a smile on his mouth.

"And I had a one-night stand with some rando in that bar and it sucked."

Mick couldn't help his frown and she caught it. "Oh really? You have something to say about how you were totally chaste while we were apart?"

There was pretty much no safe way to answer the question. So he kept is simple. "Nope, not at all." Pretty much the opposite. He fucked a lot but *felt* less than he needed to. Except guilt. That, he wallowed in. "I'm sorry."

She shrugged. "Whatever. It's not like my pussy died when you both took off. A girl likes to come, you know? Also, stop beating yourself up," she told them both. "I learned a lot about myself."

"Like what? What did you learn?" Adam asked Jessi.

Jessi thought about it a bit before she spoke. "I learned I was capable."

She chewed on her licorice and thought. "See, my whole life, people have taken care of things for me. My parents, my siblings, then Mick and Hamish and Adam. When you both left, I couldn't go to my parents. Hamish was on a world tour, so that was out. My siblings? I talked to Charlie about it a little, but I didn't have the words to explain it all. I didn't even know myself."

"You're the most capable person I've ever met, Jess." Mick shook his head.

She laughed. "I know how to mend buttons. I know how to make grilled cheese sandwiches and how to can tomatoes. But I found myself...anchorless? Yeah, that's it. I didn't know what to do with myself. I'd had you two in my life for so long I didn't know how to *not* have you around."

She played with the seam on the blanket, trying to piece together everything as she went along.

"A few days ago I had some weirdness at my shop. The electric went all wonky."

"You know you live with a guy who is handy with things, right?" Mick asked.

"Which is why I'm telling this story. Before I'd have called you, or my dad, or Leif to get advice. But when I lived in Portland, before Carey, hell, even after, I took care of my own business. That was a simple thing, just an example. But I handled it. Because I'm a grown-ass woman."

"What was it?" Adam asked. "The electrical issue."

"It was a wiring thing. The electrician had to pull out something and replace it. Whatever. My landlord has to pay for it anyway. That part was a nice reminder that leasing means someone else handles all that stuff."

"In the future, call me. For real." Mick sighed. "I feel awful that I wasn't there to do this for you all this time."

"This isn't about you!" Jessi surprised everyone—including herself—with her outburst. "I'm sorry," she told him as she took his hand. "I don't want to hurt you. I'm not trying to. But this... it's about me. And my ability to take care of my shit. I'm giving you examples of that. I don't want to argue about how I solved my own problem."

Mick was quiet a bit as they all worked through their own stuff. She felt bad for yelling. But not for speaking up.

"It's not that I survived having my heart broken. It was *more* than that. I didn't even realize the full extent of it all until recently. When I was driving up here from Portland, in a truck full of my stuff, I realized I wasn't sad. I felt bad that I'd hurt Carey's heart, but it didn't feel like the failure our breakup did."

"All right. Fair enough," Mick said.

She turned, got to her knees, and faced him, taking his face between her hands. "I never knew I was strong until my life turned upside down and pretty much everything I'd counted on was gone. I was thrown into the deep end, and I had to figure it all out. And I did. Without help from anyone. That means so much to me because I'm here as an equal to you both. I can bring something to our relationship instead of having to rely on you to do things for me."

"What if I like doing things for you?" Mick asked. "I didn't take care of you. That matters."

"But it doesn't. Because you took care of *you*. And now you're here. The fact is, none of us was ready four years ago." She kissed him and returned to her place under her blanket. "Don't worry, I'll still make you do stuff and fix things, reach up on the high shelves and carry heavy loads. And keep me pleasured, naturally."

Mick and Adam both laughed, and things were working their way back to being all right once again.

It was important to her that she was able to make her own way. More than she'd ever imagined before she found herself alone four years before. And it had taken years to get there. But she did.

Maybe it was the youngest child thing. Or the wonderful fact that people who loved her took care of her. But it took being at the lowest point to stand where she was now.

The tears threatened. She held on as hard as she could because she didn't want them to think she was sad. They were tears of letting go, of acceptance. And they were good.

"As much as I hate to say it out loud, I *needed* the breakup. We all did. Without it, in five years would I have felt helpless? Would you have tired of having to carry me all the time? Would the constant stress of being in an unconventional relationship have killed us before we had the change to strengthen and grow? It's hard enough watching you two deal with your families. I have attacks of conscience every day! But I can handle it now. I can get past those negative thoughts and know I'm here for real. For good. *I am an equal*. Not a dependent."

Adam shook his head. "I've never thought of you as weak. Or as a dependent."

"Doesn't matter. It's how I felt. I will *always* know what I'm capable of." She could believe in herself, know she could handle just about anything. She wouldn't have if they hadn't walked away.

"I love taking care of you," Mick said quietly. "When I walked away—ran away—I lost the right to. No. I gave it up."

And as she blew out a long breath, the weight of it, the pain of being left behind, lifted from her shoulders.

"You had to." And she was finally able to truly understand. It still hurt, but it was one of those things like Carmella had said. Jessi knew why it had to happen. Mick had to save himself just like she had.

"Now this is about *me*." His tone was gentle but firm as he directed her words back at her.

She wrestled her need to comfort him back.

Mick looked at her like she was the most amazing, intelligent, beautiful woman in the world. It was so tender, so raw and genuine that the edge of a sob slipped free. But that was it. She clamped her lips together, blinking back tears.

"From the first moment I saw you, you were mine. Glossy black hair always pulled back into braids or a ponytail. Always so happy. I never thought I'd have anything as fine as you. But you *gave* yourself to me from the very start. You brought me into your world and filled mine with joy."

He'd been seven years old and she five. Even then he'd been tall and broad-shouldered. So sweet and *lonely*. She'd felt it coming off him in waves. From the moment she decided to step into the trees and take his hand, she'd wanted to erase that. Fill his life with whatever it took to chase off all that loneliness.

"And then I fucked up. And I lost the right to take care of you. It meant so much. Fuck." He dashed tears away with the heel of his hands. "It was the thing, the *best* thing I've ever done and I threw it away. So." Mick licked his lips. "Having that right again, *earning* that right, that responsibility of taking care of you, keeping you safe and loved, sheltered, provided for, pleasured—obviously—is . . . it's what I crave."

She managed to laugh a little around the emotion in her throat.

"Making your life easier means I'm being the best man I can. Because I love you and I cherish you. I don't want to smother you. Or hinder you. But I want you to call *me* when something needs fixing. I want to open your door and carry your things. I know this is all what *I* want. And it's selfish."

And Mick was never allowed to be selfish when it came to his own emotions as he grew up. Not by anyone but those in the room right then. That he'd just trusted her enough to be so totally vulnerable, because he knew she wouldn't use it against him touched her deeply.

"But it's honest." Jessi searched for a way to discuss this, wanting to be careful when they all worked to find equilibrium. "I want your honesty as much as I want your love and respect."

"I need that too," Adam said. "Not just honesty, but taking care of you. I missed that. Nothing in the world feels the way making sure you're happy does."

"I don't want to be anyone's penance." It was one of the things that scared her most. "You two have made a choice to be with each other. I can see it. It's beautiful. But you deal with me differently. It *feels* amazing, but it freaks me out."

Adam cocked his head. "You're not my penance. Let's get that out of the way right now. Looking from the outside in, I suppose, yes, Mick and I have a different thing than you and I do. Does that hurt you?"

"No. Not at all. When I said I thought it was beautiful I totally meant it. It's sexy and sweet."

"So what about it makes you hesitate then?" Mick asked.

"Not hesitate. I'm sorry, I'm not saying it right."

Mick started to laugh. "Too bad there's no how-to manual for threesomes, huh?" He kissed her. "Don't apologize for not having the right words. What we feel is way more complicated than words. We're all muddling through."

"I just don't want to be a responsibility instead of a choice,"

Jessi spoke the words and realized it did make her feel better to get them out.

Mick shook his head. "You're both. Being with you is my choice, but it's where I've always been headed. But yes, you're a responsibility as well. I want that. I choose that too. Because it's important. Important that I not only *can* take care of you—my woman, my partner and mate—but that I *do*. And I do it well. For a guy like me, some fucked-up grease monkey with more tattoos than sense, it's everything that you trust me the way you do. That after everything that's happened between us, you still do. Adam is my choice and responsibility too, but in a different way."

Jessi thought that over.

"Tell us about the amazing part," Adam said.

"When you two look at me the way you do, when Mick automatically adjusts how we're walking through a crowd to be sure I don't get jostled, how you never complained that all my stuff has taken the elegant class of this house and turned it all upside down. You let me be Jessi. You love me for who and what I am."

Adam snorted. "This is our house now. Bits and pieces of whatever you're working on, candy bars in the freezer, your light-fingered ways with our clothing—*it's us*. Like Mick's favorite beer in the fridge and his beard care stuff all over the bathroom is us. This makes me *happy*. It means you're both in my life for the long haul. Putting down roots with me."

Mick had shifted so his knees touched Adam's "I want to hold you and shelter you, but I don't want to dim your light, angel. Do you understand the difference? Is that a distinction you can live with?"

"It's the perfect one," Adam agreed.

She thought so too. Jessi took their hands, linking the three of them. "That'll do nicely. And the next time there's an electrical problem, I promise to call you."

CHAPTER
Twenty-four

Adam called Jessi's phone twice, but got her voicemail. He'd stopped by her studio, but it was after six and when he'd gone inside, she hadn't been there.

The envelope with his name written across it sat on the front seat of his car. The sight of it filled him with outrage.

As he pulled up to his house, he saw vehicles in the driveway and parked out front. Most likely a houseful of Twisted Steel folks. Adam was still adjusting to the social schedules Mick and Jessi kept. He liked quiet. Liked privacy. Fortunately, they shifted houses and places to hang out at, which meant Adam could opt out or leave early if he needed to.

Each time they managed to adjust and make things work, Adam let himself believe their happy ending a little bit more.

He pulled into the garage, grabbing the envelope on his way into the house. Tonight it wasn't a houseful of Mick's friends but a whole lot of Franklins.

Addie stood in his kitchen, pots bubbling on the stove, the air full of delicious smells.

Adam gave her a one-armed hug. "Good evening, beautiful." He kissed her cheek. "What are you making? Please say spaghetti."

She grinned. "Spaghetti and meatballs. Stuffed cabbage in the oven for Mick. Jessi and Leif are with Hamish in the living room. James and Mick made a run to the grocery store. We've taken over your lovely home, Adam!" Addie tossed it out like a war cry, her spoon held aloft.

He smiled. "Like a plague, you people." He winked at her and she laughed prettily. "You're family. You're always welcome here. *Especially* when you're cooking dinner."

"Thank you for saying so, sweetheart. This house has good energy. It's nice to be here."

It had been Jessi who'd filled the place with all this joy and life, so it made sense it was her mother who felt it.

"You make her happy. Don't stop doing that," Addie said.

"She's the one who makes everyone happy. I'm just here to bask in it."

"Good answer. Now go see her. Dinner will be ready in about twenty minutes."

Having been given his orders, Adam headed in Jessi's direction.

Music played in the background as he entered the living room, where Jessi sat on the floor looking through pictures as she leaned on her brother. Hamish took up much of the couch, sprawling comfortably as they talked.

When Jessi caught sight of Adam she jumped up and rushed into his embrace. "You're home."

"Hey, angel." He kissed her quickly before raising a hand in greeting to Leif and then to Hamish, who seemed relaxed and in a good mood.

She followed him up to the bedroom so he could change, settling on the bathroom counter while he did. "I tried to call you earlier. To tell you my family was here, but I dropped my phone on the driveway. It's dead. Sad, dead phone."

"Even in that new case?" Only Jessi could manage to break a phone wrapped in a case like the one he'd given her only three weeks before when she'd nearly cracked the screen.

"I'm hopeless when it comes to keeping electronics alive."

"Good thing you're so cute otherwise."

She laughed. "I know, right? Are you really okay with all my family here?"

"I love your family. I even feel like I don't want to punch Hamish in the face. Which is a huge win. It's good. I'm pleased you're comfortable enough here to have them over." He thought about the envelope on the bed and decided to wait for Mick to come home so they could deal with it together.

It was after ten by the time everyone had left. Addie had not only cooked dinner, but made several other meals that she packaged up and filled the freezer with.

"Your mom is awesome," Mick said, closing the freezer door.

Jessi smiled, clearly pleased. "She is. It was nice to see them in my house, you know? Hamish was looking at that house two streets up. The one with all the windows?"

Mick sighed as Adam tried not to growl. "He's rich. He can afford a much more exclusive neighborhood," Adam said. "I should get him the name of a good real estate agent. I work with them all the time."

Jessi patted his hand. "In case it has escaped your notice, Adam, *you're* rich. This is a pretty swanktastic neighborhood. I bet musicians and that type already live around here. I like the idea of being close. He needs family around. People who aren't trying to get something from him."

Which was fair. Adam could understand that. Even if Hamish needed to step back. He liked to take care of Jessi too. And while Jessi indulged it, Adam didn't want to. Jessi was theirs, damn it.

"He has trouble sharing," Mick said, which made them all laugh. "Okay, correction, with anyone other than me. And it took him years to get to that point."

"You two are silly." Jessi waved a hand at them.

"Whatever." Adam waited until they'd all changed for bed before he came into the room holding the envelope. "This was in the stack of mail at the office today. But it didn't have postage on it."

Inside were pictures taken with a telephoto lens of Jessi hugging someone leaving her studio. The photo was black-and-white, taken from at least a block away. He put them down on the bed, and Mick picked them up before Jessi could.

"What the fuck?"

Jessi looked over his shoulder as she knelt behind him on the mattress. "This was last Saturday. At my shop, obviously. That's Hamish. The garment bag in his hand had a few shirts and some pants. I fitted him for it all last month." She glanced back up at Adam and he saw the alarm on her face. "Someone took pictures of me? Like watched me and creeped all over my life? Ew! Why?"

"Was there a note?" Mick asked as he shifted to put an arm around Jessi's shoulders to comfort her.

"Nothing. Just the pictures," Adam said. "Sometimes we get mail for other tenants in the building. We just leave it sitting on the ledge in the mail area. That's where it had been left, so when my assistant went down to get the mail, it was there."

"What for? What purpose does this serve?" Jessi asked.

"To make it look like you're having an affair," Mick answered. "That's what this angle makes me think of. PI shots of cheating spouses."

"It's broad daylight in these photographs. People on the sidewalk. He's carrying one of my shop bags? For god's sake! My mother was inside that day, and Hamish reeked of weed and pussy, and *neither* had anything to do with me." Jessi's outrage made Adam angrier than some coward trying to stir shit in their relationship.

Mick looked over the photographs a few times more. "Angel, think for a moment. Look at the perspective of the photos. What's down that way? Some duplexes? A café?"

Jessi got herself calmed down a bit as she thought. "A fourplex next door to a duplex. Side by side at the corner. A teahouse. Café, bookstore that sells candles and lotions. Past it to the north is more of the same. As you know to the south it's more commercial. Grocery store, restaurants, insurance place, that sort of thing."

"But from this shot, what would I be standing in front of?" Mick asked.

"Other side of the street. Must be in a car given the angle. In front of the duplex. People park there all the time. It's constantly full."

"Have you seen or felt weird?"

"Should I be scared?" Jessi asked Mick.

Adam wanted to lie to her. He was terrified to have anyone's focus on her in such a clearly unhealthy way. Was it a stalker? A vindictive person they knew? Mick's family? Adam's?

Adam settled on, "I think you should be cautious. Use common sense."

"Has there been anything weird? Someone watching you? A customer who was mad at you? Your ex?" Mick asked.

"He's on a cruise with his new girlfriend. I sent him brownies for his birthday. He e-mailed to thank me last week and said things were serious with her. The trip was her present to him. He's not . . . he would never do this. He's not malicious or creepy, much less obsessed with me. No upset customers. Things are good at work. No one is mad at me except for Mick's parents and your dad, Adam."

It had crossed his mind that Paul hired a PI to watch them. He seemed more likely than John Senior, who didn't strike Adam as the sort who would spend hard-earned money to tail Jessi.

Mick pushed from the bed and began to pace. "It's got to be Adam's dad or mine. Who else could it be?"

"Hamish is a famous person. I've been out with him before and had photographers pop from bushes and had those shots show up on gossip sites. But those people don't give their photos away. If they wanted something from you for a story, they'd come at you in the open to get a rise from you. This is sneaky. Remember that car from last weekend? When you went all black-ops agent and crept around?" Jessi asked Mick.

Despite the seriousness of the situation, Adam couldn't help but laugh, because he'd thought it was hot too.

"I thought about that." Mick blushed charmingly. "I talked to Carmella about the car you saw outside your shop too. I'm going to assume it's connected, but it might not be. Maybe you can work from home until we figure out what's going on."

"No way. This is just a picture. My eyes aren't scribbled out, there's no threatening note. I'm trying to build my business. The bulk of my work needs to be done there. I can't have fittings at the house. Not for most clients. Anyway, I *like* working there. It's comfortable. Quiet. Near most anything I'd need and ten minutes from home." Jessi's tone said she wasn't going to be moved on this.

Which didn't mean Adam wasn't going to try. "We don't know what it is. Until then, why not just take extra precautions?"

"Are *you* taking extra precautions?" she challenged. "Is Mick? Look if this is one of your father's parishioners saying *ooh look at that skanky whore, oooh*, then I'm not in danger. It's just stupid."

"At least let us take you and pick you up." Mick went for another angle.

"I'm done with this conversation." Jessi's mouth firmed and Adam knew they'd hit her limit.

"I just think we don't know yet exactly what it is. Or who it is. Until we do, we should be careful." Mick's tone went silky and Jessi's insistence gentled a little.

"You're so good at that," she told Mick. "But unless you two are working from home or are being driven in and picked up, fuck off."

Mick laughed, grabbing her around the waist and tossing her to the bed on her back. "You're awfully saucy."

"I know. I'm a menace. Someone ought to teach me a lesson." Jessi looked from Mick to Adam. "Or two."

"Are you trying to distract us with sex?" Adam asked.

"Is it working?" Her smile shot straight to his dick.

He grabbed her ankle, hauling her to him and Mick with her. "Only when I want it to."

She let her thighs fall open, a smile of challenge on that delicious fucking mouth. "And do you?"

"Hell yes." He pulled the soft sleep pants she wore from her body, along with her panties.

"Thank god," Mick muttered as he ridded himself of his clothing while dropping kisses over Jessi's face and Adam's shoulder.

"Oh yeah? What is it you need, baby?" Adam gave an order wrapped in a question.

Jessi shivered as she looked to Mick, waiting to hear his answer.

"Not really craving pain, just sweet oblivion with you two. This makes me unsettled. I need for us to raise the drawbridges and fuck like minks." Mick grabbed Adam's cock and gave it a squeeze.

"How do we know so much about minks and their sexual habits anyway?" Jessi asked. "That's weird."

Mick laughed as he took one of her nipples between his teeth and gave it a few hard tugs.

"Google it. After. For now, what about you, angel? What do you need?" Adam asked her.

The intensity of his gaze sent her silliness far, far away. "I need everything," she said on a breath.

Adam bent to kiss across her belly. "The whole night all I could think about was the taste of your skin." He licked over her hipbone and around her belly button. Walking his fingertips down her belly, her parted her labia and tugged her piercing gently. "And the way this feels against my tongue."

He raised his fingers from her pussy and drew them over Mick's bottom lip. A sweep of Mick's tongue had Jessi and Adam both groaning.

That he looked so smooth and polished but was so breathtakingly dirty rendered Jessi into a puddle of goo.

He kissed Mick then, and from her place on her back below them, she watched, enchanted.

She'd do anything necessary to keep this safe. To protect it from anyone or anything that wanted to tear it apart. If Paul Gulati or John Roberts wanted to start shit, she'd teach them to never underestimate a nice girl again.

Taking Mick's cock in her hand, she angled it to lick over the head and crown. On her other side, Adam shifted to brush his cock against Mick's, over Jessi's mouth and tongue.

It was too much. Too much sensation. Their weight was right on the verge of overwhelming. All she could see, smell, taste, and feel was them.

She drowned in it as they touched her, as Adam's fingers trailed against her temple. He spoke soft, velvet filth to her. Of her beauty and curves. Of the way she made him feel.

Every time she opened her eyes it was to find them above her, foreheads touching as they watched their cocks sliding against her lips.

Their taste changed, Mick's always stronger than Adam's. Mixed and became different.

"I don't want to come all over your pretty face." Mick pulled back and bent to kiss her and lick over Adam's cock as she did.

"You don't?" Jessi asked.

"Not right this moment. Right this moment I want to fuck you while I watch you suck Adam off."

Adam hummed his approval.

"You're better at it than I am. I mean, why have fast food when you can have a gourmet meal?" Jessi asked.

Mick and Adam were stunned silent for long moments until they both started to laugh.

"What? I'm not wrong. Mick is better at sucking cock than I am."

Mick managed to stifle his laughter to speak. "Jessi, that's not true. It's different. Not better or worse."

"Stop laughing!" She wasn't that effective at this admonition through her own gales of laughter. "You have the penis, you know how to do it better."

"Stop. Oh my god." Adam did some sort of roll thing where he flipped her and she ended up straddling his waist. "I'm going to crack a rib laughing."

"Serve you right for mocking my pain." Jessi rubbed herself all over his cock.

"You're aware this is the opposite of punishment, right?" Adam asked.

"Oh I don't want to punish you. And I don't want you to punish me either. I don't need a daddy, I have one of those. But maybe I want to tease you . . . it feels so, so good." She arched her back as she ground her clit against him.

"It really does. Mick, baby, what are you up to?" Adam reached out to find Mick had moved behind Jessi.

"I needed to kiss the back of Jessi's neck where the skin is so soft." Mick underlined that by kissing her exactly there.

Jessi let her head fall forward to give Mick access while Adam's hands skimmed over her breasts.

Damn she was blessed. Not just for the abundance of penis in her life, but the big stuff, the love and connection they brought her. The belonging.

Adam slipped into her pussy in short teasing strokes and then hissed, the muscles in his neck cording.

They'd decided that week, after two clean tests each, that they could leave the condoms behind.

He felt so good inside her naked she had no regrets about that decision. Though messier, there was something so raw and sexy about it, about his scent all over her and hers on him. All that sweat and come was sticky yes, but showering afterward was an indicator of just how much fun you had.

These boys had her washing her hair afterward, as well as changing the sheets. Pretty much—she realized—her life was fucking perfect. Sexy, sticky, full of laughter and snuggling. Yeah, life was good.

Adam snarled a curse, the sound of it made her toes curl. When he let his control go—or to be fair, whenever she managed to get him that flustered—it sent a wildfire through her.

Mick was at her back, his cock against her ass. So hot and hard. He scratched down her spine just this shy of pain and she hissed arching as she pressed into his touch.

Then his hands settled at her waist, fingers splayed there, moving with her as she undulated on Adam's cock.

Adam pinched her nipples. "I've been thinking of piercing them. What do you think?" Jessi asked them both.

"It would look gorgeous," Mick said in her ear.

Adam broke in. "The possibilities . . . oh so many toys we could play with."

The liquid heat of climax began to spread through her body. She groaned, loving the way it echoed outward from her diaphragm.

Sometimes the pleasure was so massive and so sharp it scared her. She reined it in rather than be overwhelmed. Letting herself get carried away and swept up in how they made her feel was part of why it hurt so damned much the first time.

But it wasn't four years ago. They were all different. All better.

And now she flung herself into it, grinding herself against Adam, sending sparks of sensation from her clit each time she did.

"Yes, yes, yes," she mumbled as she got closer and closer.

"When he comes, I'm next. Do you understand?" Mick asked,

his hands moving from her waist to cup her breasts. He thrust himself between his belly and her ass and back, the way already slick from pre-come.

Beyond words, she nodded enthusiastically.

Adam's hands had replaced Mick's at her waist as he controlled her angle, getting in so deep she let out a little *oof* of breath.

"So beautiful," Adam said, voice tinged with wonder. It humbled her that he'd see her that way.

Jessi reached behind herself, down to cup Adam's balls as he continued to fuck her. When she scored her nails gently over his sac he hissed and she felt the jolt of his cock.

He fucked her faster. Harder. Sweat sheened over his chest and belly, over his forehead. His eyes weren't blurred as Jessi knew hers were. No, he gazed at her with so much intensity she was bared to her soul.

There was no sound but the slap of his body against hers as he'd long taken over the thrusts, even though she was on top.

She dragged in breath after breath, holding back, riding right on the razor's edge of climax until he froze, his muscles locked, every bit of his attention on her as he came.

He held her tight enough that he'd leave a mark. That thought and the sting of the bruises forming sent her into orgasm. Adam stretched up, taking her mouth, kissing her as she continued to come, as he pulled out and Mick took his place.

A different sort of orgasm rolled through her at the invasion. Different shape and size, Mick's cock touched parts of her deep inside that Adam didn't.

"I've never dreamed of anything so hot," Adam said. He moved so that he remained under her as Mick shifted her body to her hands and knees.

The way they'd put her how they wanted was ridiculous. Anyone else on earth and she'd probably have punched them. But these two? They touched her and she wanted more. No matter how they touched her she wanted it.

That it was dirty and taboo at times and yet still managed to be comforting and safe would have been unbelievable with anyone else.

But there she was, between two men, naked, sticky, sweaty, saying all manner of filthy stuff and meaning it, oh yes. But it was beautiful because it was them.

Mick's hands slid up her back and then into her hair, tugging her back, arching her so he could kiss her while Adam licked and bit her nipple.

"Holy shit," she wheezed, "you're going to make me come again."

He did and she didn't stop coming until he began.

Everyone needed a shower and a hair wash that night.

CHAPTER
Twenty-five

Mick smiled as he watched her work. Jessi bent over a sewing machine, TV on the Radio turned up loud. He'd made up a reason to come by, knowing she'd see it for the ruse it was.

But as he stood there he realized it wasn't so much of a ruse after all, because all his agitation seemed to slide away.

She looked up at last, smiling. "Hi there!"

"Come have lunch with me." He poured on extra charm.

"You're a ways from Twisted Steel for lunch, mister."

"I am. I came to check on you. I admit it. But I do want to have lunch. That little café down the block has excellent sandwiches."

"And the servers love you." She pulled the fabric free of the machine and snipped threads before she stood and came to him, hugging him. "I'm all right. No one strange has been lurking. Been quiet so far today."

"Good to know." He'd already done a walk around the blocks surrounding her shop, so he knew that, but it was nice she was paying attention.

"Which part? How much everyone at the café loves you coming in because you're so hot? Or that I'm aware of my surroundings like an adult and as I told you and Adam I would be?"

She was teasing, but he heard the annoyance in her tone. Knew he and Adam were in her business more than she liked. Which was unfortunate, but neither man had plans to let their guard down. They'd figure out what was happening and once things were resolved, she could go back to flitting around doing her thing.

"You know Adam and I don't think you're incapable of handling yourself."

Jessi gave him a raised brow. "If I didn't, I'd be sleeping here from now on."

"You told us all how important it was to you that you were able to run your own life. Adam and I respect that. And you. But we love you and worry about you."

"Fine. You're buying lunch."

He stole a kiss. "Deal."

He'd have to be dumb and willfully blind not to see the way the servers in the café responded when they came in. Yes, they did flirt with him like crazy, but he kept his distance. He was with his woman. *And* truth was, he hated it when people did it to her or to Adam.

Luckily, it wasn't rude or invasive at the café. Just a bunch of lovely little old Ukrainian sisters who ran the place together.

Jessi gave his plate a look. "It's like four times more food than anyone else," she said with a snicker. "I don't blame them for being so taken with you."

"I can't help being charming, Jessilyn." He grinned.

"This is true. You just are. My mom was over to help this morning and she invited us all over for dinner on Saturday. Also, she invited us for Thanksgiving and Christmas. I say *invited*, which is a funny word because really, even though she's so sweet, it was an order." Jessi dug into her soup.

"Honestly, Jess? I can think of very few things I want more than to be back around that table at the holidays. I've missed that." God, he had. It wasn't as if he was alone. Asa's mother had them all over at holiday time as well as various members of his own family he still liked to be around.

But the Franklin household during the holidays was a very cool place to be. Full of love and joy. Food everywhere. Presents. They actually sang carols for fun and made popcorn and seed cakes and strings to hang in the trees for whatever animals were still around and would be hungry.

The Franklins greeted you at the door with genuine hugs and made you happy to be there. Made you feel wanted.

Jessi grinned. "Good. I did talk her out of the perceived need for us to sleep over on Christmas Eve, but if you and Adam are interested, we're all going to midnight services as always."

He nodded. Of course he'd be there.

"I said I thought you'd both be there. She knows you both have family in the area, so if you need to do that too, no one will be mad."

"I have nothing to do with any of them. I'll stop over and take presents to John and Kate, but otherwise, I'm good."

Jessi frowned. "None of your siblings other than John?"

"Maybe next year or in the future things will work out with me and Anna, but the others are aligned with my father so that's how that goes." And the more he thought about this very thing, the less it hurt that he had pulled his life back away from theirs.

"It's Thursday. Are you still beating people up tonight?" Jessi asked, changing the subject like she knew he'd want.

Mick laughed. "We lay off from November through February for all the holidays. I was thinking it might be nice to do a date-type thing. Movies and dinner. What do you say?"

Few people loved movies more than Jessi. Adam had upgraded his entertainment system at the house so they could watch movies on a big projection screen.

He was glad he suggested it when her eyes lit and she smiled so big it made him laugh.

"I love that idea. I'm having popcorn with the yellow goo on it so know right now you and Adam have to get your own and are forbidden from discussing your disgust at fake butter in my presence." Jessi gave him a look that had him blushing. Fake butter was totally disgusting. But she loved it, and as long as he could get his own non-fake-butter popcorn, he'd keep his counsel about hers to himself.

"We can make out too." Mick waggled his brows. She rolled her eyes.

"Depending on what theater we go to. Maybe. People give us dirty looks just from holding hands. I can't imagine what they'd do if we started to kiss each other."

He harrumphed and continued eating his lunch. "Carmella wanted me to tell you she was going to call you to see if you were free. She and PJ are doing something Sunday afternoon and she wants you to come. Don't ask me what it was. I can't remember."

He was just thrilled that Carmella and PJ seemed to go out of their way to make Jessi feel welcomed into their group and that Jessi seemed to really like both women.

"All right. I think she mentioned some sort of holiday market thing last week. That's probably it. I'm making a dress for PJ, did she tell you?"

The vareniki arrived along with pelmeni, extras just for them. He and Jessi both made appropriate noises of awe and appreciation, which earned him a sweet smile and a pat on the shoulder as the oldest sister, Marina, told Jessi he was a keeper.

After Jessi agreed and they were alone, neither wasted time grabbing up dumplings and getting started on lunch.

The windows were steamed but it was rainy outside, so you couldn't really tell unless you looked closely. The place was fairly busy with regulars from the neighborhood.

"She always gives me extra potato and cheese vareniki when I come in," Jessi said. "And two weeks ago when I had the sniffles she sent me back to work with an extra container of carrot soup. And it totally made me feel better. It feels like I'm at someone's kitchen table."

That was exactly it. Aside from those bullshit pictures—and Adam's silly excuses when he'd asked them to move in with him—Mick thought the area around her shop was a good neighborhood. Well lit. Well traveled. But not overly noisy or congested. The people at the espresso stand on the corner knew to start Jessi's order as well as Mick's when he came in. The Thai joint up the block knew when Mick said five stars he really meant he wanted it that hot. These sisters and this café where they pampered Jessi when she was sick had been in the same spot for thirty years.

Once he left Jessi at her studio, Mick headed back to the café to speak with Marina. She looked up when he came back in, a question on her face.

"If you have two minutes, I'd appreciate them. I'd like to ask you about something," he told her.

"Of course. For you, always. Is Jessi all right?" she asked.

Mick nodded. "She is. But this is about her, sort of. Have you noticed any cars parked around here lately that seemed out of place? Anything that might have made you look twice?"

"Not that I've noticed. Some occasional new faces, but no one frightening." She beckoned her sister over to ask if she'd seen anything unusual.

"There's a guy who sits in his car. In front of that duplex there." Dasha, the younger sister, indicated with her pen. "He just pulled up. You want we should call the police? Is this person a bad guy?"

Mick turned slowly. A dark green car, two-door, not overly flashy but not really a professional tail type of bland.

Whoever he was, whatever type car, it worked well enough that no one noticed until now. He'd stepped into their lives, far too close to Jessi.

And he could not tolerate that.

"I'm going to find out just exactly who he is right now. Don't call the police unless it looks like I'm in trouble." Mick wanted information, not to get the cops involved. The guy probably hadn't even broken any laws.

The sisters let him use the back door, out the kitchen. Mick headed over one block to come in from the rear. He let instinct take over, using parked cars and the fact that the guy's attention was on Jessi's shop to get the drop on him.

Mick yanked the door open and hauled him out, tossing his body against the side of his car hard enough to knock the breath from him. "Tell me why you're sitting out front of my girlfriend's business staring at her through the very big lens of your camera."

He made an effort to get free but eventually gave up. The guy was probably powerful in his day, but Mick was younger, far bigger, in shape, and had the heat of protective rage fueling his strength.

Still, stalker guy soldiered on. "I don't know what you're talking about. I'm just sitting here in my car. It's my lunch hour." He went for innocent and slightly hurt at being accused.

Bad strategy.

Mick shook the guy a little to underline his point. "No. You're taking pictures of my girlfriend. Don't deny it. So you're a stalker or you've been encouraged by someone—hired possibly—to watch her."

His eyes widened to the point that Mick began to believe this dude was anything but a professional. "I'm not going to tell you anything. You're crazy."

Mick looked around the guy's body into the car. That's when he saw the parking sticker on the rear window and knew exactly who hired him to watch Jessi.

"All right." Mick pulled his phone from his pocket. "I'm going to call the police."

The guy's muscles locked up and he broke out in a profuse panic sweat. Mick sighed, wanting to give this loser a break. "You're not a total moron, the pictures were pretty decent. But my father wouldn't spend the money on a professional and you're not one by a long shot. So, I'm going to tell you that if I see you around Jessi or my home again, I'm going to be really upset. And I'll take it out on you. Get me? Now run and tell my father to get his nose out of my business."

Mick stepped back and let him go, and that's when he heard Jessi yelling.

The dude had managed to get back in his car. The *thunk* of the locks engaging and the sound of the engine gave Mick the ability to turn his attention to find his woman rushing in their direction waving a baseball bat as she hollered insults and threats at the car driving as fast as it could to get away from them both.

Damn. He grinned at the sight of her, his own personal Valkyrie, as she skidded to a halt in front of him.

"Should I call the police?" she demanded. "Why are you grinning at me like that? Did you hit your head?" She reached up to touch his cheek.

"I love you so hard, angel." He kissed her, hugging her and taking the bat as he did. "Everything is okay. Let's get back inside, it's cold out here." He waved his thanks to the sisters standing in the café's front windows as he and Jessi crossed the street.

"I love you too. Now tell me what's going on. I only looked out when I did because I was staring at raindrops on the glass and caught movement outside."

He hugged her again. Staring at raindrops and threatening men with baseball bats, all beautiful, fierce contradictions, their Jessi.

"That guy goes to the same megachurch my family goes to. He's just some dude with a nice camera who my dad convinced to help him because of my sin or some likely bullshit. I scared him, and I don't think he's going to be a problem from now on."

"But he's going to tell your dad."

"That's my hope."

She made an annoyed sound. "This is only going to end in yelling."

"Not on my part. My whole life I wanted him to see me as worthy. I wanted him to be proud of me. Of who I really am, not of who he thinks I should be. I've bent into a fucking pretzel to be *enough*. That's never going to happen. You and Adam aren't the only ones who've said that. Duke and Asa and even John have said the same. And you're all right."

Jessi nodded. "Okay, so why hope for a confrontation? Why not just let it be?"

Mick considered that after the initial rage over what his dad had done to her four years before had passed. Adam had adopted that stance, to just let things drift away totally. But this absolutely had to be confronted because his father was a fucking vandal in Mick's life now, and that wasn't to be tolerated.

"Because I've had enough of his abuse." In front of anyone else, the emotion in his voice would have driven him to be embarrassed. But Jessi knew his heart. Probably better than anyone else in the world.

She took his hands in her own, squeezing. "All right." And just like that she accepted it and made everything better all at once.

"I should get back to work, but I don't want you here alone."

She counted to ten, he could tell. "If this is just some idiot taking pictures for your dad to use to break us apart, there's nothing I need to be protected from."

He blew out a breath. "How about, I need to go back to work and I really need you with me."

She smiled. "You're so charming."

Thank god for it.

"Did it work?"

"You know how hard it is for me to say no to you. But I have to finish this skirt. I need a few hours. Go to work, do your job. Then when you're done, come get me. I'll be here. I'll always be here. And I have a bat and I'm not afraid to use it."

He frowned and she burst out laughing. "You hate being told no! Oh, sweetie, I love you. But I'm saying nope to your lovely offer. I don't want to stand around Twisted Steel while you work. I have a job and I need to do it."

"I just hate being told no by you."

She giggled, throwing her arms around him. "I've spoiled you terribly, you know that?"

"You have. Thank you." He kissed her temple. "I'll be back here at six so be ready for movies and dinner."

CHAPTER
Twenty-six

PJ, Carmella, and Jessi had wandered through the huge holiday-themed market, picking up presents, looking for ideas, and pretty much having a good time.

"I need to eat," Carmella said after they'd been laden down with bags and boxes and packages.

"Yay!" Jessi aimed them all toward the lot, where a bunch of food trucks had parked.

After they'd gotten their food and found a place to sit out of the rain, PJ pulled her phone from her pocket. "Asa texted to see if we all wanted to go out tonight. He promises real, non-fistfighting fun."

All the guys had been at Twisted Steel working that Sunday afternoon and Adam was out at a job site while the women went to the holiday market, but they were supposed to all come back together that night.

"I vote for something non-bar based," Carmella said. "Like dinner at a place with tablecloths and shiny flatware. A bottle of wine. Dessert and coffee."

Oh something laid-back would be really nice. "Yes! Afterward, how about somewhere like Jazz Alley? Music, but not where I'm in the middle of two hundred sweaty dudes. I'm not knocking sweaty dudes and live shows, but I'm feeling a little raw lately," Jessi confessed.

PJ leaned over to hug Jessi tight. It was exactly what she'd needed. "I bet. Frankly, you're holding up way better than I'd be in your situation." She texted Asa back with their ideas for an outing and then put her phone away.

"PJ and I made a promise not to bring this up right away, but we wanted to know how you're doing with all this. Both PJ and I have family stuff. It's not exactly the same, but we're here for you." Carmella put the lid back on her coffee after stirring the sugar in.

"It's that all this is happening *to* Adam and Mick. I'm part of it, but I'm the weapon to hurt them more. And I can't fix it." Helplessness was part of life. Jessi understood that. The world was bigger than just one person.

But when the people she loved the most hurt, it was a lot harder to be understanding. Normally Jessi would go to her mom for help and guidance, but this wasn't a normal situation.

Carmella squeezed her hand.

"I'm biased and I try not to be. But it's impossible here. Am I relieved they're choosing me over the expectations of their family? Yes." Jessi breathed out long and slow. "I feel guilty for that. But not enough to push them to change their minds."

"Fuck that." PJ made a face. "Why should you feel guilty?"

"I get it," Carmella said. "It's something I've struggled with when it comes to my mother. Even when we know something with our heads, it's hard to let go. People take more crap from their family than they ever do from anyone else."

PJ sighed. "That's a good point. And totally true. But I don't think you should feel guilty that Mick and Adam are making the choice to be with you over the poisonous bullshit Mick's father has fed him over the years. And Adam's dad sounds like mine. Which means he's a prick with a lot of money and power and zero ability to connect with the people who should mean the most to him."

"Is it weird that this makes me feel better?" Jessi asked through a laugh. "You're right, PJ. I don't feel bad about that part. My parents have counted both Mick and Adam as their sons for a very long time. I think we're better for them both. I think we love them better. And yes, that's biased. But whatever, you *should* be biased when it comes to the people you love most."

Carmella nodded enthusiastically. "Yes, exactly that."

"That's sort of where I am. Mainly the guilt isn't weightier than the knowledge that Mick's dad can't be around to tear him down all the time. I'll protect his heart and still hold him accountable. It's not hard to love your kids. I don't understand it." Jessi tried to keep the tears from her voice.

This time it was Carmella who hugged her. "I don't understand it either. But you love them. And your family does. And we do."

"I know. And it means a lot." Jessi dabbed her eyes with a napkin and they stopped sobbing long enough to eat. "Anyway, aside from that, I've never been so happy—and so vexed—in all my life."

PJ and Carmella laughed pretty hard at that.

PJ indicated Jessi with the tip of her French fry. "Girl, I know that pain. There's a reason Asa and Adam get along so well. They're all deliciously in charge and they take care of you so well, but they're bossy and nosy and big giant babies when they're sick. God, Mick too. You must have the patience of a saint."

"Well at least you could tell what yours was before you went and fell for him. Duke is just as bossy and nosy, but he's all smooth and sneaky. I didn't know until it was too damned late and I'd gone and fallen in love with him," Carmella said.

"They're adorable. Adorable dumbasses who love me. Which is pretty much all I've ever wanted."

Mick whistled as Jessi walked to the table where he waited along with everyone else. The men had arrived first, which meant they all got the pleasure of watching Jessi, PJ, and Carmella come into the restaurant.

"We're lucky motherfuckers," Asa said in an undertone as he held a hand out to PJ.

Indeed they were.

Jessi's perfume met Mick's senses as he pulled her into a hug. Even in those long tall heels she was shorter and fit just right against him. "Hey, angel. You look gorgeous and you smell good enough to eat." She wore gray trousers and an emerald-green sweater and very little make-up and stole his breath.

"Maybe later," she said back with a wink.

Adam took over as Mick passed her into his arms. "Look at you, sexy. I love this color on you." He gave her a quick kiss before they all sat down and ordered drinks.

They all made small talk after they ordered, and Mick didn't really hide the way he watched her. "Did you all have fun today?"

Jessi tucked her hair behind an ear. "So much fun! I crossed a few people off my holiday shopping list. Picked up supplies for some holiday decorations I want to make."

"We're going to have a Twisted Steel holiday party and make things." PJ beamed at Asa, who frowned so hard Mick couldn't help but laugh.

"Don't worry, Asa. I will only ask that you let us use your finger when we need to tie bows. And you can choose whatever color glitter you want for your hair when we go out caroling. Or you can have the cute reindeer antlers." Jessi kept her face totally straight.

The panic in Asa's eyes had PJ laughing so hard she had to dab tears away.

"Oh I see. Pick on Asa because you're so cute no one would ever take you to task. Is that it, shorty?" Asa teased.

Jessi's delighted laugh had people turning heads. "It worked, didn't it?"

Duke raised his glass. "You, darlin', are absolutely perfect for this group. You can hold your own—and manage our Mick—just fine."

"He's worth the work." Jessi laid her head on Mick's shoulder a moment. "We really are planning a holiday party for Twisted Steel, but the making things part will only be for those of us who want to."

"We're making things for a shelter her parents are involved with," Carmella said. "I thought we could also do some putting together of street kits her mom told me about."

"An annual tradition with the Franklins." Mick realized this meant he got to be part of their Christmas stuff in a way he couldn't while they were broken up.

"My mom is going to be so happy to hear this."

"Tell them about the volunteer services thing," PJ said to Jessi.

"No, not right now. It's time to enjoy one another."

Mick took her hand, squeezing it a moment. "If you want to tell us, you should. We want to know."

"My parents and their church work with a bunch of different organizations in the area to help low-income and homeless people. One thing people really need are low-cost repairs, or places they could pay in installments."

Carmella interrupted. "I told her about how you fixed my stove." She indicated Duke.

"I don't expect you to do anything." Jessi put a hand up. "I know you're all busy and command top dollar for your work. But if you could put out word. If anyone wants to volunteer a few hours or would be willing to be on a contact list, that would be wonderful."

"Well, you should expect it." Mick shrugged. "None of us gets here on our own. Plenty of folks have helped me out. I'm grumpy you didn't mention this before now."

"I only talked to my mom about it a few days ago. When Carmella told me about Duke fixing her stove I remembered and mentioned it to her." Jessi dug into her crab cakes.

"What if I call your mother and let her know what sorts of things we might be able to help out with at Twisted Steel? Maybe a monthly clinic or something. We want to help, Jessi. I'm at a point in my life when I can do things to give back. I know I'm not the only one who feels that way." Asa handed his phone to Jessi, who added her mother's name and phone number.

"Thank you," Jessi said, handing the phone back. "I'll tell her to expect your call. She's really nice. Most likely my dad will bake you a pie. Oh and I hope you like gloves. She's a knitter."

Mick pulled a pair from his coat pocket. "She does good work. If you're lucky she'll have you over to meet the sheep."

"Sheep? Really?" PJ asked.

"Geese, sheep, goats, dogs, cats, a pig, chickens," Jessi supplied.

"What Jessi isn't saying is that three-quarters of the animals living on her parents' land are those she saved." Mick smiled, proud of what a giving, loving human she was.

"People just throw animals away. It's disgusting." Jessi's face darkened. "They don't deserve the way they get treated. We have a lot of land, my dad's a veterinarian, so he never minded it when we brought an animal home. Well, he drew the line at raccoons. We had to tell him where they were but not touch them or go too close. But they're really cute, if not total thieves and vandals." She looked over at Mick and blushed. "I appear to have a soft spot for bad boys."

Mick chuckled. "Lucky for us, you also have a way with keeping us all in line too. I can promise I don't have rabies, though."

"Thank goodness, since you bite sometimes," Adam said quietly, which made everyone laugh.

"Only when you ask me to nicely."

Or when he ordered it. He liked to lick after he bit too.

"Thank you, Asa. My mom is going to be so excited. No matter what help you can give, she'll appreciate it And so do I," Jessi said.

Asa's scowl eased away in response to Jessi's thank-you. "Of course, sweetheart. I know what it means to need and not to have the means or ability to take care of it. I'm not that kid anymore, but the memories are enough. If I can help, I'm happy to do it."

PJ rested her head on his shoulder a moment. Asa tried to look tough, but when it came to PJ, everyone knew he was a big softie.

"By the way, Mick and Adam, I met our new dog this morning."

Mick looked over to Adam, who didn't even wince. Heaven only knew what she'd decided to love and make theirs.

"I take it this creature is at Addie and James's place?" Adam asked with the smallest of smirks.

And Jessi didn't miss it either. "I was thinking of stopping by again on the way home. So you can meet her. Mom tossed in a dog bed, and Leif made sure all the shots and stuff have been handled."

"Can we come? Not tonight. Obviously your parents probably wouldn't appreciate a houseful of strangers uninvited. But another day. I want to see all those animals," PJ said.

"What are you all doing tomorrow afternoon? I'm supposed to go over there in the morning, but in the afternoon they're having a cookout. It's cold but my dad has a deep and intense relationship with his grill. He uses it all year round. Anyway, they'd love it if you came over. You don't have to stay for dinner or even that very long. But you can see the animals."

"We wouldn't want to impose. Four extra people is a lot," Carmella said.

Mick barked out a laugh. "You'll soon get over that."

Jessi rolled her eyes. "What Mick means is that my parents' house is pretty much always full. I've got three brothers and sisters and we've got family like Mick and Adam and Hamish, so believe me when I assure you there'll not only be plenty of food, but that they'd love for you to come. My mom loves taking care of people, and my dad loves cooking."

As Jessi, PJ, and Carmella laughed, Mick locked gazes with Adam a moment, both men pleased to see her forming friendships with people who enjoyed her as much as she did them.

It made her stronger and if for no other reason he would have favored it. But it was more because he loved them too. Their family made them all stronger and safer. Even Adam had found a place in their group. One that fit him, a genuine, natural affinity and friendship with Asa had eased the way at first. Duke was impossible not to like, so he and Adam got on from the start.

"My life is full to the gills with love. Thank you." Mick kissed her hand and she smiled so sweet and pretty he was doubly glad he'd spoken his thoughts aloud.

He'd waited forever to feel this comfortable in his own skin. It wasn't an epiphany by any means. More that since they'd come to one another once more, Mick had been less and less lost by the day. Until right that very moment when he realized he'd arrived at who he'd wanted to be all along.

The dinner was good. Carmella, PJ, and Jessi had a nice, civilizing influence as well as being really pretty to look at. Adam was pleased and relaxed. Mick realized *this* was not only possible, but it made him happy.

It wasn't as if he had plans to stop racing, or stop the bare knuckles fighting or the boxing. Or that Jessi or Adam even wanted him to. It was that there was room in his life for other things now.

More importantly, he *wanted* to use all his time for other things. For them. He didn't need as much speed and danger now. He still loved living hard and fast, but they gave him boundaries and limits, and that's what he'd needed.

CHAPTER
Twenty-seven

Jessi handed a glass of iced tea to her mother and another to Mick.

"Thank you, sweetheart. Can you take the red tray on the counter there out to your dad?"

"Sure can." Jessi grabbed the tray and ferried it out to her father, who grilled out on the back deck. The Supremes blasted, and one of the cats and two of the dogs hovered nearby, hoping to get scraps from her softhearted father.

"I bring meat!"

Duke held up a glass. "Rad."

Adam came out onto the deck, Dottie in the crook of his arm.

Dottie was what she'd named the sweet mutt who'd decided to be theirs. Some sort of hybrid of a bunch of small dog breeds made her petite but also perfectly goofy. She had an underbite and one of her eyes wasn't quite right, but she was a puppy and adored Adam so much from the very first that she nearly fell over from wagging her tail so hard at the sight of him.

He'd bent over, picked her up, and she'd been in his arms ever since. So adorable.

"Hi." She bent to kiss Dottie's forehead and then give her a scritch behind her ears.

"Am I second best already?" Adam asked.

"You asking me?" Jessi teased. "Or your new lady friend?"

Dottie made a little growly howl that made every part of Jessi say *awwww*.

"I don't believe anyone has ever successfully talked you out of an animal yet," Adam said. "Dottie here is, of course, the finest in the lot."

"I told her the exact same thing when I met her." An entire litter of puppies had been left on the doorstep of the vet clinic. The moment Jessi laid eyes on Dottie with her sassy little entire back-end tail wag and that fetching little underbite, she knew Mick and Adam would love her too.

"Mom knitted her a sweater. We should put it on her. It's cold out here." Adam's wince made her laugh. "Oh, are you too manly to put a sweater on a puppy?"

"Angel, there's nothing unmanly about it. She's so small, though. I don't want to hurt her. I've never actually put a sweater on a dog before. It's a little out of my wheelhouse."

Jessi took Dottie. "I'll take care of it. Come on, dumpling. One of these days, though, Dad," she teased Adam, "you'll need to learn. What will you do if I'm not around?"

"Wait till you get back?"

Laughing, she headed inside with the dog. "He's worried he might hurt you but you're tough, right, Dot?"

She got another kiss in answer.

"Did Asa tell you he volunteered one Wednesday a month for a car repair clinic?" her mother told Jessi when she came back through with a freshly sweatered puppy.

"He didn't. What a fantastic thing he's doing." Jessi would have to think up a way to thank the guys at Twisted Steel. She knew it wasn't just Asa, but all the guys behind it. "They're a pretty nice group over there."

Mick snorted. "I don't know if I'd go that far, but we won't miss a few hours a month and it makes a big difference. Everyone doing their part makes the work easier done."

"He *did* listen to all my sermons on manners," Addie said with a wink.

"Impossible not to." Mick grinned.

"Why do you think I gave my lessons with cookies and milk?" Jessi's mom patted his leg.

The house was absolutely full of family and friends. The table had both leaves in it, and people sat elbow to elbow as they piled their plates high and got to work on the feast.

"Your mom is really good at this," PJ said.

"My grandpa likes to say my mom started throwing parties for the family before she could walk." Jessi snickered.

"We all have our paths to bringing joy. How blessed am I that this is mine?" Addie patted PJ's hand. "It's a small thing that leaves a big mark and enriches everyone."

Later, after dinner when all the dudes were in the kitchen cleaning up, PJ and Carmella begged for a tour of the property and the animals.

"The rain has stopped, and it's still light for a while. There are plenty of rain boots at the back door. I even penned up the crew," Addie assured everyone.

"The killer geese we spoke of before," Jessi explained.

"They're really not that bad," Addie said with a look. "They're just very enthusiastic about being geese."

She loved her mother so much. Jessi hugged her. "I think that's probably true. Which means they're a lot like cats, only much more aggressive about you not being geese."

"Very diplomatic, darling." Addie kissed Jessi's cheek.

"That's me all right. Jessilyn Diplomatic Franklin. Want to come along with us? Have a nice walk? I'll even steal Rynn, so Charlie can have some free time."

Jessi's two-year-old nephew was truly a delight. She loved being around him and all his happy energy.

As it turned out, Charlie wanted to come along, so the whole group headed out, Rynn's hand in Jessi's as they both jumped in puddles.

"You have to give him a bath after this, Jessi," Charlie called out, laughing.

"Bubbles, young man, are in your future. Probably mine too, I wager."

Rynn tipped his head back and cackled with glee. That was the awesome thing about a two-year-old. They took their joy where they found it and released their grievances quickly.

"How lucky you are to have grown up here," PJ said as they checked in on the pig, who gave them a grunt and a baleful glance as she chowed down.

"Totally. I still love to run and jump and play here." All the time away, this had been part of her, had kept her heart happy. The trees and woods all around, though not as plentiful now as when she was growing up as the city continued to encroach on the wild.

"I'm not sure we can get Asa to leave tonight. He and that grill, along with all the trees and fresh air out here, are serious competition. I love animals, but living in the middle of the city and working as much as Asa and I do, it's not really fair to have a pet. Though I suppose he could take a dog to work. Carmella brings her dog to work several days a week, as do a few other people. It's like doggie day camp. With ice cream bars."

"And gorgeous men." Carmella winked.

"Goes without saying," Jessi agreed.

"And Mick's family lives near here?" PJ asked.

"Next door. Though it's about a mile and a half away. They have a few acres that abut ours." Addie tried not to look angry, but failed.

Mick had run to those woods, clinging to the wild to give him some safety from a home that drove him away every chance it got.

The bald truth of it was that the Roberts family didn't deserve someone like Mick. They'd never deserved him.

"They're jerks." PJ sniffed, clearly pissed on their behalf.

"It's uncharitable of me," Jessi whispered to her mother when Rynn and Charlie headed over to check on the chickens.

"What is?"

"I hate them, Mom. I hate that they treat him the way they do. How much damage will be enough for them?"

"I've tried—and failed—many times over the years to find it in me to forgive them. The more I loved Mick, the harder it became. Then of course, what his father did to you, well that was the last straw. But what I like to do more than hate them is love you. And Mick. And Charlotte and Leif and all my family. I try to push all that hate away with love like I'm supposed to. Focus on the love, Jessi. You can protect them in your way, but if you let the anger take over, it'll eat you alive. He gets enough negative from those who aim to hurt him. We stand sentry. That's love instead of hate."

That's what she'd needed. Both the acceptance and then the pep talk on how to do better.

"Thanks."

"All part of the service I provide, Jessilyn. Your daddy and I are proud of you. Of the person you are." Her mother gave her a one-armed hug as they took up behind everyone else to catch up.

The lights from the house called them home as twilight slowly fell into dark.

Laughter sounded on the air, speeding their steps, but the crunch of gravel out front meant they had more people arriving to the party.

They came in through the back, met with mugs of hot chocolate.

"I believe I promised a bubble bath to a certain someone." Jessi picked Rynn up and he wrapped his arms around her neck.

"I'll get you some clean clothes too. He's going to get you soaked," Charlie said, leading the way.

"You don't even sound sad about that," Jessi told her sister through laughter.

"Heck no. I plan to enjoy the heck out of being dry." She kissed the top of her son's head and left Jessi to getting him undressed while the bath ran.

"I heard someone pulling up the front drive," Addie said as she headed past Adam toward the door. "Probably Hamish."

"Let me." Adam needed to make more of an effort with Hamish, he may as well start then and help Addie out at the same time.

"Thank you. I'll come along with you." She looped her arm through his.

"I promise I won't punch him. He and I are long past that."

Addie laughed. "I should hope so being that you're smart, grown men who understand exactly what the other is to Jessi." She pulled him to a stop. Touching his cheek briefly. "And who you are to me and James. You have a place in my heart and in the heart of this family that can't be erased or diminished by anyone else."

He blushed, thinking how long past blushing he was, and yet Addie Franklin could bring one easy as she pleased.

He hugged her, even as he heard shoes on the porch. "Thank you for loving me."

She made a sound, a soft sigh, as she hugged him tighter. "Thank you for being so loveable."

The pounding on the door startled them both.

"He's probably got too much in his hands. Stop kicking my door, Hamish!" She yanked the door open but it wasn't Hamish there, it was John Senior with a face so red it was easy to make out in the light from the porch lamp.

Adam pulled her behind him, even if she squawked like Jessi would have.

John tried to come in, but Adam planted himself in the way. "You haven't been invited in."

"My boy is here. You have no right to bar the way."

"I have *every* right." Adam took a step closer, keeping John Senior out.

He knew from the sound at his back that the fracas had garnered the attention of others, who had begun to fill into the room behind him.

"I've got this," Mick said as he came to stand with Adam. Adam looked over, but Mick showed no emotion but anger.

"This is my home." James circled from the other side. "Charlie, please make sure Jessi stays out of this mess and take your mother with you."

Charlie made a growling sound, but soon enough Adam heard her retreating footsteps.

"State your business from the front porch, John, or get the hell off my land. Given what I've recently learned you've said and done to my daughter and the lifetime of misery you've shoveled at your son, I have little tolerance for you. None at all for you in my house."

Mick's dad stared at James, who may have looked like a sweet dude who wore Birkenstocks with socks, but he was big and broad-shouldered, and he was protecting what was his. Adam wouldn't have bet on anyone else in a fight.

Mick heard his father's words shaped to insult and harm as he rushed into the front room. "This is between me and my son. None of you homosexuals or false Christians has anything of use to say to me. You will not stand between us." John's face got redder.

"I've turned the other cheek a number of times with you, sir." James stood forward, but Mick put his hand out.

"No. Please. I'll speak with him outside. I don't want anyone else involved." Mick didn't bother to address his father. It wasn't his leave Mick was seeking. He needed to handle this himself.

James searched Mick's features and clasped his forearm. "You *have* a father who loves and respects you," he murmured and Mick was grateful for what he had with a clarity he very much needed. "We'll be right here. You do what you need to."

Mick swallowed back emotion. But then he turned to Adam, whose ferocity sent a shiver through him.

Adam cupped his neck, pulling him closer so they were forehead to forehead. "I love you. Do you want me out there with you?"

"I love you too. Just . . . be close."

"Remember, Mick, you get what you need at home." Adam squeezed the back of Mick's neck to underline. Message received. And thank god for it, knowing he'd get to work out all of this shit under Adam's skillful—and loving—hands, meant Mick had plenty of reasons to keep this from driving off the road.

His father made a derisive sound. "They didn't waste any time getting you back in their clutches. This is an abomination."

Mick walked out to the porch, past his father, shutting the door at his back. There was no way anyone was going to contain Jessi in that bathroom once she knew Mick was out there with his father, so he wanted to make it quick.

"Why are you here?" Mick asked as he led his father down the porch steps.

"Why are *you* here? This is a den of the worst sort of sin. These people care nothing for you. You're running from your family because you don't like what we have to say. Ask yourself why."

"*These people* have done nothing but care for me. You don't have to like my life. You don't have to like who I am. But this is not okay. You having your church buddies stalking Jessi, using those pictures to try to break us up, none of that is okay. You're terrorizing a woman, my woman. There's nothing loving about that. They *are* my family. You're just a guy who contributed DNA and a whole lot of junk I'll have to get over."

His father grabbed his upper arms, and inside the house, Mick heard Adam telling Jessi to get away from the door.

"*She's a whore*. Michael, that girl is the source of all your problems. These people, these pick-and-choose Christians, they're the problem. They encourage your sin. Can't you see that? Even pictures of her engaged in an affair with another man isn't enough for you?"

"That's her foster brother. She was hugging him on a public sidewalk in broad daylight. Do you even hear yourself? Why are you here?" Mick yelled it this time, shoving himself free, balling his fists, but keeping them at his sides for the time being. "We aren't close. You don't even like me, for god's sake."

"Don't compound your troubles with blasphemy. I'm your father, the leader of our family. These people have tried to steal you away and it's high time I stopped them."

High time. "Oh like that time you broke into Jessi's apartment, shoved her against a wall and screamed in her face that she was trying to seduce you after *you* tore her shirt?"

"Is that what she told you?"

"Is that what happened?" Mick challenged, knowing Jessi hadn't lied.

"I will protect my family from those who mean it harm."

"So the answer is yes. You did that. Does Mom know?"

"I do my best to shield your mother from the depravity you've wallowed in."

That's what he'd figured. Though, to be honest, Mick was fairly sure his mother would be just fine with it.

"Here's the situation as it now stands," Mick told his father. "*These people* as you call them, they're my family. They have been for years and you barely noticed. The only time you really seem to get worked up is when I'm happy and living my life without being the subject of your exhortations on sin. What does that say about you?"

"I make the hard choices. Sin is easy. That's why everyone does it. You aren't some sort of tattooed freak who loves men! You're a good, Christian boy and you come from a good home. Act like you have some self-control. Give yourself over to a better life. Find a real woman to settle down with, marry her. Have grandchildren. This"—Mick's father indicated the Franklin house—"isn't who you are."

Mick blew out a breath. "This isn't who I am? How do you talk about what I am and aren't? You barely know me."

"I'm your father. I know you plenty because I raised you. You made mistakes, and it's my job as your father to set you right."

"Like those times you whipped the backs of my legs until I got welts and then had to kneel and pray for hours? Or when you made me sit in another room to eat because you didn't want me to infect the rest with my sinful ways? Like that, right? Because been there done that, had the T-shirt. I have no desire to go back."

"Spare the rod, spoil the child," John intoned.

"The rod is what the shepherd uses to *guide* the sheep, not shame and harm the sheep." Mick stopped himself before getting drawn into this dead-end argument with this man. "Who I am is a bisexual man in a committed relationship with his best friends. I'm not interested in having any relationship with a person who stalks my girlfriend and puts his hands on her. Even if you were drunk or whatever your excuse is for shoving a woman a foot shorter than you." He shrugged. Normally that would call for a punch in the nose. But this was his father, and people Mick cared about were feet away, watching.

That's what kept him from landing a fist in his father's face.

"This isn't what you were meant for. This isn't what you were raised to do. You can make your own choices, boy. It's your soul, you're the only one who can keep from throwing it away."

Mick sought his patience, knowing Addie was inside. "I've made it clear what I'm doing. I don't ask you to accept it. Or to like it. I'm saying this is who I am and what I'm doing. So stop harassing these kind people. I don't want this with you. Not anymore. It's not healthy. It's not love."

"It *is* love, damn you!" His father grabbed his arm once more and this time, the front door opened and Jessi burst out to the porch.

"Take your hands off him or I'm calling the cops," Jessi called out, tears in her voice.

Adam spoke softly to her, urging her back inside. But Jessi wasn't going to be moved and Mick knew that as well as Adam did.

"You can't have his soul!"

Jessi, who hadn't gone inside, replied. "I don't want his soul. Are you so blinded by your fear and hatred that you can't truly see your son? Look at him. How can you not see his light? The capacity for love and compassion within him is limitless. I feel sorry for you, Mr. Roberts, that you can't see Mick for the truly amazing person he is. I have his heart. His soul is his business."

It was the kindness in her response, even when his father had been so awful to her, that enabled Mick to pull back from the precipice of rage he'd been teetering on.

She'd bolstered him. Defended him. Reminded him, and she hadn't done it by tearing anyone down.

And in doing so, she'd underlined the now over the then. His present and his future were this. Love and compassion. His past—the Mick he was—had to be let go of.

"Go home. Be a better father and husband to the family you still have and leave me be." Mick turned his back and walked up to the path, where Jessi waited with Adam.

James moved past them, heading straight to Mick's father.

Everyone froze, waiting to see what would happen. James leaned close and spoke too quietly to be overheard.

His father's spine stiffened. He stepped back, but the expression on his face was one of anger and shame all at once. Then he turned and walked to his car without another word, and drove away.

EPILOGUE

Six months later

Adam held his glass up to toast their friends' announcement. "To Asa and PJ." The room they took up near to bursting at a favorite local restaurant was lit with pretty candles he was sure Jessi had a part in.

The room was her doing along with Carmella, who'd helped Asa with this engagement dinner.

Mick leaned his head on Adam's shoulder a moment as he looked on at the newly engaged couple with a smile.

PJ, standing hand in hand with Asa at the head of a very long table, took a drink of her champagne. "What a bunch of mugs in this room, eh? Thank goodness for every last gorgeous, inked-up, pierced, and muscled inch of you."

Asa put an arm around her waist. "My family. Our family."

"Now let's eat. I'm starving," PJ said with a laugh as she sat, picked up her fork, and dug in.

"When's the wedding?" Duke called out.

"Penelope Jean tells me she's up for Valentine's Day. I didn't say I thought this was too *schmoopy*." Asa's mouth did a thing, as if he tested the word out and Adam couldn't help but laugh. "But I aim to marry her on whatever day she chooses."

"I said I knew some people would say it was dumb. Or whatever. But I don't care. I love Valentine's Day, and I want to have my anniversary be February fourteenth," PJ said.

"My position on what other people think of me is, fuck what other people think." Asa had voiced Adam's position exactly.

"Hear, fucking hear." Duke rapped his knuckles on the tabletop. "If our PJ wants it, that's what matters."

Carmella nodded.

Jessi spoke in between bites. "Well, I think it's romantic and wonderful. So there."

"It's a good thing I know someone who can make my wedding dress. Someone I trust to create exactly what I want that will be beautiful and totally me." PJ looked over to Jessi.

"I'd absolutely love to make your wedding dress!" Jessi grinned so hard everyone else had to join in.

"I'd want you to work in that purple. From your dream, remember?" PJ asked.

"Oh! I have several ideas about that. We can talk about it whenever you're ready."

Four hours later, Adam collapsed to their bed with a happy groan. "Nice to see ours happy, isn't it?"

Jessi snuggled into his body, his chin settling on the top of her head.

"It's very nice." Mick hopped in after bending to grab Dottie so she could settle with them too.

"Oh, it's the princess," Adam crooned as he let the dog lie on his belly so everyone could love on her.

"I love how you say that like it's everyone else who spoils her instead of you." Jessi rubbed Dottie's belly.

"*Instead of* makes it seem like I'm the only one. *In addition to*, I say, is more accurate."

"You love to spoil all your women, I think, is probably the closest to the truth." Mick kissed Adam and then Jessi before he paused to snuggle Dottie too. "And your men."

"I have to do my best to keep you all pleased and satisfied. A big job, but someone has to do it, and thank heaven it's me." After a few moments of contented silence, Adam gave up the words he'd been working on for months.

"After you left there was a storm. Inside me. Churning. I never knew how I'd feel. And even when I did manage to have a good day, it could change at any moment. You know enough about my father to understand I come by this power and trouble harnessing it from him. A blessing and a curse, I guess. Back then I had no control.

"Oh, I thought I did, of course. I thought if I learned how to wield a crop or a flogger I had control. But that window dressing was a lie. It took pretty much the entire time—years—that we were apart until I found useful ways of keeping my shit together. I had to relearn myself. I had to find a way to respect my choices. Which led me back to both of you. I had to let it go, let myself wallow. Give up all pretenses that I had control. So I could earn it. Day by day."

Jessi shifted, resting her chin to look up into his features.

"I needed to be worthy of this. To know if someone came to try to take it from me I could fend them off and protect what was mine. Because I deserved it."

Mick kissed his forehead, which got Dottie all excited as she hopped over Jessi's head to get to Adam.

"Here we all are. Improved but not perfect. Holding fast to one another to be the best we can possibly be. And that's why I trust it. That's why it's special. That's why I love you both more than I ever thought possible to love anyone and not die from it. This is our house. This is our bed and our stunningly gorgeous Jessi with our supermodel dog. This is where we're supposed to be," Mick said.

Dottie barked, her butt ping-ponging from side to side as she wagged her stumpy little tail.

"He included you. Don't be silly." Jessi kissed Dottie's head and the dog wriggled to lick Jessi.

This was silly and wonderful and more than he'd ever imagined having in his life. This was worth everything and more.

"I love you," Adam told Jessi and then Mick, petting Dottie to let her know she was included.

"Well, good. Because it wasn't as if I was moving out or anything. I like it here." Jessi shifted, backing into Adam's body.

"I love you too. Now, who's going to bring me a candy bar?"

Asa Barrons, co-owner of the
Twisted Steel custom motorcycle and
hot rod shop, never allows his after-hours
affairs to interfere with business—until he meets
racing royalty PJ Colman. Under Asa's expert
touch, PJ is initiated into a world of wicked
desire. But as perfect as their passion seems, a
new challenge awaits, forcing them to ask
just how far they are willing to go...

Please see the next page
for an excerpt from

OPENING UP.

CHAPTER
One

I don't even know who that is, but I'd like to take several large bites." PJ took in the ridiculously badass alpha male across the room from where she and her sister had just been handed drinks at the bar.

"Who?" Julie asked as she paid and they moved to the side. "Point him out. In a non-attention-seeking way!" she added, like PJ was a beast.

PJ blinked a few times before she spoke. "You're a terrible human being."

"I get it from Dad."

PJ tilted her head to indicate the guy whose sheer charisma she felt from across the room. A brunette with a body straight out of a pinup calendar stared up into his face as she stroked a hand up and down his arm.

"She's all right in a totally voluptuous, drop-dead-sex-bomb way. I mean, for those who like that sort of thing." Julie's dry delivery made PJ smile.

"Let's saunter by that fantastic Camaro over there so I can get a closer look." PJ started off.

"At the guy or the car?"

"Two birds. One stone," PJ called lightly over her shoulder.

"Will this end up in some sort of terrible misunderstanding that will embarrass me for years to come? Or, better yet, am I going to have to explain what happened to the police?"

"That only happened once."

Julie's brow rose very slowly. Julie was the elegant one. The one who played the piano perfectly. She'd gone to the schools their parents had told her to. Wore tasteful, perfectly tailored clothes. Now had a corner office at their family's tire company and was set to lead it into the future with their other siblings.

Whereas Penelope Jean Colman had been a "terrible disappointment" because she just never fit anywhere her parents tried to put her. And maybe because she'd gotten her big sister into some trouble once or twice.

"Okay, three times. But I had good reasons for two of them."

"The other was you being innocent?"

"Heck no. Which isn't to say how pleased it makes me that I got away with it."

"He's standing with Duke Bradshaw. The dark-haired one."

Julie did a very nice job of looking natural as she shifted to stand next to PJ, giving her an unobstructed view.

"Duke owns Twisted Steel with someone else. Maybe that's him," Julie said.

There really was no other word for the man but dominant. Easily six foot three, he stood, feet apart, a beer in one hand as he spoke to Duke. This was a man you could dress in a tux, and while he'd look fantastic, you'd know he could punch you in the face without losing a cufflink.

She wasn't entirely sure why that made him so hot, it just did. There was a sort of barely restrained...*something* about him that made her take notice.

Dark hair, shaved close at the sides, longer on the top. He had it pulled back from his face, exposing masculine features.

"You have that goofy look." Julie poked her in the side.

"Ow! What?" PJ asked without tearing her gaze from *him*.

"You get it at the sight of tacos, too."

PJ nearly choked on her drink. Thank goodness he hadn't noticed her almost dying.

Once she could breathe again, PJ glared at her sister through still-watering eyes. "You're on a roll tonight. Did you take allergy medication before you started drinking?"

Her normally serene sister had a twinkle in her eye. "Someone has to keep me entertained at these things. You seem to like them. I, on the other hand, would rather be home catching up on my *Housewives*."

"What a waste that would be. There are handsome single men here. A bar. Food that's being served from a tray instead of a buffet a hundred people of questionable hygiene have pawed over. Me, of course. All of these things are better than being at home alone watching TV."

"Says you."

"Witty. That expensive Ivy League education was totally worth it."

"I need to dumb it down for state college dropouts to understand." Julie stuck out her tongue.

PJ turned back to look at *him* again. He was too far away for her to see the color of his eyes, but she figured they'd be brown or green maybe. She took note of the septum piercing and the tattoos on both arms visible from the elbows, where he had his shirtsleeves rolled up. It was necessary, for reasons of some sort, that she get a better look.

"Since he's standing with Duke, I say you go on over and introduce yourself. This is an industry party. You're here for Colman Enterprises. It's your job to network. Give him your card." Julie got a little closer, lowering her voice. "And it's good for you to make some connections for your custom work."

It meant a lot that Julie was on her side, excited about the direction PJ's life was headed.

"Come with me."

Julie shook her head. "I see a few people I should at least buy a drink for. Send out a distress call if they're weird and you need me to mace them."

With a wave, Julie headed off in the direction of one of their other clients. Well, all right then.

Ever since PJ met Duke Bradshaw nearly a year before at a race, she'd coveted his work. All the people at Twisted Steel were beyond good at what they did, so the cars and bikes they created and restored were absolutely beautiful. It was art.

Their work had one more thing, the most important thing as far as PJ was concerned. It wasn't just the money or even the art. It was that they loved cars. And motorcycles and racing and engines.

It was that passion that she wanted more of for Colman Enterprises. Her family was great at selling tires. But it wasn't the same as it had been when her grandfather had founded the company. He'd raced, too. He'd understood the heart of his customer in a way no spreadsheet ever could.

For PJ, it was a belief system. It was a love of cars, of speed and chrome and the rumble of engines that was the heart of Colman. That would never change, even if the products and services they offered did.

PJ shook that off as she approached, hearing his voice before she got close enough to say hello.

Mmmmm. Deep and gravelly.

Dark brown eyes—and she bet that when he had his hair down it slanted over them so he'd look hot and mysterious all at once—took her in.

His gaze locked with hers and a smile marked a mouth so carnal she probably would have to light a candle in penance for her very naughty thoughts.

She smiled back and the moment between them heated and

slowed. He was *holy shit hot damn and wow* sexy. One of his brows rose. Confident and not a small bit cocky.

He was older. Probably late thirties, early forties. Which was absolutely okay with her. Didn't matter though, because all it took was a close-up view of this male to know he was totally out of her league. He'd rock her world. Maybe set it on fire.

Just having his full attention left her a little shaky. What would sex with him be like? Wrong. Wrong thing to start to wonder right then. Her cheeks heated and she hoped it was dark enough that he missed her blush.

And yet there she continued to stand, finally breaking that moment and turning to Duke. Also ridiculously hot.

"PJ Colman, how are you?" Duke showed perfect white teeth. The dimple to the left of his mouth made PJ bet it tasted sweet.

"I'm doing all right. You?"

"As well as you can be at one of these things."

"Asa Barrons," Manly Man said as he held out a hand.

A *big* hand that engulfed hers as he shook it.

Duke grinned, making him look like a charming wayward boy. No one could stay mad at that face, she bet. "Sorry about that. I figured you already knew PJ. Asa, this is PJ Colman. PJ, this is Asa; he co-owns Twisted Steel with me."

"Colman, as in Colman Enterprises?" Asa let go of her hand slowly and she was proud she didn't gulp audibly.

"Yes." She looked back over her shoulder toward the Camaro and then back to Asa and Duke. "That's one seriously delicious machine."

Asa used that moment to take her in, from the pointed toes of her black heels, up shapely legs, over mouthwatering curves at her hips, to one of the finest racks he'd ever beheld.

The neckline of the dark blue dress she wore—a dress that

lovingly caressed her body and yet stayed pretty and feminine—showed off her collarbone and the uppermost curves of her breasts.

And she had good taste. That Camaro was a project they'd finished just a few weeks before. The owner was taking it home to Oregon the following day, so Asa and Duke figured it'd be a good idea to show it off while they could.

PJ stepped to the side to allow a server to pass with a tray of something, and without thinking Asa reached out to take her elbow to steady her. Her skin was warm and soft, and with her so close it wasn't a struggle to breathe her in. Spice and heady flowers.

"Thanks," he said, referring to her compliment about the car. "I'll be a little sad to see it go."

"We argued about the racing stripe." Duke grinned.

"What do *you* think about the racing stripe?" Asa asked her.

He'd liked her smile, but the smirk she gave in response to his question made his cock hard. Christ.

She walked to the car and he followed, barely conscious of anything but the metronome switch of her hips and the long braided rope of her hair hanging to her waist. Purple hair. Light at the top and then darker at the ends.

"I think it's always more about the car." Her voice dropped so that only he could hear. "In general I like racing stripes well enough. My car has them. Though my car is purple, so it's not all stock."

"That so?" He wanted to brush an errant tendril of her hair away from her face, but he resisted.

This was a *work* event. She was the granddaughter of one of the most influential men in racing, and she couldn't have been any more than twenty-five years old. All of that should have been an ice-cold slap of reality.

But his cock didn't give a shit. His cock agreed with his brain that her freckles were fucking hot and wanted to see if she had them all over. And she liked cars. He could tell by the way she looked at his Camaro. Her gaze seemed to caress the curves and lines.

A woman who liked cars on the same level he did was hot. Even if she was totally off the menu.

"Purple?"

"Can I tell you a secret?"

Oh yes, yes she could.

"Go on ahead." He tried to keep the grin off his face.

"I'm kind of a rebel."

He laughed. "That so? I figured, given your hair, that you just liked purple a lot."

"Maybe that too. As for this particular car? The racing stripes are exactly what it needed."

"Duke likes racing stripes on American muscle. The client is a friend of his."

"The paint is fantastic. Perfect work." She walked around, peering closely here and there. "No skimping or cut corners."

"Were you going to judge me harshly if there had been?"

She ran her tongue over her bottom lip before she sank her top teeth into it briefly. He felt it to his toes.

"Absolutely. Paint is a serious thing. Do you need to be reminded of that?"

Christ.

He liked to do the reminding. And he surely would like to remind this woman while she was naked and in his bed. There was something striking about her. An air of confidence that grew as they flirted over machines. Her energy was vibrant. Sensual.

And still, not for him.

He probably should be breaking away to go back over to where Duke stood. Instead he kept talking. "So what do you do at Colman central?"

"I manage accounts. Which is a fancy way of saying I sell tires to people like you and Duke. They send me to industry events like this." She cocked her head and paused before speaking again. "Who does your paint work?"

That was a quick change of topic. "We have paint done on-site. Specialty stuff goes out to contractors. Are you looking for any kind of work in particular? I could give you a better idea if I knew more."

She laughed and . . . it surprised him. Low and sultry. Not what he expected at all. A brief touch of her hand to his forearm. "*I* do custom paint work. Just wondering who my competition was."

An image of her bent over, breasts heaving against the front of a very tight shirt as she worked on one of his cars, settled in, and he let it.

"This a new service Colman is offering?"

"It's a way to do what I like to do and to expand our reach into new sectors of this business."

Young? Yes. He probably had wrenches older than she was. But she had intelligence to go with the looks. It wasn't as if he thought Colman was the huge success it was without a lot of smart, hard-working people at the helm. But he'd taken one look at that face and body and misjudged her as spoiled, pretty, and rich, and therefore totally useless.

"At some point I'd like to talk with you and Duke about that direction."

"Give the shop a call and set something up." At least he'd get another chance to see that face.

"All right." She looked up, and the upward curve to her lips urged his own to do the same.

Neither of them spoke. It felt as if she waited for him. *That* hit hard. Unexpected to be so moved by this wisp of a woman he'd just met minutes before. It wasn't until she hummed low in her throat, a sound of pleasure, that he realized he'd taken a step closer.

"Excuse me. I'm sorry to interrupt, PJ, but do you have any of Shawn's cards?"

Asa wrestled back his instinct to shove this guy away and have PJ all to himself again.

And was doubly glad when she turned with a smile that was totally different than the one she'd just given Asa. That's when he took in the strong resemblance between her and the guy who'd spoken and figured this had to be one of her brothers.

"Jay, this is Asa Barrons. He's one of the co-owners of Twisted Steel." She looked back to Asa. "This is my brother Jay, CEO at Colman."

Duke dealt better with guys like this one. Asa kept his head in his machines as much as he could. He loved gear with a passion, but people? Not so much.

"Nice to meet you. PJ sings the praises of Twisted Steel frequently." Jay shook Asa's hand.

PJ handed her brother a few cards.

"She was just educating me on her view of racing stripes."

Jay appeared apprehensive, but PJ just laughed and patted her brother's arm. "Don't worry. I'm sure he's not going to stop doing business with us. I didn't tell him I thought they were boring or overdone."

It was Asa's turn to laugh. "Boring?"

Her eyes seemed to light up as her laugh continued to drive him nuts. "Oops, cat's out of the bag now. Please continue to buy our tires."

Jay's eyes widened and Asa wanted to tell the dude to lighten up.

Asa gave her brother a look and made an X over his heart. "I promise we'll continue to buy your tires even though your sister is so irreverent. Maybe *because*." He winked at her and she poked her brother's upper arm.

Jay looked back over his shoulder and then to them once more. "I need to get back to my conversation. It was nice to finally meet you, Asa." He held the cards up. "Thanks."

Before Asa could say anything else, the woman he'd actually

been planning on taking home came back through the room looking for him.

"I need to get back to it as well." He held his hand out, shaking PJ's, and then he handed her a business card and took hers.

"Have an excellent evening, Asa Barrons."

The buxom brunette making her way over to him would probably guarantee that. But he couldn't deny the pull as PJ walked away.

He *really* couldn't deny it when she was stopped not even half a room away by Scott Elroy, one of the guys in town who custom-built bikes. And by the looks of it, Asa wasn't the only one who found PJ Colman rather delightful.